W9-BGV-011

BIG SKY

KATE ATKINSON

BIG SKY

Doubleday Canada

Doubleday Canada and colophon are registered trademarks of Penguin Random House Canada Limited

Library and Archives Canada Cataloguing in Publication

Title: Big sky / Kate Atkinson.
Names: Atkinson, Kate, author.
Identifiers: Canadiana (print) 20190050918
| Canadiana (ebook) 20190050926 | ISBN 9780385691550 (hardcover)
| ISBN 9780385691567 (EPUB)
Classification: LCC PR6051.T56 B54 2019 | DDC 823/.92—dc23

This book is a work of fiction. Names, characters, places and incidents are products of the author's imagination or are used fictitiously. Any resemblance to actual events or locales or persons, living or dead, is entirely coincidental.

Jacket design: Kelly Hill
Jacket images: clouds © Paul Robinson/EyeEm/Getty Images;
East Yorkshire/Alamy Stock Photo; texture © foxie/Shutterstock

Printed and bound in the USA
Published in Canada by Bond Street Books,
a division of Penguin Random House Canada Limited
www.penguinrandomhouse.ca

10 9 8 7 6 5 4 3 2 1

Before Enlightenment I chopped wood and carried water.
After Enlightenment I chopped wood and carried water.

Zen saying

'I'm for truth, no matter who tells it.
I'm for justice, no matter who it is for or against.'

Malcolm X

For Alison Barrow

Eloping

'So what now?' he asked.

'A quick getaway,' she said, shucking off her fancy shoes into the passenger footwell. 'They were killing me,' she said and gave him a rueful smile because they'd cost a fortune. He knew – he'd paid for them. She had already removed her bridal veil and tossed it on to the back seat, along with her bouquet, and now she began to struggle with the thicket of grips in her hair. The delicate silk of her wedding dress was already crushed, like moth wings. She glanced at him and said, 'As you like to say – time to get the hell out of Dodge.'

'Okay, then. Let's hit the highway,' he said and started the engine.

He noticed that she was cupping the bowl of her belly where she was incubating an as yet invisible baby. Another branch to add to the family tree. A twig. A bud. The past counted for nothing, he realized. Only the present had value.

'Wheels up, then,' he said and put his foot down on the gas.

On the way, they made a detour up to Rosedale Chimney Bank to stretch their legs and look at the sunset that was flooding the vast sky with a glorious palette of reds and yellows, orange and even violet. It demanded poetry, a thought he voiced out loud, and she said, 'No, I don't think so. It's enough in itself.' The getting of wisdom, he thought.

There was another car parked up there, an older couple, admiring the view. 'Magnificent, isn't it?' the man said. The woman smiled at them and congratulated the 'happy couple' on their wedding and Jackson said, 'It's not what it looks like.'

1

One Week Earlier

Anderson Price Associates

Katja scrutinized Nadja's make-up. Nadja posed for her as if she were taking a selfie, cheeks sucked in like a corpse, mouth pouted extravagantly.

'Yeah. Good,' Katja pronounced finally. She was the younger of the two sisters but was by far the bossier. *They could be twins*, people always said. There were two years and one and a half inches between them. Katja was the smaller and the prettier of the two, although they were both petite and shared the same shade of (not entirely natural) blonde hair, as well as their mother's eyes – green irises encircled by grey.

'Hold still,' Nadja said and brushed an eyelash off Katja's cheek. Nadja had a degree in Hospitality Management and worked at the Radisson Blu, where she wore a pencil-skirted suit and two-inch heels and tidied her hair away in a tight bun while she dealt with complaining guests. People complained all the time. When she got home to her shoe-box apartment she shook her hair free and put on jeans and a big sweatshirt and walked around barefoot and no one complained because she lived on her own, which was the way she liked it.

Katja had a job in Housekeeping in the same hotel. Her English wasn't as good as her older sister's. She didn't have any qualifications beyond school and even those were mediocre because she had spent her childhood and most of her teenage years ice-skating competitively, but in the end she just wasn't good enough. It was a cruel, vicious world and she missed it every day. The ice rink had made her tough and she still had a skater's figure, lithe and strong. It drove men a little crazy. For Nadja it had been dancing – ballet – but she had given it up when their mother couldn't afford to pay for lessons for both of them. She had sacrificed her talent easily, or so it seemed to Katja.

Katja was twenty-one, living at home, and couldn't wait to fly the stifling nest, even though she knew that a job in London would almost certainly be the same as the one she had here – making beds and cleaning toilets and pulling strangers' soapy hair out of plugholes. But once she was there things would change, she knew they would.

The man was called Mr Price. Mark Price. He was a partner in a recruitment agency called Anderson Price Associates – APA – and had already interviewed Nadja over Skype. Nadja reported to Katja that he was attractive – tanned, a full head of attractively greying hair ('like George Clooney'), a gold signet ring and a heavy Rolex on his wrist ('like Roger Federer'). 'He'd better look out, I might marry him,' Katja said to her sister and they both laughed.

Nadja had emailed scans of her qualifications and references to Mark Price and now they were waiting in Nadja's apartment for him to Skype from London again to 'confirm all the details' and 'have a quick chat' with Katja. Nadja had asked him if he could find work for her sister too and he said, 'Why not?' There was plenty of work in British hotels. 'The problem is no one wants to work hard here,' Mark Price said.

'I want to work hard there,' Nadja said.

They weren't stupid, they knew about trafficking, about people who tricked girls into thinking they were going to good jobs, proper jobs, who then ended up drugged, trapped in some filthy hole of a room having sex with one man after another, unable to get home again because their passports had been confiscated and they had to 'earn' them back. APA wasn't like that. They had a professional website, all above board. They recruited all over the world for hotels, nursing homes, restaurants, cleaning companies, they even had an office in Brussels, as well as one in Luxembourg. They were 'affiliated' and recognized and had all kinds of testimonials from people.

From what you could see of it on Skype, their office in London looked very smart. It was busy – you could hear the constant murmur of staff in the background, talking to each other, tapping keyboards, answering the ringing phones. And Mark Price himself was serious and businesslike. He talked about 'human resources' and 'support' and 'employer responsibility'. He could help to arrange accommodation, visas, English tuition, ongoing training.

He already had something in mind for Nadja, 'one of the very top hotels', but she could decide when she arrived. There were plenty of opportunities 'for a bright girl' like her. 'And my sister,' she had reminded him.

'And your sister, yes, of course,' he'd laughed.

He would even pay their airfares. Most agencies expected you to pay *them* money up front for finding you a job. He would send an e-ticket, he said, they would fly to Newcastle. Katja had looked it up on the map. It was miles from London. 'Three hours on the train,' Mark Price said, it was 'easy'. And cheaper for him this way – he was paying for their tickets, after all. A representative of Anderson Price Associates would meet them at the airport and take them to an Airbnb in Newcastle for the night as the Gdansk flight came in late in the day. Next morning someone would escort them to the station and put them on a train. Someone else would pick them up at King's Cross and drive them to a hotel for a few nights until they got settled. 'It's a well-oiled machine,' he said.

Nadja could probably have got a transfer to another Radisson but she was ambitious and wanted to work in a luxury hotel, somewhere everyone had heard of – the Dorchester, the Lanesborough, the Mandarin Oriental. 'Oh, yes,' Mark Price had said, 'we have contracts with all those places.' Katja wasn't bothered, she just wanted to be in London. Nadja was the more serious of the two, Katja the carefree one. Like the song said, girls just wanted to have fun.

And so now they were sitting in front of Nadja's open laptop waiting for Mark Price to call.

Mark Price was on time, to the second. 'Okay,' Nadja said to Katja. 'Here we go. Ready?'

The tiny delay in transmission seemed to be making it harder for her to translate what he was saying. Her English wasn't as proficient as her sister had claimed. She laughed a lot to compensate, tossing her hair and looming nearer the screen as if she could persuade him by filling it with her face. She was pretty, though. They were both pretty, but this one was prettier.

'Okay, Katja,' he said. 'Time's getting on.' He tapped his watch to illustrate because he could see the blankness behind her smile. 'Is your sister still there?' Nadja's face appeared on the screen, squashed against Katja's, and they both grinned at him. They looked as if they were in a Photo-Me booth.

'Nadja,' he said, 'I'll have my secretary email you the tickets first thing in the morning, okay? And I'll see you both soon. Looking forward to meeting you. Have a good evening.'

He turned the screen off and the girls disappeared. He stood up and stretched. Behind him on the wall was the smart 'APA' logo for Anderson Price Associates. He had a desk and a chair. There was a print of something modern but classy on the wall. Part of it was in view in the camera on the laptop – he had checked carefully. On the other side you could see an orchid. The orchid looked real, but it was a fake. The office was a fake. Anderson Price Associates was a fake, Mark Price was a fake. Only his Rolex was real.

He wasn't in an office in London, he was in a mobile home in a field on the East Coast. His 'other office', as he thought of it. It was only half a mile inland and sometimes the screaming gulls threatened to spoil the illusion that he was in London.

He turned off the recording of *Office Ambience Sounds*, switched off the lights, locked up the mobile home and climbed into his Land Rover Discovery. Time to go home. He could almost taste the Talisker that his wife would have waiting for him.

The Battle of the River Plate

And there's the Ark Royal, *keeping a good distance from the enemy* . . .

There were a couple of quiet explosions – *pop-pop-pop.* The noise of tinny gunfire competing unsuccessfully with the gulls wheeling and screeching overhead.

Oh, and the Achilles *has taken a hit, but luckily she has been able to contact the* Ark Royal, *who is racing to her aid* . . .

'Racing' wasn't quite the word that Jackson would have used for the rather laboured progress the *Ark Royal* was making across the boating lake in the park.

And here come the RAF bombers! Excellent shooting, boys! Let's hear it for the RAF and the escorts . . .

A rather weak cheer went up from the audience as two very small wooden planes jerked across the boating lake on zip wires.

'Jesus,' Nathan muttered. 'This is pathetic.'

'Don't swear,' Jackson said automatically. It *was* pathetic in some ways (*the smallest manned navy in the world!*), but that was the charm of it, surely? The boats were replicas, the longest twenty foot at most, the others considerably less. There were park employees concealed inside the boats, steering them. The audience was sitting on wooden benches on raked concrete steps. For an hour beforehand an old-fashioned kind of man had played old-fashioned kind of music on an organ in a bandstand and now the same old-fashioned man was commentating on the battle. In an old-fashioned kind of way. ('Is this ever going to end?' Nathan asked.)

Jackson had come here as a kid once himself, not with his own family (when he had a family) – they never did anything together,

9

never went anywhere, not even a day-trip. That was the working class for you, too busy working to have time for pleasure, and too poor to pay for it if they managed to find the time. ('Didn't you hear, Jackson?' Julia said. 'The class war's over. Everyone lost.') He couldn't remember the circumstances – perhaps he had come here on a Scouts outing, or with the Boys' Brigade, or even the Salvation Army – the young Jackson had clung to any organization going in the hope of getting something for free. He didn't let the fact that he was brought up as a Catholic interfere with his beliefs. He had even signed the Pledge at the age of ten, promising the local Salvation Army Temperance Society his lifelong sobriety in exchange for a lemonade and a plate of cakes. ('And how did that work out for you?' Julia asked.) It was a relief when he eventually discovered the real Army, where everything was free. At a price.

'The Battle of the River Plate,' Jackson told Nathan, 'was the first naval battle of the Second World War.' One of his jobs as a father was to educate, especially on his specialist subjects – cars, wars, women. ('Jackson, you know *nothing* about women,' Julia said. 'Exactly,' Jackson said.) Nathan met any information conveyed to him by either rolling his eyes or appearing to be deaf. Jackson hoped that, somehow or other, his son was unconsciously absorbing the continual bombardment of advice and warnings that his behaviour necessitated – 'Don't walk so close to the edge of the cliff. Use your knife and fork, not your fingers. Give up your seat on the bus.' Although when did Nathan ever go anywhere on a bus? He was ferried around like a lord. Jackson's son was thirteen and his ego was big enough to swallow planets whole.

'What do they mean – "manned"?' Nathan said.

'There are people inside the boats, steering them.'

'There aren't,' he scoffed. 'That's stupid.'

'There are. You'll see.'

Here comes Exeter *as well. And the enemy submarine is in trouble now . . .*

'You wait,' Jackson said. 'One day you'll have kids of your own and you'll find that you make them do all the things that you currently despise – museums, stately homes, walks in the countryside – and they in turn will hate you for it. That, my son, is how cosmic justice works.'

'I won't be doing *this*,' Nathan said.

'And that sound you can hear will be me laughing.'

'No, it won't. You'll be dead by then.'

'Thanks. Thanks, Nathan.' Jackson sighed. Had he been so callous at his son's age? And he hardly needed reminding of his mortality, he saw it in his own boy growing older every day.

Looking on the bright side, Nathan was talking in more or less whole sentences this afternoon, rather than the usual simian grunts. He was slumped on the bench, his long legs sprawled out, his arms folded in what could only be described as a sarcastic manner. His feet (designer trainers, of course) were enormous – it wouldn't be long before he was taller than Jackson. When Jackson was his son's age he had two sets of clothes and one of those was his school uniform. Apart from his gym plimsolls ('Your what?' Nathan puzzled), he had possessed just the one pair of shoes and would have been baffled by the concept 'designer' or 'logo'.

By the time Jackson was thirteen his mother was already dead of cancer, his sister had been murdered and his brother had killed himself, helpfully leaving his body – hanging from the light fitting – for Jackson to find when he came home from school. Jackson never got the chance to be selfish, to sprawl and make demands and fold his arms sarcastically. And anyway, if he had, his father would have given him a good skelping. Not that Jackson wished suffering on his son – God forbid – but a little less narcissism wouldn't go amiss.

Julia, Nathan's mother, could go toe to toe with Jackson in the grief stakes – one sister murdered, one sister who killed herself, one who died of cancer. ('Oh, and don't forget Daddy's sexual abuse,' she reminded him. 'Trumps to me, I think.') And now all the wretchedness of their shared pasts had been distilled into this one child. What if somehow, despite his untroubled appearance, it had lodged in Nathan's DNA and infected his blood, and even now tragedy and grief were growing and multiplying in his bones like a cancer. ('Have you even tried being an optimist?' Julia said. 'Once,' Jackson said. 'It didn't suit me.')

'I thought you said you were going to get me an ice-cream.'

'I think what you meant to say was, "Dad, can I have that ice-cream you promised and seem to have temporarily forgotten about? Please?"'

'Yeah, whatever.' After an impressively long pause he added, reluctantly, 'Please.' ('I serve at the pleasure of the President,' an unruffled Julia said when their offspring demanded something.)

'What do you want?'

'Magnum. Double peanut butter.'

'I think you might be setting your sights quite high there.'

'Whatever. A Cornetto.'

'Still high.'

Nathan came trailing clouds of instructions where food was concerned. Julia was surprisingly neurotic about snacks. 'Try and control what he eats,' she said. 'He can have a small chocolate bar but no sweets, definitely no Haribo. He's like a Gremlin after midnight if he gets too much sugar. And if you can get a piece of fruit into him then you're a better woman than me.' Another year or two and Julia would be worrying about cigarettes and alcohol and drugs. She should enjoy the sugar years, Jackson thought.

'While I'm getting your ice-cream,' Jackson said to Nathan, 'make sure you keep an eye on our friend Gary there in the front row, will you?' Nathan showed no sign of having heard him so Jackson waited a beat and then said, 'What did I just say?'

'You *said*, "While I'm gone make sure you keep an eye on our friend Gary there in the front row, will you?"'

'Right. Good,' Jackson said, slightly chastened, not that he was going to show it. 'Here,' he said, handing over his iPhone, 'take a photograph if he does anything interesting.'

When Jackson got up, the dog followed him, labouring up the steps behind him to the café. Julia's dog, Dido, a yellow Labrador, overweight and ageing. Years ago, when Jackson was first introduced to Dido by Julia ('Jackson, this is Dido – Dido, this is Jackson'), he thought the dog must have been called after the singer, but it turned out she was the namesake of the Queen of Carthage. That was Julia in a nutshell.

Dido — the dog, not the Queen of Carthage — also came with a long list of instructions. You would think Jackson had never looked after a child or a dog before. ('But it wasn't my child or my dog,' Julia pointed out. 'I believe that should be *our* child,' Jackson said.)

Nathan had been three years old before Jackson was able to claim any ownership of him. Julia, for reasons best known to herself, had denied that Jackson was Nathan's father, so he had already missed the best years before she admitted to his paternity. ('I wanted him to myself,' she said.) Now that the worst years had arrived, however, it seemed that she was more than keen to share him.

Julia was going to be 'ferociously' busy for nearly the entire school holiday, so Jackson had brought Nathan to stay with him in the cottage he was currently renting, on the east coast of Yorkshire, a couple of miles north of Whitby. With good wi-fi Jackson could run his business — Brodie Investigations — from just about anywhere. The internet was evil but you had to love it.

Julia played a pathologist ('*the* pathologist,' she corrected) in the long-running police procedural *Collier. Collier* was described as 'gritty northern drama', although these days it was tired hokum thought up by cynical metropolitan types off their heads on coke, or worse, most of the time.

Julia had been given her own storyline for once. 'It's a big arc,' she told Jackson. He thought she said 'ark' and it took him a while to sort this mystery out in his head. Now, still, whenever she talked about 'my arc' he had a vision of her leading an increasingly bizarre parade of puzzled animals, two by two, up a gangplank. She wouldn't be the worst person to be with during the Flood. Beneath her scatty, actressy demeanour she was resilient and resourceful, not to mention good with animals.

Her contract was up for renewal and they were drip-feeding the script to her, so, she said, she was pretty certain that she was heading for a grisly exit at the end of her 'arc'. ('Aren't we all?' Jackson said.) Julia was sanguine, it had been a good run, she said. Her agent was keeping an eye on a Restoration Comedy that was coming up at the West Yorkshire Playhouse. ('Proper acting,' Julia said. 'And if that fails there's always *Strictly*. I've been offered it twice already. They're obviously scraping the bottom of the barrel.') She had a lovely throaty laugh, especially when being self-deprecating. Or pretending to be. It had a certain charm.

'As suspected, no Magnums, no Cornettos, they only had Bassani's,' Jackson said, returning with two cones held aloft like flambeaux. You might have thought that people would want their kids to stop eating Bassani's ice-cream after what had happened. Carmody's amusements were still there as well, a rowdy, popular presence on the front. Ice-cream and arcades – the perfect lures for kids. It must be getting on for a decade since the case was in the papers? (The older Jackson grew, the more slippery time became.) Antonio Bassani and Michael Carmody, local 'worthies' – one of them was in jail and the other one had topped himself, but Jackson could never remember which was which. He wouldn't be surprised if the one in jail wasn't due to get out soon, if he hadn't already. Bassani and Carmody liked kids. They liked kids too much. They liked handing kids around to other men who liked kids too much. Like gifts, like forfeits.

An eternally hungry Dido had waddled back hopefully on his heels and in lieu of ice-cream Jackson gave her a bone-shaped dog treat. He supposed it didn't make much difference to her what shape it was.

'I got a vanilla and a chocolate,' he said to Nathan. 'Which do you want?' A rhetorical question. Who under voting age ever chose vanilla?

'Chocolate. Thanks.'

Thanks – a small triumph for good manners, Jackson thought. ('He'll come good in the end,' Julia told him. 'Being a teenager is so difficult, their hormones are in chaos, they're exhausted a lot of the time. All that growing uses up a lot of energy.') But what about all those teenagers in the past who had left school at fourteen (nearly the same age as Nathan!) and gone into factories and steelworks and down coal mines? (Jackson's own father and his father before him, for example.) Or Jackson himself, in the Army at sixteen, a youth broken into pieces by authority and put back together again by it as a man. Were those teenagers, himself included, allowed the indulgence of chaotic hormones? No, they were not. They went to work alongside men and behaved themselves, they brought their pay packets home to their mothers (or fathers) at the end of the week and— ('Oh, do shut up, will you?' Julia said wearily. 'That life's gone and it isn't coming back.')

'Where's Gary?' Jackson asked, scanning the banks of seats.

'Gary?'

'The Gary you're supposed to be keeping an eye on.'

Without looking up from his phone, Nathan nodded in the direction of the dragon boats where Gary and Kirsty were queuing for tickets.

And the battle is over and the Union Jack is being hoisted. Let's have a cheer for the good old Union flag!

Jackson cheered along with the rest of the audience. He gave Nathan a friendly nudge and said, 'Come on, cheer the good old Union flag.'

'Hurrah,' Nathan said laconically. Oh, irony, thy name is Nathan Land, Jackson thought. His son had his mother's surname, it was a source of some contention between Julia and Jackson. To put it mildly. 'Nathan Land' to Jackson's ears sounded like the name of an eighteenth-century Jewish financier, the progenitor of a European banking dynasty. 'Nat Brodie', on the other hand, sounded like a robust adventurer, someone striking west, following the frontier in search of gold or cattle, loose-moraled women following in his wake. ('When did you get so fanciful?' Julia asked. Probably when I met you, Jackson thought.)

'Can we go now?' Nathan said, yawning excessively and unselfconsciously.

'In a minute, when I've finished this,' Jackson said, indicating his ice-cream. Nothing, in Jackson's opinion, made a grown man look more of a twit than walking around licking an ice-cream cone.

The combatants of the Battle of the River Plate began their lap of honour. The men inside had removed the top part of the boats – like conning towers – and were waving at the crowd.

'See?' Jackson said to Nathan. 'Told you so.'

Nathan rolled his eyes. 'So you did. *Now* can we go?'

'Yeah, well, let's just check on our Gary.'

Nathan moaned as if he was about to be waterboarded.

'Suck it up,' Jackson said cheerfully.

Now that the smallest manned navy in the world was sailing off to its moorings, the park's dragon boats were coming back out – paddle boats in bright primary colours with long necks and big dragon heads, like cartoon versions of Viking longboats. Gary and Kirsty had already mounted their own fiery steed, Gary pedalling heroically out into the middle of the boating lake. Jackson took a couple of photos. When he checked his phone he was pleasantly surprised to find that Nathan had taken a burst – the modern equivalent of the flicker-books of his own childhood – while Jackson was off buying the ice-creams. Gary and Kirsty kissing, puckered up like a pair of puffer fish. 'Good lad,' Jackson said to Nathan.

'*Now* can we go?'

'Yes, we can.'

Jackson had been following Gary and Kirsty for several weeks. He had sent enough photographs of them *in flagrante* to Gary's wife, Penny, for her to have divorced her husband for adultery several times over, but every time Jackson said to her, 'I think you've got enough evidence now, Mrs Trotter,' she always said, 'Just stay on them a bit longer, Mr Brodie.' Penny Trotter – it was an unfortunate name, Jackson thought. Pig's trotters. A cheap meal from a butcher. His mother had cooked pig's feet, the head too. Snout to tail and everything in between, nothing wasted. She was Irish, the memory of famine engraved on her bones, like the scrimshaw he had seen in the museum in Whitby. And, being an Irish mother, of course the men of the family were fed first – in order of age. Next it was his sister's turn, and then, finally, their mother would sit down with her plate, dining on whatever was left – often nothing more than a couple of potatoes and a drop of gravy. Only Niamh ever noticed this maternal sacrifice. ('Come on, Ma, have a bit of my meat.')

There were occasions when Jackson's sister appeared more vivid to him in death than she had been in life. He did his best to keep the memory of her alive as there was no one else left to tend the flame. Soon she would be snuffed out for eternity. As would he, as would his son, as— ('For Christ's sake, Jackson, give it a break,' Julia said crossly.)

Jackson had begun to wonder if Penny Trotter took some kind of masochistic pleasure in what amounted (almost) to voyeurism. Or did she have an endgame that she wasn't sharing with Jackson? Perhaps she was simply waiting it out, Penelope hoping Odysseus would find his way home. Nathan had a school project for the holidays about the *Odyssey*. He didn't seem to have learned anything, whereas Jackson had learned quite a lot.

Nathan attended a private school (mostly thanks to Julia's fee for *Collier*), which was something that Jackson objected to on principle but was secretly relieved by as Nathan's local comp was a sink school. ('I can't decide which you are,' Julia said, 'a hypocrite or just a failed ideologue.' Had she always been so judgemental? That used to be the job of his ex-wife Josie. When had it become Julia's?)

Jackson had grown bored with Gary and Kirsty. They were creatures of habit, going out together every Monday and Wednesday evening, in Leeds, where they both worked at the same insurance company. The same pattern: a drink, a meal and then a couple of hours closeted in Kirsty's tiny modern flat, where Jackson could guess what they were up to without, thank goodness, having to actually witness it. Afterwards Gary drove home to Penny and the brick-built, character-free, semi-detached house they owned in Acomb, a flat suburb of York. Jackson like to think that if he was a married man conducting an illicit affair – something he had never done, hand to God – then it would have been a little more spontaneous, a little less predictable. A little more fun. Hopefully.

Leeds was a long drive over the moors and so Jackson had contracted a helpful youth called Sam Tilling who lived in Harrogate and had been kicking his heels between university and joining the police when Jackson recruited him to do some legwork for him. Sam cheerfully carried out the more tedious assignments – the wine bars, the cocktail lounges and the curry houses where Gary and

Kirsty indulged in bridled passion. They occasionally tottered off on a day-trip somewhere. It was Thursday today so they must have bunked off work on account of the good weather. Jackson, with no real evidence, imagined that Gary and Kirsty were the kind of people who would deceive their employers without any qualms.

As Peasholm Park was practically on Jackson's doorstep, he had chosen to follow them himself today. Plus, it gave him something to do with Nathan, even if Nathan's preferred default position was to be inside playing *Grand Theft Auto* on his Xbox or chatting online with his friends. (What on earth did they find to *say* to each other? They never *did* anything.) Jackson had tried dragging Nathan (almost literally) up the hundred and ninety-nine steps to the gaunt ruins of Whitby Abbey in a vain attempt to make him understand history. Similarly the museum, a place that Jackson liked for its quirky medley of exhibits from fossilized crocodiles to whaling memorabilia to the mummified hand of a hanged man. None of that interactive, keep-the-ADHD-kids-amused-no-matter-what stuff. Just a gallimaufry of the past, still in its original Victorian cases — butterflies pinned, birds stuffed, war medals displayed, dolls' houses open to view. The odds and ends of people's lives, which, when all was said and done, were the things that mattered, weren't they?

Jackson was surprised that Nathan wasn't attracted by the gruesomeness of the mummified hand. 'The Hand of Glory' it was called and it carried an elaborate, confusing folktale of gallows and opportunistic housebreakers. The museum was full, too, of Whitby's maritime heritage, also of no interest whatsoever to Nathan, and obviously the Captain Cook Museum was a non-starter. Jackson admired Cook. 'First man to sail round the world,' he said, trying to engage Nathan's interest. 'So?' he said. (So! How Jackson hated that contemptuous *So?*) Perhaps his son was right. Perhaps the past was no longer the context for the present. Perhaps none of it mattered any more. Was this how the world would end — not with a bang but a *So?*

While Gary and Kirsty were gallivanting, Penny Trotter was seeing to business — a gift shop in Acomb called the Treasure Trove, the interior of which smelt of an unholy mix of patchouli-scented incense and artificial vanilla. The stock consisted mostly of cards and wrapping paper, calendars, candles, soaps, mugs and a lot of twee objects whose function wasn't readily apparent. It was the kind of business that kept going by staggering from one festivity to the next – Christmas, Valentine's Day, Mother's Day, Hallowe'en, back to Christmas again, and all the birthdays in between.

'Well, it has no *purpose* as such,' Penny Trotter had said when Jackson questioned the raison d'être of a stuffed felt heart that had *Love* picked out in sequins across its scarlet surface. 'You just hang it up somewhere.' Penny Trotter had a romantic nature – it was her downfall, she said. She was a Christian, 'born again' in some way. (Once was enough, surely?) She wore a cross around her neck and a band around her wrist with the initials WWJD printed on it, which baffled Jackson. 'What Would Jesus Do?' she explained. 'It makes me stop and think before I do something I might regret.' Jackson reckoned he would find one of those useful. WWJD – What Would Jackson Do?

Brodie Investigations was the latest incarnation of Jackson's erstwhile private detective agency, although he tried not to use the term 'private detective' – it had too many glamorous connotations (or sleazy, depending how you looked at it). Too Chandleresque. It raised people's expectations.

Jackson's days consisted of some dog-work for solicitors – debt tracing, surveillance and so on. Then there was employee theft, DBS, background checks, a bit of due diligence, but really when he hung up the virtual shingle for Brodie Investigations he may as well have suspended one of Penny Trotter's stuffed hearts because the majority of his work was either following cheating spouses (infidelity, thy name is Gary) or trapping unsuspecting would-be Garys in the sticky insides of honeypots (or fly-traps, as Jackson thought of them) to test fiancés and boyfriends with temptation. Even Jackson, long in the tooth though he was, had not realized just how many suspicious women there were out there.

To this end, he primed his man-eating traps with an agent provocateur. This took the form of a particularly enticing yet lethal honey bee – a Russian woman called Tatiana. More hornet than honey bee, actually. Jackson had first encountered Tatiana in another lifetime when she had been a dominatrix and he had been fancy-free and – briefly, ludicrous though it seemed now – a millionaire. Not sex, not a relationship, God forbid, he'd rather go to bed with the aforesaid hornet than Tatiana. She had simply been on the fringes of an investigation he had got caught up in. And anyway he had been with Julia at the time (or had been under the impression that he was), busily creating the embryo that would one day sprawl its legs and fold its arms sarcastically. Tatiana had been a child of the circus, she claimed, her father a famous clown. Clowns in Russia were not funny, she said. They aren't here either, Jackson thought. Tatiana herself, unlikely as it seemed, had once been a trapeze artist. Did she still practise? Jackson wondered.

The world had grown darker since he first met her, although the world grew darker every day as far as Jackson could make out, yet Tatiana remained much the same, although she, too, had reincarnated. He had come across her again by chance (he presumed, but who knew?) in Leeds, where she had been working as a waitress in a cocktail bar (there was a song in there somewhere), dipping and puppy-dogging for customers in a tight black sequinned dress. 'Legitimate,' she told him later, but the word was rendered implausible on her lips.

Jackson had been having a professional after-hours drink with a lawyer called Stephen Mellors for whom he did sporadic work. The bar was the kind of modish place where it was so dark that you could hardly see your drink in front of you. Mellors, a modish sort himself, metrosexual and proud of it, something Jackson could never be accused of, ordered a Manhattan while Jackson settled for a Perrier. Leeds had never struck Jackson as the kind of place where you could trust the tap water. Not that he had anything against alcohol, quite the opposite, but he had very strict self-imposed drunk-driving rules. You only had to scrape a carload of over-the-limit teenagers off the tarmac once to see that cars and alcohol don't mix.

A waitress had taken their order and a different waitress had brought it to their table. She had bobbed down with her tray of drinks, a potentially precarious move for a woman in four-inch heels, but it did allow Mellors to eye up her cleavage as she put his Manhattan down on their low table. She delivered Jackson's Perrier in the same manner, pouring the water slowly into his glass as if it were an act of seduction. 'Thanks,' he said, trying to behave like a gentleman (a lifelong project) and not look at the cleavage. Instead he looked her in the eye and found that she was smiling at him in a feral way that was startlingly familiar and saying, 'Hello, Jackson Brodie, we meet again,' as if she were auditioning for a part as a Bond villainess. By the time Jackson had recovered the power of speech she had stalked off on those killer heels (they weren't called stilettos for nothing) and disappeared into the shadows.

'Wow,' Stephen Mellors said approvingly. 'You're a lucky man, Brodie. Thighs like a nutcracker. I bet she does a lot of squats.'

'Trapeze, actually,' Jackson said. He noticed a fallen sequin, glinting on the table in front of him like a calling-card.

They made their way out of the park, Nathan loping along like a puppy, Dido gamely hirpling as if she could do with a hip replacement (she could, apparently). At the gates of the park there was a noticeboard on to which several posters had been affixed advertising the various delights of the summer season – Lifeboat Flag Day, Tom Jones at the open-air theatre, Showaddywaddy at the Spa. There was some kind of Eighties revival show, a variety thing, at the Palace, with Barclay Jack topping the bill. Jackson recognized his gurning face. *'The North's very own side-splitting laughter-maker. Parental guidance required.'*

Jackson knew something dodgy about Barclay Jack, but he couldn't get the knowledge to rise up from the seabed of his memory – a dismal place that was littered with the rusting wreckage and detritus of his brain cells. Some scandal to do with kids or drugs, an accident in a swimming pool. There'd been a putative raid on his house that had come to nothing and then a lot of apologizing and backtracking from the police and the media, but that was his career pretty much ruined. There was something else too, but Jackson had exhausted his powers of retrieval.

'That guy's a wanker,' Nathan said.

'Don't use that word,' Jackson said. Was there an age limit, he wondered, when you let your child swear with impunity?

On the way to the car park they passed a bungalow with its name proudly on the gate – Thisldo. Nathan took some time decoding it and then snorted with laughter. 'That's crap,' he said.

'It is,' Jackson agreed. ('Crap' was allowed, he judged – too useful a word to ban completely.) 'But, you know, perhaps it's quite, I dunno . . . Zen' (*Zen* – was he really saying that?) 'to know when you've got somewhere and realize that it's enough. Not striving, just accepting.' A concept Jackson struggled with every day.

'It's still crap.'

'Yeah, well.'

In the car park there were what Jackson always thought of as 'bad boys' – three of them, only a couple of years older than Nathan. They were smoking and drinking cans of something that would definitely be on Julia's taboo list. And loitering far too near Jackson's car for his liking. Although in his head he drove something more virile, his actual vehicle of choice was currently a tragically uninspiring mid-range Toyota that endorsed his parental, Labrador-sitting status.

'Lads?' he said, suddenly becoming a policeman again. They sniggered at the authority in his voice. Jackson could sense Nathan shrinking towards him – for all his bravado, he was still a child. Jackson's heart filled at this sign of vulnerability. If anyone laid a finger on his son or upset him in any way Jackson had to suppress the urge to rip their head off and stick it where the sun never shone. Middlesbrough, perhaps.

Dido growled instinctively at the boys. 'Really?' Jackson said to her. 'You and whose wolf?'

'That's my car,' he said to the boys, 'so hop it, lads, okay?' It would take more than a posturing teenage prat to scare Jackson. One of them crushed his empty can underfoot and bumped the car with his arse so that the alarm went off and they all exploded into laughter like hyenas. Jackson sighed. He could hardly beat them up, they were still – technically – children and he preferred to restrict his acts of violence to people old enough to fight for their country.

The boys slouched away slowly, still facing him, their body language an insult. One of them was making an obscene gesture with both hands so he looked as though he was trying to do one-fingered juggling with an invisible object. Jackson turned the alarm off and unlocked the car. Nathan got in the car while Jackson gave Dido a leg-up into the back. She weighed a ton.

As they drove out of the car park they overtook the trio of boys, still sauntering along. One of them was imitating an ape – *oo-oo-ooo* – and tried to climb on to the bonnet of the Toyota when it crawled past them, as though they were in a safari park. Jackson put his foot down hard on the brake and the boy fell off the car. Jackson drove off without looking back to see if there was any damage done. 'Wankers,' he said to Nathan.

Albatross

The Belvedere Golf Club. On the green were Thomas Holroyd, Andrew Bragg, Vincent Ives. Butcher, baker, candlestick-maker. Actually, the owner of a haulage company, a travel-agent-cum-hotelier and a telecom-equipment area manager.

It was Vince's turn to tee off. He took up a stance and tried to focus. He heard Andy Bragg sighing impatiently behind him.

'Maybe you should stick to mini golf, Vince,' Andy said.

There were different categories of friends in Vince's opinion. Golf friends, work friends, old school friends, shipboard friends (he'd been on a Mediterranean cruise a few years ago with Wendy, his about-to-be-ex-wife), but *friend* friends were harder to come by. Andy and Tommy were in the golf-friends box. Not with each other – with each other they were friend friends. They had known each other for years and had a relationship so tight that Vince always felt as though he was on the outside of something when he was with them. Not that he could put his finger on what it was that he was excluded from exactly. He wondered sometimes if it wasn't so much that Tommy and Andy shared a secret as that they liked to make him *think* they shared a secret. Men never really left the snigger of the schoolyard, they just grew bigger. That was his wife's opinion, anyway. Soon-to-be-ex-wife.

'The ball won't move by telepathy, Vince,' Tommy Holroyd said. 'You have to hit it with the club, you know.'

Tommy was a big, fit man in his forties. He had a brawler's broken nose which didn't detract from his looks, indeed seemed to add to them where women were concerned. He'd started to run to flesh a

24

bit, but he was still the sort you'd definitely want in your corner rather than in the other bloke's. He'd had a 'misspent youth', he laughed to Vince, leaving school early and working the doors on several of the rougher northern clubs and hanging around with 'the wrong people'. Vince had once inadvertently overheard him refer to 'protection work' – a vague term that seemed to cover a multitude of either sins or virtues. 'Don't worry, those days are over,' Tommy said with a smile when he realized that Vince had heard what was being said. Vince had raised his hands meekly as though he was surrendering and said, 'No worries, Tommy.'

Tommy Holroyd was proud of being 'a self-made man'. Although wasn't everyone self-made, by definition? Vince was beginning to think that he hadn't made much of himself.

As well as being a bouncer, Tommy had been an amateur boxer. Combat seemed to be in the family – Tommy's own father had been a professional wrestler, a well-known 'heel', and had once beaten Jimmy Savile in the ring, at the Spa Royal Hall in Brid, something his son boasted about on his father's behalf. 'M'dad beat the nonce to a pulp,' he told Vince. 'If he'd known what he was really like he'd have killed him, I expect.'

Vince, for whom the world of wrestling was as arcane and exotic as a Chinese emperor's court, had to google the word 'heel'. A villain, an antagonist, someone who cheated or showed contempt. 'It was a role,' Tommy said, 'but m'dad didn't have to do much acting. He was a nasty bastard.' Vince felt sorry for Tommy. His own father had been as meek as a half of Tetley's Mild, his favourite tipple.

Tommy's narrative continued its rapid upward climb, from boxing to promoting, and when he'd made enough money from the ring he acquired an HGV licence and bought his first truck and that was the beginning of his fleet – Holroyd Haulage. It might not be the biggest flotilla of freight trailers in the North but it certainly seemed to be amazingly successful, if Tommy's lifestyle was anything to go by. He was flashily affluent, with a swimming pool and a second wife, Crystal, who, rumour had it, had once been a glamour model.

Tommy wasn't the kind of bloke who would pass you by on the street if you were in trouble, although Vince wondered if there might be a price to pay later. Vince liked Tommy though, he was easy-going and had what Vince could only think of as *presence*, a kind of northern swagger that Vince often coveted, feeling the singular lack of it in his own make-up. And Crystal was stunning. 'A Barbie doll' was Wendy's verdict on her. Vince thought that Wendy's idea of stunning would be to taser him, her once benign indifference to him having turned to loathing. And what had he done to provoke that feeling? Nothing!

Not long before Vince was first introduced to Tommy, Lesley – Tommy's first wife – had died in an awful accident. She had fallen off a cliff, trying to rescue the family pet – Vince remembered reading about it in the *Gazette* ('Wife of prominent East Coast businessman killed in tragedy' and so on), remembered saying to Wendy, 'You should be careful if you take Sparky up on the cliff.' Sparky was their dog, a puppy at the time. 'Who are you more worried about – me or the dog?' she said, and he had said, 'Well . . .' which he could see now was the wrong answer.

The Merry Widower, Andy had called Tommy, and he had indeed seemed surprisingly unmarked by the tragedy. 'Well, Les was a bit of a burden,' Andy said, rotating his index finger against the side of his head as if he was trying to screw a hole through to his brain. 'Looney Tunes.' Andy wasn't the sentimental sort. Quite the opposite. At the time, there had still been a desiccated bunch of flowers attached to a bench close to where Lesley Holroyd had gone over the cliff. It had seemed an inadequate kind of memorial.

'Earth to Vince,' Tommy said. 'A seagull's going to land on you if you don't move off that tee soon.'

'What's your handicap on the mini golf course, Vince?' Andy laughed, obviously not willing to let the subject go just yet. 'That windmill's tricky, those sails are a bugger to get through. And, of course, you have to be a real pro to face the rocket. It's a killer, it'll get you every time.'

Andy wasn't showy like Tommy. 'Yeah, he's a quiet one, our Andrew,' Tommy chuckled, putting his arm round Andy's shoulders and giving him a (very) manly hug. 'It's the quiet ones you've got to watch, Vince.'

'Piss off,' Andy said good-naturedly.

I'm a quiet one, Vince thought, and no one needs to worry about watching me. Andy was a small, wiry sort of bloke. If they were animals, Tommy would be a bear – and not a harmless soft teddy like the ones Vince's daughter, Ashley, covered her bed with. The bears were still there, waiting patiently for his absent daughter's return from her gap year. Tommy would be one of the ones you had to watch out for, like a polar or a grizzly. Andy would be a fox. That was a nickname Tommy sometimes used for Andy: Foxy. And Vince himself? A deer, he thought. Caught in the headlights of the car that was about to mow him down. Wendy at the wheel, probably.

Had either of them actually *played* mini golf? he wondered. He'd spent hours – enjoyable (mostly) – with Ashley when she was young, stoically encouraging her while she repeatedly missed the tee or mulishly insisted on attempting a putt, over and over, while a queue built up behind them, wailing *'Daaaad'* every time he signalled to the people who were waiting that they should play through. Ashley had been an obstinate child. (Not that he'd been resentful. He loved her!)

Vince sighed. Let Tommy and Andy have a laugh if they wanted to. Male banter – it used to be fun (more or less), all that swank and strut. Cocks of the North, all of them. It was in blokes' DNA or their testosterone or something, but Vince was too depressed these days to join in with the (mostly) good-natured jeering and one-upmanship.

If Tommy was still curving upward on the graph of life then Vince was on a decidedly downward gradient. He was grinding towards fifty and for the last three months he had been living in a one-bedroom flat behind a fish-and-chip shop, ever since Wendy turned to him one morning over his breakfast muesli – he'd been on a short-lived health kick – and said, 'Enough's enough, don't you think, Vince?' leaving him slack-mouthed with astonishment over his Tesco Finest Berry and Cherry.

Ashley had just set off on her gap year, backpacking around South-East Asia with her surfer boyfriend. As far as Vince could tell, 'gap year' meant the lull between him funding her expensive private school and funding her expensive university, a remission that was nonetheless still costing him her airfares and a monthly allowance.

When Vince was young he had been taught the worthy noncon-formist virtues of self-discipline and self-improvement, whereas Ashley (not to mention the surfer boyfriend) simply believed in the 'self' bit. (Not that he was resentful. He loved her!)

As soon as Ashley had fledged, on an Emirates flight to Hanoi, Wendy reported to Vince that their marriage was dead. Its corpse wasn't even cold before she was internet dating like a rabbit on speed, leaving him to dine off fish and chips most nights and wonder where it all went wrong. (Tenerife, three years ago, apparently.)

'I got you some cardboard boxes from Costcutter to put your stuff in,' she said as he stared uncomprehendingly at her. 'Don't forget to clear out your dirty clothes from the basket in the utility room. I'm not doing any more laundry for you, Vince. Twenty-one years a slave. It's enough.'

This, then, was the return on sacrifice. You worked all the hours God gave, driving hundreds of miles a week in your company car, hardly any time for yourself, so your daughter could take endless selfies in Angkor Wat or wherever and your wife could report that for the last year she had been sneaking around with a local café owner who was also one of the lifeboat crew, which seemed to sanc-tion the liaison in her eyes. ('Craig risks his life every time he goes out on a shout. Do you, Vince?' Yes, in his own way.) It clipped at your soul, clip, clip, clip.

Wendy enjoyed shaving and shearing, slicing and trimming. She had the Flymo out on the lawn almost every night in summer – over the years she had spent more time with the lawnmower than she had with Vince. And she might as well have had secateurs for hands. One of Wendy's weird hobbies was growing a bonsai tree (or stop-ping it growing, Vince supposed), a cruel pastime that reminded him of those Chinese women who used to bind their feet. That was what she was doing to him now, snipping at his soul, trimming him down to a dwarf version of himself.

He had trudged through his life for his wife and daughter, more heroically than they could imagine, and this was the thanks he received. Couldn't be a coincidence that 'trudge' rhymed with 'drudge'. He had presumed that there was a goal to be reached at the end of all the trudging, but it turned out that there was nothing – just more trudging.

'You again?' the jolly, bustling woman behind the chip-shop counter said to him every time he came in. He could probably have reached out of his back window and into the chip shop and scooped the fish out of the fryer himself.

'Yes, me again,' Vince said without fail, brightly, as if it was a surprise to him too. It was like that film *Groundhog Day*, except that he didn't learn anything (because, let's face it, there was nothing to learn) and nothing ever changed.

Had he complained? No. In fact, that had been the refrain of his adult life. 'Can't complain.' A British stoic to the core. Mustn't grumble. Like someone in an old-fashioned sitcom. He was making up for it now, even if only to himself, because he still felt impelled to put on a good face for the world, it seemed bad manners to do otherwise. 'If you can't say something nice,' his mother had tutored him, 'then don't say anything at all.'

'One of each, please,' he said to the woman in the chip shop. Was there anything more wretched than an about-to-be-divorced middle-aged man ordering a single fish supper?

'Do you want scraps with that?' the woman asked.

'If you've got them, please. Thank you,' he said, grimacing inwardly. Yes, he was not blind to the irony of her question, he thought, as the woman shovelled up the crispy remnants of batter. That was all that was left of his life now. Scraps.

'More?' she asked, the scoop still poised, prepared to be generous. The kindness of strangers. He should learn her name, Vince thought. He saw more of her than he did anyone else.

'No, thanks. That'll do.'

'Thisldo' they had called their house, a jokey idea that seemed stupid now, but they had been a jokey kind of family once. A unit that functioned at the top of its game – barbecues in the back garden, friends round for drinks, trips to Alton Towers, foreign holidays at four-star resorts, a cruise or two. Living the dream, compared to a lot of people. The dream of a middle-aged, middle-of-the-road, middle-class man.

They had loaded up the boot every weekend at Tesco's and never stinted on Ashley's dance classes, horse riding, birthday parties, tennis lessons. (School skiing trips. You needed a second mortgage for them!) And all the time he spent ferrying her to 'sleepovers' and 'playdates'. She didn't come cheap. (Not that he was resentful. He loved her!)

And driving lessons – hours, days, even, of his life that he would never get back, teaching both his wife and daughter to drive. Sitting in the passenger seat of his own car with one of them in the driving seat, neither of whom could tell left from right or even backwards from forwards. And then suddenly Ashley was in the back of a tuk-tuk and Wendy had a Honda with a UKIP sticker on the back that she zipped around in, looking for the new Mr Right now that Vince was suddenly Mr Wrong. Craig, the lifeboatman, had been jettisoned apparently in favour of the smorgasbord of Tinder. According to his wife, Vince could have had a whole Mr Men series of his own – Mr Boring, Mr Overweight, Mr Exhausted. And to add insult to injury, Wendy had gone back to her maiden name, as if he was to be erased entirely from existence.

'Thisldo,' he snorted to himself. Now it didn't do at all and even Sparky treated him like a stranger. Sparky was an indeterminate kind of lurcher that had chosen Wendy as its alpha male even though Vince was inordinately fond of it and was the one who had usually taken it for walks or cleaned up its crap or fed it its expensive food – which in retrospect seemed of a higher quality than the tins of supermarket-own-brand stew he had been reduced to buying nowadays for himself when he wasn't dining on fish and chips. He should probably just buy dog food for himself instead of the stew, it couldn't be any worse. He missed the dog more than he missed Wendy. In fact, he was surprised to find that he hardly missed Wendy at all, just the home comforts she had taken away from him. A man bereft of his home comforts was just a sad and lonely bastard.

Vince had still been in the Signals when he met Wendy, at an Army mate's wedding down South. He'd had a Balkans suntan and newly promoted sergeant's stripes and she had giggled and said, 'Oh, I do like a man in uniform,' and two years later they were at their own wedding and he was on civvy street, working for a telecoms firm, first as an engineer, running the IT, before moving into the suit-and-tie end of the business, in management, ten years ago. He thought of Craig, the lifeboatman, and wondered now if it had been the uniform all along that she had liked about Vince and not the man inside it.

'My mother warned me not to marry you,' she had laughed as, exhausted and drunk, they had stripped themselves of their wedding finery in the bedroom of the hotel where they had their reception – a lacklustre venue on the outskirts of Wendy's home town of Croyden. As a seductive prelude to their first night as a married couple the words didn't augur well. Her mother – a mean-spirited, lazy widow – had indulged in a disproportionate amount of wailing and gnashing of teeth over Wendy's choice of husband. Sitting in the front pew in an appalling hat, she may as well have been at a funeral from her aspect of grief. In subsequent years she had strived hard for the award for 'Most Critical Mother-in-Law in the World'. 'Yeah, competition's stiff for that one,' Tommy said, although he had managed two marriages with no mother-in-law in sight. It was a huge relief for Vince when she died a couple of years ago from a lingering cancer that transformed her into a martyr in Wendy's eyes.

'If only I'd listened to my poor mother,' Wendy said as she itemized the belongings he was allowed to take with him. Wendy who was getting so much money in the settlement that Vince barely had enough left for his golf-club fees.

'Best I can do, Vince,' Steve Mellors said, shaking his head sadly. 'Matrimonial law, it's a minefield.' Steve was handling Vince's divorce for him for free, as a favour, for which Vince was more than grateful. Steve was a corporate lawyer over in Leeds, and didn't usually 'dabble in divorce'. Neither do I, Vince thought, neither do I.

Vince shared history with Steve Mellors – they had gone to the same school, in Dewsbury, home of the coarse recycled-wool industry known as shoddy. Appropriate, Vince thought, considering how his life was turning out. After school their paths had diverged markedly. Steve's took him to Leeds to do Law while Vince went straight into the Army, at his father's behest, 'to get a decent trade'. His father owned a plumbing business, he *was* the business, he'd never even taken on an apprentice. His father was a nice man, a patient man, who never raised his voice to Vince or his mother, did the football pools every Friday and came home with a box of cakes every Saturday from the baker's next to his shop. Lemon squares and sponge drops. Never grumbled. It was in the genes.

His father hadn't encouraged Vince to follow him into the plumbing business. 'You'll spend half your life up to your elbows in other people's shit, son.' And Vince had indeed got a trade, the Signals was good for that. He had rarely been deployed to the heart of a conflict. Ulster, the Gulf, Bosnia – Vince had been behind the lines in a support unit, fiddling with technical equipment or trying to resuscitate ailing software. It was only in his last deployment in Kosovo that he had gone in with the front-line troops and come under fire. He had tasted conflict and he hadn't liked it. Hadn't liked the fallout from war either – the women, the children, even the dogs, who constituted 'collateral damage'. After Kosovo he decided to get out of the Army. Unlike a lot of the other guys, he had never regretted leaving.

Steve Mellors had always been the clever, popular one. It had been enough for Vince to be his sidekick and let some of Steve's self-assured aura rub off on him. Watson to Steve's Holmes, Tenzing to his Hillary. In Vince's animal lexicon, Steve would have been a young lion in those days.

They used to ride their bikes home from school together along the canal towpath, a lot of larking around, until one day Steve hit a bump, went head over handlebars, banged his head on the dried-mud towpath and toppled into the water. Slipped under. '*Just like that,*' Vince said later in the retelling of the incident, doing his best Tommy Cooper impression. He used to be the class jester. Something that was hard to believe now.

Vince waited for Steve to resurface, to swim to the bank – he was a good swimmer – but there was nothing, just a few bubbles rising to the surface as if it was a fish down there, not a person.

Vince jumped in the canal and pulled his friend out. He laid him down on the bank and after a couple of seconds half the canal gushed back out of his mouth and he sat up and said, 'Fuck.' He had a bruise the size of a duck egg on his forehead from where he had knocked himself unconscious, but apart from that he seemed fine.

It hadn't seemed a particularly heroic act to Vince at the time, he'd done a life-saving class at the local swimming pool so he was hardly going to stand there and watch his friend drown. It made a bond between them (saving someone's life would do that, he supposed) because they had stayed in touch, however tangentially – sporadic Christmas cards mostly. They both, in their different ways, shared the trait of loyalty – not always a good thing, as far as Vince could see. He had been loyal to Wendy, he had been loyal to Sparky. Had they been loyal to him in return? No. And, sadly, he had no doubt that Ashley would take her mother's side in the divorce. They were two peas in a pod.

He had reconnected in person with Steve at a school reunion a couple of years ago, a hellish event that confirmed Wendy's belief that men didn't grow up, they just got bigger. And balder. And fatter. Not Steve though, he had the look of a thoroughbred who groomed himself every morning, nothing shoddy about Steve. 'Are you keeping your portrait in the attic then, Steve?' someone said at the school reunion. He laughed the comment off ('Tennis and the love of a good woman') but Vince could see that he preened himself a little at the compliment. Girls and money – those had always been the twin targets that Steve had aimed for, Vince supposed, and it seemed he had hit bullseyes in both.

He had morphed into 'Stephen' these days, although Vince found it hard to call him that. It was Steve who had introduced Vince to 'my good friends' Tommy and Andy. They made an odd trio – the lion, the bear and the fox, like something out of Aesop's Fables. In Vince's hierarchy of friends, Tommy and Andy and Steve would be friend friends. There was a pecking order at work though, Vince soon realized. Steve looked down on Tommy because Steve was better educated. Tommy looked down on Andy because Tommy had a gorgeous wife, and Andy looked down on him because, well, because he was Vince. Vince had no one to look down on. Except himself.

'Andy and Tommy live in your neck of the woods,' Steve said.

'You should get to know them. They might be useful to you.' (For what? Vince had wondered.) And it was Steve, too, who had proposed him for the Belvedere Golf Club.

In Vince's complex hierachy of friendship, Steve was a school friend, not a friend friend – too much time had elapsed, too many experiences hadn't been shared. 'Old school chum,' Steve had said, thumping him (rather hard) on the back when he introduced him to Tommy and Andy. It made Vince feel young for a moment and then it made him feel old. 'This guy saved my life,' Steve said to Tommy and Andy, 'and I mean literally. You could say that I owe him everything.'

'Long time ago now,' Vince said, staring modestly at his feet. He didn't think they'd ever used the word 'chum' when they were in Dewsbury. He doubted that anyone in West Yorkshire ever had. It was a word more suited to the playing fields of Eton than the shoddy capital of the North.

Steve lived now in an old farmhouse outside Malton, with an attractive, sophisticated wife called Sophie, a strapping rugby-playing teenage son called Jamie and a pony-obsessed, rather sullen daughter called Ida. 'Princess Ida,' Sophie laughed as if that was some kind of family joke. 'It's a Gilbert and Sullivan opera,' she explained when she saw Wendy looking blank. ('Pretentious cow,' Wendy said in the evening's debrief later.)

They'd been invited over for dinner, him and Wendy, but it had been a slightly awkward evening, just the four of them, that had left Wendy feeling churlish because Vince hadn't done as well in his life as his old 'chum'.

'Showing off, if you ask me,' Wendy said. 'Silver cutlery, crystal glasses, damask tablecloth,' she inventoried. 'I thought it was supposed to be a simple kitchen-table supper.' (What was that? Vince wondered. Something she'd read about in a colour supplement?) He, too, had been a little surprised at Steve's lifestyle, but you could hardly hold it against a man for doing well.

They had forgotten to take a gift with them and arrived with a last-minute bottle of wine and bunch of flowers from a garage en route as well as a hastily chosen box of After Eights. ('How lovely,' Sophie murmured.)

They'd had a little tabby called Sophie, got as a kitten before Ashley was born. She had died only a couple of years ago and Vince still missed her undemanding companionship. Every time Steve mentioned his wife, Vince was reminded of the cat, although the name was the only thing she had in common with Steve's svelte spouse, apart from a penchant for a brindled colourway. Before her marriage, Sophie had been a high-ranking accountant 'with Deloitte', but she had given up work to look after her family. 'It's a full-time job, after all, isn't it?' she said.

'Tell me about it,' Wendy said. In retrospect, Vince could see that his wife had inherited her mother's predisposition to martyrdom.

He had castigated himself for not bringing better wine but was relieved in the end because Steve made a big deal out of the 'Pommard, 2011' he was decanting, even though to Vince it tasted like any old red you could have grabbed off the shelf in Tesco's.

'And her, *Sophie*,' Wendy said disdainfully (no sisterhood for Wendy), 'she was wearing Dries Van Noten, while the best I can do is Marks and Spencer's Autograph.' Although Vince didn't understand the specifics of this sentence, he understood the implication. It wasn't the best Wendy could do, it was the best Vince had done on her behalf.

They had reciprocated, rather reluctantly. Wendy had cooked some kind of fancy lamb dish and an even fancier dessert. Thisldo had a poky dining room that was only used on high days and holidays and the Ercol dining table was usually covered with Vince's paperwork (not any more!), which had to be cleared away. Wendy had fretted uncharacteristically about flowers and 'tapered dinner candles' and cloth napkins, all of which Vince had to go and find on his way to a 'proper' wine merchant.

In the end, Vince's verdict was that it was a pleasant enough evening. Sophie had arrived with roses 'from the garden' and Steve was clutching a bottle of 'Dom', ready chilled, and they managed to avoid politics and religion (although who talked about religion these days?) and when Brexit had momentarily reared its ugly head Vince managed to quash it quickly back down.

★

Vince tried to focus. *Be the ball.* He took his shot and chunked it.

'Keep up, Vince!' Andy Bragg yelled at him as they hauled their trolleys across the green. 'Eighteenth's in sight, last one pays.'

It was a beautiful afternoon. Vince struggled to appreciate it despite the cloud of despondency hanging over him. From here, high up on the cliff, the whole of the town was visible, the castle on the cliff, the sweep of the North Bay. A great blue sky as far as you could see.

'Makes a man glad to be alive,' Tommy Holroyd said as he lined his own ball up. He was a good golfer, three under par at the moment. *Thwack!*

'Good shot,' Vince said generously.

And All Things Nice

Crystal was having a fly cigarette in the conservatory. There had been a bake-sale at Candy's playgroup, they had one every month. It helped to pay for outings and the rent for the church hall. Everyone made something except for Crystal, who doubted that the other mothers would appreciate her 'vegan zucchini mud cake' or 'gluten-free parsnip cup cakes' – she was a zealous convert to 'clean eating'. To make up for her perceived shortcomings she bought tons of other people's sickly offerings and then binned them when she got home or let Candy feed them to the ducks. Crystal felt bad for the ducks, they should be eating pond weed or whatever it was that ducks ate.

Today she had brought home flapjacks, a Victoria sponge, and something labelled as a 'traybake fluffle slice'. Crystal couldn't even begin to imagine what that might be. Was 'fluffle' even a word? She'd have to ask her stepson, Harry. Whatever it was, it looked figging awful. Crystal had made a massive effort not to swear after Candy was born. There was a whole list of stupid substitutes online. Sugar, fudge, fig, fiddlesticks, crackers. The 'c' word – carrots. Yes, she had been on fucking Mumsnet. Figging Mumsnet. There you go, you see – it was hard work retraining yourself. It turned out you could take the girl out of Hull but you couldn't take Hull out of the woman.

Tommy didn't think swearing and smoking were 'ladylike', although what Tommy knew about ladies could be written on a postage stamp. If he'd wanted a lady perhaps he should have gone shopping for one at a tea dance or a WI meeting or wherever it was you found them, and not in a nail bar in the ailing back streets of a seaside town.

Before she became Mrs Thomas Holroyd, Crystal had clawed her way up, hand over hand, to reach the dizzying heights of nail technician. She had run Nail It! for an owner she never saw. A big gruff bloke called Jason called in every week and, opposite to what would happen in a regular business, deposited cash rather than collecting it. He wasn't what you would call a conversationalist. She wasn't stupid, she knew it was a front. Was there a nail bar or tanning salon in the world that wasn't? But she had kept her mouth shut and run a nice place, although you had to wonder why the Inland Revenue didn't question the fact that she was shifting so much money. And it was just Crystal, no trafficked Vietnamese kids enslaved to the file and polish, like you saw in other places. 'More trouble than they're worth,' Jason said, as if he knew about these things.

For work, Crystal had worn a spotless white uniform – tunic and trousers, not the sexy-nurse kind of outfit that you could get for hen nights – and kept everything clinically clean. She was good at what she did – acrylics, gels, shellac, nail art – and was proud of the attention she gave to her job, even if trade was sparse. It was the first thing she'd ever done that didn't involve selling her body in one way or another. Marriage to Tommy was a financial transaction too, of course, but to Crystal's way of thinking, you could be lap-dancing for the fat sweaty patron of a so-called 'gentlemen's club' or you could be greeting Tommy Holroyd with a peck on the cheek and hanging his jacket up before laying his dinner before him. It was all part of the same spectrum as far as Crystal was concerned, but she knew which end of it she preferred. And, to quote Tina Turner, what does love have to do with it? Fig all, that was what.

There was no shame in marrying for money – money meant security. Women had been doing it since time began. You saw it on all the nature programmes on TV – build me the best nest, do the most impressive dance for me, bring me shells and shiny things. And Tommy was more than happy with the arrangement – she cooked for him, she had sex with him, she kept house for him. And in return she woke up every morning and felt one step further away from her old self. History, in Crystal's opinion, was something that was best left behind where it belonged.

And she had lots of shells and shiny things in the form of a huge wardrobe of clothes, a diamond bracelet and matching pendant, a gold Cartier watch (given to her by Tommy on their first anniversary, inscribed *From Tommy with love*), a high-spec white Range Rover Evoque, a black American Express card, a child, Candace – Candy – whom she adored. This was not the order that Crystal ranked her assets in. The child came first. Always and for ever. She was ready to kill anyone who touched a hair on Candy's head.

She had met Tommy when he came into the salon one wild and wet afternoon, looking attractively dishevelled on account of the force-eight gale outside, and said, 'Can you give me a quick manicure, love?' He was on his way to a meeting, he said, but couldn't turn up with his hands 'covered in oil and muck'. He'd had to change 'a bugger of a tyre' in a lay-by, apparently, on his way back from Castleford.

Tommy was surprisingly chatty and so was Crystal, if only professionally ('So are you going on holiday this summer?'), and one thing led to another. As it does. And now here she was mashing a tell-tale stub of a cigarette into a Swiss cheese plant – an ugly thing that refused to stop growing – and wondering if the washing-machine with his shirts inside had finished its spin cycle.

Tommy's first wife – Lesley – had been a smoker and he said that the smell of cigarettes reminded him of her. He didn't say whether this was a bad thing or a good thing, but either way it was probably best not to summon up the ghost of the first Mrs Tommy Holroyd in his presence with a packet of Marlboro Lights. 'She was a bit unstable, Les was,' Tommy said, which, considering what happened to her, could have been funny if it wasn't so horrible. It was an accident (Crystal hoped), but you never knew in this life when you might slip and lose your footing and find yourself going over the edge. Crystal trod a very careful path these days.

Crystal was hovering around thirty-nine years old and it took a lot of work to stay in this holding pattern. She was a construction, made from artificial materials – the acrylic nails, the silicone breasts, the polymer eyelashes. A continually renewed fake tan and a hairpiece fixed into her bleached-blonde hair completed the synthetic that was Crystal. A hairpiece was less trouble than extensions and it wasn't as if Tommy was bothered either way. The hair was real, Crystal had no idea who it had once belonged to. She'd worried it might have come from a corpse but her hairdresser said, 'Nah, from a temple in India. The women shave their heads for some kind of religious thing and then the monks sell it.' Crystal wondered if the hair got blessed before it was packed up and sent on its way. Holy hair. She liked the idea. It would be nice if a bit of holiness were to rub off on her.

Crystal was never sure where the 'glamour model' thing had come from, she must have mentioned something in the throes of courtship. 'Topless only,' Tommy said if he told people – he liked to tell people, she wished he wouldn't. It was true she had done some photographic stuff, some films as well, early on, but there'd been precious little that was glamorous about it, quite the opposite. And it wasn't just her top that had been off.

'The bimbo,' she'd heard someone say at their wedding. It didn't worry Crystal, it was the way Tommy liked her and she'd been called far worse names in her time. And, let's face it, 'bimbo' was a step up from most things that had gone before. Nonetheless you had to wonder when the cracks would start to show.

On the plus side, Tommy loved Candy and, as an extra bonus, he had a cheerful nature, not to mention being easy on the eye. Women found him attractive, although Crystal was pretty numb to the charms of men on account of her personal history, but she was adept at faking so it hardly mattered. And they lived in a fantastic house – High Haven. Tommy bought it after their wedding and renovated it, top-to-toe, all his workmen off the books, the interior décor left to Crystal so that it was like playing with the doll's house she'd never had as a child. It had a huge kitchen, an indoor swimming pool, all the bedrooms en suite. The swimming pool was just for her and the kids as Tommy didn't swim, although even Crystal thought it was a bit too bling as it had a kind of Roman theme with a gold mosaic of a dolphin in the middle of the pool and a couple of fake classical statues that Tommy had picked up in the local garden centre.

Crystal loved swimming, loved the way that when she moved

through the water it felt as if she was washing everything away. She'd been baptized once – full immersion – at the insistence of this Baptist minister that she'd known. 'Wash away your sins,' he said and she thought, What about yours then? No! She didn't need to revisit that memory, thank you very much.

The pool had been built into the basement of the house, so all the light was artificial, but in the rest of High Haven there were big windows everywhere and everything was painted white and it was like living inside a big box of light. Clean and white. Crystal believed in cleanliness – that was her religion, not some mumbo-jumbo God stuff. And, thank you, but she didn't need a psychiatrist to tell her that with every drop of Domestos and every wipe of Dettol-soaked J-cloth she was disinfecting the past.

The house was at the end of a long drive and perched high on a cliff, hence its name. It got battered by the weather in winter, but it had a great view of the sea. You wouldn't do anything to jeopardize living in a house like this.

She had side-stepped the après playgroup in Costa this morning. Sometimes it was too much like hard work. She knew that the play-group mothers regarded her as a curiosity (trophy wife, glamour model, et cetera), like a flamingo amongst a flock of chickens. They were all on Mumsnet. Enough said. She only suffered playgroup for Candy's sake, not to mention Baby Ballet and Gymini and Turtle Tots and Jo Jingles – it was a full timetable that left her hardly any time for her own martial arts classes. The only reason she'd chosen Wing Chun a couple of years ago was because it was at the local leisure centre and they ran a daycare. It sounded like something you would order in a Chinese restaurant. It wasn't. It was all about balance and strength and finding your power, both inner and outer. Crystal liked that idea. She was surprisingly good at finding her power.

It was important to Crystal that Candy had friends and fitted in and didn't grow up to be an odd one out. The flamingo amongst chickens. She was trying to give her daughter the childhood that she herself had been robbed of. A few weeks ago Harry had asked her what it had been like for her when she was young and she had

41

said, 'Oh, you know, Harry, fairground rides and ice-creams all the way.' Which was not in itself a lie, of course. Harry was sixteen, Tommy's son from the ill-fated first marriage. He was a funny boy, young for his age but also old for his age. He was a bit of an odd-bod, but Crystal was fond of him. He was nothing like his father, which was probably a good thing.

Instead of Costa, they had gone to the swings. Candy could sit on a swing for hours. Crystal understood, she felt the same about swimming laps in their pool. Up and down, up and down, nothing but the movement. It was soothing. And driving. She would drive all day if she could, she didn't even mind traffic jams and roadworks. Tommy – surprisingly patient – had taught her before they got married. She'd taken to it like a duck to water. What would it be like, she wondered, to live somewhere like Texas or Arizona where all you had ahead of you was the empty horizon, mile after mindless mile beneath your wheels, slowly erasing everything behind you?

When they got back in the car she said to Candy, 'Don't go to sleep back there, sweetheart, you'll spoil your nap,' although stopping a small child from nodding off in a warm car was pretty nigh impossible. She reached back and handed Candy her little pink portable DVD player and matching headphones and her *Frozen* DVD. She was, appropriately, dressed as Elsa today. In the wing-mirror Crystal could see there was a car behind them. A silver BMW 3 series. Crystal knew her cars.

She was pretty sure it was the same car she had noticed yesterday when she had given Harry a lift to Transylvania World. And then prowling after her as she came out of the car park in Sainsbury's. And then *again* later in the afternoon when she'd popped out to pick up the dry-cleaning. Too many times to be a coincidence, surely? Was someone following her? Watching her? Or was she being paranoid? Maybe she was going mad. Her mother had drunk herself into madness, leaving Crystal to the clutches of a so-called 'care home'. After that happened to you at the age of ten, nothing could surprise you.

In the back of the Evoque, Candy was in a world of her own, headbanging along to her DVD and yelling tunelessly to what might have been 'Do You Want To Build A Snowman?' but without being able to hear the music it was pretty much impossible for Crystal to tell.

Crystal tried to read the number plate of the BMW in the rear-view mirror, squinting because she couldn't locate her sunglasses in the glove compartment. They were Chanel, fitted with prescription lenses. She had terrible eyesight although she hardly ever wore her regular specs, it was a bad look on her (librarian slut) and her optician said she couldn't have contacts because she had 'dry eyes'. Must be all that crying she'd done as a child. Emptied the well.

She could make out a T and an X and a 6, it was like taking an eye test at the opticians, except backwards and on the move. The car had blacked-out windows and gave off a sinister air. Was it stalking her? Why? Had Tommy hired someone to follow her? A private detective? But why would he do that? She hadn't given Tommy any cause for suspicion, never would. He never asked her where she'd been or what she'd been doing, but that didn't mean he didn't want to know, she supposed. Henry VIII and Anne Boleyn sprang into her mind. The only bits of history Crystal knew seemed to involve women having their heads lopped off – Mary, Queen of Scots, Marie Antoinette.

'Don't forget Lady Jane Grey,' Harry said. 'The Nine Days' Queen, they called her.' They'd done the Tudors at school, he added apologetically. He tried not to show off his general knowledge around her general ignorance. She didn't mind, she'd learned a lot from Harry. His mother, Lesley, had 'lost her head' too, according to Tommy. 'After the baby.' There'd been a stillbirth, a sister for Harry. Harry didn't remember. Tommy loved Candace – his 'princess'. Her birth had secured Crystal's position as Queen of High Haven, Harry said. 'Like a character in *Game of Thrones*,' he added. It wasn't one of the TV programmes that they watched together. It was too much like real life for Crystal.

Before she could decipher anything else, the BMW took a sudden left turn and was lost to her.

Not Tommy, she decided. Hiring a private detective wasn't his style. He'd confront her head on. (*What the fuck, Crystal?*) Something more menacing than a suspicious Tommy? Some*one* more menacing than Tommy? There were plenty of those, but they were all in the past. Weren't they? She braked suddenly to avoid a cat that had pranced nonchalantly into the road. Candy gave a little squeal, halfway between delight and fear. She pulled off her headphones and Crystal could hear the music continuing tinnily within them. 'Mummy?' she said, a worried look on her little face.

'Sorry,' Crystal said, her heart racing. 'Sorry, sweetheart.'

When they got home Crystal fed Candy lunch — wholemeal toast with almond butter and a banana — and then put her down for a nap.

She knocked on Harry's bedroom door to see if he wanted anything. He always had his head in a book or was drawing little cartoons. 'He's artistic,' she said to Tommy, and he said, 'They're still calling it that, are they?' You didn't get to choose your children, you took what you were given, she said. Tommy didn't have a sense of humour, but Harry did, always coming out with silly jokes. ('Why didn't the cheese want to get sliced?' 'I don't know,' Crystal said obligingly, 'why didn't the cheese want to get sliced?' 'Because it had grater plans!') Nearly all his jokes were about cheese, for some reason.

There was no answer when she knocked on his door. He must be out. Harry was always busy — if he wasn't reading or drawing he was working at the vampire place. And at the theatre, too, this year. Tommy didn't give him much pocket money because he thought he should 'learn to stand on his own two feet', but Crystal slipped him the odd twenty. Why not? He was a good kid and the poor lad had lost his mum, you couldn't help but feel sorry for him.

'I lost my mum too,' she told Harry, but didn't add that for all she knew her mother was still alive. She imagined her not as a person but as a heap of gin-soaked, urine-stained rags in a forgotten corner somewhere. And as for her father, well, not a good idea to go there either. There wasn't even a path.

'Did you get on with your mum?' Harry had asked her the other day. He was always asking questions. She was always having to make up answers. 'Course I did,' she said. 'Who doesn't?'

She didn't like the idea that Harry was working for that old goat Barclay Jack at the Palace Theatre, but she could hardly explain her objections to Harry without revealing things that were best left to rot in the dark of the past. Barclay was a dirty old bugger, but at least he wasn't into boys. She wouldn't have let Harry near him if he had been. Still, he shouldn't really be allowed to carry on walking the earth. Crystal had met Barclay a couple of times – been 'introduced' to him. Nothing had happened, he hadn't been interested because she was 'too old' for him, apparently. She must have been all of fourteen by then. She shuddered at the memory. Bridlington, of course. It didn't matter how far you travelled, the road always led back to Bridlington.

Once Candy was asleep Crystal made herself a cup of mint tea and reviewed her bake-sale trawl. After much deliberation she freed the Victoria sponge from its suffocating cling film and placed it on the breakfast bar. Then she stared at it for a long time, tapping her false nails on the polished granite as if she were waiting impatiently for the cake to do something. Her heart began to hammer in her chest and her ribs felt like a corset that was being tightened by the second. It was as if she were about to perpetrate a murder. The cake was unresponsive and after some more silent debate with herself, Crystal cut herself a modest slice. She ate it standing up to lessen her commitment to it. It was disgusting. She put it back in the cupboard.

'You're beefing up there, love, aren't you?' Tommy had laughed the other night. She had been brushing her teeth in the en suite when he had put his arms round her from behind and grabbed a handful of her midriff beneath her lovely La Perla nightgown. As a kid she'd never had nightclothes, she'd had to sleep in her vest and knickers in her little bunk in the trailer.

Beefing up? What the duck? (A few pounds maybe, but it was muscle, from the Wing Chun.) Cheeky bugger. Badger. Cheeky badger, she corrected herself. (That sounded worse, somehow.) 'I don't mind,' Tommy said, moving his hands down to her hips. 'I like a bit of flesh on a woman. Gives you something to grab on to so you don't fall off. They don't call them love handles for nothing.'

Crystal retrieved the cake from the cupboard and placed it on the breakfast bar. She unwrapped it again, cut another modest slice. She sat down to eat it this time. Cut another slice, less modest. Ate it. And then another and another, stuffing them in her mouth. It was surprising how quickly you could eat an entire cake if you put your mind to it.

When the cake was finished Crystal stared at the empty plate for a while and then went to the downstairs cloakroom and threw it all back up again. She had to flush the toilet twice to sluice it away. She scrubbed the toilet bowl with bleach. You could have eaten out of her toilet, it was so clean. She refolded the towels and smoothed them down on the rail, realigned the spare toilet rolls in the cupboard beneath the sink and sprayed J'Adore around the small room. She felt lighter, cleansed. She returned to the kitchen and loaded the dishwasher. Then she went back to the conservatory and lit up another cigarette. Up to some of your old tricks again, Christina, she thought. What brought that on? she wondered.

Saving Lives at Sea

Collier's unit base was a couple of streets away. They'd commandeered half a municipal car park – at great cost, Jackson imagined. They were filming here all week – Julia's 'arc' involved being kidnapped by a raging psychopath who had escaped from prison and was on the run. Jackson couldn't remember why the raging psychopath had chosen to bring her to the seaside, he had stopped paying attention to the arc after a while.

It was five o'clock and Julia had said she thought she would be finishing about then. She had a day off tomorrow and Nathan was going to stay with her tonight in the Crown Spa. Jackson was looking forward to an evening of peace – living with Nathan was like living inside an argument. Jackson hadn't realized until recently how much he relished solitude nowadays. ('Some might call it reclusivity,' Julia said. 'Big word,' Jackson said.) And there were still several weeks of the school holidays to go. His son missed his friends, he was bored. He was *dying* of boredom, in fact, he said. No autopsy had ever resulted in 'boredom' being put on a death certificate, Jackson told him.

'Have you seen an autopsy?' Nathan asked, perking up at the idea.

'Plenty,' Jackson said.

How many dead bodies had he seen? 'Like in the whole of your life?'

'Too many,' Jackson said. And they all looked like they would have gladly opted for boredom rather than the slab.

As he cruised along the Esplanade looking for a parking place, Jackson peered up at the houses that lined the street. This was Savile territory – 'Jim'll Fix It' had owned an apartment along here

47

somewhere. There had been a plaque on the Esplanade railings, overlooking the sands, that said *Savile's View*. Long since removed, of course. Buried with the honours befitting a Catholic saint and now rotting in an unmarked grave to prevent desecration. So it goes, Jackson thought, just a shame it took so long. Just a shame there were so many other predators still out there. You might catch one, but then ten seemed to rush in to fill the vacuum and no one seemed able to fix that.

It was amazing how many deviants you could pack into one geographical area. Jackson had never forgotten being at a talk, a lifetime ago, given by a child protection officer. 'Look around at any seaside beach in summer,' she had said, 'and there'll be a hundred paedophiles enjoying themselves in their natural hunting-ground.'

It *was* a great view though, a panorama of the South Bay laid out before them. 'Great view,' Jackson said to Nathan, although he knew you had to be at least thirty before you could appreciate a good vista. And anyway Nathan was busy consulting the oracle of his iPhone.

Jackson spotted a parking space just as a Bassani's ice-cream van began to make admirably stately progress along the Esplanade towards them. It was pink and the tune it was playing was 'The Teddy Bears' Picnic'. The chimes sounded as though they were running down, making the music — if you could call it that — mournful rather than merry. Jackson had a vague memory of singing it to his daughter when she was little. He had never previously thought of it as a sad tune. *If you go down to the woods today, you'd better go in disguise.* Or threatening, even. He found it unnerving now, somehow.

There'd been something about those pink ice-cream vans, hadn't there? It had been one of the ways they'd enticed the kids. Could you hypnotize children with ice-cream-van chimes? Jackson wondered. Beguile them like the Pied Piper and lead them away to some horrible fate? (Had he read that in a Stephen King novel?) Who ran Bassani's now? Was it still in the family or was it just a name now?

How had Bassani and Carmody met each other? A council meeting, a black-tie charity event? They must have been delighted to discover they shared an appetite for the same fodder. It was a story that was depressingly familiar, a tale of girls – and boys – beguiled out of care homes and foster families or their own dysfunctional households. As council officials and respected charity supporters, Bassani and Carmody were in the perfect position to be welcomed into those places, they were *invited* in, for God's sake, like vampires. They came bearing gifts – offering Christmas parties, outings to the countryside and the seaside, camping and trailer holidays – Carmody had owned trailer sites all along the East Coast. The kids were given free entrance to amusement arcades and funfairs. Ice-cream, sweets, cigarettes. Treats. Deprived kids liked treats.

There'd always been rumours of a third man. Not Savile, he'd had his own show, separate from Bassani and Carmody. The pair of them had been on the go for decades without being caught. There used to be a TV programme, *The Good Old Days*, a tribute to the defunct music hall. The old programmes were still – for some reason, God knows why – being rebroadcast on BBC4. ('Post-irony,' Julia said, a term that was mysterious to Jackson.) Bassani and Carmody had had their own show. *The Bad Old Days*.

Bassani and Carmody had run this coast once. It was funny how so many men were defined by their downfall. Caesar, Fred Goodwin, Trotsky, Harvey Weinstein, Hitler, Jimmy Savile. Women hardly ever. They didn't fall down. They stood up.

'Can I have an ice-cream?' Nathan asked, the Pavlovian response to the chimes kicking in straight away.

'*Another* ice-cream? What do you think?'

'Why not?'

'Because you've just had one, obviously.'

'So?'

'*So*,' Jackson said, 'you're not getting another one.' It was never enough. It was the dominant trait in Nathan's friends too. It didn't matter how much they were given, how much stuff they acquired, they were never satisfied. They had been bred to consume and one day there would be nothing left. Capitalism would have eaten itself, thereby fulfilling its raison d'être in an act of self-destruction, aided by the dopamine feedback loop – the snake swallowing its own tail.

Still, his son had his virtues, Jackson reminded himself. He was good with Dido, for example. Sympathetic to her ailments, always ready to brush her or feed her. He had known her since she was a puppy. Nathan had been a puppy himself, sweet and playful, but now Dido had left him far behind. It wouldn't be long before her path ran out, and Jackson dreaded how Nathan would react to that. Julia would be worse, of course.

Jackson was distracted by the sight of a girl, walking on the other side of the road. She was wearing trainers, jeans and a T-shirt with a sequinned picture of a kitten's head on it. A brightly coloured backpack. Twelve years old? Jackson didn't like to see girls on their own. The ice-cream van slowed to a halt and the girl turned to look both ways (good) before crossing the road, and Jackson thought that she was going to get an ice-cream but then she stuck out her thumb (bad) at the passing cars.

She was hitching, for Christ's sake! She was a child, what was she thinking? She ran towards the ice-cream van, her backpack bumping against her skinny shoulders. The bag was blue and had a unicorn on it, amongst a scattering of little rainbows. Kittens, unicorns, rainbows – girls were curious creatures. He couldn't imagine Nathan carrying a bag with a unicorn on it or wearing a T-shirt displaying a kitten's head. Unless it was the logo of a global brand, in which case the sequins would probably have been sewn on by hand by a child in a Third World sweatshop. ('Must you always see the dark side of everything?' Julia said. 'Someone has to,' Jackson said. 'Yes, but does it have to be *you*?' Apparently, yes. It did.)

The girl didn't stop at the ice-cream van but instead ran past it, and that was when Jackson spotted the unassuming grey hatchback that had pulled to a halt in front of the Bassani's van, and before he could even think, *Don't do that!* she was climbing in the passenger side and the car was driving off.

'Quick!' Jackson said to Nathan. 'Photograph that car.'

'What?'

'That *car*, get the number plate.'

Too late. Jackson started the engine and threw the Toyota into a U-turn just as the ice-cream van moved off slowly and – lo and behold – a garbage truck appeared, straddling the road with no intention of making way for anyone and cutting Jackson off at the pass. Between the pink ice-cream van and the garbage truck, Jackson had lost all chance of following the car.

'Shit,' he said. 'I didn't even notice what make it was.' He was losing his touch.

'A Peugeot 308,' Nathan said, his eyes already back on his phone.

Despite his frustration, Jackson felt a twinge of pride. That's my boy, he thought.

'I don't know why you're so worked up,' Nathan said. 'It was probably her dad or her mum picking her up.'

'She was *hitching.*'

'She might have been joking with them.'

'Joking?'

Nathan passed his phone to Jackson. There was a photograph, after all, too blurred to read the number plate.

'Can we *go*, Dad?'

No sign of Julia at the unit base. 'Still on set,' someone said. The cast and crew were used to Jackson. The guy who played Collier was always pumping him for information about how a 'real' detective would behave and then not taking the advice. 'Well, why should he?' Julia said. 'It's years since you were in the police.' Yes, but I'll always be a policeman, Jackson thought. It was his default setting. It was knitted into his *soul*, for heaven's sake.

He was the second guy to play Collier, the original actor had had a breakdown, left and never come back. That was five years ago, but Jackson still thought of the new guy as the new guy, and he had one of those names – Sam, Max, Matt – that had never stuck in Jackson's brain.

The catering van had put sandwiches out and Nathan wolfed down a handful with no trace of a please or thank-you. He could give Dido a run for her money. 'Nice there in the pigsty, is it?' Jackson said, and Nathan scowled at him and said, 'What?' as if he was an irritation. He was, Jackson knew it. An irritation and an embarrassment. ('It's part of your job description as father,' Julia said. 'And, anyway, you're an old man.' 'Thanks.' 'In *his* eyes, I meant.')

Jackson thought he looked quite good for his age. Full head of hair, which – genetically – he would be donating to Nathan one day, so he should be grateful (as if). And with his Belstaff Roadmaster jacket and his Ray-Bans, Jackson thought he still cut quite an attractive figure, some might even say cool. 'Of course you are,' Julia said, as if she were soothing a fractious child.

Julia pitched up eventually, looking as if she'd come straight from the battlefield. She was dressed in scrubs, which was a good look on her except that she was smeared with blood and had a nasty slash across her face, courtesy of the make-up department. 'Been attacked by a serial killer,' she said cheerfully to Jackson. Nathan was already shying away from her as she approached him with arms open for a hug. 'Hold him down for me, will you?' she said to Jackson. He chose sides and declined. Nathan ducked and dived but Julia managed to get hold of him and plant a noisy, smacking kiss on him while he wriggled like a fish on a hook in an attempt to escape the maternal embrace. 'Mum, please, stop.' He broke free.

'He loves it really,' Julia said to Jackson.

'You look disgusting,' Nathan said to her.

'I know. Brilliant, isn't it?' She dropped to her knees and embraced Dido almost as effusively as she had embraced her son. The dog, unlike the child, responded in kind.

They were running late, she said, she was going to be ages. 'You'd better go home with Dad.'

'No problem,' 'Dad' said.

Julia made an excessively pouty clown-face of sorrow, and said to Nathan, 'And I was so looking forward to spending time with my baby. Come back and see me tomorrow, sweetie?' To Jackson, less pouty, more efficient, she said, 'I've got a day off tomorrow. Can you bring him down to the hotel?'

'No problem. Come on,' Jackson said to Nathan. 'We'll go and get a fish supper.'

They ate their fish and chips on the hoof, out of cardboard boxes while walking along the foreshore. Jackson missed the greasy,

vinegary newspaper of the fish suppers of his boyhood. He was becoming a walking, talking history lesson, a one-man folk museum,
except that nobody was interested in learning anything from him.
Jackson pushed their finished boxes into an overflowing bin. So
much for the obstructive garbage truck.

There were still a lot of people on the beach, making the most of
the balmy early-evening weather. In the part of Yorkshire in which
Jackson had been born and bred it had rained every day, all day,
since time began, and he had been pleasantly surprised how literally
bright and breezy the East Coast could be. And it had been a great
summer too, the sun showing his face, sometimes even with his hat
on, for at least a few hours every day.

The tide was currently halfway out, or halfway in, Jackson couldn't
tell which. (Was this a glass-half-full/half-empty kind of thing?)
He was still learning what it meant to live on the coast. If he stayed
here long enough perhaps he would feel the ebb and flow of the sea
in his blood and would no longer need to consult the tide table every
time he went for a run on the beach.

'Come on,' Jackson said to Nathan. 'Let's walk on the sand.'

'*Walk*?'

'Yeah, walk, it's easy. I'll show you how, if you like. See – this
foot first, and then follow it with the other one.'

'Ha, ha.'

'Come on. Then we'll catch the funicular back to the car. It's fun,
that's why it's called that.'

'No, it's not.'

'True, but you'll like it.'

'Oh, hold me back,' Nathan muttered, which was something Jackson
himself said, in moments of high cynicism. Strange and rather flat-
tering to hear the boy speaking like the man.

'Come on,' Jackson encouraged when they reached the beach.

'O-*kay*.'

'Do you know that "okay" is the most recognizable word in the
world?'

'Yeah?' Nathan shrugged his disinterest but trudged along beside him. Men had trekked across deserts beneath a boiling sun with more enthusiasm.

'Go on, ask me,' Jackson said, 'because I know you're dying to – what's the second most recognizable word in the world?'

'Dad?' The cynical teenager was gone and for a moment he was just a boy again.

'What?'

'Look.' Nathan pointed out to the bay, where there was some kind of commotion taking place in the water. 'There's no sharks here, are there?' he said doubtfully.

'Plenty, but they're not necessarily in the sea,' Jackson said. Not a shark attack, but the trio of bad boys from earlier in the car park. Two of them were in a ramshackle-looking inflatable, more of a kids' toy than a seaworthy vessel. The third was presumably the one causing pandemonium by inconveniently drowning in the water. Jackson looked around for a lifeguard, but couldn't see one. Surely they didn't keep office hours? He sighed. Just his luck to be the one on watch. He pulled off his Magnum boots and handed his jacket to Nathan – no way was he about to ruin a Belstaff for one of these numpties. He ran down to the water's edge and kept on running, splashing in a rather ungainly fashion until he could launch himself on the waves and start swimming. A man running into the sea in his socks was almost as undignified as a man walking along licking an ice-cream cone.

The boy (or the wanker in the water, as he preferred to think of him) had gone under by the time Jackson got there. The other two bad boys were yelling like useless idiots, their bluster gone, replaced by blind panic. Jackson took a great breath and forced himself under the water. The sea had looked calm from the beach, but out here, less than a hundred feet from shore, it felt brutishly in command. The sea took no prisoners, you won or you lost.

Jackson, an awkward merman if ever there was, bobbed up and pushed himself back down again. He managed to hook the boy by grabbing a handful of hair and then snagging the back of his jeans until finally, somehow, God knows how, he was able to get them both up to the surface. It was not the most elegant piece of lifesaving, but it would have worked fine if Jackson hadn't then tried to hold on to the worse-than-useless dinghy. It proved far too frail for the job and the other two boys were tipped, screaming, into the water. More drowning commenced. Had *none* of them ever learned to swim? They were a waste of space, all three of them, but not to their mothers, he supposed. (Or perhaps they were.) Waste of space or not, the instinct was to save them.

One was not so bad, but three was impossible. Jackson could feel exhaustion kicking in and for a brief second he thought, *Is this it?* But luckily for all of them, the inshore lifeboat motored up and started hauling them out of the water.

Back on dry land someone gave the drowned boy CPR on the sand, while people stood around offering mute encouragement. The other two boys – a pair of sodden water rats – stepped away from Jackson when he approached, ill-equipped to deal with gallantry, his or anyone else's.

The drowned boy spluttered back to life – a miracle, Jackson thought, waste of space or not – reborn right there on the sands. He thought of Penny Trotter who was 'born again'. Jackson himself had once been dead. He had been injured in a rail crash and his heart had stopped. ('Briefly,' the doctor in A&E had said – somewhat dismissively in Jackson's opinion.) He had been revived by someone – a girl – at the side of the railway tracks and had for a long time afterwards felt the euphoria of the saved. It had worn off now, of course, the commonplace of everyday life having eventually defeated transcendence.

A paramedic draped Jackson in a blanket and wanted to take him to hospital, but he refused. 'Dad?' Nathan was hovering, pale and worried. Dido moved to Jackson's side to offer silent, stoic support, which involved leaning rather heavily on him. 'All right?' Nathan asked.

'Yeah,' Jackson said. 'Can we go now?'

Sugar and Spice

The scent of his dad's breakfast – sausage, bacon, egg, black pudding, baked beans, fried bread – still lingered rather threateningly throughout the house (and it was a big house). 'It's going to kill you one day, Tommy,' Crystal said nearly every time she put it in front of him. 'Hasn't happened yet,' his father said cheerfully, as if that was a logical argument. (Harry imagined his mother saying, 'Well, I haven't fallen off a cliff yet,' when warned about the dangers.)

His dad had driven off first thing this morning to the Port of Tyne to meet a DFDS ferry coming in from Rotterdam. 'White goods,' he said. He quite often met his trucks himself at Customs if they were coming in from the Continent. 'Quality control,' he said. 'Vital if you're going to keep customer loyalty.' His dad used to express the wish that Harry would join the firm – 'Holroyd and Son,' he said – but he hadn't mentioned this idea much lately, not really since Harry had said he wanted to do Theatre Studies. ('Why not Engineering or something?')

The other day Harry overheard him asking Crystal if she thought his son was gay. 'I mean, he's a bit light in his loafers, isn't he?' 'Dunno,' Crystal said. 'Does it matter?' To his dad it did, apparently. Harry didn't *think* he was gay – he liked girls (although perhaps not in *that* way) – but he also felt so unformed as a person, as a character at the centre of his own drama, that he didn't feel ready to be definitive about anything. Perhaps his father could persuade Candace into the business instead. Holroyd and Daughter. Paint his trucks pink to tempt her.

Harry was alone in the house. Crystal and Candace were at

playgroup, which was usually followed by the park or coffee in Costa with the other mothers – which was basically just the play-group in a different, less suitable location. In the school holidays Harry sometimes did the playgroup run. It was interesting having coffee with the playgroup mothers. Between the mothers and the chorus girls at the theatre he had learned a lot, most of it anatomical and confusing.

He had an afternoon shift at Transylvania World, or 'the World' as it was known to its underpaid employees – basically Harry and his friends. ARE YOU PREPARED TO BE SCARED? it said on a poster outside. It was one of the attractions on the pier, although 'attractive' was not a word anyone would have used to describe it. Harry had worked there for the last couple of summers, taking the money, issuing the tickets. It was hardly challenging and, due to the lack of customers, he spent most of the time reading. He was starting his A levels in September and had a long reading list that he was currently trawling his way through. He went to a posh school – that was how his father referred to it. 'Is that posh school teaching you anything?' or 'I'm paying that posh school to teach you *ethics*, for fuck's sake? I can teach you ethics: Don't kick a man when he's down. Don't let your right hand know what your left hand's doing. Women and children first.' As moral codes went it was a mixed bag and Harry wasn't sure that Socrates would have entirely concurred with it, or even that his father adhered to it.

Despite it being a 'posh school', nearly everyone Harry knew worked during the summer holidays. There were so many seasonal jobs going it seemed criminal not to have one. The cool kids – or rather the kids who considered themselves to be cool – all spent their time bodyboarding or trying to qualify as lifeguards, while the nerdy ones, like Harry and his friends, manned ticket booths, scooped ice-creams, trowelled chips and waited tables.

The World was owned by Carmody's, the amusement people, and was the lowest of the low where attractions were concerned – a few moth-eaten figures acquired from an old waxworks and a couple of badly modelled tableaux. It advertised 'with live actors' but there was only one, not an actor but a fellow nerd called Archie who was in Harry's History class and was paid peanuts to lurk around and jump out at the (few and far between) paying customers in a rubber Dracula mask. *True Blood* it wasn't.

The town was known for vampires, it was where the original Count had landed – in fiction, at any rate, although the way people went on you would think it had been an actual historical event. The souvenir shops were full of skulls and crosses and coffins and rubber bats. Several times a year the town was flooded with Goths in thrall to the living dead, and now there was Steampunk Week and a Pirate Week so that the whole town seemed like the venue for a fancy-dress party. The 'pirates' all wore shabby greatcoats and big hats with feathers stuck in them and carried cutlasses and revolvers. Harry wondered if the cutlasses were sharp. In reality, Harry's friend Emily said sarcastically, 'they're men called Kevin who work in the data mines all week. Living out their fantasies for the weekend.'

Harry supposed there was nothing wrong with that, although why anyone would want to be a pirate or the bride of Dracula he couldn't imagine. ('Well, lots of women are married to vampires,' Crystal said.) But Steampunk was something Harry had yet to come to terms with. Only last weekend a man had bumped into Harry. He was wearing a full-face metal mask with hoses and tubes coming out of it. 'Ee, sorry, lad,' he said cheerfully. 'I can't see a thing in this.' Harry didn't want to be someone else, he just wanted to be himself. That was hard enough.

Harry still had some time before he had to get going. He could have a swim in the pool, he supposed, or sit in the garden and read – but it was a lovely day and he didn't feel much like sticking his head in a book. That was how Crystal referred to it – 'Got your head stuck in a book again, Harry?' It would be funny if his head did actually get stuck in a book.

Between the theatre and the World he had a series of laborious journeys most days. High Haven was stranded high on the cliffs in a no-man's-land between Scarborough and Whitby, and Harry had spent most of the summer shuttling between the two. If he had lots of time he sometimes cycled on the old railway cinder track, but usually he caught the bus. He couldn't wait for the day he passed his driving test and was allowed a car. His dad had started to teach him on back roads, letting him drive his S-Class. ('What's the worst you can do? Crash it?') Tommy was surprisingly (astonishingly) patient and it turned out to be an arena in which they got on like, well, like father and son. ('You're not as crap at this as I thought you would be,' Tommy said. High praise indeed.) It felt nice to have discovered an activity in which they were not a disappointment to each other.

This summer Crystal had driven him in to work a few times, 'Because I'm going in anyway, Harry,' or sometimes she 'just felt like a drive'. Crystal said she would list driving as one of her hobbies if she ever had to fill in a form for 'a job application or something'. Was she thinking of getting a job? Harry wondered what she was qualified for. She enjoyed driving and Harry enjoyed being driven by her. He usually sat in the back of the Evoque with Candace and all three of them sang 'Let It Go' at the top of their voices. Harry had a nice, modest voice − he was in the school choir − but Crystal was tone deaf and Candace was a screecher. Nonetheless it felt bonding. Like being a family. He caught sight of the clock and realized he had spent so much time dawdling that he was about to miss the bus.

There had been hardly any visitors to Transylvania World all afternoon. It was dead, Harry thought. Ha, ha. Plus it was sunny and no one, apart from the occasional pervy type, wanted to be inside when the weather was good. Rain was best for business, people came in to find shelter and it was only a two-pound entry fee, although even that often proved too much once they had sampled the meagre amount of horror on offer. The exit was on a different street so Harry didn't usually have to deal with the disappointed customers. By the time they'd worked out where they were and how to get back to the beginning they'd lost the will to live and two pounds didn't seem worth arguing about.

Archie, the so-called 'live actor', hadn't turned up. When this happened − which was unsurprisingly often − Harry would guide people towards the entrance ('It's quite dark in there.' It was!) and then he would race along a back corridor to a concealed door, grab the Dracula mask and jump out just as they rounded the corner, making gargling noises in his throat (*Yaargh!*) like a vampire trying to cough up phlegm. People were never impressed and rarely frightened. Fear was not a bad thing, his father said. 'Keeps you on your toes.'

Harry's mother – Lesley – died six years ago when Harry was ten, and his dad had got married again, to Crystal, and a year later they had Candace. She was three years old now and got called Candy by everyone except Harry, who thought it was a bit of a sexist sort of name. He thought girls should have straightforward names like Emily and Olivia and Amy, which were the names of the girls at his school who were his friends. 'Hermiones,' Miss Dangerfield called them, rather dismissively, especially considering they were in her 'fan club' as she called it. 'A wee bit Jean Brodie for my liking,' she said. (Was Miss Dangerfield in her prime yet? Harry wondered. He hadn't asked.)

Miss Dangerfield was their Drama and English Lit teacher at school. 'Call me Bella,' she said to Harry when she gave him a lift home from rehearsals. ('I live in the same direction.') At the end of the summer term they had put on a production of *Death of a Salesman*. Harry had a small part – Stanley, the waiter in the chop house – although he had auditioned (poorly) for both Biff and Happy. He wasn't very good at acting. ('Don't worry, Harry,' Crystal said, 'you'll learn as you get older.')

They ran *Death of a Salesman* for three nights. Harry's dad couldn't make it, but Crystal came for the first night. ('Depressing play, isn't it? But you were very good, Harry,' she added. He knew he wasn't, but it was nice of her to say so.)

'How did Hamlet start his soliloquy about cheese?' he asked Miss Dangerfield as she gave him a lift home on the last night. 'To Brie or not to Brie.' She had laughed and then when she parked her car outside his house she put her hand on his knee and said, 'You have no idea what a special boy you are, Harry. Remember – your whole future's ahead of you, don't waste it,' and then she had leant over and kissed him on the mouth and he had felt her tongue, probing his, like a sweet, mint-flavoured slug.

'Was that your precious Miss Dangerfield?' Crystal frowned when he came in the house, still reeling from the kiss. 'I can see you on the security cameras.' Harry blushed. Crystal gave him a sympathetic pat on his shoulder. 'You know she's transferring to another school next year, don't you?' Harry didn't know whether to be disappointed or relieved at the news.

Girls with names like Bunny and Bella could be confusing. And a name like Candy might lead to all kinds of unfortunate things. (Being eaten, basically.) Of course, you might grow up to be a drag queen. Bunny Hopps, who had a drag act at the Palace, knew someone called Candy Floss, although Harry presumed that wasn't his (or her) real name.

Everything in Candace's bedroom (in her life, in fact) was pink and themed on fairies and princesses. She slept in an elaborate bed that was meant to be Cinderella's carriage and had an entire rack of Disney fancy-dress outfits that she liked to wear in rotation – Belle and Elsa, Ariel, Snow White, Tinker Bell, Moana, Cinderella – an endless, virtually interchangeable inventory of sequins and artificial satin. They had been to Disneyland Paris last year and pretty much cleared the rack in the shop.

'Better than looking like JonBenét, I suppose,' Bunny said. If anyone knew about fancy-dress it was Bunny, of course. He – she – Harry had to watch his pronouns around Bunny – was Harry's confidante. It was weird but he was the one Harry had started going to for advice, for confession. It was almost like having a mother again. One who wore a wig and size-twelve heels and 'tucked his undercarriage away' (something that required a masculine pronoun, even in Bunny's lexicon).

Harry often read Candace her bedtime story and he had retrieved his own books from one of the old outbuildings where his child-hood had been boxed up (rather badly) and left to moulder. His father had converted two of the outbuildings into garages and he was trying to get permission to convert a third, but was prevented from doing so because there were bats roosting in there (or 'the fucking bats' as they were always referred to) and the bats were protected. ('Why? Why would you protect a fucking bat, for fuck's sake?') Harry liked to watch them flitting around the barn in the summer evenings, catching insects. They were tiny and seemed vulnerable and Harry worried that his father intended them clandestine harm.

Harry had found a very nice illustrated edition of the Grimm Brothers (inscribed *From Mummy with Love*) in one of the boxes in the Batcave and he was employing it to introduce Candace to the more evil side of fairies – tales where people were cursed or abandoned or had their toes chopped off and their eyes pecked out. Ones where there was a noticeable absence of sugar and spice. Not because he wanted to scare Candace – and to her credit she didn't scare easily – but because he felt that someone ought to counter the fluffy pink marshmallow world she was being swallowed up by, and in the absence of anyone else he supposed it would have to be him. Plus, they had been his own introduction to literature and he thought it would be nice if she turned out to be a reader too.

He had had a conversation with the dangerous Miss Dangerfield about fairy stories and she said they were 'primers' for girls so that they would know how to survive in a world of 'male predators'. ('Or wolves, as we might call them.') A handbook of what to do, she said, when a girl found herself alone in the dark wood. Harry supposed the dark wood was a metaphor. Not many dark woods around these days, but nonetheless he liked to think that Candace might grow up knowing how to avoid the wolves.

No matter how hard he tried to conjure her up, his own mother was no longer much more than a smudge of memory and it was becoming more and more difficult to re-create her. Occasionally something would break through this miasma, a sudden sharp fragment – a recollection of sitting beside her in a car or being handed an ice-cream – although the 'context', as Miss Dangerfield would have called it, was entirely missing. His mother had never lived at High Haven, so he had no sense of her here either. She had been a smoker, he remembered that. He remembered, too, a hoarse laugh, dark hair. And her dancing round the kitchen once, not like waltzing, more like poor cursed Karen in *The Red Shoes*. (Too horrible a tale for telling to Candace, Harry had judged.)

Emily seemed to have more of a connection to his mother than Harry did and she was always saying things like, 'Remember that fire-engine cake that your mother made for your birthday?' or 'That was good when your mother took us on the Christmas steam train, wasn't it?' and so on. Was it? He didn't know, it was as if most of his memories had been erased along with his mother. Like a book that no longer possessed a narrative, just a few words scattered here and there throughout its pages. 'Sometimes it's best to forget, Harry,' Crystal said.

Harry sometimes wondered if she would have died of cancer eventually, given the smoking, instead of falling off a cliff, which was what actually happened to her.

No one had seen her fall, she had been out walking the dog. Tipsy – a sweet little Yorkshire terrier that Harry could recall more clearly than he could his mother. A prescient name given what happened to the dog. ('Prescient' was another of Miss Dangerfield's words.) Tipsy was found on a ledge below the cliff and it was presumed that the dog had gone over and his mother had tried to get her back and had slipped and fallen.

Tipsy was found alive, but his mother's body had to be rescued from the sea by the inshore lifeboat. Harry had recently come across his mother's death certificate when he had been looking for his own birth certificate – to prove his age for his under-eighteen bus pass – and it said her cause of death was 'drowning'. Which was a surprise as he had always imagined that the tide had been out and she had dashed her head on the rocks, which would have been awful but better somehow because it would surely have been quicker. Sometimes he wondered if Tipsy had seen her when she plummeted past, if they had exchanged a look of surprise.

His dad got rid of the dog, gave it to one of his drivers. 'Can't look at it, Harry, without thinking about Les.' Two years later and he was married to Crystal. Harry wished he hadn't given Tipsy away.

His mother had been replaced, but not the dog. There was just a Rottweiler now called Brutus that his dad had bought to be a guard dog for the Holroyd yard, and at first they weren't allowed near him. It was Candy his father was concerned about, he seemed less bothered about Crystal or Harry being mauled to death by the dog. Actually Brutus turned out to be not quite the savage that his dad had hoped he would be, he was a big softie and seemed especially fond of Harry, although Crystal remained suspicious of him. She had never had a pet when she was growing up, she said. 'Not even a hamster?' Harry asked, feeling sorry for her. 'Not even a hamster,' she confirmed. 'Lot of rats around, though.'

Crystal wasn't a wicked stepmother. She didn't nag ('Live and let live') and she took a benign interest in his life ('How's it going, Harry? All right?'). She didn't walk around the house in her underwear or anything, God forbid. Nor did she make jokes about the absence of stubble or the presence of spots on his face. In fact, she had discreetly left an expensive antibacterial facewash in his en suite. He did his own laundry these days though, it would have been embarrassing if Crystal had washed his underpants and socks. 'Don't mind, Harry,' she said. 'I've handled a lot worse.'

She didn't treat him as a child, more as an adult who happened to share the house with her. There were times when Harry would really have liked to be treated as a child, but he didn't say so. (He was 'young for his age', according to his father.) They were 'pals', Crystal said, and it did feel companionable when they flopped on the sofa together after Candace was in bed and watched their favourite programmes – *America's Next Top Model*, *Countryfile*, *SAS: Who Dares Wins*. They had eclectic taste, Harry said to her. ('Electric?' Crystal puzzled. 'Kind of,' he said.)

They hardly ever watched the news. ('Turn it off, Harry, it's all bad.') They watched nature programmes though, oohing and aahing at anything cute and furry, changing channels the minute it looked as though something sad or gory was about to happen. It went without saying that Harry's father wasn't on the sofa with them. ('What's this shit you're watching?') He was working a lot of the time, and if not he was in his 'den' with his eighty-inch TV and Sky Sports. He lifted weights in there too, grunting and sweating as he heaved barbells above his head or jabbed at the big Everlast punching-bag that hung from the ceiling. Sometimes it felt as though Harry and Crystal were conspirators, although Harry never felt sure what it was they were in league against. His father, he supposed. His dad liked to think he was 'the masterful type', Crystal said.

'Like Mr Rochester,' Harry said, and Crystal said, 'I don't think I know him. Is he a teacher at your school?'

Crystal worked overtime on Candace and Harry sometimes wondered what her own childhood had been like. There was no evidence of it — no photos, no relatives, no grandparents for Candace — it was as if Crystal had come into the world fully formed, like Botticelli's Venus. That was an unfortunate thought — Harry went to great lengths not to think about Crystal naked. Or any other female, for that matter. He had a huge coffee-table art book he'd asked for last Christmas. The nudes in it were the nearest he got to porn. Looking at nude women embarrassed him even when he was on his own. ('The boy's not normal,' he heard his father say to Crystal. Perhaps he wasn't. 'Show me normal,' Crystal said.) He'd asked Crystal about her childhood and she'd laughed and said something about fairgrounds and ice-cream, but she didn't make them sound attractive.

Crystal cooked the kind of food his father liked — the 'full English' which she made every morning, the Sunday roast ('and all the trimmings'), and in between steaks and burgers, although his father spent a lot of time at work or 'out and about' when he picked up takeaways. Or he came in late and took a pizza or a ready-meal from the freezer (a Meneghini, the price of which would have bought Harry his first car when the time came).

Crystal and Candace didn't eat any of 'that muck', as Crystal called it. The arrival of Candace had made her a 'convert' to healthy eating. 'Clean eating,' she said. 'I like those words.' She was on the internet all the time, blogs and vlogs and recipes. Salads and fruit and veg. Cashew milk, tofu. Quinoa, chia, goji berries — food that sounded as if it should be eaten by tribesmen in the Amazon, not a sixteen-year-old boy in Yorkshire. Last week Crystal had made a 'chocolate' cake from black beans and avocados and yesterday she had offered Harry a 'meringue', saying, 'I bet you can't tell what that's made from.' No, he couldn't. Something that had died at the bottom of a well a hundred years ago, perhaps. 'The water from a tin of chickpeas!' Crystal said triumphantly. 'It's called aquafaba,' which sounded to Harry's ears like something the Romans might have built.

Harry was generally free, however, to choose what he ate. Crystal was always pushing broccoli and sweet potatoes on him. 'You're a growing boy, Harry. You are what you eat.' Which meant he was pretty much an American hot pizza. Clean eating hadn't stopped Crystal smoking, Harry noticed ('Just the odd one here and there, Harry. Don't tell on me'), although she never smoked in front of Candace or in the house, just the conservatory, which they hardly ever went in. And he'd never seen her drink much, not like his father.

If Crystal was in a fire, the first things she would save – apart from Candace, obviously – would be her Vitamix blender and her Kuvings juicer, the Lares and Penates of High Haven as far as she was concerned. ('How about a glass of kale and celery juice, Harry?') Who would save him? Harry wondered. His dad, he hoped. Or perhaps Brutus. 'Don't be daft,' Crystal said. 'I'd save you.'

Crystal loved doing housework and, despite Harry's dad's insistence, she refused to employ a cleaner because they wouldn't be as 'thorough' as she was. 'I married a dolly-bird,' Tommy complained, 'and I ended up with Mrs Mopp.' 'Dolly-bird' and 'Mrs Mopp' were words that Tommy had learned from his own father, apparently, and were utterly mysterious to both Harry and Crystal.

High Haven itself was Edwardian, although you could only tell from the outside as Crystal had stripped it of all its original fittings and fixtures and made it look more like the white and shiny interior of a spaceship. ('I know,' Crystal said, regarding the kitchen island fondly, 'you could operate on that.')

High Haven had been built as the holiday retreat of a long-dead Bradford wool baron and his family, and Harry liked to imagine how it must have once looked – the ferns in brass pots, the Vaseline glass lampshades, the Arts and Crafts friezes. And the swishing of silk skirts and the tinkle of teacups instead of the built-in Miele coffee machine that sounded like a steam train when it was pumping caffeine into his father. ('Why not put in a drip?' Crystal said to Tommy.)

Harry had a feel for the way things looked in the past. He had helped to design the set for a school production of *The Importance of Being Earnest*. ('That was quite an avant-garde take on the play,' he overheard the headmaster say to Miss Dangerfield.) Miss Dangerfield said to Harry that she suspected his future lay in theatre design rather than acting.

Crystal was a 'neat freak', according to his dad. 'Yeah, OCD,' she said triumphantly, as though she'd worked hard to acquire it. Everything folded and sorted and lined up exactly. Tins, ornaments, clothes, everything 'just so'. She had come into Harry's room once to ask him something (she always knocked, unlike his dad) and started putting the books on his bookshelves into (not quite correct) alphabetical order, and he didn't have the heart to point out that he had already arranged them according to subject. ('I'm not a reader, Harry. School and me didn't really get on. *Marie Claire*'s my limit.')

The bricks in the wall of frozen food in the Meneghini, Harry had realized one day when he was looking for oven chips, were arranged in a complex categorical system that could have put a librarian to shame. He'd had Olivia and Amy round to the house one afternoon and Olivia had opened up the fridge to get a juice and she had screamed, actually screamed, when she saw the inside of the fridge. Harry had to admit he felt a certain amount of pride in being the stepson of a woman whose ranks of labelled Tupperware and glass could impress a sixteen-year-old girl that much. Wait until she saw the bathroom, he thought.

His friend Amy appeared, to take over the World from him as Harry had to get to the Palace in time for the evening performance.

'There's someone in,' he said, indicating the entrance to the dark tunnel. 'Mum, dad, one kid.' The 'kid' was about ten years old, a lumpish scowling boy who had been gnawing on a stick of rock candy like a dinosaur chomping on a bone. 'He won't be scared, will he?' his timid mother had asked.

'Unlikely,' Harry said.

'Archie isn't here,' he said to Amy. 'You'll have to put the mask on.'

'No way,' Amy said. 'It's disgustingly unhygienic. They can do without a vampire.'

Amy had an eating disorder and Harry had read a lot about it online so that he'd know the kinds of things he shouldn't say to her – like 'Eat up, you need some meat on your bones,' or 'At least finish what's on your plate, for heaven's sake,' which were things Amy's mother said to her all the time. Harry, on the other hand, said things like, 'I'm not going to be able to eat all of this apple, would you like half of it?' Half an apple didn't alarm Amy the way a big plate of pasta did.

'They've been in there a long time – longer than usual anyway.'

'Maybe they've been scared to death. That'll be the day. You're going to be late, Harry.'

'Oh, by the way,' Harry said casually as he was going out of the door, 'there's a hummus and salad sandwich here I couldn't eat. Crystal made it so it's all good. Just toss it if you don't want it.'

'Thanks, Harry.'

The Kray Twins

Reggie had brought in coffee in a Thermos flask. The coffee at the station was bogging, more like brown water than actual coffee. Ronnie drank hers black, but Reggie had brought a little jar of soya milk to put in hers. She'd been a vegan for quite a long time, nearly ten years, before celebrities made it fashionable. People always seemed to want to quiz her about her diet and she found the best response was a vague 'Oh, you know – allergies,' because everyone was allergic to something these days. What she really would have liked to say was, 'Because I don't want to put dead animals inside my body' or 'Because cow's milk is for baby cows' or 'I don't want to add to the death of the planet,' but for some reason people didn't like it when you said that. Mind you, it was hard work being a vegan and Reggie was no cook. She'd probably be dead of starvation by now if it wasn't for her go-to meal of beans on toast. Reggie was twenty-six, but she didn't think that she had ever been the right age.

'Thanks,' Ronnie said when Reggie poured her a coffee. They had their own mugs. They had already had coffee that morning, 'at home' as they had already started calling it, although they had so far only spent two nights in the little tumbledown Airbnb cottage in Robin Hood's Bay that had been rented for a week – which was how long this part of the investigation was expected to take.

They perched side by side on the one desk they had been allotted in a sparse office that was on the top floor of the station. There was a computer on the desk and that was pretty much it apart from a pile of boxes that had appeared out of nowhere yesterday and contained paperwork pertaining to the original investigation into Bassani and

Carmody. It was a chaotic jumble of receipts and bills and mysterious notes that their DI, Rod Gilmerton, had asked the local force to sweep up for them. 'Paperwork' would be an obsolete word one day. Reggie very much hoped so anyway. Another reason for not partaking of the station coffee was that Gilmerton had instructed them to keep themselves to themselves. 'Discretion's the better part of whatever,' he said.

'Valour,' Reggie supplied. 'Although what Shakespeare actually said is "The better part of valour is discretion." People always misquote.'

'You need to get a life, Reggie,' Gilmerton said.

'Contrary to popular opinion, I do have one,' Reggie said.

There had been no flags and bunting out for them when they arrived. They were interlopers from another force and they had not been exactly welcome in this neck of the woods. The case they had been tasked with had originated here over ten years ago now. It had been closed for some time – the guilty punished, the innocent compensated, the stain scrubbed away, although, as any SOCO will tell you, there's always a trace left behind. Nonetheless, everyone behaved as if it were closed, and not just closed, but put in a locked box on a high shelf where everyone involved had tried to forget about it and move on, and now here were Ronnie and Reggie breaking the locks and opening the box again.

It was still early and it was relatively quiet, although down below at the front of the house a small knot of last night's drunks were being processed by the desk sergeant so they could be released back into society and become tonight's drunks. Reggie and Ronnie spent a few rather futile minutes looking over their notes from yesterday. They had spent the previous afternoon interviewing a pro at the Belvedere Golf Club whose memory might as well have been wiped clean by aliens. In fact, the aliens seemed to have been quite busy in the amnesia business around here.

Ronnie was usually based in Bradford and Reggie in Leeds, and although they had only been working together for a couple of weeks, out of Reggie's station in Leeds, they had already discovered how harmonious they were. Reggie could imagine them being friends outside of work, but had kept that thought to herself as she didn't want to appear too eager.

They had been brought in as part of a small outside task force that went by the name Operation Villette. Actually they pretty much *were* Operation Villette. Gilmerton was bouncing on and off other investigations as well. He was pleasant enough and at first Reggie had liked the way he made light of things, and then after a while he had begun to seem more lightweight than light.

Reggie and Ronnie had been recruited to interview potential witnesses and contacts. Some new accusations had recently come to light and the accuser herself lived on their patch. Their job was to talk to people who had been mentioned by other people who in turn had been mentioned by other people, a bit like a game of Chinese whispers. It was an ever-expanding jigsaw, one with a lot of missing pieces as it dialled all the way back to the Seventies and many of the people mentioned were dead. Unfortunately. The new accusations involved Establishment figures – big cheeses, 'head yins' in Reggie's native patois – and yet the investigation couldn't be more low-profile. Perhaps for good reason. Or perhaps not.

Gilmerton was on the edge of retirement, demob happy, and was pretty much leaving them to 'get on with things' on their own. He wasn't expecting much in the way of results, he said ('We're just dotting some "i"s and crossing some "t"s'), which made Ronnie and Reggie more determined than ever to solve the puzzle.

'We'll find all the pieces,' Reggie said. 'They'll be under a carpet or down the back of a sofa. But we'll finish it.'

'Perhaps they've been swept under the carpet on purpose,' Ronnie said.

Ronnie liked to be organized almost as much as Reggie did, and that was saying something. They were both newly promoted, fast-tracking 'all the way to the top', Ronnie said. Two years in uniform and then a training period in CID. Keen as mustard. Reggie planned to apply for a job with the National Crime Agency. Ronnie wanted to join the Met.

Reggie was Scottish, but did not have the exile's longing for her homeland. Some of the worst years of her life had been spent in

Edinburgh, where she came from. And anyway, her family were all dead now, so there was no one to go back to. At eighteen, she'd flown south and landed in Derby, where she did a degree in Law and Criminology. Before she went there she couldn't have found Derby on the map. She hadn't really minded where she went as long as it wasn't where she came from.

Ronnie had studied for a Master's in Forensic Science from the University of Kent. Her name was Veronika, spelled Weronika. Her parents were Polish and her mother called her Vera, which she hated. She was second generation. Her parents talked a lot about going back, but Ronnie wasn't interested. Yet one more thing she had in common with Reggie.

They were the same height – short. ('Petite,' Ronnie amended.) Reggie wore her hair bobbed to her ears and Ronnie wore hers in a bun held tidily in place by a scrunchy. The older female detectives were, on the whole, a sartorial mess – jeans or ill-fitting skirts, washed-out shirts and unfashionable jackets on bodies softened by too many takeaways and packets of crisps. Reggie and Ronnie were spick and span. Today Ronnie was wearing a white shirt and a pair of navy-blue trousers. Despite the warm weather, Reggie was wearing a black suit in 'summer-weight wool' (no such thing, she had discovered – wool was wool).

When she was younger, Reggie had hoped that one day she would have a life that involved a black suit. Her mentor and employer at that time, Joanna Hunter, had gone to work every day as a GP in a black suit. Reggie had worked as Dr Hunter's nanny and they still kept in regular contact, even though Dr Hunter had moved to New Zealand with her son Gabriel for a 'fresh start'. (You could hardly blame her when you thought about what had happened to her.) 'Why don't you come, Reggie? Come for a visit. You might even think about getting a job here.' New Zealand seemed to Reggie to be awfully far away. 'Well, not when you're actually here,' Dr Hunter wrote. 'Then it's not far away at all. Then it's just where you are. You're here.' Not so much a mentor as a guru.

Reggie did Taekwondo, Ronnie boxed. You had to do something when you were small and you were female and you were police. A triple whammy. Reggie was fast-tracking in Taekwondo as well as CID, already a third dan. Reggie harboured a daydream. The dark night, the sinister alley, the unexpected attack – and the surprise of her assailant when he was knocked to the ground. *Hi-yah!* Not that anyone said that in her class. And not that she was violent, but if you'd spent your life being referred to as a 'wee lass', or as 'poor little Reggie Chase', you were allowed the occasional fierce fantasy.

Reggie had been offered a scholarship to Cambridge but hadn't taken it up. She knew she'd have sunk amongst all that privilege and entitlement, and even if they had accepted her they would still have looked at her and seen her unfortunate background every day of her time there. Her father had been killed before she was born in a 'friendly fire' incident (not very friendly at all, in Reggie's opinion) in a futile war that everyone had pretty much forgotten now. And her mother had drowned in a swimming-pool accident when Reggie was fifteen, leaving just a brother for her to lose to drugs.

Derby had been a revelation: people her own age who liked her (She had friends!) and a relationship (Sex! Not embarrassing!) with a funny, polite boy who had studied Computer Science and was now working as an anti-hacker for the same evil multinational corporation that he had hacked when he was a post-grad, because of course that was what happened to every good hacker – coerced to work for the devil under threat of a long jail sentence or extradition. He was called Sai and had Asian good looks and they no longer saw each other because he was having an arranged marriage and had been poached by the FBI and was going off to work at Quantico, all of which seemed to Reggie to be an excessively dramatic way of ending a relationship.

Her heart wasn't shattered, just cracked, although cracked was bad enough. And she had her career, and the black suit, as a comfort. 'That's the important thing,' Ronnie said. Ronnie herself was 'between girlfriends'. Reggie often found herself wishing that she was gay too, it might make life simpler, but Ronnie laughed her head off and said, 'And how exactly?'

Reggie had started with the Taekwondo at uni. There were clubs for anything you fancied learning. Dr Hunter had been in the running club at her university – as well as shooting – and Reggie knew how useful those two things could be because Dr Hunter had demonstrated how.

Dr Hunter had been the nicest, kindest, most sympathetic person that Reggie had ever known, and Reggie knew for a fact that Dr Hunter had murdered two men with her bare hands (literally) and only Reggie and one other person knew about it. So it just went to show. 'Justice has nothing to do with the law,' Dr Hunter had told her once, and Reggie understood what she meant, as would that one other person who knew about Dr Hunter's short career as an assassin.

Ronnie and Reggie drained their coffee cups, both finishing at the same time. They left a message for Gilmerton to tell him what their plans were for today, ditto with Control here. More of an operational issue, really, as Reggie got the feeling that no one actually cared.

'Right then,' Ronnie said. 'We'd better get started.'

They had their warrant cards ready when Ronnie rang the doorbell of the Seashell. A woman answered and Ronnie said, 'Good morning, I'm DC Ronnie Dibicki and this is DC Reggie Chase.' Reggie smiled at the woman and held her warrant card higher for scrutiny, but the woman barely glanced at it. 'We're looking for a Mr Andrew Bragg?' Ronnie said.

'Andy? What do you want him for?'

'Are you Mrs Bragg?' Reggie asked.

'Maybe,' the woman said. Well, you either are or you aren't, Reggie thought. You're not Schrödinger's cat.

'And is Mr Bragg here?' Ronnie asked. 'We just need a quick word,' she mollified. 'Tidying up a few loose ends in a historic case. Paperwork, really.' Ronnie raised a questioning eyebrow at the woman. She was very good at the raised-eyebrow thing. Reggie had tried it, but she just ended up looking as though she were trying to do a poor (really poor) impression of Roger Moore. Or Groucho Marx.

Andy Bragg's wife conceded to the eyebrow. 'I'll go and see if he's here,' she said. 'You'd better come in,' she added reluctantly, parking them in the residents' lounge before disappearing into the bowels of the house.

Tourist information leaflets were fanned out on a sideboard. Boat trips, horse riding, local restaurants and taxi numbers. Reggie took a seat on a sofa and picked up a tide table from the coffee table. The cushions on the sofa and the curtains at the window were made from a fabric that was adorned with seashells. Once you started looking you could see that they were everywhere. It was strangely disturbing. Reggie perused the arcane information contained in the tide table. 'Low tide at three today,' she said. Neither Ronnie nor Reggie had ever lived by the sea. It was a mystery to them. In and out, out and in, in thrall to the moon.

A dog the size of a carthorse wandered into the room and examined them in silence before wandering out again.

'That was a big dog,' Ronnie said.

'It was,' Reggie agreed. 'Almost as big as you.'

'Or you.'

Reggie looked at her watch. 'Do you think Mrs Bragg has forgotten that she's looking for Mr Bragg?'

A man came into the lounge and looked startled at the sight of them.

'Mr Bragg?' Reggie said, jumping to her feet.

'No,' he said. 'Have you seen him anywhere? There's no hot water in the shower.'

The Nineteenth Hole

'Your round, I believe, squire,' Andy said.

'Again?' Vince said. How could that be? he wondered. Hadn't he just bought a round? His bar bill must be through the roof by now – Tommy and Andy were drinking double malts. Vince had tried to restrict himself to pints but nonetheless he was feeling woozy with drink.

'You're a bit of a lightweight today, Vince,' Tommy said. 'What happened to you?'

'Skipped lunch,' Vince said. 'Too busy to eat.' Hardly true. Well, the lunch part was true, but not 'busy' at all, because on top of everything else – and he had confided this to no one – he had lost his job a week ago. He had reached the bottom of the curve. Rock bottom. Woe piled upon woe. It felt biblical, as if he were being tested by some vengeful Old Testament God. The suffering of Job, he thought. He had been brought up as a West Yorkshire Baptist and his Sunday School Bible lessons had taken root.

It was a funny coincidence, if you thought about it – 'Job' and 'job' being the same word. Not that funny when you didn't have one any more. Redundant.

'Sorry, Vince,' his boss, Neil Mosser, had said. 'But you know . . .' He shrugged. 'The takeover and everything.' Vince thought a shrug was an inappropriate response to a man losing his livelihood. 'Cuts were bound to happen as soon as they started consolidating,' Mosser said. ('Rhymes with tosser,' they all said behind his back. It was true. He was.)

And, on the other hand, everyone *liked* Vince, their faces lit up when he walked in, they were always glad to see him – *Can I get you a cup of coffee, Vince? How's that daughter of yours, Vince? Ashley, isn't it?* Not like Wendy, who for the last year had barely looked at him when he walked in the door. There was one particularly nice woman who worked up in the York office, Heather was her name. On the chubby side, always seemed to be dressed in purple, not that either of those things counted against her. She always gave him a hug and said, 'Look who's here, if it isn't Vince!' as if no one was expecting him.

'I've worked for the company twenty years,' Vince said to Mosser. Didn't it all count for something? 'And isn't it supposed to be first in, last out? Not first in, first out?'

Another shrug from the tosser. 'They want fresh meat, you know. Young and hungry, guys who are prepared to bleed for the company.'

'I have bled! I have no blood left! I'm like a vampire's victim after it's feasted!'

'Don't make it more difficult than it is, Vince.' (Why not?) 'You'll get a good redundancy package.'

Good, my arse, Vince thought. It wouldn't keep him going for a year. The universe was having a laugh at his expense. An unemployed divorced man nudging fifty – was there a lower life form on the planet? A year ago he was a fully functioning human being – husband, father, worker – now he was redundant, in every sense of the word. A scrap at the bottom of the fryer.

'Get a move on, Vince!' Tommy Holroyd's voice boomed in his ears, interrupting his thoughts. 'Thirsty men here.'

'Did you hear the news?' Tommy asked casually as they sat at a table near the window that had a great view of the fairway. (Tommy always got the best table, the club's female staff liked him.) 'Someone said that Carmody's up for early release. They're going to let him out on licence.'

'Jesus,' Vince said. 'How did he wangle that?'

'Compassionate grounds. His wife's dying. Supposedly.' Tommy and Andy exchanged a look that Vince found hard to interpret. Both Bassani and Carmody had been members of the Belvedere.

They were never mentioned at the club now, but their ghosts still lurked somewhere in the shadows. They had left something tainted behind, a question mark over everything they'd touched. And, of course, there'd always been rumours of a third man. Was it someone who was still here? Vince wondered, casting his eye around the clubhouse, alive now with alcohol and the leisurely exchanges of the self-satisfied. Vince had never really felt like he belonged here, even less so now that he had had his own fall from grace.

Bassani and Carmody had been charged with awful things, the kind of things that made Vince feel sick to think about, mostly to do with underage kids. There'd been all kinds of accusations – 'parties' that had been held, children that had been 'supplied', trips abroad to somewhere 'special' that they owned. A black book that contained the names of judges and bankers and policemen. The great and the good. Not to mention corruption: they had both spent years in local government. Most of it hadn't been proved, just (just!) indecent assault on underage girls, prostitution of children and possession of child pornography. It was enough to send them down, or at any rate to send Carmody down, because Bassani had hanged himself in Armley Gaol while on remand. Carmody had been found guilty on all counts and been shipped off to Wakefield Prison, still protesting his innocence. Neither of them gave up the contents of the little black book, if it existed at all.

'I heard,' Tommy said, 'that Carmody's sick.'

'Who told you that?' Andy asked.

'A little bird. Or quite a big bird – that retired ACC who drinks in here.'

'The tall bloke with the gay beard?'

'Yeah, that one. He says Carmody's not got long left. He'll be eligible for parole in a few months and wants out early. Says there's talk of him making a deal.'

'Deal?' Andy said sharply. 'What kind of deal?'

'I dunno,' Tommy said. 'Naming names, maybe.'

'Who?' Vince asked, trying not to be left out of the conversation. 'Like the third man?'

Both Tommy and Andy turned to look at him as if they were seeing him for the first time that evening. It took a beat before Tommy laughed and said, 'The third man? That's a film, isn't it, Vince?'

Tommy and Andy exchanged another look, one that entirely excluded Vince. Friend friends.

Holding Out for a Hero

As soon as he got home Jackson stripped off his sodden clothes and threw them in the washing-machine, then he stepped into the shower and blasted himself with hot water. It might be summer but a dip in the North Sea was still enough to give you hypothermia.

It felt good to be back safely on land. The sea really wasn't his element, Jackson would take earth over water any time. Good to be in a nice warm cottage, too. Logs in the wood store, honeysuckle round the door. The cottage was on an estate dating back hundreds of years to when the Normans appropriated this land. Everything well kept. Jackson liked that. It wasn't where he would have predicted that he'd end up. Not that he had necessarily ended.

The cottage was set back three hundred yards from the sea, tucked in at the end of a small valley, a cleft in the landscape, which meant it was sheltered from the worst of the wind. There was a view of a wood on one side, a hill to shelter behind on the other. A stream ran through the valley. Sometimes there were cows on the hill. The disappearance and reappearance of the cows was a mystery that Jackson spent more time dwelling on than a younger man might have.

He had been living here since the spring and liked it enough to think about making it more permanent. They got cut off when it snowed, a neighbour told him when he moved in, you could go days without seeing anyone. It seemed an inviting idea. ('Reclusivity,' Julia said. 'I rest my case.')

'All right?' Nathan asked, glancing briefly at him when he came into the living room, towel-drying his hair. This show of concern was heartening – they hadn't raised a sociopath, after all.

'Yes. Thanks,' he replied.

Nathan was slouching on the sofa – on a chat site, by the look of it – while on the TV there was some kind of game show – complicated and moronic at the same time. ('Like you, then,' he heard Julia's voice say in his head.) There were people dressed as animals – chickens, rabbits, squirrels, with oversized heads – running around while other people screamed encouragement at them.

'Meanwhile in Aleppo,' Jackson murmured.

'What?'

'Nothing,' Jackson sighed.

'It was cool,' Nathan said, after a while.

'What was?'

'What you did today.'

'Just another day at the office,' Jackson said, although inside his heart swelled with pride. The son honoured the father.

Julia had neglected to have an opinion on crisps, so they shared a large bag of Kettle sweet chilli and sour cream, quite companionably, and watched the giant squirrels and rabbits chasing each other. It was a good day, Jackson thought, when you saved someone's life. Even better when you didn't lose your own.

Summer Season

Barclay Jack was in his dressing room, spading Rimmel foundation on to his face. He paused to gaze gloomily into the mirror. Did he look his age? (Fifty-eight.) Yes, he did, every minute of it and more. Barclay (real name Brian Smith) felt a drooping of the spirits. His stomach swooped around inside him. Stage fright? Or a dodgy curry?

There was a knock on the dressing-room door. It opened tentatively and Harry put his head round it. Barclay had been given an 'assistant' for the season, a volunteer, a school kid who wanted to 'get into theatre'. Well, this isn't the path, sunshine, Barclay thought. Harry. Harry Holroyd. It was the name for someone in silent comedies. Or an escape artist.

'That's your ten minutes, Mr Jack.'

'Fuck off.'

'Yes, Mr Jack.'

Harry shut the door and hovered in the corridor. Next year he was applying to the University of Sunderland to do Film and Theatre Studies and so he thought of the Palace as a kind of work experience that would look good on his application form. It was certainly an *experience* – Harry only realized what a sheltered, naïve life he'd been living when he came to work here. 'The Palace' was a bit of a misnomer. It couldn't have been less like a palace if it tried.

Bunny Hopps sashayed towards him along the narrow corridor, teetering on his colossal red sparkly heels. Honeybun Hopps – but everyone called him Bunny – was enormous, well over six foot and built like a rugby forward. 'No relation to Lady Bunny,' he said, rather mysteriously. 'I've been Bunny since I was a bairn.' His real name was Clive but his surname really was Hopps. He was billed as a 'female impersonator' – a description that seemed to infuriate him. 'I'm not fucking Danny La Rue,' he said to Harry. Harry had no idea who that was, but he'd found him – her – on an old TV programme called *The Good Old Days*. 'It was a bit . . . *weird*,' Harry reported to Bunny. 'Aw, pet,' Bunny said (he was a Geordie), 'wait until you come across Fanny Cradock.' The show at the Palace was an Eighties revival thing – a variety show that in its own weird way echoed *The Good Old Days*.

'I'm a drag queen, for fuck's sake,' Bunny said. 'Why haven't they billed me as that?' Out of curiosity, Harry had sought out *RuPaul's Drag Race* and discovered that Bunny, despite his protestations, was quite an old-fashioned participant in the shape-shifting world of drag, more Lily Savage than RuPaul. Of course, his father, who took no interest in anything Harry watched, would choose that moment to barge into his room. 'Jesus Christ,' he said. 'Couldn't you watch porn like everyone else?'

Bunny trawled for cigarettes somewhere inside the corset he was stuffed into. Smoking was strictly forbidden in the theatre – it was a 'tinderbox' waiting to catch fire, according to the ASM. What smoke alarms there were had run out of battery long ago and there was a singular lack of sprinklers backstage, allowing for a good deal of illicit smoking from the performers. The chorus girls were the worst, lighting up like chimneys in their dressing room amidst a health-and-safety nightmare of hairspray and polyester.

Bunny offered his pack of cigarettes to Harry, saying, 'Go on, pet, it won't kill you.'

'No, I'm all right, Bunny, thanks,' Harry said. They had pretty much the same exchange every night and Harry kept a box of matches in his pocket so that he could light Bunny's cigarettes. He (she, *she*, he corrected himself) could manage the cigarettes but there wasn't room in her costume for anything to light them with. 'Too tight,' Bunny growled. 'The friction it would cause if I tried to squeeze anything else in there would be dangerous. You might see a case of spontaneous combustion.'

Harry knew that just about everything Bunny said was salacious but he wasn't always sure what was intended by the double entendres. There was something oddly Shakespearean about Bunny. They'd done some stuff about gender swapping at school – 'Compare and contrast male and female roles in *Twelfth Night* and *The Merchant of Venice*.'

Harry had studied Bunny's act as he might indeed have studied Shakespeare. It had an interesting trajectory (one of Miss Danger-field's favoured terms). Bunny's act closed the first half of the show and was based around the concept that he – she – was an opera diva, a screechy soprano, who never quite got round to singing her big aria. (It was more entertaining than it sounded.) For the first half of Bunny's performance the audience was restless, cat-calling and muttering – a lot of them were only there for Barclay Jack, not a big man in heels.

'But you always win them over,' Harry told Bunny.

'Thanks for explaining my own act to me, pet,' Bunny said.

'Sorry,' Harry said, pressing on anyway. 'But I really like the way that you do it – you really *are* funny, and kind of . . . reckless.' Harry would have liked to learn how to be reckless. 'And then by the time you get to your big ending—' ('Oo, Betty,' Bunny said mysteriously) 'they're cheering you on like you're a hero. It's brilliant.'

Harry liked the transformative nature of what Bunny did. He wondered whether if he changed his own name he would become a different person. What name would he choose for himself if he took on the identity of a drag queen? (An unlikely idea, he would never have the nerve.) 'Hedda Gobbler?' he offered Bunny. 'Lynn Crusta?'

'A bit obscure, pet.'

Bunny knew a drag queen called Auntie Hista-Mean, and another one called Miss Demena, which were definitely not real names. And Anna Rexia, which was just plain wrong. He wondered if Amy had eaten the hummus sandwich he'd left for her.

Crystal was called Crystal Waters before his dad married her. It seemed an unlikely name. She confided to Harry that it was her 'stage name'. Had she been on stage? Harry asked eagerly. 'Well, you know . . .' she said vaguely. His dad had said that she'd once been a glamour model, 'topless only', as if that was an achievement, although more on his part than hers.

Not an achievement but a debasement, according to Emily. Emily could be harshly opinionated, especially on the subject of Crystal. 'An ersatz woman,' she called her. Harry had known Emily since primary school, so it was a bit late to start standing up to her. 'I mean, your stepmother's not exactly a feminist icon, is she, Harry?' 'No, but she's a nice person,' Harry defended weakly. And you had to admire the effort she put into her appearance – almost as much as Bunny did. ('Donatella, eat your heart out,' Bunny said when Harry showed him a photo. He was actually showing him a picture of Candace, but Bunny was more interested in Crystal, who also happened to be in the frame.) Harry recognized 'ersatz' as one of Miss Dangerfield's words. Emily was going to be very put out when she learned that Miss Dangerfield wasn't returning to school after the summer. Emily was scarily clever. She was reading *Ulysses* and *Finnegans Wake* 'for fun' during the summer holidays. She would have been appalled by the show at the Palace.

Crystal was cleverer than Emily gave her credit for, cleverer than she gave herself credit for. For example, she played a mean, albeit reluctant, game of chess, although she was always making out that she was thick. And you had to be pretty savvy to digest (as it were) all that science about 'clean eating'. Sometimes she sounded as if she had a degree in advanced nutrition. 'You see the thing about B12, Harry, is that . . .' and so on. Harry thought she was 'hiding her light under a bushel' – that was what Miss Dangerfield had said about Harry to his parents at last term's PTA.

'Miss Dangerfield's bush,' his father grinned when he came home. 'That would be a sight for sore eyes.' His father could be horribly crude sometimes. He seemed to think it would make a man of Harry.

'And is that what you want to be, pet?' Bunny asked. 'To be a man? Because, believe me, it's not all it's cut out to be.'

'How about Polly Esther?' Harry suggested to Bunny (he was on a roll). 'Or Aunty Rhinum? Phyllis Tyne! That's a good one. It would suit you, Bunny, being a Geordie.'

('You seem very into the whole drag thing, Harry,' Emily said. 'You should beware of cultural appropriation.' Which was definitely something she'd got from Miss Dangerfield.)

From Barclay Jack's dressing room came the sound of something crashing to the floor, followed by the man himself roaring with anger.

Bunny pointed her cigarette at the dressing-room door and said, 'Has that bastard been giving you trouble again?'

Harry shrugged. 'It's all right.'

'He's raging 'cos he's not on the telly any more,' Bunny said. 'Plus he's a fat cunt.'

If Harry's father heard Bunny use language like that he would probably deck him. His dad used terrible language himself, as bad as anything that came out of Bunny's plumped-up lips, but that didn't seem to count. He had standards for other people, especially Harry. 'It's about bettering yourself,' he said. 'Do what I say, not what I do.' Harry hoped his father never came across Bunny. He couldn't imagine them in the same room together.

Harry knocked again on Barclay Jack's door and shouted, 'Two minutes, Mr Jack!'

'Well, if he does give you trouble,' Bunny said, as they listened to the expletive-fuelled response from Barclay Jack, 'just mention Bridlington to him.'

'Bridlington?' Harry asked. 'What happened in Bridlington?'

'Never you mind, pet. You know what they say – what happens in Brid stays in Brid. If you're lucky, that is.'

The lights went down on a couple of singers – husband and wife – who had once been the (failed, needless to say) UK entry to Eurovision. Jesus, Barclay thought, it was like stepping back in time. Well, it *was*

stepping back in time – they were billed as a 'Blast from the Past', aka the dregs of Seventies and Eighties TV. Good decades for Barclay then, but not necessarily now. There were chorus girls kicking their legs up and a ventriloquist whose 'doll' was a chicken (Clucky) and who used to inhabit the soul-destroying corridors of kids' TV. A glitter band that had been – literally – a one-hit wonder and who had been touring in revival shows for the last forty years on the strength of it. A magician who had once had a regular guest spot on something on TV – a magazine programme? Cilla Black? Esther Rantzen? Barclay couldn't remember. Neither could the magician. Everyone thought he was dead. ('Me too,' the magician said.)

And, of course, bloody Bunny Hopps fannying around like a third-rate pantomime dame. It was enough to make a man puke. The theatre was trying to make it into a family show, but they'd been forced by the powers-that-be to put a warning out before the interval that parents with children in the audience should use their discretion about allowing them to stay for the second half as Barclay Jack was 'somewhat risqué'. Management had asked him to 'tone it down' for the matinées. Fucking cheeky buggers. He didn't bother, he knew they wouldn't be back. The whole show, the whole season, was written off as something from the Dark Ages. As was Barclay himself.

He'd risen. He'd fallen. He used to be on television all the time, he'd won an 'audience choice' award. He'd received hundreds of fan letters a week, emceed *Saturday Night at the London Palladium*, met the Prince of Wales. Twice. He'd had his own ITV game show for a while. And a short-lived quiz on Channel 5 in its early days. The contestants were not the brightest, even the simplest general knowledge question seemed to be beyond them. (Question: What was Hitler's first name? Answer: Heil?)

And now look at me, Barclay thought. Bottom-feeding. ('Well, Barclay,' his manager Trevor said, 'crack cocaine and underage girls, it can be a long road to redemption.'

'Rumours, Trevor,' Barclay said. 'Nothing ever proved.' And it was the Seventies, for heaven's sake. Everybody was at it then.)

The lights went up again. He could feel the excitement, like a hot vapour rising and filling the auditorium. It was a raucous lot that were in tonight, a couple of hen parties by the sound of it. That was the thing, he was still popular – wildly so, if this audience was anything to go by. Why couldn't TV executives see that?

He walked out on to the stage and took a moment to appreciate it, his stomach settled now. He waggled a leering eyebrow at a woman in the front row and she looked as if she was going to wet herself. 'How do you get a fat bird to go to bed with you?' he shouted to the back row of the balcony. They were laughing already, even before the punchline.

'Easy!' he yelled. 'A piece of cake!' He was loved.

Time, Gentlemen

'Well,' Andy said, 'I suppose it's time to get home to the old ball and chain.' Tommy clucked sympathetically. Andy's wife, Rhoda, was built to very different architecture from Crystal, whose blueprint was that of a goddess. 'You would think,' Andy said to Vince once, out of Tommy's hearing, 'that if Crystal *had* been a glamour model there'd be nudie photos of her all over the web, but I haven't been able to find anything. I think our Tommy's telling porkies.'

'You've *looked*?' Vince said, horrified.

'Course I have. Don't tell me you haven't.'

He hadn't. He wouldn't. It was disrespectful. He would never be able to look at Crystal again without imagining her naked.

'That's kind of the point, Vince,' Andy said.

The denizens of the Belvedere clubhouse bar made their tardy way home. Mindful of the law, Tommy Holroyd had phoned for a cab.

Andy, as usual, was happy to take his chances of being stopped. The Belvedere was second home to quite a few members of the force who would probably turn a blind eye to his transgressions. He offered Vince a lift to the hovel Wendy had forced him into, but he declined.

If he was going to die – and to be quite honest he wouldn't be that bothered if he did – then Vince didn't want it to be with his face in the airbag of Andy Bragg's Volvo. There were better places for it – deep in the purple-clad cleavage of Heather in York, for example. He could imagine himself plunging his head into her fat balloon-like bosom. *Look who's here, if it isn't Vince!* And then he would—

Andy Bragg hooted at him as he drove past. He slowed and rolled down the passenger-side window. 'Are you sure you don't want a lift, Vince?'

'Nah, I'm all right, Andy. Thanks. I fancy some air. It's a nice evening. I might drop by the house, take the dog for its walk before bedtime. Haven't seen Sparky for a while.'

'As you wish, squire.' Andy roared off into the night. He lived a forty-minute drive up the coast in his hotel – the Seashell – but Vince knew he would be trying to do it in thirty.

The Seashell. They'd bought Sea View a couple of years ago, changed the name and relaunched it as a boutique hotel. ('Luxury boutique,' Rhoda insisted.) It had been an old-fashioned, very tired hotel when they bought it. Red and blue figured carpet, nicotine-stained Lincrusta wallpaper, wall lamps with fringed shades and candle light bulbs. They stripped it bare, made the seven bedrooms en suite, painted everything in muted greys and blues and greens, sanded and whitewashed floorboards. 'Cape Cod style,' Rhoda said, although neither of them had ever been to Cape Cod. In a nod to something more British they had called the rooms after shipping forecast areas – Lundy, Malin, Cromarty and so on. Not the weird ones like German Bight or Dogger, which sounded vaguely pornographic.

It was Rhoda's baby, really. Andy did the 'heavy lifting', as she called it – driving to the Cash and Carry, the endless maintenance, not to mention the more awkward guests who had to be placated. He was good at appeasement – Mr Congeniality, Rhoda called him sometimes, although it didn't always seem to be a compliment. Conflict resolution was not Rhoda's forte. She was more likely to start a fight than to end one.

Andy's travel agency – the eponymous Andy's Travel – had gone bust some time ago and now he ran his reincarnated business from home, with Rhoda's name on the company documents, under the anonymous epithet of Exotic Travel.

He'd been in travel longer than he cared to remember. After serving an apprenticeship with Thomas Cook he started his own business, with a desk in someone else's agency – he was in Bridlington at the time – until he scraped together enough money for his own storefront further up the coast. In those days it was still mostly packages – two weeks in Lanzarote, the Algarve or the Costa Brava, clutching your travellers' cheques in one hand and a bottle of Hawaiian Tropic in the other.

Life was simple then. People needed travel agents. Now they were dead in the water, killed by the internet. It had been dog eat dog out there for a long time and you could only survive if you evolved. So Andy had evolved, focussing on the more niche aspects of the business – 'a bespoke service catering for individual taste' was how he had described his approach. Sex tourism, basically. Trips for blokes to Thailand, Bali, Sri Lanka, where they could pick up girls in bars, boys on beaches, even find a wife if that was what they were after. Now that, too, had gone the way of all flesh, as it were. The blokes were doing it for themselves and Exotic Travel didn't exist in much more than name only. Andy's business had gone underground. These days it was all about import rather than export. Rhoda took no interest in Andy's business, which was just as well, considering.

It was a slippery slope. You started off selling Club Med packages to eighteen-year-olds who wanted a bit of fun and sun, and you ended up on the end of a pitchfork being toasted like a pikelet. Sins of commission. Andy knew what was waiting for him. He'd been brought up a strict Catholic, his mother was ferocious in her faith. It was going to take more than a few Hail Marys to wipe his slate clean.

The Seashell was in a village, or what passed for a village, although it was mostly holiday rental properties nowadays, strung out along the road or, in the case of the more expensive ones, hiding up the valley. There was none of the tacky carnival atmosphere you found further down the coast, no arcades or fish-and-chip shops or amusements. The air wasn't polluted by the stench of frying fat and sugar. This was where dog-walkers came – middle-aged retirees, day-trippers (unfortunately) and young couples with small children who wanted old-fashioned bucket-and-spade holidays. 'Staycations' (he hated that word). None of them were the ideal clientele for the Seashell. They were licensed though and did 'light lunches', which helped, but he supposed that Airbnb would be the death of them eventually. It wouldn't matter, it wasn't as if there wasn't plenty of money, he was swilling in cash, it was just unfortunate that he couldn't find a way of explaining any of it to Rhoda.

Rhoda had made a feature of the shell thing. Big conches in the en suites, scallop shells for soap dishes, wind chimes made of periwinkles and slipper shells. Andy didn't know a winkle from a mussel. The table mats in the dining room were expensive with a classical-style painting of shells on each one. They wouldn't have looked out of place in Pompeii. A large shell adorned the centre of every table. Rhoda had personally glued seashells on to the Ikea lamp bases. Andy thought that she had taken the theme too far, but she was like a woman possessed. In TK Maxx in the Metrocentre in Gateshead she'd seen shower curtains with seashells on them (there was a tongue-twister if ever there was) and was now contemplating custom-made towels, embroidered with the hotel's logo – a seashell above a pair of entwined 'S's. Andy worried about the Nazi connotations. Rhoda, a bit of a Stormtrooper herself, thought he was being oversensitive – not something Andy was usually accused of.

Andy had met Rhoda ten years ago when she came into his agency to book a singles holiday in Fuerteventura. She had been passing through – she was a traveller for a pharmaceutical company and was a formidable woman in many ways, not least in size. She was wearing an ill-fitting tight grey trouser suit (that made the word 'haunches' spring unexpectedly into his mind) and was enveloped in a choking fog composed equally of Elnett hairspray and Dior Poison. After Andy had secured the booking and taken the deposit he'd said, 'A gorgeous woman like you shouldn't be single.' Rhoda had laughed dismissively at him in the same way that the girls at school used to. Then she picked up her heavy black case of samples and got back in her company car. Nonetheless his chat-up line must have had some effect because a year later they were on honeymoon in a hotel in Crete that he'd secured a great trade discount on.

Rhoda had been living in Luton ('a hell-hole') at the time, but was from Filey originally and was relieved to move back to the East Coast. The magnetic pull of the North. 'Like a spawning salmon,' Rhoda said. 'Except I'm not going to actually spawn. God forbid.' It was a second marriage for them both and Rhoda hadn't wanted children. 'I think that ship has sailed anyway,' she said, without any sign of regret. Andy did sometimes wonder what fatherhood would be like – seeing his own DNA blossom in a child. But then, he thought, perhaps the world was better off without another Andy Bragg in it.

Instead of a child they had a dog, a Newfoundland called Lottie who was as big as a pony and featured on their website as if she was one of the attractions of the Seashell, yet she remained stoically indifferent to guests. Andy and Rhoda projected a variety of emotions on to her, although in fact her expression – a kind of resolute blankness – never changed. Andy thought it was a shame she didn't play poker. She tended to block your path, like a large, impassive piece of furniture. In some ways Lottie reminded Andy of his wife.

Rhoda knew her own mind, it was one of her best features. Also one of her worst, of course. She was determined to make the Seashell a success, even if she had to drug the passing trade and drag them through the doors. Like a tiger with prey, Andy thought.

The front door was locked by the time Andy got home – residents had a key. It took him several minutes to find his own key and a few drunken attempts before he managed to get it in the lock. There was no way he was going to ring the bell and get Rhoda out of bed – she was a nightmare if her sleep was disturbed. She was a lark, not an owl, she said. The differences between Rhoda and a lark were too great to contemplate.

Finally he managed to get inside, not before tripping over the giant spider conch that was acting as a doorstop for the inner porch door.

He passed the open door of the dining room where everything was neatly laid out for tomorrow's breakfasts. Little individual jars of ketchup and jams that were expensive and wasteful, but that's what defined 'luxury', apparently. High season and only three of the seven bedrooms were occupied. It was amazing what one poor review on TripAdvisor could do.

He had to negotiate his way round Lottie, who was sleeping soundly on the landing, before he could tiptoe up to the attic room that served as the office for Exotic Travel. He paused on the threshold and listened to make sure that Rhoda wasn't stirring in the room beneath. He switched on his computer. He logged on. The screen was the only light in the room and he stared at it for a long time before typing in a website address. It wasn't the kind of website you could find on Google.

❧

Crystal had been having a fly cigarette on the doorstep when she heard the sound of a car turning into the driveway. Squinting into the darkness, she felt a little flutter of fear. Was it the silver BMW?

The motion-sensor lights that lined the drive were suddenly activated and she could see that it was only a local taxi approaching – Tommy home from the Belvedere. 'Fig,' she muttered, grinding out the cigarette beneath her foot.

She gave herself a quick skoosh of mouth-freshener and took up a pose on the doorstep as if she were on the catwalk, and when Tommy had exited the taxi she said, 'Hello, babe. Did you have a good day?'

'Yeah, great day,' Tommy Holroyd said. 'I hit an albatross.'

Crystal frowned. She couldn't imagine a scenario in which that could lead to a great day, particularly not for the albatross, but she said, 'Oh, well done you. I didn't even know we had them in Britain.'

❧

Thisldo. 'The marital home', as it was now known in Steve Mellors' legalese. The pigeon part of his brain guided Vince's feet there automatically. Perhaps he could have a word with Wendy, ask her to dial down the divorce so he didn't lose everything, especially his dignity.

The lights were on, a fact which irritated him as he was still paying the electricity bill. Wendy could show a little mercy, even if only by turning a light off. She had a job, after all, only part-time, but she could easily go full-time and make some more money instead of taking all of his. (And half his pension! How could that be fair?) Wendy worked in the office of a local college, although you would think she spent her day hewing coal with her bare hands from the dramatic way she used to fling herself on the sofa when she came in from work. ('I'm knackered, Vince, fetch me a glass of prosecco, will you?')

Vince peered through the front window but couldn't see anything between the finger-thin gap in the curtains. It seemed unlikely that Wendy was in there with a new man, she would surely have been canoodling by the soft light of a lamp or a forgiving candle rather than in the full glare of their five-armed BHS ceiling chandelier. British Home Stores may have gone bust now but their light fittings blazed bravely on. It was a Saturday night, he supposed Wendy was out painting the town.

He rested his head against the cold glass of the window for a moment. The house seemed deathly quiet. No chatter from the television, no crazed barking from Sparky.

'Vince!'

Vince jumped away from the window but it was only a neighbour – Benny. Ex-neighbour.

'You all right, mate?'

'Just checking in on the old homestead, you know.'

'We miss you round here.'

'Yeah, I miss me too,' Vince said.

'How are you doing anyway?' Benny asked, an expression of concern on his face, a doctor with a terminal patient.

'Oh, you know,' Vince said, mustering an attempt at bonhomie, 'can't complain.' He had lost the appetite for confrontation with Wendy and said, 'Better get going anyway. See you around, Benny.'

'Yeah, Vince, see you around.'

Vince crawled between his stale-smelling sheets. Yes, there *was* something more pathetic than an about-to-be-divorced middle-aged man ordering a single fish supper – it was an about-to-be-divorced middle-aged man lugging a bag of dirty washing through the streets to a launderette. The company car had disappeared with the job, the dog with the marriage and the washing-machine with the house. What would be taken from him next? he wondered.

He lay awake, staring at the ceiling. The pubs had just emptied and it was far too noisy to sleep. He could hear the nerve-jangling noise of Carmody's amusement arcade across the way. The Carmody family still ran it. Every time he passed it Vince could see Carmody's stringy daughter sitting in the change booth, looking bored to death. They used to call it Carmody's 'empire', just because he had more than one arcade in more than one town. Four amusement arcades do not an empire make, Vince thought. And now where was Carmody? Sitting in a jail cell somewhere, an emperor deposed. 'Look on my works, ye Mighty, and despair!' Vince thought. He had learned that poem at school. He had an excellent memory, more curse than gift. Was Carmody really going to name names? Depose more emperors? Or just their minions?

He was dog-tired, but he expected that as with most nights since he had moved here he would have a tortured, restless sleep. The usual pattern was that just as he managed to forget his troubles and drop off, he would be rudely woken by the seagulls performing their morning tap-dancing routine on the pantiled roof above his head.

Vince sighed. He was reluctantly coming to the realization that nobody would care if he didn't wake up in the morning. Vince wasn't sure that he cared himself. If he fell off a cliff, like Lesley Holroyd, he doubted that there would even be a bunch of withered flowers to mark the spot. A tear ran down his cheek. I am very sad, he thought. A very sad man. Perhaps it was time to call time on it all.

Encore

'How do you get a nun pregnant?'

Harry had never listened to the punchline to this joke because when he heard it on the backstage speaker it was his five-minute cue to make sure everything was in place for Barclay Jack's exit, stage left. No bear to pursue him. Barclay Jack himself was the bear. As soon as he was off-stage he had to have a cigarette and a gin – three ice cubes, splash of tonic. ('And I mean a splash, kid. The tonic just waves at the gin from a distance – *capiche*?') Harry also had to have a clean towel ready for Barclay Jack to mop the sweat off his face (and his bald pate) and the make-up-remover wipes out. After that Barclay always had to have a burger. Harry had already slipped out and bought one and now it was reheating in the little microwave that the chorus girls kept in their dressing room, where they wandered around half-naked without any embarrassment. ('Zip me up, Harry, will you?') He was like a puppy to them, amusing and quite cute but utterly sexless. He sometimes dreamt about them at night, but not in a good way.

They were already queuing in the wings for the finale. Everyone complained about the curtain call, especially the chorus girls, as it wasn't a proper finale and they had to hang around for most of the second half just to take a bow after a ten-second reprise of can-can kicks. Barclay Jack had insisted on it, said he wasn't going to be alone on-stage at the end as if he had no friends. 'But you *have* no friends, Barclay,' Bunny said to him.

Harry joined the girls (women, really) in the wings, where they were jostling like a flock of giant restless birds, squashing him with their muscular, fishnetted legs – it wasn't just the plumes in their headdresses and tails or their enormous eyelashes (almost as big as Bunny's) that made him think of ostriches. They smelt ripe because their costumes only got dry-cleaned once a week. Their hair lacquer and make-up were industrial strength and gave off an odd chemical aura, like ozone.

'Because a man will actually search for a golf ball!' Barclay Jack yelled. Conversely, Harry had never heard the first line of this particular joke, not that he wanted to. One of the girls snorted with derision, even though she had heard the act dozens of times – Barclay's set was the same every night, no changes, no variation. And he hated hecklers because he had no witty ripostes. It was funny, Harry thought, but for a comedian he seemed to have very little sense of humour. Harry liked jokes. He had lots of them. ('Go on then, make me laugh,' Barclay said. 'What cheese would you use to disguise a horse?' 'I don't know.' 'Mascarpone. Get it? Mask a pony.' 'Jesus, kid, don't give up the day job.')

Just the iceberg-lettuce joke to go and it would be over. Even from here you could see the pearls of sweat on Barclay Jack's face. He looked horribly unhealthy. From the opposite wing, Bunny, in full sequin mode, winked at Harry and made a rude gesture in the direction of Barclay Jack. Bunny was second on the bill, closing the first half of the show. He'd had a standing ovation tonight – his act finished on such a crescendo that sometimes the audience seemed unable to stop themselves leaping to their feet. Barclay fumed every time Bunny had a good show.

'A man walks into a doctor's surgery with a piece of lettuce hanging out of his arse!' Barclay yelled. 'And so the doctor says, "I'd better have a look, drop your trousers and bend over. Hm," he says, "I see what you mean. It certainly looks as if you've got a problem there." And the man says, "It's just the tip of the iceberg, doctor."' The audience howled their approval.

'That's all, folks. Ladies and gentlemen, you have been a fucking brilliant audience, see you all again soon, I hope.' Barclay Jack walked off-stage to rowdy applause before pirouetting in the wings and walking back out and taking a bow. The lights were killed before he'd got off-stage a second time, giving him no chance to milk the applause. Harry knew the ASM would be in for it later.

Harry watched as Barclay's audience-pleasing grin turned to a grimace. 'Get my drink,' he growled at Harry. 'And get your skates on.'

'Yes, Mr Jack.'

WWMMD?

Jackson was idling on his phone. He was on a messaging app, but no one had a message for him. There were two sofas in the living room of the cottage, Jackson occupied one, a snoring Queen of Carthage the other. The television was still on, one of those channels aimed at the insomniac elderly that showed old crime shows, presumably because they were cheap to buy. An ancient *Midsomer Murders* gave way to an early episode of *Collier*. Jackson was keeping a weather eye out for an appearance by Julia. When it came it was fleeting. She was in the mortuary, holding what was meant to be a human heart in her hand. ('Healthy male,' she said. 'No sign of heart problems.') There was a metaphor in there somewhere but he wasn't sure what it was. Did she hold his heart in her hand? (And was he a healthy male?)

Since he'd started living up here and seeing her regularly on account of the endless dropping off and picking up of Nathan, they'd fallen into a comfortable routine with each other. 'Like putting on a pair of old slippers,' she said. 'Thanks,' Jackson said. 'Just what I've always wanted to hear from a woman.' They had kissed once – no, twice – but it had gone no further, and one of those times had been Christmas, which didn't really count.

He'd finally managed to persuade Nathan to go to bed – the same tedious tussle every evening. 'Why? I'm not tired,' repeated endlessly in the hope of wearing Jackson into indifference. He'd gone up to say goodnight, stifling the instinct to hug his son for fear of rejection. He should be more hands on, like Julia. (*Hold him down for me, will you?*) He was probably still awake up there, Snapchatting by the light of the silvery moon. It was more golden than silver tonight, fat and round, dominating the dark night sky above the wood. Jackson hadn't drawn the curtains and he could see it climbing up the window. He heard an owl. He had thought before living here that owls made gentle, fairy-tale sounds – *twit-ta-whooo* – but this one sounded like an old man with a bad smoker's cough.

The phone rang. Jackson sighed. There was only one person who called him this late.

'Are you in bed? Shall I tell you story? Bedtime story?' Tatiana purred. Jackson wished she didn't always sound like a sex-phone operator. And, no, he had never phoned a sex line – but he always imagined they were manned (or womanned) not by the Tatianas of this world but by harassed yet practical women, mothers who were talking filth to their unseen clients while sorting out their son's football kit or stirring a spaghetti sauce for tea. Older women, supplementing their pension, half an eye on a muted *Countdown* while pretending to be in the grip of ecstasy.

'No, I'm not in bed,' he said. Even if he had been he would have denied it. It would have made him feel vulnerable and weirdly unsexed when talking to Tatiana. 'How about you just tell me what happened,' he said. 'Everything all right?'

'Everything okey-dokey.'

'Where are you?'

'In taxi. Just left Malmaison. Robbie is very naughty boy.' Sometimes – often, in fact – Jackson got the feeling that Tatiana was perfectly capable of using tenses and articles and all the other little bits and pieces of grammar but she just preferred to sound like a comedy Russian. 'I meet him in hotel bar and say, "You want to buy lady drink?" and then after drink, I say I have room here, does he want to come up? He say *da*. I say, "Do you have girlfriend?"'

'And he say?'

'*Nyet*. Says he's single and fancy.'

'Fancy-free,' he corrected. 'Did you record all this?'

'*Da*. Don't worry.'

Should he worry? His job was to protect women (yes, it was), not pay them to put themselves in positions where they might be at risk.

What if it got her into trouble? She wasn't most women, of course, she was Siberian and could probably smash a man's head like a walnut with those nutcracker thighs.

Tatiana was off the books, although Jackson was more than willing to pay her and gather PAYE and National Insurance and whatever else was legally required, but she was Russian, which was synonymous with cash. There was no cliché she couldn't live up to. He sometimes imagined that one day he would discover she wasn't Siberian at all but had actually been born somewhere like Scunthorpe or Skegness and had worked on the counter at Greggs before deciding to reinvent herself.

'Poor girlfriend – whatshername.'

'Jenna,' Jackson said. 'You know her name very well.'

'No wedding bells now.' Tatiana was entirely devoid of sympathy. She would make a perfect assassin. In fact, he wouldn't be surprised if she didn't moonlight as one.

'Where is he now?' he asked. 'Robbie.'

'In hotel room waiting for me. Ha. Long wait. I'm going home.'

Jackson had no idea where Tatiana lived. 'Home' sounded far too cosy a word for her. It was easier to imagine her in a forest lair or lying on a tree branch, one eye open even in sleep, ready to swoop on an unsuspecting victim, but no, she was a creature of surprises. 'Going to have hot chocolate and watch old *Marple*,' she said.

As he ended the call, Jackson suddenly remembered the girl on the Esplanade. He thought about the backpack with the rainbows and the unicorn and the speed with which she'd slipped into the Peugeot and disappeared. He felt a surge of guilt. He still had some contacts in the police. Tomorrow he'd try to find out if any girls were missing, perhaps see if anyone could do anything with that blurred number plate. He felt bad for having forgotten about her, but it had been a long day.

Barclay Jack was still niggling away at him, struggling to rise free of the anchor that was keeping him on the neglected seabed of Jackson's memory. Oh, yeah. He'd done a gig for Britain First. That would be about right.

On the TV Miss Marple was dead-heading roses in her garden in

St Mary Mead. What would she have done about the girl? he wondered. He was distracted from this line of thought by the herald of a little *ding* from his phone. He had a message.

EWAN: Hi. How u doing? u good?
CHLOE: Yh, good. WUUP2?
EWAN: Not much? Sos u 14?
CHLOE: 13.
EWAN: U don't look it.
CHLOE: Lols wish i wasn't.
EWAN: Btw. Send more photos. No clothes, yh?!
CHLOE: Don't know. Do u—

'Dad?'
Shit. Jackson signed off hastily:

CHLOE: Gtg. Parents here.
EWAN: TLK2UL8R

Nathan smirked and said, 'Catch you watching porn, did I?'
'Ha, ha. Work actually, for my eyes only.' It was true, it was work. A different version of the honeypot. Jackson was masquerading as a teenage girl called Chloe, which was precisely as challenging as he had envisaged it would be when he took on the job. 'Why aren't you in bed?'
'Couldn't sleep. There's something making a racket outside.'
'It's an owl.'
'And I thought I heard screaming.'
'A fox. It's a jungle out there, son.'

Darcy Slee

On a dark street the nondescript grey hatchback slithered quietly to a halt beneath a streetlight that was helpfully broken. The car's engine was killed and the driver, almost as anonymous-looking as the Peugeot itself, climbed out and shut the car door with a quiet clunk. The passenger door opened and a girl climbed out. The driver waited on the pavement for her to heave her backpack from out of the footwell. The colours of the little rainbows had all turned to grey in the dark and the unicorn had been rendered almost invisible. She closed the car door and heard the little *chirrup* as the man locked it. He went ahead of her, then turned and smiled and said, 'This way, follow me.' He approached a house, the door key ready in his hand. Darcy hesitated for a moment. Something told her that she should run, but she was only thirteen and hadn't learned to listen to her instincts yet, so she slung her backpack over one shoulder and followed the man into the house.

Beachcombing

Jackson took Dido for her usual morning constitutional. He'd left Nathan sleeping in bed. He was old enough, surely, to be left on his own? It wasn't illegal and anyway Jackson could guarantee that he'd still be fast asleep when he returned. When Jackson was thirteen – he could almost hear Julia sighing at whatever he was about to think, so he caved in and let the thought go free, where it floated down to join the rest of the jetsam lying on the seabed of his memory. He'd go home in a minute, turf Nathan out of his pit, feed him breakfast, and then drive him and the dog over to Julia. Twenty-four hours of freedom, he thought.

He tossed a ball for Dido, a gentle throw that went just far enough to remind her that she was still a dog, but not so far that her rusty hips seized up altogether. She trotted ponderously off in pursuit before returning with the ball and dropping it at his feet. It was covered in slobber and sand, and Jackson made a mental note to buy one of those ball-launcher doo-dahs.

The beach was pretty empty at this hour, just Jackson and the congregation of early-morning dog-walkers. They acknowledged each other with a murmured 'Morning' or 'Lovely morning' (it was). The dogs were more enthusiastic, sniffing each other's nether regions like connoisseurs. Thank God the owners didn't have to do that, Jackson thought.

He could see Whitby from here, two miles south along the beach, the skeleton of the Abbey standing on top of the cliff. The tide was definitely going out, he decided. The beach was clean and gleaming in the morning sun. Every morning was a promise, Jackson thought, and chided himself for sounding like a greeting card. No, not a card – it was something he had seen written in Penny Trotter's shop, the Treasure Trove – on a sign, a painted wooden one. She had a lot of them, along the lines of *Caution – Free Range Children* and *Count the Memories, not the Calories* (a motto she lived by, if her waistline was anything to go by), not to mention the ubiquitous *Keep Calm and Carry On*, banal advice that particularly raised Jackson's ire.

A little further ahead something had been washed up by the tide. Dido was dipping her paws in the water as delicately as a dowager taking a paddle, and sniffing at whatever it was. It looked like a bag. Jackson called for Dido to come back to him because he didn't like abandoned bags, even ones that looked as if they'd spent the night at sea. He had a sinking feeling as he approached it. Despite the fact that it was sodden and water-darkened, he could still make out the little rainbows. And a unicorn.

'Shit,' he said to Dido. She gave him a sympathetic if uncomprehending look.

'I used to be a policeman.'

'Yeah, they all say that,' the desk sergeant said.

'Really?' Did they? Jackson wondered. And who were 'they'? Men who came into the police station claiming that something bad had happened, which was what he had been asserting for the last ten minutes, to no avail.

'I really was,' he protested. 'With the Cambridgeshire Constabulary. And now I'm a private investigator. I've got a licence,' he added. It sounded lame, even to his own ears.

He had taken the unicorn-and-rainbow backpack home to the cottage and examined it while Nathan was shovelling Crunchy Nut Cornflakes into his mouth like a fireman stoking the boilers on the *Titanic*. They were on the forbidden list, but where was granola when you needed it? 'Don't tell your mother,' Jackson said to him.

'What is that? It looks gross.'

'It's not gross, just wet.' The backpack had dried out quite a bit by now, as it had spent the last hour hanging on the rail of the Aga. Yes,

Jackson was living with an Aga. He liked it. It was a more manly object than he had previously been led to believe.

'Don't you recognize it?' Jackson asked.

'Nope.'

'That girl yesterday – the one on the Esplanade who was hitching?'

Nathan shrugged. 'Kind of. The one you *thought* was hitching.'

'Yes, that one. She was carrying one just like it. It's seems too much of a coincidence to think it's not hers.' Jackson didn't believe in coincidences. 'A coincidence is just an explanation waiting to happen' – that was one of his mantras. Also 'If you get enough coincidences they add up to a probability,' which he'd got from an old episode of *Law and Order*. 'Why would it be in the sea?' he puzzled.

'Dunno,' Nathan said.

He would get a less one-sided conversation with Dido, Jackson thought. 'No, neither do I,' he said. 'But it doesn't feel good.'

The first time Jackson had seen the unicorn it had been in Scarborough, twenty miles further south. Had the currents brought it this far? Or had it been lost – or jettisoned – closer to here? Winds and tides and currents – they were the engines that drove the world, weren't they? And yet he had no understanding of them at all.

The Girl with the Unicorn Backpack. It sounded like one of those Scandi noir books that he didn't read. Jackson didn't like them much – too dark and twisted or else too lugubrious. He liked his crime fiction to be cheerfully unrealistic, although in fact he hardly read anything any more in any genre. Life was too short and Netflix was too good.

The unicorn backpack had yielded no clues. No purse, not so much as a hairbrush or soggy bus pass. 'I'll take it into a police station later,' he said to Nathan. There was no police station where he was living. Just the valley, the wood, a shop, a string of estate-worker and holiday cottages. Sometimes the cows. There was a hotel of sorts, too – the Seashell. He'd had a so-so pub lunch in the beer garden with Julia and Nathan. Fish pies, sticky toffee puddings, that kind of thing. They were served in individual pottery dishes. 'Freezer to microwave,' Julia said dismissively, even though that pretty much described her own cuisine.

'Okay,' Nathan said with a shrug, interested in neither the genesis nor the exodus of the unicorn backpack. His own backpack was enormous, with a huge swoosh on it. Even his phone cover was branded with logos. Teenage boys were like living sandwich boards, covered in free advertising for corporate evil. Whither individuality? Jackson wondered. ('Oh, enough with the *Anthem for Doomed Youth*,' Julia said.)

'Come on, eat up,' he said. 'Time to go.'

'In a minute.'

'Now.'

'In a *minute*. I've got to do this.' He was Instagramming his cereal. No, actually he was photographing himself, the cornflakes just happened to be in the shot. Teenage boys didn't photograph the food in front of them, that wouldn't have been cool – it was what the very uncool Garys and Kirstys of this world did, snapping every meal that passed in front of their faces. Lamb Kandhari in the Bengal Brasserie on the Merrion Way. Chicken Pad Thai in Chaophraya. Kirsty and her favourite cocktail – lime daiquiri – in Harvey Nichols. The daiquiri photographed better than Kirsty. Jackson had been on holiday in South Africa a few years ago (long story) and the bar staff couldn't understand the way the woman he was with (even longer story) pronounced her drink of choice – a daiquiri or, in her thick accent, a 'dackerree'. She was unrepentantly from the wrong side of the Pennines, so the whole trip had been damned from the start. Her considerable thirst was finally quenched when she learned to communicate by pronouncing it 'dikeeree', courtesy of Jackson, channelling a non-PC version of himself. ('What do you call a nest of lesbians? A dyke eyrie.' The court of women gave no relief to him on this one.)

Jackson himself would never have drunk anything so frivolous. A straight malt, a pint of Black Sheep, a Ricard or a Pernod on occasion.

Kirsty put all her food and drink on her private Instagram account in the misplaced belief that Penny Trotter would never see it. 'Fat Rascals in Bettys in Harlow Carr – yum!' ('Fat Bastards,' Julia called them.) 'Nothing's ever private,' Sam Tilling, Jackson's helpmeet, said – because apart from covering the more tedious aspects of sur-veillance, the boy detective was also a boy wizard – not in the Potter sense (although unfortunately for his love life he was a bit Potterish), but he knew more about computing than Jackson ever wanted to.

'He'll kill himself,' Penny Trotter said, perusing the photographs with him the last time Jackson had visited the Treasure Trove. Gary's wedding-ringed hand was in the picture as he reached for a vanilla slice. He was diabetic. Type 2, Jackson presumed – it was how the human race was going to end, on a tide of sugar and vis-ceral fat – but no, his faithful wife said, type 1. 'The full Monty, daily injections of insulin,' which she had to remind him about. 'He's the sort of man who needs mothering,' Penny said. Did Kirsty know? Jackson wondered. Would she be plying him with Fat Ras-cals if she did? Did she mother him? It seemed unlikely.

'Come on,' Jackson said to Nathan.

'In a minute.'

'Because, like, photographing yourself's important,' Jackson said sarcastically.

'Yeah. It is.' ('You can't impose your own values on him,' Julia said. I can damn well try, Jackson thought. It was his job to make a man out of the boy.)

Jackson supposed he should be grateful that he didn't have to wrangle his son to school every morning. Grateful, too, that Nathan wasn't climbing into strangers' cars and driving off into the night. Jackson had installed a GPS location tracker on his son's phone, but he would have had a tracking chip inserted into his scruff if he could. He'd looked into it, but it turned out it wasn't that simple, and he would need to implant a receiver and a bulky battery pack as well. He didn't suppose Nathan would be too happy about that.

He set about marshalling his troops, Nathan in the passenger seat, Dido in the back. He would feel better if the dog had a seat belt. She always sat up straight like an alert back-seat driver on the lookout for danger, but she would catapult like a boulder through the wind-screen if he had to brake hard. He tossed the empty backpack into the boot.

Starting the engine, he said, 'Some music?' to Nathan, but before you could even say 'playlist' Nathan was yelling his protests. 'Dad, please, not that miserable crap you listen to.' They compromised on Radio 2 – quite a big compromise on Nathan's part.

When they arrived at the Crown Spa Hotel on the Esplanade, Jackson googled the whereabouts of the nearest police station while he was standing in the lobby waiting for Julia.

'My two favourite people!' she exclaimed when she appeared. Jackson felt quite pleased until he realized that she was referring to Nathan and Dido. 'Dogs aren't people,' he said.

'Of course they are,' she said. 'Doing anything nice with your free day?'

'Chasing unicorns.'

'Great,' she said, so he knew she wasn't listening. An increasing number of people, Jackson had noticed lately, were not listening to him.

'But surely you can tell me if any girls have gone missing in the last twenty-four hours?' he persisted with the desk sergeant.

'No, sir, I can't tell you that,' he said. He wasn't even looking at Jackson, but was making a show of being busy with the paperwork on his desk.

'"No, there haven't been any girls gone missing" or "No, you won't tell me even if they have"?'

'Exactly.'

'What – no girls missing?'

'No girls missing,' the desk sergeant sighed. 'Now will you go away and "investigate" something else?'

'No CCTV up on the Esplanade that might have captured a young girl getting into a car?'

'No.'

'No CCTV footage or no CCTV?' There was CCTV everywhere. You couldn't move in Britain without being filmed. Jackson loved that.

'Neither.'

'You're not going to look up that car registration number on the DVLA?'

'No, sir, but I am considering arresting you for wasting police time.'

'No, you're not,' Jackson said. 'Too much paperwork.'

Despite his protests the desk sergeant had taken the backpack, saying he was going to log it into Lost Property.

'No one's going to claim it,' Jackson said.

'Well, then, leave your name and address, sir, and if no one does then in six months it's all yours.'

Jackson had taken a photograph of the backpack before leaving the cottage – he photographed everything these days, you never knew when you would need evidence. Nonetheless he resented having to give the backpack up, it was the one tangible link to the elusive girl and now it was disappearing into the dark of a storage room somewhere.

He retrieved the Toyota and set off back up the coast. Back to the ranch to make some phone calls, he thought, call in a few favours. Free of Nathan's musical prejudices he searched through his music and put on Lori McKenna. He always imagined that Lori was someone who would understand his melancholy streak. *Wreck you*, she sang. That's what people did all the time, wasn't it? One way or another.

He sighed. The day was still relatively young, but it felt as if it contained less promise now. There was no sign for that in Penny Trotter's shop.

Lady with Lapdog

To their surprise Control called them, asking if they were still on the A165.

'Yeah,' Ronnie said. 'Just coming off the Burniston Road.'

'Well, turn the car round and head west, will you? There's been a report of a murder. Everyone's tied up with something that's kicked off in town – day-tripping bikers or rioting youth, it's not clear. You're the closest we've got.'

Ronnie and Reggie looked at each other, features all over the place, eyes popping out of their heads. Sometimes it was like they were telepathic. Ronnie eagerly tapped the address into their GPS.

'Serious Crimes'll be on your heels, but can you hold the fort until they get there?' They were to secure the scene, nothing else. This wasn't their back yard, after all.

'No problem, we're on our way.'

They grinned at each other and hit their blues and twos. Reggie pushed her sunglasses further up her nose, checked for other traffic and accelerated. She was a careful driver. Understatement. 'Jeeso,' she said, and in her best imitation of Taggart, 'There's been a murrrder.'

'Eh?' Ronnie said.

If they were being honest, which they nearly always were, Ronnie and Reggie would have admitted that they were a tad nervous. They'd both attended at plenty of deaths – drugs, drink, fires, drownings, suicides – but not much in the way of proper murders.

The 999 call had come in from a Leo Parker, a tree surgeon, who had arrived at the premises 'to take down a tree' (which sounded like a mob hit to Reggie). Instead he had found a body – a woman lying on the lawn. Felled, Reggie thought.

'That's all we know,' Control had said. 'Ambulances are snarled up in this big incident but the caller's adamant she's dead.'

In the driveway of the bungalow there was a van with the name Friendly Forestry written on the side, and parked in front of it was a huge machine that Reggie guessed was a woodchipper of some sort. It looked like you could feed a tree into it whole. Or a body, for that matter.

A man was sitting in the passenger seat of the van, smoking and looking a bit green around the gills (Reggie loved that expression). 'Mr Parker?' Reggie asked but he signalled towards another man, less green about the gills, who was standing next to the side gate to the garden. He had a man bun, pseudo-Viking style, and was wearing a tool belt and a harness. 'Doesn't he love himself?' Ronnie murmured. He looked doubtful when they approached, holding up their warrants. They were often told by members of the public, or even criminals (sometimes the two overlapped, of course – quite often, in fact) that they were 'very small' or 'very young' or both. And Ronnie would answer, 'I know, aren't we lucky?' and Reggie thought, *Hi-yah!*

'Mr Parker? I'm DC Reggie Chase and this is DC Ronnie Dibicki.'

'I thought I'd better stand guard here, you know,' Man Bun said. 'Secure the scene.'

Was he the one who had phoned the Emergency Services?

He was.

And did he know if there was anyone in the house?

He didn't.

Ronnie went round the front, rang the doorbell and knocked hard on the door. All the lights were on, but no one was home.

And who was Mr Parker due to meet here?

'The lady of the house. I haven't met her, only spoken to her on the phone. A Ms Easton.'

'As in Sheena?' Reggie said, writing the name down in her notebook. 'Do you know her first name?'

He didn't. All he knew was that she had asked him to cut down a tree, Man Bun said. 'A sycamore,' he added, as if that might be relevant. He took a mangled roll-up from behind his ear and lit it. 'In there,' he said, gesturing with the cigarette towards the garden. Through the open gate Reggie could see the immobile body of a woman lying on the lawn.

'Did you go in, Mr Parker?' Reggie asked.

'Yes, of course, I thought she might be injured or ill.'

Ronnie returned. 'No answer from the house,' she said.

'Ms Easton,' Reggie told Ronnie. 'That's the name of the lady who lives here, apparently. Carry on, Mr Parker.'

'Well, then I came straight out again. I didn't want to disturb anything. You know, for the forensic team.' Everyone an expert, thanks to TV. *Collier* and its ilk had a lot to answer for, Reggie thought. Still, it meant he'd done the right thing.

'Good,' Reggie said. 'You stay here, Mr Parker.' They put on gloves and blue shoes and had a good look around before entering the garden. If someone was murdered then there had to be a murderer, and if there was a murderer he might still be lurking in the garden, although it wasn't the kind of garden that encouraged lurking. No trees, apart from one that stood out from the neat, bland borders like the proverbial sore thumb. The unloved sycamore, Reggie presumed. There was a big patio with lots of paving that only served to make the planet's job harder.

Why was Mr Parker so sure that it was a murder and not an accident?

'You'll see,' Man Bun said.

She was wearing an almost transparent nightdress and negligée, the kind of garments you wore to have sex in, not get a good night's sleep. Both Ronnie and Reggie wore practical nightwear for their solitary bedtimes. Ronnie wore hiking socks and pyjamas, Reggie went to bed in a tracksuit. Ready to run. Dr Hunter had taught her that.

There was a garage, which they approached carefully. Just enough room for a small Honda and a Flymo lawnmower. No killer hiding in there. They turned their attention to the woman.

She was lying on her side and looked as if she might have simply fallen asleep on the grass because she lacked the energy to get herself into bed. That was until you drew closer and saw that the back of her skull was smashed in. The blood had drained on to the grass, where it made an unattractive muddied colour that you wouldn't find in a paintbox.

And a dog. Not dead, thank goodness, Reggie thought, but lying Sphynx-like, as if guarding the body. 'Fido,' she said.

'What?' Ronnie asked.

'The Greyfriars Bobby of Italy. Faithful unto death. Dogs, you know, stay by their master's side after they've died.' Fido, Hachiko, Ruswarp, Old Shep, Squeak, Spot. There was a list on Wikipedia. Reggie read it sometimes when she needed a good cry and didn't want to dip into her own personal well of sorrow.

Sadie, that was the name of Dr Hunter's German Shepherd. Long dead now, but if Dr Hunter had died Sadie would have stayed by her side, no matter what. Dr Hunter said that apart from a few exceptions (Reggie was on the list, thank goodness) she preferred dogs to people. And that one of the great tragedies about dogs was that they didn't live as long as humans. Dr Hunter had had a dog when she was a child. Scout. 'Such a good dog,' she said. Scout had been murdered along with Dr Hunter's mother and sister and baby brother one hot summer's day long ago now. This scene was so vivid to Reggie that sometimes she thought she had been there that day.

'Reggie?'

'Yeah, sorry. Good boy,' she said to the dog. The dog gave her a slightly shame-faced look as if it knew it didn't deserve such a beneficent adjective. That was when Reggie noticed that the dog's muzzle was covered in blood. It had been lapping at the lady of the house. Perhaps the dog wouldn't make the cut for the Wikipedia list after all.

Neither Ronnie nor Reggie quailed at the sight. They had surprisingly strong stomachs for this kind of thing. No green gills. Despite the extreme deadness of the woman, Ronnie crouched down and checked for a pulse in her neck. 'To be absolutely sure. In case anyone asks. Any sign of a weapon?' she asked Reggie.

Reggie scanned the lawn and then walked over to one of the neat, bland borders. Ronnie joined her and said, 'Wow,' when she saw the bloodied golf club lying amongst the uninspiring bedding plants. A fragment of skull still adhered to it and a bit of grey mince-like brain.

And then, before they had a chance to say 'smoking gun', the cavalry came rushing in. Uniforms, paramedics, Serious Crimes, a pathologist, CSU, Uncle Tom Cobley and all. There were some people Reggie recognized – a couple of uniforms and a DI called Marriot whom they had encountered before and who said she was the SIO in charge. 'Oh, Gawd,' they heard her say as she advanced like a tank towards them, 'it's the Kray twins.'

'U-uh, the Fat Controller,' Reggie murmured to Ronnie.

The DI was a woman who liked to throw her weight around and she had quite a lot of it to throw. You could have fitted both Ronnie and Reggie inside her and there would probably still have been room for Ronnie's kid sister, Dominika.

'You'd better not have gone all *Prime Suspect* on this,' DI Marriot said. 'And you can bugger off now, the grown-ups are here.'

They both felt a little deflated. To have been so near to a murder investigation. And yet so far. DI Marriot wanted a written report from them of everything they had done before she arrived, so they drove off and parked on the Esplanade and wrote it up on Ronnie's iPad.

'You know, Jimmy Savile used to have a flat up here,' Reggie said.

'Hell must be quite full these days,' Ronnie said.

'There's always room for one more.'

They'd had to leave the scene before any ID had been made, which was frustrating. 'It must have been Man Bun's lady of the house – Ms Easton – surely?' Reggie mused.

'I guess we'll find out,' Ronnie said.

When they'd pointed out the golf club to the DI she'd peered at it speculatively before saying to no one in particular, 'What's that? A putter?'

'"We arrived at the premises at ten twenty-two,"' Ronnie read back from her iPad, '"and found a Mr Leo Parker waiting for us on the premises." What was the other guy called? The one in the van. I didn't write it down.'

Reggie consulted her notebook again. 'Owen. Owen Watts.'

When they had arrived Ronnie had puzzled over the name of the bungalow, on a sign affixed to the gate. She raised an enquiring eyebrow.

'Just say it out loud,' Reggie said.

'Thisldo,' Ronnie pronounced carefully. Enlightenment dawned. 'Ah. That's a bit crap, isn't it?'

'Yeah. It is,' Reggie agreed. Her stomach was rumbling like a train.

'We can grab lunch after the next one on the list,' Ronnie said.

Reggie consulted her notebook again. 'I've got a little list,' she said.

'Eh?'

'Gilbert and Sullivan. Never mind. Next is a Mr Vincent Ives, lives in Friargate.'

'As in chip fryer?'

'As in monk.'

The Final Straw

'Mr Ives? Mr Vincent Ives? I'm DC Ronnie Dibicki and this is my colleague, DC Reggie Chase. Can we come in?'

Vince let them in, offered them tea. 'Or coffee, but it's only instant, I'm afraid,' he apologized. Wendy had retained custody of the Krups bean-to-cup machine.

'That's very kind,' the one with the Scottish accent said, 'but we're fine, thank you.'

Had he done something that merited a visit from the police? Off-hand Vince couldn't think of anything, but he wouldn't be surprised. The general malaise he had been experiencing recently meant that he felt vaguely guilty all the time. He looked around, tried to see the flat through the detectives' eyes. It was a mean, scruffy place, something that wasn't reflected in the rent.

'Sorry,' he said. 'It's a bit of a mess.'

'Shall we sit?' the one who wasn't Scottish said.

'Sorry. Of course.' He moved some papers from the sofa, brushed the crumbs off and gestured towards it in a way that he realized made him seem like Walter Raleigh laying a cloak over a puddle. He felt foolish, but they didn't seem to notice. They sat down, crossing their ankles neatly, notebooks ready. They looked like keen sixth-formers doing a school project.

'Have I done something?' he asked.

'Oh, no. It's okay, nothing to worry about,' the one who wasn't Scottish said. Vince had already forgotten both their names. 'You're not suspected of anything. We're conducting an investigation into a historic case and this is just a routine interview. We're looking into several individuals and would like to ask you a few questions, if that's all right? We're trying to build a picture, fill in some background details. A bit like doing a jigsaw. Your name was mentioned by someone . . .'

'Who? Who mentioned my name?'

'I'm sorry, sir. We're not at liberty to disclose that. Are you all right? To answer some questions?'

'Yes,' Vince said cautiously.

'First of all, I'm going to ask you if you have heard the name Antonio or Tony Bassani?' the Scottish one said.

'Yes. Everyone has, haven't they?' Was this what Tommy and Andy had been talking about? That Carmody had been 'naming names'? But surely not *my* name, Vince thought.

'Did you ever meet Mr Bassani?'

'He was a member of my golf club, but that was long before I joined.'

'Which golf club is that?'

'The Belvedere.'

The Scottish one was writing down everything he said in her notebook. It made him feel even more guilty somehow. *Anything you say can be used in evidence against you*, he thought. She was working her way through a checklist, writing his answers neatly next to each question. The other one, the not-Scottish one, was making freehand notes to supplement this. He imagined her notes were more on the descriptive side ('He said "yes" warily,' or 'He said he didn't know, but looked shifty'). Vince felt like he was taking an oral exam.

'And have you heard the name Michael – or Mick – Carmody?'

'Yes. Again, everybody has.'

'Everybody?'

'Well . . .'

'And have you ever met Michael Carmody?'

'No.'

'Not at the Belvedere Golf Club?'

'No. He's in jail.'

'Yes, he is. What about Andrew Bragg? Have you heard that name?'

'Andy?' How could Andy be mentioned in the same breath as Carmody and Bassani? 'I golf with him. At the Belvedere.'

'The Belvedere Golf Club?'

'Yes.'

'Is he a friend of yours?' the Scottish one coaxed.

'Well, not a *friend* friend.'

'What kind of friend, then?' the not-Scottish one puzzled.

'A golfing friend.'

'So you don't see him outside of the Belvedere?'

'Well, I do,' he admitted.

'So *not* just a golfing friend. How about the name Thomas – or Tommy – Holroyd? Have you heard of him?'

Vince could feel his throat getting dry and his voice growing squeaky. Bassani and Carmody was an abuse case. Why were they asking about Tommy and Andy? That was ridiculous, they weren't like *that*. Oh, dear God, he thought, do they mean me? He would never do anything like that. Vince felt an icy waterfall of fear in his insides. He'd never abused anyone! Who would say that? Wendy, probably, just to get back at him for having married her. 'I haven't done anything,' he said.

'Not you, Mr Ives,' the Scottish one soothed as Vince jumped agitatedly to his feet. He would have paced the room if it had been big enough for pacing. 'Do sit down. Mr Ives?' she nudged. 'Thomas Holroyd?'

'Yes. At the Belvedere. Tommy's a member. We play together.'

'The Belvedere Golf Club?'

'Yes.'

'With Mr Bragg?'

'Yes.'

'A *golfing* friend?'

'Yes.'

'And have you ever been to Mr Holroyd's house?' the Scottish one asked, consulting her notes. 'The Haven.' She tilted her head to one side like a little bird when she asked a question. A sparrow.

'High Haven,' he corrected. 'A few times.'

'And can you tell me, when you were at Mr Holroyd's house – High Haven – were there other people present?'

'Usually.'

'Was Mr Bragg there?'

'Usually.'

'Mr Bassani?'

'No.'

'Mr Carmody?'

'No, I told you. I never met him. He was before my time.'

Vince was beginning to feel sick. How much longer was this cat-echism going to go on? What were they trying to dig out of him?

'Nearly finished, Mr Ives,' the Scottish one said, as if reading his thoughts. She smiled sympathetically. Like a dental nurse assisting with a root canal.

'And when you were at Mr Holroyd's house,' the one without the Scottish accent continued, 'can you name anyone else who was present? At any time?'

'Well, Tommy's wife – Crystal. His son, Harry. Andy – Andy Bragg – and his wife, Rhoda. A lot of people go to his house – Christmas drinks, there was a party on bonfire night, one for Tommy's birthday. A pool party.'

'A pool party? Like snooker?'

'No, like a swimming pool. They've got an indoor one, heated, dug into the basement. Tommy put it in when they bought the house. It was a party for Crystal's birthday.' Tommy had seen to the barbecue outside, hadn't gone into the pool. 'Never learned how to swim,' Crystal said. 'I think he's a bit scared of water. It's his – what's it? – Achilles heel. That's from the Greek, you know,' she said. 'It's a myth, Harry told me about it.' She was standing talking to him in a bikini so it had been quite hard to concentrate on Greek myths. She was a bit like one herself, a statuesque blonde goddess who had wandered down from Olympus. The mere thought of Crystal made Vince fanciful, the way she moved through the water with her mag-nificent breaststroke.

The memory of her in a bikini made him blush, the word 'breast-stroke' made him blush too, and he worried that the two detectives had noticed. Both detectives cocked their bird heads in unison and regarded him with curiosity. 'A barbecue in the garden,' he said.

'Steaks, burgers. Chicken. Chops,' he added weakly. He had to make an effort to stop himself from itemizing an entire butcher's counter. The Scottish detective was writing it all down, like a shopping list.

'Anyone else? That you met at his house? High Haven?'

'Lots of people. Ellerman – that wholesale grocer guy, Pete Robinson – he runs that big hotel on the front. All kinds. A guy who's a councillor – Brook, I think. Someone in social work. Oh, and Steve Mellors. Stephen Mellors. He's a solicitor, he's handling my divorce, plays at the Belvedere with us sometimes.'

'The Belvedere Golf Club?'

'Yes.'

'And he's your—?'

'Solicitor. He's my solicitor. And a friend.'

'A friend?' the not-Scottish one said.

'We went to school together.'

'A *friend* friend, then?'

'School friend,' he murmured. He felt like a total idiot.

'You go back a long way, then?'

'Yes.'

'Anyone else at all? At these parties? Anyone else associated with the legal profession?'

'Well, a policeman. A superintendent, I think he said.'

'A superintendent?' they said in harmony.

'Yeah, I think he was a Scot. Like you,' he added to the Scottish detective as if she might not know what he meant by a Scot.

The detectives both sat up straighter and looked at each other. Stared, really, as if they were communicating telepathically.

'Can you remember his name?' the not-Scottish one asked.

'No, sorry. I can't even remember yours and you only told me five minutes ago.' Although it felt like hours.

'DC Reggie Chase and DC Ronnie Dibicki,' the not-Scottish one reminded him.

'Right. Sorry.' (Did she say 'Ronnie the Biscuit'? Surely not. It sounded like a London gangster from the Sixties.)

There was a pause as if they were gathering their thoughts. The

Scottish one – Reggie Chase – frowned at her notebook. The other one, the biscuit one, said, 'Mr Ives, have you ever heard the term "the magic circle"?'

'Yeah, it's magicians.'

'Magicians?'

'Like a magicians' union. Not a union, like a – an organization. You have to prove you can do tricks to get in.'

They both gazed at him. 'Tricks?' the biscuit one echoed coolly, arching a surprisingly threatening eyebrow.

Before he could say anything else the doorbell rang. All three of them looked towards the door as if something portentous was on the other side of it. Vince felt unsure, did he need permission from them to open it? The doorbell rang again and they looked at him enquiringly. 'I'll get that, shall I?' he said hastily.

The front door opened directly into the flat, not even the luxury of a hallway. Two uniformed constables – women – were standing there. They took their hats off and showed him their IDs, their faces solemn.

'Mr Ives? Mr Vincent Ives? Can we come in?'

Oh, Jesus, Vince thought. Now what?

Treasure Trove

Andy Bragg knew Newcastle Airport like the back of his hand. He spent enough time there, usually hanging about in a coffee shop. His travel agency used to be about taking people out of the country, nowadays it was about bringing them in.

The flight he was waiting for had been delayed and he was on to his third espresso, beginning to get jittery. He knew which table to sit at to get a good view of the Arrivals board. Shedloads of flights from Amsterdam in the air at this time of day, ditto Charles de Gaulle. Heathrow, Berlin, Gdansk, Tenerife, Sofia. One from Malaga that was taxiing. The one he was waiting for flashed up 'Landed' so he finished his coffee and strolled towards the Arrivals hall.

There was no hurry – they had to clear Immigration and it always took for ever, even though they were on tourist visas and had an address in Quayside that they could give. Then, of course, they had to collect their luggage and they always brought massive bags. Still, he didn't want to miss them so he took up a position behind the barrier, his iPad at the ready with their names on. Nice and professional – no barely legible writing scribbled on a bit of paper.

After half an hour he was beginning to think they had missed the flight or hadn't managed to clear Passport Control, but then the doors swished open and two girls – looked like sisters – stood there looking around uncertainly. Jeans and sneakers, branded, almost certainly fake. Ponytails, lots of make-up. They could have been twins. Huge suitcases, naturally. They caught sight of the iPad and he saw the look of relief on their faces.

They trotted eagerly up to him and one of them said, 'Mr Mark?'

'No, love, my name's Andy. Mr Price sent me – Mr Mark, that is.' He put out his hand and she shook it. 'Jasmine?' he hazarded, smiling. Let's face it, they all looked alike. He'd guessed right. He hadn't bothered with surnames, he wasn't about to start learning how to pronounce Tagalog. (Was that really what they called their language? It sounded like the name of a kids' TV programme.) 'You must be Maria, then,' he said to the other one. She gave him a big grin. She had a surprisingly firm handshake for someone so small.

'Good flight?' They nodded. *Yes.* Unsure. On their application forms they had both said that they had 'good' English. They'd probably lied. Most girls did.

'Come on then, girls,' he said, full of false cheer. 'Let's get out of here. Are you hungry?' He mimed spooning food into his mouth. They laughed at him and nodded. He grabbed the suitcase handles, one in each hand, and started dragging them behind him. Jesus, what did they have in there – bodies? They followed, free of baggage, their ponytails bouncing as they walked.

'So this is it, girls,' Andy said, opening the door to the apartment. It was a Quayside studio flat they'd bought a couple of years ago that they used a lot for one thing or another. It was on the seventh floor, clean and modern, and had a great view, if you liked views of Newcastle. Maria and Jasmine seemed impressed, which was the intention. Andy thought of it as 'buttering up' – keeping them docile. He would have taken them straight to Silver Birches but neither Jason nor Vasily – Tommy's henchmen – had been available to process them and the place was 'in lockdown', Tommy said.

'One night only,' he warned as the girls explored. That was a song, wasn't it? From something he'd seen with Rhoda in London. They'd had a weekend away, done all the tourist things, the London Eye, an open-top bus, a West End show – a musical. Rhoda knew London better than Andy did and he had felt a bit like a hick up from the provinces, fumbling with his Oyster card and walking around with his eyes glued to Google Maps on his phone. Still, over all they'd had a good time and the weekend had reminded Andy that most of the time he quite enjoyed being married to Rhoda, although whether Rhoda felt the same way towards him was uncertain.

They'd left the Seashell in the hands of Wendy Ives. It was out of season and there was only one booking. They could have saved the money they paid her and put Lottie in charge for all the work that was involved. That was before the split with Vince, and Wendy was already having an affair with that bloke who was on the lifeboats. Rhoda suspected that Wendy had wanted to babysit the hotel so she could have somewhere to go with her new man while her old man stayed home and walked the dog and looked like a bit of a tit for not knowing. He knew now, all right. Wendy was taking Vince to the cleaners.

Wendy had come on to Andy once when she was drunk – well, they were both drunk, but he wouldn't have dared even if he'd wanted to, which he didn't. Rhoda was more than enough woman for him. Literally. A quarter of Rhoda would have been enough for any man. Besides which, she would kill him if she ever found out that he'd been unfaithful to her. Torture him first, probably. That was the least of his worries. He had a much bigger secret he was keeping from her, a secret that was getting bigger and more cumbersome every day.

'Mr Andy?'

'Yes, Jasmine, love?' He was able to tell the difference between them now. He'd surprised himself by managing to learn their names – something he usually had difficulty with.

'We stay here tonight?'

'Yes, love. One night only though.' (*Dreamgirls* – that was what the show was called.) 'First thing tomorrow we'll go to Silver Birches. They're getting your room ready for you.'

He was exhausted. He'd taken them shopping in Primark, not that they needed new clothes, those suitcases were stuffed, but he'd steered them towards some skimpy sequinned stuff that attracted them like magpies. They'd taken endless selfies. Tried to get him to pose with them. No way, he laughed, pulling away from them. He wasn't going on anyone's Facebook page, but nonetheless it was good that they did post a photo, then everyone back home could see they were alive and well and safely arrived in Britain and having a great time. They weren't bar girls, they worked in a garment factory in Manila and they were coming here to be care workers. British care homes were full of Filipinos because British people couldn't take care of anything, least of all their own families.

They'd shopped in Sainsbury's and he'd helped the girls choose stuff for their tea. Ready-meals – there was a microwave in the Quayside flat. They ate all kinds of crap where they came from – chicken feet and fried insects and God knows what. They were excited by the supermarket. Easily excited, both of them.

His phone rang. Stephen Mellors. Aka Mark Price. 'Steve?'

'All still okay with Bumbum and Bambi?'

'Mr Price,' Andy mouthed to the girls, indicating the phone. They smiled and nodded. 'Jasmine and Maria?' he said to Steve. 'Yeah. Good. I'm just settling them in for the night.' The girls had put the TV on and were watching *Pointless*. They seemed hypnotized, although surely they couldn't understand a word of what was going on. 'We've had a good day, eh, girls?' Andy said, raising his voice and giving them a thumbs-up and a big grin. They giggled and gave him exaggerated thumbs-up back. It was criminally easy to hoodwink them. They were innocents, like children or baby rabbits, he thought. Little lambs. He caught sight of himself in a mirror on the wall and felt a spasm of something. Guilt? It was a new emotion to him. Sometimes he wondered where his humanity had gone. Oh, yes, he remembered – he'd never had any.

'Talk to you later,' he said, pressing the Call End button. The phone lit up again almost immediately and the caller ID came up – a photo of Lottie. It wasn't actually Lottie calling him, of course, it was the photo he used for Rhoda. He took the call in the narrow hallway.

'Hello, love,' he said, trying to keep the weariness out of his voice. It was no good looking to Rhoda for sympathy. She had the energy of a Japanese train.

'Are you going to be long, Andrew? Doing whatever it is you're doing?'

Why had Rhoda started addressing him as Andrew instead of

Andy? He associated 'Andrew' with his mother, as previously she had been the only one to call him that, and then only when she was annoyed with him (although that was often), so now he felt as though Rhoda was always irritated with him about something. (Was she?)

'Is that Alexander Armstrong's voice I can hear? Are you watching *Pointless*?' she asked suspiciously. 'Where *are* you, Andrew?'

In a meaningless void, he thought. 'On my way home,' he said brightly. 'Do you want me to pick anything up on the way? How about an Indian? Or a Chinese?'

Paperwork

'I mean, what are the chances?' Reggie said to Ronnie after they had left Vincent Ives's flat in Friargate. 'That the man we were there to interview for Operation Villette would be the very same man who was married to our dead body. When she wasn't a dead body.'

'I know — talk about a coincidence,' Ronnie agreed. 'Weird. Very weird.' Vincent Ives wasn't suspected of anything, at least not by Reggie and Ronnie. He was a tiny tick on their checklist, a dull piece in the jigsaw — featureless sky or grass — who had been mentioned by a barman at the Belvedere, and yet now he was the husband of a murdered woman. It certainly made you question his innocence in general.

The two uniforms who had come to Vincent Ives's door had been confused by the presence of Ronnie and Reggie. At first they thought they were friends of Ives, and then they seemed to think they were social workers of some kind, and it was only when they produced their warrants and Reggie said, 'DC Reggie Chase and DC Ronnie Dibicki' that it clicked with the uniforms. 'Have you informed him already?' one of them asked.

'Informed him what?' Ronnie puzzled.

'About his wife,' the other one said.

'What about his wife?'

'Yes, what about my wife?' Ives said.

'Ms Easton,' one of the policewomen said gently to him. 'Wendy Easton, or Ives — is that the name of your wife, Mr Ives?'

'About-to-be-ex-wife,' he murmured.

'Would you like to sit down, sir?' one of the uniforms said to Vincent Ives. 'I'm afraid we have some bad news about Ms Easton.'

Murdered! Ronnie and Reggie stared at each other, communicating silently, eyes on stalks. For who was the person most likely to have murdered their lady on the lawn if not the about-to-be-ex-husband? The man who was sitting on a sofa right there in front of them! Reggie thought of the golf club lying in the garden border. 'The Belvedere,' she murmured to Ronnie. 'I know,' Ronnie murmured back.

Then the uniforms had taken Vince Ives away, saying they wanted him to accompany them to identify his wife. And, just like that, the murder of Wendy Easton slipped through their fingers again.

What was really peculiar, they were agreed on afterwards, was that when they told him that his wife had been murdered, the first thing Vincent Ives said was, 'Is the dog okay?'

They drove back to the Seashell.

'See if we can catch our Mr Bragg in this time,' Ronnie said.

The sun was beginning to set, streaking across the sky. '"See where Christ's blood streams in the firmament,"' Reggie said.

'Eh?' Ronnie said.

'Hello again, Mrs Bragg. Is Mr Bragg home now?'

'No.'

'Are you expecting him home soon?'

'No.'

'I'll leave you my card, then. Could you ask him to give us a call?'

'"They seek him here, they seek him there,"' Reggie said when they were back in the car. They shared a packet of nuts and raisins. 'The Scarlet Pimpernel,' she added. 'He was known for being elusive. Like our Mr Bragg.'

'Perhaps we should check in as guests,' Ronnie said. 'We might be able to catch hold of him then.'

They finished the nuts and raisins. Ronnie folded up the packet and put it in the little plastic bag they kept for rubbish. Even their rubbish was neat.

'We should go home, I suppose,' Ronnie sighed. 'Make a start on the boxes.'

'Yeah.' Reggie was beginning to really like the way they called it 'home' without thinking twice.

They had loaded the boxes of paperwork on to the back seat of the car – in fact they took up the whole car, apart from the space Reggie and Ronnie had carved out for themselves. The boxes, unwanted back-seat passengers, were beginning to feel oppressive. Reggie and Ronnie had done their homework, they knew the Bassani and Carmody case inside out, not to mention backwards and forwards and up and down, and it seemed unlikely they could find anything in the boxes that hadn't been raked over already, and most of the important stuff was computerized anyway.

'Well I never,' Ronnie said. 'Speak of the devil.'

'What?'

'Over there, sitting on that bench. That's none other than our old friend Mr Ives, isn't it?'

'He's a long way from home. What's he doing here, do you suppose?' Reggie puzzled.

'Odd, isn't it? Perhaps he's looking for Andy Bragg as well? Of course, they're not *friend* friends,' Ronnie laughed.

'Maybe he's come to tell him that we were asking questions about him. Or tell him about his wife's murder. I wonder if he's being treated as a suspect.'

'Hey-up,' Ronnie said. 'He's on the move.'

They watched as Vincent Ives went into the car park behind the sea wall, craning their necks to see where he was heading. He plodded up the set of steps that led from the car park to the cliff path.

'Evening stroll,' Ronnie said. 'He might be wanting some peace to mourn the soon-to-be-ex-Mrs Ives.'

'No longer soon-to-be,' Reggie said. 'Now completely ex.'

They decided to hang around a bit longer in case Andy Bragg came home or Vincent Ives came back and did something interesting. They got out of the car and leant on the sea wall to get some air and appreciate the remains of the sunset and the vastness of the North Sea. The tide was fully in now, swelling and heaving against the sea wall and the promenade. 'It makes you wonder what it must be like in winter,' Ronnie said.

'Pretty dramatic, I expect,' Reggie said. She thought she might go mad living in a place like this. A runner caught her eye, jogging through the car park. A middle-aged man, headphones clamped to his head. She gave a little gasp of surprise.

'What?' Ronnie said.

'That guy,' Reggie said.

'The one running up the cliff?'

'Yeah. That one. I know him.'

'It's a day for coincidences, all right.'

'You know what they say,' Reggie said.

'No, what do they say?'

'A coincidence is just an explanation waiting to happen.' Or at any rate, Reggie thought, that was what the man who was running up the cliff always said.

'Have you seen this?' Ronnie said.

They were truffling through the dross in the bottomless evidence boxes, the task mollified a little by the extra-large pizza and the bottle of Rioja they had picked up in the Co-op in Whitby. It wasn't cold enough for a fire, but Reggie had lit one anyway and it was crackling away fiercely in the little hearth. It seemed the right thing to do when you were in a seaside cottage. She'd never made a fire before and had to google how, but was quite proud of the end result.

'Seen what?' she asked.

Ronnie held up a creased and worn piece of paper. 'It's a record of a court case in 1998. It looks like a conveyancing thing, about a flat in Filey. Something about a "flying freehold" – what's that?'

'I think it's when you don't actually own the ground beneath your property. If you had a room above a passage or some kind of void.'

'How do you even know that?'

'I'm a repository of useless knowledge,' Reggie said. 'A hundred years ago I'd have been treading the boards of a music hall. Like Mr Memory in *The Thirty-Nine Steps*.'

'The what?'

'*The Thirty-Nine Steps*. It's a Hitchcock film. It's famous.' Reggie sometimes wondered if Ronnie had ever opened a book or watched a film or a play. She was a total philistine. Reggie didn't hold it against her, in fact she rather admired it. As someone who had read and seen everything from the *Iliad* to *Passport to Pimlico*, Reggie didn't feel that any of it had done her much good. It certainly hadn't helped to keep Sai.

'Anyhoo,' Ronnie said, 'it says here that the buyer wasn't informed about the flying freehold and the buyer's solicitor is suing the seller's solicitor. For misrepresentation or something. The buyer was Antonio Bassani, but that's not what's interesting. The solicitor representing him in court was Stephen Mellors. Remember that name?'

'Vincent Ives's solicitor,' Reggie said. She reached for her notebook, flipped through the pages and read out loud, '*He's a solicitor, he's handling my divorce, plays at the Belvedere with us sometimes.*'

'Also a *school* friend, remember,' Ronnie said. 'They go back a long way.'

'There's more old stuff like that in here,' Reggie said, passing over a flimsy folder, the cardboard soft and furry now with age. 'Just bits and pieces from Bassani's property portfolio from the Seventies mostly. Trailer parks. A nursing home. Flats in Redcar, Saltburn, Scarborough. You can imagine him being the kind of landlord who gave Rachman a bad name.'

'Who?'

'Never mind. This stuff must have been raked over by forensic accountants at the time of the trial, don't you think?'

'Dunno. Do we need to open another bottle?'

There were two small bedrooms beneath the eaves, each containing a narrow bed, the kind a maiden aunt might have found herself relegated to. Or a nun.

'Beguinage,' Reggie said.

'Eh?'

'It's like a lay convent for women, a religious community from medieval times. There's one in Bruges. It's beautiful. I mean, it's not a thing now. It would be quite nice if it was.' Reggie had been to Bruges with Sai, on an overnight ferry that rolled its way across the North Sea to Zeebrugge. She had been seasick all the way and he had held her hair back while she vomited into the stainless steel toilet in the tiny shower room in their cabin. 'No greater love has a boy-friend,' he'd laughed. After he left her to marry the girl his parents had chosen for him, Reggie went to the hairdresser and asked him to cut her hair short, a ritual women had undergone since time im-memorial, or at least since the first man dumped the first woman. Adam and Eve, perhaps. Who knew how their union had gone after Adam had tattle-taled to God that Eve had been flirting with the tree of knowledge?

'I mean – who wants a woman who *knows* anything?' Reggie said crossly to Ronnie.

'Dunno. Another woman?'

Tipping Point

Murdered? Vince had expected they would take him to a morgue or even the murder scene (or 'my home' as he still thought of it) and show him a corpse, but no, they took him to a police station and showed him a Polaroid. You would have thought that getting divorced from a woman would free you of the obligation to identify her corpse, but apparently not.

You couldn't really see what was wrong with Wendy in the photograph. You might not have concluded that she was asleep, but given a multiple-choice questionnaire you wouldn't necessarily have opted for 'dead'. They said she had a head injury, but they must have posed her in a way that concealed whatever horror was there. They wouldn't tell him how she had acquired this 'head injury'. What they did say was that she had been found in the back garden and they thought she had been killed either late last night or in the early hours of this morning. They had to prompt him into identifying her as he just kept staring at the photograph. *Was* it Wendy? It struck him that she didn't have particularly distinctive features. He'd never really noticed that before.

'Mr Ives?'

'Yes,' he said eventually. 'That's her. That's Wendy.' Was it? He still felt doubtful. It looked like her, but the whole thing seemed so unlikely. Murdered. By who?

'Do you know who did it?' he asked the detective who said she was in charge of the investigation. 'DI Marriot,' she said when she introduced herself. She asked about 'your daughter' but Ashley was in the middle of a jungle somewhere with no phone signal. 'Helping to protect orang-utans,' she'd said before she went off-grid. You would think there were plenty of things closer to home that she could have found to protect. Her mother, for one. (Not that he was resentful. He loved her!)

'We'll contact the British consul in Sarawak.'

'Thank you. She'll be devastated,' Vince said. 'They were close.'

'And you weren't?'

'Wendy was divorcing me. So, no, I think that means we weren't close, don't you?'

The uniformed WPCs (were they still called that?) had taken him to a police station, where he had been asked a lot of questions. He had already been interrogated once that morning, twice in one day seemed unfair. He had been surrounded all day by women with odd names asking him questions, although he had begun to think almost fondly of the two bird-like detectives and their fascination with the Belvedere. In retrospect their questions seemed almost innocuous, and at least they hadn't suspected him of murder. Just golfing, apparently.

DI Marriot was interested in golf too, she kept asking him about his golf clubs. They were kept at the Belvedere, he told her. They had a (costly) storage facility for members, which was just as well as there was no room in the flat. No room for anything, hardly any room for Vince himself. Certainly not enough room for Vince and four policewomen, no matter how small they were. He had felt as if he was suffocating. *I'm afraid we have some bad news about Ms Easton.*

'Attacked,' they said at first, as if working their way up to the really bad word. Murdered. The house had been quiet when he'd gone there last night. Was she already dead? If he'd gone round to the back, looked in the garden, would he have found her? That was where she'd been discovered this morning, apparently. He thought of all that internet dating Wendy had been doing. Was it some stranger she had picked up and brought back to the marital bed? Was she in the middle of being murdered when he had been peering through the living-room curtains? Could he have stopped it? But then wouldn't Sparky have been barking his head off? He was a good guard dog, it would have been curious for him not to react to a stranger.

'Mr Ives? Sir?'

'Yes, sorry.'

It had taken a while for it to dawn on Vince that he might be a suspect. When it did dawn, it seemed such an astonishing idea that he tripped up in the middle of the answer to one of their questions ('And is there someone, Mr Ives, who can verify where you were last night? Or in the early hours of this morning?') and he started to babble nonsense. 'Asleep, I was asleep, I'd only just dropped off, because the amusement arcade is so noisy. I sleep alone, so no, no one can verify my alibi.' Oh, God – *I sleep alone.* It sounded so pathetic.

'Alibi?' the inspector said placidly. 'No one's talking about alibis, Mr Ives. Only you.'

He felt a fleeting frisson of fear, as if he perhaps *had* murdered Wendy and then somehow forgotten all about it, his usually good memory failing in the face of trauma.

'The Belvedere,' he said. 'I was in the clubhouse, drinking with friends. Tommy Holroyd and Andy Bragg.'

He didn't mention to DI Marriot that he'd been there, at the house. It was stupid of him, he realized now. He'd been seen, after all, he'd talked to Benny next door, there was probably CCTV everywhere that he hadn't noticed. Unfortunately, by the time he thought to correct his mistake they had moved on and Inspector Marriot was asking for his DNA, 'for elimination'. His fingerprints too. 'While you're here,' she said, as if it was for his convenience.

That used to be a joke between him and Wendy. They'd be sitting on the sofa together watching TV and she'd say, 'While you're up, love, can you make me a cup of tea?' somehow managing to make it sound as if she was the one doing him a favour. He used to respond like one of Pavlov's dogs, jumping up and putting the kettle on before he'd even realized he had been no more 'up' than Wendy had been. He could hear her laughing (fondly, or so he'd thought at the time) as he dutifully got the tea-bags out of the Queen's Golden Jubilee commemoration caddy that she had sent off for. She was a faithful monarchist. She did bonsai. She went to a twice-weekly

Callanetics class and liked television programmes about women seeking revenge. And she was dead. She would never sit on the sofa again.

They had spent a lot of time on that sofa together, watched a lot of television on it, eaten a lot of takeaways on it, drunk a lot of tea, not to mention wine, on it. The dog used to lie flopped between them like an arm rest. Yes, it was a dull and pedestrian existence, but there was something to be said for that. Better than starving or being shot at or being swept away by a tsunami. Better than being a murder suspect. Definitely better than being dead.

Afterwards, after he was ejected from the self-same sofa, Wendy told him that their home life together had become 'a living death', which Vince thought was going a bit far. Now she'd probably happily settle for a living death instead of, well, a dead death. Vince missed that sofa. He had felt safe and comfortable on it. It had been a lifeboat and now he was drowning.

'You don't remember being at Ms Easton's house – Thisldo – last night at about eleven p.m.?' the Spanish Inquisitor pressed on relentlessly. 'You were seen on a neighbour's security camera.'

'My house as well, not just Wendy's,' he corrected dully. 'I'm still paying the mortgage. And I'm not not living there by choice.' Was that a double negative? he wondered.

'Or,' she said, ignoring this remark, 'do you remember speaking to a man who lives in the neighbouring house, a Mr . . . ' – she consulted her notes – 'a Mr Benjamin Lincoln?'

'Benny. Yes. It slipped my mind. Sorry.'

'Slipped your mind?'

Vince had half expected Inspector Marriot to arrest him on the spot, but he was told he was free to go. 'We'd like you to come back in tomorrow, if you don't mind, Mr Ives.'

'How was she killed?' he asked. 'I mean I know it was a head injury, but how? What did they use as a weapon?'

'A golf club, Mr Ives. A golf club.'

What was he supposed to do now? he wondered. Perhaps he could go for a walk, he thought, clear his head. They wouldn't let him have the dog, it was 'being tested for DNA'. Did they think *Sparky* had killed Wendy? No, the inspector said, looking at him sadly as if she felt sorry for him being such a fool. 'In case the dog attacked the killer.'

He didn't walk, he caught a bus. By chance he was hovering indecisively next to a stop when a bus drew up and, in an uncharacteristic act of spontaneity, he simply stepped on board. It was the first time he'd been on a bus in twenty years. Who was driving his company car now? he wondered as he settled in the seat. He had given it no thought when it was his, now he thought of it fondly, almost the way he thought of Sparky.

The bus said Middlesbrough on the front but it may as well have said The First Circle of Hell. And what did it matter anyway? He just needed to get away, leave it all behind. If only he could leave himself behind. Vince supposed that if he disappeared the police would presume he was guilty, but he was past caring. Perhaps they would issue one of those things they had on American cop shows? BOLOs, that's what they were called, wasn't it? Be on the lookout for. Running for the border, he thought, like a man in a book or a film, although he was neither, he was a man in his own life, and that life was falling apart. And there was no border to run for, unless you counted the invisible administrative one between North Yorkshire and Teesside. Vince didn't even get that far. He got off the bus in Whitby in case he fell asleep and ended up in limbo, or Middlesbrough, which was much the same thing, and then walked along the beach as far as he could before the tide started chasing him and he climbed up a set of steps slippery with seaweed on to the pavement that ran along the front.

He passed a small hotel overlooking the sea and, to his surprise, realized that it was the Seashell – Andy Bragg's place. He'd only been here a couple of times, and in the car. Everything seemed different when you were on foot. (Much slower, for a start.) He wondered about going in and drowning his sorrows, unburdening his problems to a sympathetic ear (*You'll never guess what happened to me today, Andy*), but he knew that Andy didn't have much of a sympathetic ear, his wife, Rhoda, even less of one. Times like this you needed a (friend) friend, but he couldn't think of a single one. He had tried Tommy's house phone, hoping that perhaps Crystal would be there, but only the answering-machine spoke to him, or rather Harry, Tommy's son, whose voice announced, 'You have reached the number for the Holroyd family.' He had tried Tommy's mobile too, but that just rang out, didn't even go to voicemail. He had no one he could talk to. Not even the dog.

He walked past the Seashell, found a bench near the car park by the sea wall. The bench had a view of the sea and Vince stared at it until his mind was as blank as the sea wall itself.

After a while he roused himself and looked around. From the car park there were steps that led up to the cliff. You could walk for miles up there, it was part of the Cleveland Way. They had come here with Ashley when she was small. Eaten a picnic in a freezing wind, sitting on a bench in the middle of Kettlewell. There had been nothing there, not even a café, and they had all been miserable, but the passage of time had transformed it into an almost pleasant memory. There were going to be no more pleasant memories, were there? Wouldn't it be easier all round if he followed Lesley Holroyd over the cliff?

Vince shivered. The sun had begun to dip into the sea. He needed to keep moving. He sighed and stood up stiffly from the bench and began to climb the steps up to the cliff. A man going nowhere. Trudge, trudge, trudge.

Curtain Call

Jackson was running. He had returned to the cottage, sans unicorn backpack, feeling rather defeated. Time to regroup the little grey cells. He tipped an invisible hat in Poirot's direction. Jackson preferred the Belgian to Miss Marple. He was more straightforward, whereas Miss Marple was endlessly devious.

He had Miranda Lambert on his headphones. She was his absolute favourite. She was blonde and curvy and sang about drink and sex and heartbreak and nostalgia and he suspected he would be slightly nervous of her in real life. But she was still his absolute favourite. He was running in the wood near his cottage. It was shady in the wood, damp and mushroomy, the scent of autumn. A foretaste of the change in the season that was lurking threateningly around the corner. Winter was coming. Always. With neither cease, nor desist.

The wood had two entrances. A main one, off the road, with a car park and a café, and a much smaller one close to his cottage — a path so well hidden that it seemed almost like a secret and Jackson had begun to think of it as his own private entrance. Both routes into the wood had official estate signs about respecting the wood, days of opening, warning against dogs off the lead, and so on. You weren't allowed in every day, the estate had shooting parties, and when they didn't have shooting parties they were raising things that could be shot. The pheasants wandered around tamely in Jackson's front garden, completely unaware of their final destination. The males were gorgeous in their finery, but Jackson preferred the more modest speckled females.

He was running a lot these days, despite the protests from his knees.

'Your knees are too old to run,' his GP had bluntly informed him. She was young. Nice knees on show. Nice, young knees. She would learn.

He ran in the wood, he ran on the beach. He ran on the clifftop. If he went north he could run to Kettlewell, Runswick Bay, Hinder-well, Staithes. He could probably have run all the way to Saltburn, but he hadn't tried that. He could have veered away from the cliff path and run to Middlesbrough, but he definitely wasn't going there. It wouldn't just be his knees that would protest if he did that.

In the other direction he could run along the cliff from Whitby Abbey to Robin Hood's Bay. He liked Robin Hood's Bay. There used to be a lot of smuggling going on there. Smuggling in the past seemed romantic – barrels of rum, chests of tea, bales of silk, transported from the shore through secret tunnels by the locals. Brandy galore. He seemed to remember reading a book about it when he was young (or more likely, knowing the young Jackson, it had been a comic). Contraband had lost its fanciful charm these days. Counterfeit goods, heroin, endangered animals, endangered people.

The arrival of a teenage boy and an elderly dog tended to get in the way of his running. Nathan couldn't see the point of walking, let alone running ('There is no point,' Jackson said), and although Dido would have made a game attempt to go with him, the Queen of Carthage could really only run in her sleep now.

Running wasn't pointless, of course. Sometimes you did it to try to outrun your thoughts, sometimes you did it to chase them and bring them down. Sometimes you did it so that you didn't think at all. Jackson had tried meditation (he had, honestly), but he just couldn't sit and think of nothing. Could anyone, really? He imagined the Buddha cross-legged beneath his tree with a cartoon speech balloon filled with things like 'Remember to buy dog food, check tyre pressures, phone my accountant.' But running – running was meditation.

Although at the moment his mind was full, rather than empty – consumed by the girl with the backpack. Or now, of course, without the backpack. He had trawled his police contacts – fewer than he thought, most were retired now or in some cases dead – and had come up with no one. He'd been out of the real business of detecting for too long. Entrapping unfaithful boyfriends and husbands wasn't dealing with criminals, just high-functioning morons.

And as for image-enhancement software, he didn't know where to start with that, so he had sent the photo of last night's Peugeot's number plate to Sam Tilling, his eager young apprentice. He was pretty sure he would know what to do with it. If he could decipher the number plate then Jackson could apply to the DVLA for the owner's details – having a private investigator's licence was useful for something, although not much. Not for the first time, Jackson found himself regretting leaving the police, where he'd had all those resources at his fingertips. Why did he leave? He honestly couldn't remember. A whim, probably.

If he hadn't retired from the field so prematurely he would be in clover by now. Out to pasture with a good pension, savings, lots of leisure time. He could be learning new things – hobbies, something he'd never had time for. Tree identification, for one. He was surrounded by them at the moment but he would have been hard-pressed to identify a single species. He could manage oak because the leaves were distinctive and because they had occupied such a central position in British history – all that shipbuilding, King Harry's great navy. Heart of oak. *Steady, boys, steady.* The future Charles II hiding in an oak tree. When he was younger, Jackson's politics had been on the side of the Roundheads, now he felt a certain sympathy towards the Royalists. It was the trajectory of age, he presumed.

As for the rest of the trees in the wood, they were just generic 'trees', he couldn't tell a birch from a beech. Someone should invent a Shazam for trees and plants. (They probably had.) 'Gap in the market, Jackson thought. Quite a niche market though, National Trust members mostly. Middle class, middle income – the frail and overburdened backbone of England. The kind of people who owned Labradors and listened to *The Archers* and couldn't abide reality TV. Me, Jackson thought. Even if the Labrador was on loan and he didn't actually listen to *The Archers* ('As if,' as Nathan would say), just to

Julia's endless précis of the programme. Jackson was the first person in his entire family to elbow their way into the middle class and if anyone questioned his right to be there he could wave his National Trust membership card in their face as proof. Perhaps Julia was right about the class war being over but not about everyone having lost.

He hadn't encountered a single soul on his run. This wasn't a popular part of the wood. You could probably die here and not be found for weeks. If ever. The same was true for a tree, he supposed. If a tree fell in the forest and there was no one to hear it, did it make a sound? Although it sounded like a Zen koan (yes, he knew the word 'koan'), really it was a scientific question, to do with vibration and air pressure and the physiology of the ear. If a man fell in the forest—?

He went flying, tripping on a tree root that had been waiting in hiding to ambush him and exact revenge for his ignorance. More punishment for his knees. At least there was no one around to see his pratfall, although if he listened carefully Jackson thought he could hear the sound of one hand clapping.

He picked himself up, dusted himself down and so on, and continued running, out of the wood, past his own cottage, along the bank of the stream, past the Seashell and up on to the cliff.

He'd switched to Maren Morris on his headphones. She was singing about how her car was her church. It was not a sentiment you often heard from women. If she hadn't been young enough to be his daughter (not to mention laughing him out of court), Jackson would have tried to marry her. *Hallelujah.*

The remains of a handsome sunset were still staining the sky. He was running on the old railway line. It had been built to serve the alum quarries that had given wealth to this part of the coast. The line had never been used, his little local guidebook informed him, because it was realized that it was too close to the crumbling cliff. Jackson had had no idea what alum was when he first moved here. It was obtained from shale and had been used to fix dyes, apparently, and needed quantities of urine to process it. The urine used to be shipped here in barrels. Funny business to be in. Up on the cliff you could still see the piles of shale left behind when the quarrying had finished. The old railway line had been incorporated into the Cleveland Way now and during the day Jackson encountered hearty types with backpacks and hiking sticks, but now in the late evening he was the only person up here. Once or twice he had encountered a deer, but at the moment, at bay on the cliff, was a man.

The man was standing on the tip of the promontory, staring out to sea as if he were waiting for his ship to come in and that ship was not only carrying his fortune but also the answer to the meaning of life. Or possibly he was contemplating flight, like a bird waiting for an updraught. He was very near the edge. Very near, considering all that crumbling. Jackson pulled his headphones off and veered off out along the promontory, running on shale that shifted underfoot. He slowed down as he neared the man. 'Nice evening,' the running man said to the standing man. The standing man looked round in surprise.

A jumper? Jackson wondered. 'You should be careful,' he said, feigning casualness. 'This promontory is crumbling.'

Ignoring the advice, the man took a step nearer the edge and the shale underfoot fell away in a little shower. Yeah, Jackson thought, this one had a death-wish. 'You should maybe move back from the edge a bit,' he coaxed. You had to approach would-be jumpers like you would a nervous dog. Don't alarm them, let them get the measure of you before you reach out. Most importantly of all, don't let them take you down with them.

'Do you want to talk about it?' Jackson asked.

'Not really,' the man said. He took another step nearer to flight. And then another. Jackson disobeyed his own rules and made a lunge for the man, grabbing him in a kind of clumsy bear hug so that the standing man and the running man became one as they went over the edge together. The falling man.

Stage Fright

'And that's just the tip of the iceberg, doctor!'

'Drink, please, Harry, if you would be so good,' Barclay Jack said with affected politeness as he came off-stage. He was in a good mood, full of the milk of human kindness. Trevor, his manager, had been in to see the show last night without telling him beforehand ('Didn't want to put you off your stride') and he'd brought a TV guy in with him, from a backwater channel with a handful of viewers, but TV nonetheless, and the guy 'liked what he saw', according to Trevor.

The phone in Barclay Jack's pocket vibrated as Harry handed him his tumbler of gin.

'Oo, Barclay,' Bunny Hopps said. 'Is that your phone or are you just pleased to see me?'

'Fuck off, Widow Twanky.' His good mood had been abruptly terminated, the milk of human kindness curdled by the text on the phone screen. He stared at it uncomprehendingly for a moment before understanding what it meant. His blood dropped into his boots. His legs started to shake and then collapse like columns in an earthquake. He was going down. In the literal sense.

'Harry, quick,' he heard Bunny say. 'Grab the St John's Ambulance bloke before he leaves the theatre. This stupid bugger's having a heart attack.'

And then it all went dark.

Everyone Wants to Be the Wolf

EWAN: WUU2TPM?
CHLOE: Nothing. Meet u?
EWAN: What time good 4u?
CHLOE: 4?
EWAN: Yh?? Great? Sos where?
CHLOE: Spa?
EWAN: Gud. Bandstand?
CHLOE: OK
EWAN: SYS! LOLO!

It was like learning a foreign language. It *was* a foreign language. Chloe – the real Chloe – was locked in her bedroom and grounded for the rest of her life after her mother had discovered that she was being groomed online. 'Ewan' purported – unlikely in the extreme – to like puppies and Hello Kitty and a slick Korean boy band that Jackson had watched on YouTube with a kind of fascinated horror. 'Getting down with the kids, Dad?' Nathan said sarcastically when he spotted him watching it. In reality, Jackson supposed, Ewan was probably a pitiful fortysomething sitting in front of his computer in his underpants. ('Well, you know,' Julia said, 'a large proportion of paedophiles are quite young.' How on earth did she know that? 'We covered it in an episode of *Collier*. Didn't you see it?' 'Mm, must have missed that one,' he said. He did know that, actually, and somehow he wished he didn't. The idea of boys not that much older than Nathan stalking girls on the internet was too disturbing.)

Chloe's mother, a terrifying woman called Ricky Kemp, had opted not to follow the conventional route of calling the police, mainly because her partner, Chloe's father, was a certified member of the East Coast criminal fraternity. 'I know some really bad people,' she said. Jackson didn't doubt her.

Jackson had been handed Chloe's laptop and phone by Ricky and was now masquerading as her in an attempt to net Ewan. Reverse grooming in the strange world of dark justice.

'And then when you've collared him just hand him over to me,' Ricky instructed. Jackson wasn't against entrapment – it took up the bulk of his business – nor was he against clearing the streets of one more pervert, but he wasn't at all sure about the handing-over bit. He wasn't a vigilante, he really wasn't, although his idea of right and wrong didn't always conform to the accepted legal standard. Which was a nice way of saying that he had broken the law. On more than one occasion. For the right reasons.

Ewan might be a sad loser, but did Jackson want to be responsible for him being beaten to a pulp – or worse, probably – by Chloe's father and his underworld friends? If he did manage to rendezvous with Ewan, Jackson planned to risk the wrath of the local mafia and make a citizen's arrest, before calling the police and letting the cold dead hand of the law take care of him.

Hopefully it would all be resolved this afternoon at four o'clock when they met for their 'date'.

He made coffee on the Aga with the help of his faithful old friend Bialetti and sat in the morning sun on the bench outside his front door. Dido bumbled out after him and stretched at his feet on the small lawn in front of the cottage. Jackson scratched her behind her left ear, a favoured spot, and her fur quivered down the length of her spine. ('You quiver if I scratch behind your ear?' Tatiana asked. She had met Dido. She liked dogs, she said. When she was 'little child' she had been part of a dog troupe act. 'We turn tricks together,' she told him. 'Do tricks,' he corrected her. 'Whatever.')

Jackson wondered idly how Vince was getting on. It took him a moment to retrieve his surname, proceeding methodically through the alphabet until he got to 'I'. Ives. St Ives, he thought. Jackson had never been to Cornwall, there were still large patches of the map of

Britain that remained unexplored by him. (Leicestershire – a mystery. Ditto Suffolk. And many other places as well, to be honest.) Perhaps he should go on a road trip. A grand tour of the kingdom. Perhaps he'd find St Mary Mead if he looked hard enough.

Vince Ives probably wasn't a saint, but Jackson didn't feel he was a sinner either. But who knew?

It wasn't every day you fell off a cliff. Luckily, it turned out that there was a handy life-saving shelf of sloping rock beneath and they had only fallen a few feet, although they had both yelled enough to start an avalanche before slithering to a halt inches from the edge.

For fuck's sake, Jackson had thought, lying on his back staring at the darkening sky. His heart was racing as if he'd just run a sprint and his 'old' knees hadn't been done any favours again when they had hit the unforgiving rock. He struggled to a sitting position and said to the standing man, now a lying-down man, 'That's a sheer drop and I'm not going to try and stop your acrobatics a second time. Okay?' The guy had the decency to look shame-faced.

Jackson thought it was probably a good idea to get a guy with a death-wish off a cliff. 'Come on,' he said, clambering carefully to his feet and offering Vince a hand up – warily, in case he suffered another moment of madness and decided to yank him over the edge with him.

Vince was his name, 'Vince Ives,' he said, holding his hand out to shake as if they were at a party or a conference rather than teetering in a death-defying manner on the edge of a cliff. He was very sorry, he said. 'A moment of madness. I just sort of reached a tipping point.'

'How about a drink?' Jackson offered when they had come down from the cliff and hit what passed for civilization again. 'That place looks like it's still open for business,' he said, indicating the Seashell to Vince Ives. Vince didn't seem impressed, in fact he seemed positively averse, saying, 'The Seashell? No, thanks,' with what looked like a little shudder, so Jackson took him back to his cottage, like you would a stray dog. He lit the fire and offered him a whisky, which he refused. It seemed that Vince hadn't eaten all day, so Jackson made them both tea and toast.

It was a good day when you saved someone's life, Jackson thought as he put the kettle on the Aga. Even better when you didn't die saving them. He really hoped this wasn't going to become the regular thought of the day because sooner or later he was bound to fail at one or both parts of the equation.

Eventually Vince started to pull himself together and it turned out they had something in common. They were both from the same neck of the woods and were both alumni of the band of brothers. 'We happy few,' Vince said, looking as far from happy as you could. He didn't strike Jackson as much of a soldier.

'Royal Signals,' he explained. 'In another lifetime.'

'Yeah, well,' Jackson said, 'I used to be a policeman.'

It was a familiar story. Mid-life crisis, sense of meaninglessness, depression, etcetera. He was a failure, Vince reported. 'We've all been there,' Jackson said, although in truth he'd never allowed himself more than a glimpse over the edge of the abyss. Jackson had never really seen the point of existential angst. If you didn't like something you changed it and if you couldn't change it you sucked it up and soldiered on, one foot after the other. ('Remind me not to come to you for therapy,' Julia said.)

'Trudged through my life,' Vince went on. 'Never did anything interesting, anything important. I've led a very *little* life. Never been top dog, you know?'

'Well, I don't think being the alpha male is all it's cut out to be,' Jackson said. 'There's nothing wrong with remaining in the ranks. *They also serve*, and all that.'

Vince sighed gloomily. 'It's not just that. I've lost everything – my job, my wife, my home, my dog. Pretty much lost my daughter too,' he added.

It was a long list, but a familiar one to Jackson. 'My first wife divorced me,' he said in solidarity.

'You married again then?'

'Well, yeah,' Jackson said, immediately regretting having mentioned Tessa, or whatever her real name was. A she-wolf. A certain manly pride stopped him from admitting to a stranger that his second wife had been a scheming, hustling conwoman who had removed him from his money with surgical precision before disappearing into the night. Instead he said, 'No, well, that one didn't work out either.'

'Life just seems to be against me,' Vince said. 'Like I'm cursed.'

'Sometimes you're the windshield, Vince,' Jackson said, 'sometimes you're the bug.' That was what Mary Chapin Carpenter sang anyway, *pace* Dire Straits.

'I suppose,' Vince agreed, nodding slowly as he chewed on the last bit of toast. A good sign in Jackson's book. People who were eating weren't usually about to top themselves.

'And there's no point in clinging on to things if they're over,' Jackson continued. (Julia was right, perhaps counselling really wasn't his forte.) 'You know what they say' (or what Kenny Rogers would say), ' "You've got to know when to hold them and know when to fold them." ' This was better, Jackson thought, all he had to do was utilize the lyrics from country songs, they contained better advice than anything he could conjure up himself. Best to avoid Hank, though – *I'm so lonesome I could cry. I'll never get out of this world alive. I don't care if tomorrow never comes.* Poor old Hank, not good mental fodder for a man who had just tried to jump off a cliff. Although had Vince known, Jackson wondered, about that life-saving shelf of rock? Was he aware, in a way that Jackson hadn't been, that it was a less treacherous scenario than it appeared? A cry for help rather than full-on suicide? He hoped so.

'Wendy – my wife – was walking away with everything, treating me as if I was nothing. Nobody.'

'She caught it by the handle, Vince, you caught it by the blade.' (Thank you, Ashley Monroe.)

'And they made me redundant. After twenty-odd years. Nose to the grindstone, shoulder to the wheel, every cliché in the book – never complained.'

'You'll get another job, Vince.' Could he? Jackson wondered. The guy was pushing fifty, nobody wanted you once you'd achieved a half-century on the pitch. (Jackson had started to watch cricket on TV. He kept that fact to himself, it felt like a secret vice.)

'And they took the company car,' Vince said.

'Ah, well, yeah, that is bad,' Jackson agreed. There weren't any country songs that could deal with that catastrophe. A man couldn't worship without a church.

It was only when Jackson had offered Vince Ives a lift home (insisted on it, in fact, in case he decided to wander off up the cliff again) and Vince was strapping on his seat belt that he said, 'My wife died today.'

'*Today?* The one who's divorcing you?'

'Yeah, that one.'

'Jesus, I'm sorry, Vince.' So perhaps they'd finally got to the real reason for the guy wanting to take the high jump. Cancer, Jackson thought, or an accident – but no, apparently not.

'Murdered.'

'*Murdered?*' Jackson echoed, and felt the little grey cells snap to attention. He used to be a policeman, after all.

'Yeah. Murdered. It sounds ridiculous just saying it.'

'And *you* didn't do it?' (Just checking.)

'No.'

'How? Do you know?'

'Beaten with a golf club, the police said.'

'Jesus, that sounds violent,' Jackson said. Not to mention personal. Although he had seen worse. (*How many dead bodies have you seen? Like in the whole of your life?*)

'I'm a golfer,' Vince said. 'The police were very interested in that.'

Cricket was one thing, but golf was a quite different enigma as far as Jackson was concerned. He was prepared to bet the future of the universe on the fact that he would never play the game. He had never even set foot on a golf course, except for once when he'd been a detective in Cambridge and a dead body had been discovered in the rough at the Gog Magog golf course. (Was there a more bizarrely named golf course anywhere? he wondered.)

'Plenty of people play golf,' Jackson said to Vince. 'That doesn't make them killers. Not usually, anyway.' Vince Ives played golf, his wife was killed with a golf club, therefore Vince Ives killed her. Wasn't that called something – a logical fallacy? (Was he just making that up? His little grey cells put their thinking caps on, but – unsurprisingly – came up with nothing.)

'And where *are* your golf clubs, Vince?'

'Can we just drive? I've been answering questions all day.'

'Okay.'

'Christ, I've just remembered,' Vince said. 'I had a putter, a spare one, I kept it in the garage. Used it to practise on the lawn. Wendy hated me doing that. I'm surprised she didn't put a "Keep Off the Grass" sign on the lawn.' He sighed. 'My fingerprints will be all over it, I suppose.'

'I suppose they will.'

It was late by the time they hit the road. Jackson had been up and down the A171 so much lately that he was beginning to feel as though he knew every inch of the tarmac. It hardly seemed worth going home again as he had to be back here again first thing tomorrow to pick up Nathan and resume the burden of parental duties. He wondered about staying in the Crown Spa overnight – he could sleep on the floor of Julia's hotel room. Perhaps she would even let him sleep in her bed. Was that a good idea or a bad idea? Tide in or tide out? He didn't know.

He offered to drop Vince off at his flat, but somewhere in a wasteland of back streets he said, 'No, leave me here. This'll do.' He laughed grimly and Jackson wondered what the joke was.

Jackson had phoned Julia from outside the Crown but her groggy response hadn't been exactly encouraging ('Sod off, Jackson'), and he was about to wend his weary way back when his phone lit up. He thought she had changed her mind, but it was only to tell him that Nathan had decamped to stay with a school friend for the night whose family was camping near by, but would he still take Dido?

'I'll come up,' he said, but Julia said, 'No, I'll come down,' and he had to wonder at that. Did she have someone up there with her? Or was she worried that she would be so overwhelmed by lust at his proximity to her bed that she would swoon into his arms? Fat chance of that.

She appeared in the hushed reception area barefoot, her hair all over the place and wearing a pair of pyjamas so old that he recognized them from when they had been together. She was not in the mood for seduction. 'Here,' she said, handing him the dog lead, the dog at the other end of it. Then she turned tail and said, 'Night,' sleepily and padded back up the stairs. ('When you last sleep with woman?' Tatiana demanded of him a few evenings ago. 'With real woman?' He took the Fifth on that.)

'Tails between our legs, eh?' he said to Dido in the rear-view mirror as they drove away, but she was already asleep.

So now he had the dog but not the boy, and surprised himself with how disappointed he felt about the absence of the latter.

He drained his coffee and checked his phone and found that Sam Tilling had got back to him with that number plate for the Peugeot. It was nice and readable and Jackson got an email off to DVLA, applying for the owner's details. He wasn't expecting a swift response. He phoned Sam and thanked him. 'How's Gary and Kirsty?' he asked.

'Same old, same old,' Sam replied. 'Chicken burritos in All Bar One Greek Street yesterday.'

'Photos?'

'Yep. Sent them to Mrs Trotter. She says to say hello to you.'

'Keep up the good work. There'll be a sherbet fountain in this for you when you finish.'

'Ha, ha.'

Penny Trotter had amassed an enormous dossier of evidence proving Gary's adultery. Is this What Jesus Wanted her to Do? Seemed unlikely, but his not to reason why. Wronged wives were a law unto themselves. And they paid the bills and kept the wolf from his door. ('Have you ever considered that you might be the wolf?' Julia said. 'Yeah, the lone wolf,' he said. 'I know you like to think so, but there's nothing heroic about a lone wolf, Jackson. A lone wolf is just lonely.')

More photos popped up on his phone. He had a shared album with Sam Tilling specially dedicated to Gary and Kirsty. They were all over each other in public places – 'Canoodling,' Julia would have called it. ('I love that word,' she said.) It seemed Julia wasn't prepared to canoodle with him any more in either public or private. Perhaps she wanted commitment. Perhaps he should ask her to marry him. (Did he *really* just think that?)

He finished his coffee. He had a lot of time on his hands until his tryst with Ewan and was wondering what to do with it – a run? He regarded Dido doubtfully, snoring gently in the sun at his feet. A slow stroll was probably the best they would manage together.

His phone buzzed. He wondered if it might be Julia, apologizing for being offhand last night. It wasn't. It was a client. A new one.

Girls, Girls, Girls

'Did you hear the news?' Rhoda asked when Andy entered the Seashell's kitchen the next morning. She was busy with the breakfasts, juggling pans and spatulas in a way that looked surprisingly threatening. She was ruthlessly efficient in the morning. Well, every hour of the day, really. He supposed she was annoyed with him for not coming straight home from Newcastle last night. He had taken a detour via the Belvedere instead, where he had indulged in some solitary drinking. Better to drink than think sometimes. Often, in fact. Rhoda had been fast asleep and snoring louder than Lottie when he finally stumbled through the door.

'News?' Andy said, reaching for the lifebuoy of the coffee pot. He inhaled the scent of frying bacon as if it were oxygen. His brain was still bleary with sleep, not to mention a slow-developing hangover. 'News about what?' News was rarely good, in Andy's opinion. News invariably carried consequences with it.

He tried to pinch some bacon from the frying pan to make a sandwich but Rhoda slapped his hand away. She was already bombarding him with a list of commands. 'Can you keep an eye on the sausages? I've got eggs three-ways to see to. And get some toast on, will you? The couple in Fastnet are having the full English – fried eggs for him, scrambled for her. The man in Lundy is having the full English as well, but his wife only wants poached eggs. And the vegetarian lesbians in Rockall are now claiming to be vegans. There's veggie sausages in the freezer – get four out. And open a tin of baked beans.'

'What news?' Andy persisted, resisting Rhoda's onslaught.

'About Wendy,' she said, cracking eggs into a pan of spluttering fat.

'Wendy. Wendy Ives?' Andy puzzled. 'Or Easton, or whatever she's taken to calling herself. What's she done now?'

'Only gone and joined the dead wives' club.'

'The what?'

'Murdered,' Rhoda said, making a meal of the word.

'Murdered?' Andy's alcohol-addled brain wandered around the word, trying to make sense of it. 'Murdered?' Repeating it didn't seem to help much.

'Yes, murdered. Killed.' Rhoda took a moment to consult her inner thesaurus. 'Butchered,' she retrieved, slicing through a black pudding. 'Slaughtered,' she added with some satisfaction. 'Don't just stand there, get the sausages.'

'*How* was she murdered?' Andy asked. The bacon no longer smelt so appetizing. (*Slaughtered?*) 'When? And who by, for heaven's sake? I don't understand.' He vaguely remembered hearing something on the local news on the car radio on the way home last night. *A woman has been murdered . . .* But not a name, not *Wendy* – Vince's wife, for God's sake! He got the sausages out of the freezer and read the ingredients on the packet. 'Says they contain egg white,' he said.

'Too bad, that's all I've got. The lezzies won't be able to tell.' Rhoda had quite a few gay friends, of both denominations, but it didn't stop her using derogatory language about them behind their backs. She wore the men of that persuasion on her arm like designer handbags – of which she had several criminally expensive ones that Andy had bought her for birthdays and Christmases. A couple of watches, too. It was a way (pretty insignificant in the bigger picture) of spending the money that was piling up. There was only so much cash he felt safe hanging on to. It was in the roof space in the attic. And there was only so much he could pass through the business or offload on a nail bar. He didn't think of the bags and watches as laundering, just a kind of safekeeping, and they had resale value if push came to shove. He told Rhoda that the Rolexes and the Chanel bags were fakes, when in fact they were genuine. It was a topsy-turvy world he inhabited these days.

He'd given her a Patek Philippe last year for her birthday, the real McCoy, bought it in a jeweller's in Leeds. The man behind the counter was suspicious of his cash, but he explained it away by saying he'd won on an accumulator bet. 'A Yankee at Redcar,' he felt it necessary to elaborate. The watch cost a small fortune. You could have bought a whole terrace of houses in Middlesbrough for the same price. Could probably have bought Middlesbrough itself, if you'd been so inclined. He told Rhoda it was a fake that a client had brought back for him from Hong Kong. Rhoda had only worn it once, said it was too obvious that it wasn't genuine. ('And stop buying me watches, for heaven's sake, Andy. I've only got one wrist and it's you that has the problem with timekeeping, not me.' She had two wrists, he thought, but didn't point that out.)

'Oh, and by the way,' Rhoda said, 'I forgot to tell you, because you came in so *late* last night . . .' She paused to make the point.

'Yeah, yeah. Very sorry, etcetera. What?' he prompted. 'What did you forget to tell me?'

'The police were looking for you yesterday.'

'The police?' he repeated cautiously.

'Yes, the police. Two detective constables. Girls. Looked like they should be in primary school. They came by in the morning and then they were back again in the evening.'

'I wonder what that could have been about,' Andy murmured, reaching for the coffee pot again. He noticed a little tremor in his hand as he poured. He wondered if Rhoda saw it.

'Maybe they think you murdered Wendy,' she said.

'What? I didn't kill Wendy!' he protested.

'Are you sure?'

'*Sure?* Of course I'm *sure*. I haven't seen her in weeks.'

'You daft ha'p'orth,' Rhoda snorted with laughter. 'I was joking. Do you honestly think they'd suspect *you*? They said something about paperwork. Have you not been paying your parking fines again?'

'Yeah, that was probably it.'

'Or maybe they were asking about Vince – you know, if you'd seen him. You were drinking with him, weren't you? Night before last? You might be able to provide an alibi.'

'You think they suspect *Vince*?'

'Well, it's usually the husband, isn't it?' Rhoda said.

'Is it?'

'Those sausages are about to catch, by the way.'

'But *Vince*? Surely not.' He removed the sausages from the grill, scorching his fingers. 'I don't think he's got it in him. Wouldn't have the nerve, would he?'

'Oh, I don't know,' Rhoda said. 'I've always thought Vince was a bit of a dark horse.'

'Really?'

'It was pretty nasty – her head was bashed in with a golf club. She was found in the back garden, wearing next to nothing. Makes you wonder what she was up to.'

'How do you *know* all this?' Andy puzzled.

'Trish Parker,' Rhoda said. 'She's the mother of one of the blokes that discovered the body. She's in my book club.'

'Your *book* club?' Andy didn't know which was more startling – that Wendy Ives had been murdered or that Rhoda was in a book club.

'First rule of book club,' Rhoda said, 'there is no book club. Are you going to let that toast burn as well?'

'So that's the full English for you, squire, or the full Yorkshire as we like to call it here,' Andy said, delivering a plate weighty with the promise of a heart attack to the man in Lundy. 'And for your good lady, two perfectly poached eggs. Free-range, organic, sourced from a farm up the road.' (Or Morrisons supermarket as we also like to call it, he thought.) What did the police want? His stomach was flip-flopping with fear and the smell of the eggs wasn't helping. The performance of breakfast bonhomie wasn't coming as easily as it usually did.

Had the police been in touch with Tommy as well? As soon as he could, he darted out into the hallway and called him, but his phone went straight to voicemail. Before he could think of a message to leave he heard a shriek coming from the breakfast room, closely followed by Rhoda's shrill *hulloo* as she hunted him down.

'Andrew! For Christ's sake, you gave one of the lesbians black pudding!'

It took Andy nearly three hours to get to Newcastle. A truck had shed its load on the A19 and the police were still directing traffic around the carnage of white goods. He felt a twinge of sympathy for the big cardboard boxes that were scattered along the hard shoulder like so many fallen soldiers. One box had split open to reveal a washing-machine lying forlornly, battered and bruised. It made him think of Wendy Ives, her head *bashed in with a golf club*.

What kind of club? he pondered idly as he crawled past the shamble of boxes. What would he choose himself for that kind of job? A wood, perhaps, but then you wouldn't be looking to drive Wendy's head any distance on to the fairway, would you? A short iron might be best, an 8 or a 9? He decided on a putter. The thin end of the wedge, he thought. Would crack a skull like an egg. His thoughts were interrupted by the sudden realization that it was a Holroyd Haulage truck that had lost its cargo. Tommy would give that driver hell.

Andy tried Tommy again, but he still wasn't answering his phone.

He felt as though he'd already put in a long shift by the time he was hustling Jasmine and Maria out of the Quayside flat and into his car. Their belongings seemed to have bred overnight in the dark and it took him for ever to load all their stuff into the boot. His phone rang with a number he didn't recognize and he let it go to voicemail.

They'd hardly got going before he had to stop at a service station and buy them burgers. He had one himself because his stomach was howling with hunger, having been cruelly deprived of its bacon sandwich, but the burger only served to make him feel more queasy. He took the opportunity to listen to the voicemail. A Detective Inspector Marriot needing a quick chat with him. If he could call her back? No, he couldn't. Hadn't Rhoda said that the police who were round at the house were constables? And now an inspector was calling? He was beginning to feel hounded. He tried Tommy again, but he still wasn't answering his phone – either of them. He had a bad feeling and it wasn't just on account of the burger. Why was the long arm of the law reaching out for him?

They passed the Angel of the North and he pointed it out to Jasmine and Maria, 'That's the Angel of the North, girls,' as if he were a tourist guide. They oohed and aahed a bit as if they understood.

Was it male or female? he wondered. Angels were sexless, weren't they? Andy liked to think the Angel was standing over him protectively, but in reality he supposed it was standing in judgement. Really, if he hadn't been driving he would have put his head on the steering wheel and wept at the pointlessness of it all. 'Soon be there,' he said, grinning encouragingly at them in the rear-view mirror.

He had to stop again at a Roadchef outside Durham so the girls could go to the toilets. While he was waiting he bought bars of chocolate and cans of Fanta, which seemed to be their drink of choice. They took for ever in the Ladies and for one paranoid moment he wondered if they'd absconded, but they returned eventually, giggling their heads off and chattering in their incomprehensible language.

'Can I offer you a cold beverage, ladies?' he said with ironic chivalry after he'd herded them back into the car. More giggling.

They reminded him of a Thai girl he knew in Bangkok a couple of years before he married Rhoda. She laughed at everything he said, admired everything he did. It made him feel like the most amusing, interesting man who ever lived. It was all an act, obviously, but did that matter?

He'd thought about bringing her home, marrying her, having kids – the whole shebang. It hadn't worked out, though. 'Changed my mind,' he told Tommy at the time. The truth was that it was the girl who'd changed her mind. She had one of those weird Thai nicknames – Chompoo. Something like that anyway. Shampoo, Tommy always called her. Tommy was out there with him at the time, they were dealing with 'the Retreat' as they'd always referred to it, although in fact it had no name, just a street number on the outskirts of Pattaya. Chompoo was a Buddhist nun now, apparently.

Tommy had got involved with Bassani and Carmody a few months before Andy had been drawn in. He'd been doing a bit of protection work for them – he was still in the ring at the time and he was a handy pair of fists if they got themselves into trouble. A heavy, a 'minder'. Nowadays he refrained from the dirty work. He had a couple of 'deputies' as he called them – a couple of sociopathic thugs called Jason and Vasily. Andy always presumed Vasily was Russian but he'd never been interested enough to enquire. They did anything that was asked of them. It was disturbing.

The so-called Retreat in Thailand had been a place for Tony Bassani and Mick Carmody and their like-minded friends and acquaintances to go and 'relax'. A lot of those friends and acquaintances were in high places, exalted even – at least one judge, a chief magistrate, a handful of local councillors, senior policemen, barristers, an MP or two. At the Retreat they could indulge themselves with a compliant, docile local population. Perhaps 'compliant' and 'docile' weren't quite the right words. Abused and exploited, maybe. Underage kids mostly – they were ten a penny out there. And at the end of the day, Andy had justified to himself, nobody was holding a gun to their heads. Except that one time, but that was best forgotten. That had been the beginning of the end for Tommy and Andy. 'Time for a sharp exit, don't you think?' Tommy said.

Andy had never met any of them, not even Bassani and Carmody themselves. Sure, he'd seen them at the Belvedere – on the green, in the clubhouse with their wives on a Saturday evening – but introductions were not made, discretion being the order of the day.

It had been Bassani and Carmody's solicitor who approached Andy. He was an ambitious greenhorn of a bloke who'd only just finished his articles. Bassani and Carmody had recently jumped ship from an older, established legal firm and presumably the pair of them chose the new guy because he was keen on money and not at all keen on moral scruples. He'd acted for them in a conveyancing dispute and they'd 'liked the cut of my jib', he said.

His clients, he told Andy, needed a travel agent and he would be acting as their intermediary. 'Fair enough,' Andy said. He thought the solicitor was a bit of a pillock. (Andy had a good ten years of maturity and cynicism on him.) The bloke was acting as if he was in the Mafia and Al Capone was his client. This was the late Nineties and, if anything, he reminded Andy of Tony Blair. Smooth hail-fellow-well-met Teflon type. His clients, he said, wanted to set up a holiday property, a retreat from their stressful lives in the UK. They and their friends would need their travel arranged. He was doing the paperwork ('the legals') and he was looking for someone to do the legwork out there.

'Like an estate agent?' Andy puzzled.

'Kind of,' the solicitor said.

'So,' Andy said, 'where do these clients of yours fancy for this holiday property? Benidorm? Tenerife? How about Ayia Napa – that's increasingly popular.'

'We were thinking Thailand.'

'Oh, very exotic.'

'Well, they're gentlemen with exotic tastes. We'd like you to go out there and have a look.'

'Me?' Andy said.

'Yes, you,' Steve Mellors said.

The property was not to be in their names, Steve Mellors informed him, Bassani and Carmody had a company for the purpose – SanKat – which sounded like a hygiene company to Andy's ears, one of those where they went in and changed the roller towels in the Gents or emptied the contents of 'feminine hygiene' bins. It was years before he learned that it was an amalgam of the names of their eldest daughters – Santina and Kathleen. You had to wonder about that.

Andy knew who Bassani and Carmody were, of course. Everyone did. They were influential all the way along the East Coast, fingers in lots of pies. Bassani the ice-cream emperor, Carmody the owner of amusement arcades and funfairs. They were in local government, well known for their charity work, Carmody had even been Lord Mayor for a term, clanking and swanking around in his regalia. They were the kind of men who wore gold signet rings on their fat fingers and had more than one flatteringly tailored dinner-jacket hanging in their wardrobe. The kind of men people fawned over because they do you favours – building warrants, planning permissions, liquor licences, private-taxi-hire contracts – it was all in their purview, for a price. Sometimes that price was silence.

Andy hadn't known much about the other stuff, the earlier stuff that had formed the basis of their trial. The 'parties', the kids. He knew now that there was a lot more that hadn't come out, a lot of people in their circle who hadn't been identified. Years of wrong-doing, going all the way back to the Seventies and Eighties. All those friends and acquaintances in high places had been trading kids with each other for years. Untouchables. Were they the men that Carmody was supposedly getting ready to name now? Most of them were dead – perhaps that was why he was prepared to talk.

It was years after the Retreat had been disposed of that Bassani and Carmody were arrested, and by then Andy and Tommy had cut themselves free and no one ever discovered the connection between them. Steve too, of course, had long since ceased to be their legal counsel. When they went to trial they had a pair of North Square wankers defending them in court and there was no sign of the young solicitor who used to handle their affairs. They kept schtum, named no names, and Andy wondered if it was because they were afraid of retribution – on themselves or their families. They'd dealt in some nasty business with some powerful men over time, the kind of men who could easily arrange for you to be accidentally knifed in a prison shower.

During their trial there'd been rumours flying all over the place. A 'little black book' was one of them, but no one had ever produced it and no one ever discovered the names of those men who had traded kids for decades, men who had gathered in each other's houses for 'special parties'. But Andy knew their names because he'd arranged their travel when they'd flown in and out of Bangkok. He'd seen their passports. He had photocopies. And he'd kept all the paper-work. You never knew when you might need insurance. The little black book. Not little, nor black, nor a book, but a computer file, on a memory stick, hidden with Andy's overflow of cash in the attic of the Seashell.

After they had parted company with Bassani and Carmody, the three of them – Steve, Tommy and Andy (the Three Musketeers, Steve called them, stupid name) – had started with the girls.

Anderson Price Associates was Steve's idea. A recruitment agency, legit-looking, 'completely kosher'. Just girls, because there was always a demand for girls, always had been, always would be. Not job lots. Bring them in one at a time, two by two at the most, like on the Ark. Straightforward trade, no small children, no refugees. Just girls.

Tommy was quick to agree, but then he thought the sun shone out of Steve's arse, for some reason.

Andy hadn't been so sure, but Tommy said, 'Don't worry so much, Foxy, it's the gift that keeps on giving.' And it was.

Anderson Price Associates was the official shiny recruitment face of the operation. Andy's firm, Exotic Travel, funnelled the girls into the country. Supply and demand, that was the foundation of capitalism, wasn't it? They had girls coming out of their ears. 'Exponential,' Steve said.

They weren't press-ganged or shanghaied off the street, they came of their own free will. They thought they were coming to real jobs – nursing, accountancy, care homes, clerical work, translators even. People sold bread or shoes or cars. Anderson Price sold girls. 'It's just business,' Tommy shrugged. 'No different to anything else, really.'

Anderson Price Associates, in the shape of Steve, recruited them on Skype from what he referred to as his 'second office'. It was a mobile home really, on an old site of Carmody's, but it was impressive, right down to the authentic background noises of a busy office.

A lot of the girls had skills and qualifications. Much good that did them once they were shackled to an old hospital bed in Silver Birches and being forcibly injected with drugs. Steve called it 'breaking-in', as if they were horses. After that they were distributed. Sheffield, Doncaster, Leeds, Nottingham, Manchester, Hull. The choice ones to contacts in London, some even found their way back into Europe. The white slave trade, alive and well in the new Jerusalem.

And, after all, who was going to suspect a bunch of middle-aged white blokes in a seaside town? The focus for the police, for the security services, was elsewhere – Asian paedophile gangs, Romanian slavers. So here they were, hiding in plain sight, supplying the limitless needs for sex in pop-up brothels, saunas and places that were even less legitimate, less salubrious. (You wouldn't think that was possible, but it was.) Trade was good.

Figures were meticulously kept, all the accountancy done beneath the cloak of the dark web. Anderson Price Associates was the umbrella that oversaw everything, but Anderson Price was, essentially, just Steve. The thing about Steve was that he enjoyed the game – the power and manipulation and lies, he enjoyed fooling the girls. That old mobile home of Carmody's was more like a hobby to him – a refuge too, perhaps. Other men had sheds or allotments, Steve had the mobile home.

They stopped again at a Sainsbury's Local on their way into town and he bought the girls a Ginsters pasty each and more Fanta, and some rancid coffee for himself. He couldn't believe how much they could eat. 'Hollow legs, eh, girls?' he said. Still, he thought, they probably weren't going to get much from now on, may as well treat them. They twittered something unintelligible in response that he supposed translated as gratitude. He could feel his unlooked-for conscience trying to push its way out of the darkness and into the light. He pushed it back down and said, 'Here we go, girls, we've reached our final destination,' as the sprawling, dilapidated building that was Silver Birches came into view.

It was indeed a nursing home of sorts. It had begun its life in the nineteenth century as a private mental hospital for the well-off, but in its latter days had been a home for the 'confused and elderly'. It had belonged to Tony Bassani, in the days when he had run several nursing homes along the coast. It had closed years ago and been bought by a 'shell corporation'. The shell corporation was registered to an empty tenement flat in Dundee, but there were other ghostly shells behind that. 'Like the dance of the bloody seven veils,' Tommy said. Tommy and Andy had no idea what happened beyond the Dundee shell – the legal side of things was Steve's domain. Tommy, always the happy-go-lucky sort, thought their ignorance might be protection, Andy doubted that ignorance had ever protected anyone.

Jasmine and Maria peered doubtfully at the building. Most of the windows were boarded up. The peeling paint was a depressing shade of institutional magnolia. There were bars on most of the windows, although it reminded Andy not so much of a prison as a bonded warehouse – somewhere where you stashed goods until they were ready to be sent on. Which was kind of what it was.

'This sillerburtches?' Jasmine asked, frowning.

'It's better inside,' Andy said. 'You'll see. Come on now, out of the car.' He was a shepherd with two reluctant sheep. Lambs, really. To the slaughter. His conscience sprang up again and he hit it back down. It was like playing whack-a-mole.

Someone tapped on his window, making him flinch. Vasily. He had Tommy's Rottweiler on a short chain and the girls started making little twittering noises. They didn't need to worry, the stupid mutt was just for show.

'Don't worry, Brutus is a pussycat,' Andy said, although they didn't understand a word of what he said. 'Come on, girls, let's be having you. Chop, chop. Time to start your new life, eh? A home from home.'

Wuthering Heights

Morning in the prison dubbed Monster Mansion by the tabloids. The smell of institutional breakfast – a bouquet of egg and porridge – was still permeating the wretched halls of HM Prison Wakefield, making Reggie feel nauseous.

They'd been expecting to find Prisoner JS 5896 in the hospital wing as he was supposedly at death's door, but they were shown into an ordinary interview room. A warden brought them a coffee each and said, 'He's being fetched now, he's a bit slow.' In this depressing, blank-walled room the smell of breakfast had been overlaid with the piney scent of commercial disinfectant as if someone had recently thrown up there. The coffee was gruesome, but at least it provided some kind of sensory antidote.

The object of their attention eventually shambled in, heralded by a kind of clanking, metallic noise that for a moment made Reggie think that their interviewee must be in shackles. Wakefield was a high-security prison but it turned out that Michael Carmody was free of restraint, other than being tethered to a large oxygen cylinder on wheels.

'Emphysema,' he wheezed, collapsing into one of the hard chairs at the table. A warden stood guard at the door but it seemed unlikely that Michael Carmody was about to make a bid for freedom. The only way he was getting out of this place was feet first.

'Mr Carmody,' Ronnie said. 'We are here today because certain new information has been brought to the attention of the police in regard to your case. A number of individuals have been named who were not part of the original investigation into your crimes, for which you are now serving a prison sentence.'

'Oh, I hadn't noticed,' Carmody said sarcastically.

Despite his scornful attitude he was a shadow of the man he must once have been, Reggie thought. She had seen photos of him when he was in his mayoral pomp, and even in the mugshot after his arrest – when, let's face it, most people didn't look their best – he had still looked hale and hearty, albeit florid and overfed. Now his cheeks were sunken and the whites of his eyes were a sickly yellow. He must be into his eighties by now, of course. A harmless old-age pensioner, you would have thought if you had encountered him in the street.

'We believe that you may be able to provide us with some information about the individuals we are investigating and we would like to ask you some questions. Is that all right, Mr Carmody?'

'Jeeso,' Reggie said.

'I know. I thought he wanted to talk,' Ronnie puzzled when they climbed back in the car a mere twenty minutes later. ('Have you got any antibacterial handwipes? I feel tainted.')

'He was supposed to be about to sing like ye olde proverbial canary, yet it seemed to be the last thing he wanted to do.'

'Do you think someone got to him? Threatened him?'

'Maybe,' Reggie said. 'Prison's full of criminals, after all. Do you want to drive or shall I?'

'You can if you want,' Ronnie said – generously, given that she spent a lot of time pressing her foot on an imaginary accelerator when slowhand Reggie was at the wheel. It was a two-hour drive here, two hours back. 'For nothing,' Ronnie said.

'Well, some good scenery,' Reggie said. The moors. *The wiley, windy moors.* Haworth was thirty miles in the opposite direction. Reggie knew because she had gone there on a day's outing from uni with Sai, before he opted for a full five-day Indian wedding feast instead of beans on toast and a box set of *Mad Men* with Reggie. ('It's you, not me,' he said.) There was no such word as 'wiley' in the

169

OED (Reggie had looked). You had to admire people who made words up. 'Have you ever been to Haworth?'

'No,' Ronnie said. 'What is it?'

'Haworth Parsonage. Where the Brontës lived.'

'The Brontë sisters?'

'Yeah.'

'I suppose that's who our Bronte's named after. I'd never thought about it.'

'I guess so,' Reggie said. 'Although there's a town in Sicily called Bronte, supposedly named after one of the Cyclops, who were said to live beneath Mount Etna. Admiral Nelson was given the title Duke of Bronte by King Ferdinand for helping recover his throne during the Napoleonic period. Our Bronte doesn't spell her name with a diaeresis, though.'

'A what?'

'Diaeresis – the two little dots above the "e", it's not an umlaut. Actually it was an affectation applied to the name by their father.'

'You don't get out much, do you, Reggie?'

'Honestly? No. Not any more.'

They had interviewed 'their' Bronte – Bronte Finch – at her house in Ilkley, in a lovely lemony drawing room where Bronte had served them tea in nice mugs and individual strawberry tarts from Bettys, which they couldn't resist despite an unspoken pact to eat or drink nothing while on the job. And she'd bought them specially, so it would have been rude not to have eaten them, they agreed afterwards. She was their patient zero, the first piece in the jigsaw.

There had been squashy sofas and real art on the walls and a lovely old rug ('Isfahan') on the oak parquet. A big vase of dark-pink peonies stood in the fireplace. Everything tasteful, everything comfortable. It reminded Reggie of Dr Hunter's house. It was the kind of home that Reggie would like to have herself one day.

The diaeresis-free Bronte was a small, pretty woman in her forties, mother of three ('Noah, Tilly and Jacob'), dressed in Lululemon. Her hair was tied up in a messy top-knot and she looked as if she'd just come from the gym. 'Hot yoga,' she laughed apologetically as if the idea was faintly ridiculous. A big dark-grey cat was luxuriating on the sofa. 'Ivan,' Bronte said. 'As in the Terrible. Watch him, he's a biter,' she added affectionately. She picked the cat up and carried him through to another room, 'Just in case. He doesn't like strangers.'

'Who does?' Reggie said.

Bronte was a vet. 'Small animals only. I don't want to spend my time with an arm up a cow's arse,' she laughed again. Her husband, Ben, was an A&E consultant at Leeds General. Between them they treated all creatures great and small. She had a wonderful smile, that was the thing Reggie remembered about her.

Ilkley just made it over the border into West Yorkshire, which was why they had picked up this case. They both liked Bronte immediately. You couldn't help but like a woman who said 'cow's arse' in a posh accent and who bought you strawberry tarts from Bettys.

The sun coming in at the windows flashed off the modest diamond engagement ring on her thin finger. It made little fragmented rainbows on those lemony walls as she poured the tea. Ronnie and Reggie drank the tea and ate the strawberry tarts and then they got out their notebooks and took dictation from Bronte Finch as she recited the litany of all the men who had abused her during her childhood, starting with her father, Mr Lawson Finch, Crown Court judge.

'It's a gloomy place.'

'Wakefield Gaol?'

'Haworth. I think the Brontë sisters felt imprisoned by their lives there,' Reggie mused. 'And yet in a funny way it made them free.'

'I've never read their books.'

'Not *Wuthering Heights* for school?'

'Nah. I just know the Kate Bush song.'

'DC Ronnie Dibicki and DC Reggie Chase. We're looking for Mr Stephen Mellors.'

'I'm sorry,' the receptionist at Stephen Mellors' law firm in Leeds

171

said, 'Mr Mellors isn't in today. I think he's working from home.' It was a new building, all steel and chrome and weird artwork. A church to money.

'Thanks. If you could tell him we were here.'

'Can I tell him what it's about?'

'Just some questions about clients of his. Old clients. I'll leave my card.'

They retrieved their car from the multi-storey car park. 'There's a lot of money in Leeds,' Ronnie observed.

'Sure is.' For a moment Reggie had considered inviting Ronnie to her flat 'for a quick coffee', but then she realized how unprofessional that might seem. She worried that Ronnie would think it was an invitation to some kind of intimacy and Reggie would have to do the whole embarrassing 'I'm not gay, if I was I would' spiel. But it was absurd to think that just because Ronnie was gay she would make a pass at her, and anyway why would Ronnie find her attractive when no one else on the planet did? (What if she *was* gay and she was just suppressing it in some weird Scottish Presbyterian way?) It wasn't something she ever denied anyway, whenever people presumed she was gay (they often did, she wasn't sure why), because denial implied that there was something wrong with it. And why was she tying herself in a Knoxian knot like this?

'Are we going to sit in this car park all day, looking at concrete?'

'Sorry. Where's next? You can drive if you like.'

'Felicity Yardley. Known to the local police – prostitution, drugs.' There was an ancient entryphone system, it looked filthy.

'She's in,' Reggie said. 'I saw a curtain move upstairs.'

Ronnie pressed the doorbell. There was no answer. They weren't sure that the entryphone system was working but Ronnie spoke into it anyway. 'Miss Yardley? My name's DC Ronnie Dibicki and I'm here with DC Reggie Chase. We're conducting an investigation into a historic case. This is just a routine interview, you're not in trouble in any way. We're looking into several individuals connected to the case because new accusations have surfaced.'

Nothing. Ronnie rang the bell again. Still nothing. 'Well, we can't *make* her talk to us. Let's come back later. Can I have another hand wipe? God knows who's been pressing that buzzer. I'm starving, by the way. We are going to get chips, aren't we?'

'You betcha,' Reggie said.

'Who's next?'

Reggie consulted her notebook. 'Kathleen Carmody, Carmody's daughter. She was never interviewed, but Bronte said she attended some of the parties. They're about the same age, so I think we can guess what that might mean. I don't like calling them parties,' she added.

'Because parties are something that you should enjoy.'

'Well, not me personally,' Reggie said, 'but yeah.'

Kathleen Carmody was sitting in the middle of the amusement arcade, like a spider in a web. Occasionally someone came up to her booth and changed notes for coins. There were machines that did the same thing, so it seemed like a redundant role for Carmody's daughter. She had the unhealthy complexion of someone who never saw daylight.

The arcade was a mess of noise and strident colour. It could have been designed as one of those CIA secret operations to drive people mad.

'Miss Carmody? Kathleen Carmody?' Reggie said, raising her voice so she could be heard above the din. 'My name's DC Reggie Chase and this is DC Ronnie Dibicki. We're conducting an investigation into a historic case that involved your father – Michael Carmody. This is just a routine interview, you're not in trouble in any way. We're looking into several individuals connected to the case because new accusations have surfaced and we would like to ask you a few questions, if that's all right? We're trying to build a picture, fill in some background details. A bit like doing a jigsaw. Is there somewhere a bit more private that we can go?'

'Fuck off. And if you show your faces here again I'll rip them off. Okay?'

'Do you get the feeling that she didn't want to talk to us?' Reggie said when they were back in the car.

'DC Reggie Chase and DC Ronnie Dibicki, Mrs Bragg. Remember us? Is Mr Bragg home?'

'You just missed him.'

'Any idea when he'll be back?'

'No.'

'Will you tell him we called? Again.'

A pair of disgruntled-looking hikers, women, were adjusting each other's huge rucksacks in the reception of the Seashell. They made Reggie think of the giant snails she'd seen in a zoo one time.

'You should arrest her,' one of the women said to Ronnie, nodding in the direction of Rhoda Bragg. 'The prices here are criminal and then they try to poison you.'

'Piss off,' Rhoda said cheerfully as the women pushed their encumbered bodies awkwardly out of the front door. 'Bloody lesbians,' she said to Ronnie and Reggie. 'Well, you pair would know all about that.'

'Yes,' Ronnie said, to annoy. 'The police force is the UK's biggest LGBT employer.'

'And I bet you voted against Brexit as well. You're all the same.'

'Remainers and lesbians?'

'Yes.'

'She's probably right about that,' Reggie said when they were back in the car.

'Probably.' Ronnie held a Leninesque fist in the air and said sardonically, 'Make Britain great again. You've got to laugh.'

'That's one of Barclay Jack's catchphrases.'

'"You've got to laugh"? And do they?'

'Let's find out.'

The Unicorn in the Room

There was a café in town that Jackson had suggested might be a good place to meet. He knew they allowed dogs, although that was true of just about everywhere, no one would have had any trade in this town if they didn't embrace the canine customer, but this particular place also managed a decent pot of coffee. He had arrived early and had already drained the cup sitting in front of him while Dido, at his feet beneath the table, was still chewing her way industriously through the cooked sausage he had ordered for her. ('Losing her teeth,' Julia said sadly.)

He had bought a copy of the *Yorkshire Post* from a nearby newsagent and was perusing it idly, wondering if Vince Ives's wife's murder had made it into its pages. He eventually found it inside, a small piece about 'Wendy Easton, also known as Ives'. A police spokesman said it was 'a particularly brutal murder. We are asking anyone who may have information to come forward.' Nothing about the golf club that she was attacked with, they must be keeping that detail back. Jackson's inner policeman was still interested in the golf club. Was it Vince's spare putter – a weapon of opportunity – or did the killer bring it with him in a premeditated act? If—

'Mr Brodie?'

'Mrs Holroyd?'

'You'll recognize me,' Jackson had told the new client over the phone, 'because I'll be the man with the yellow Labrador.' He should probably have been wearing a red carnation in his buttonhole or carrying a copy of the *Guardian*, both of which, around here, would have been less likely than a man in the company of a yellow Lab.

She was called Mrs Holroyd and she hadn't reciprocated with a means of identifying herself to him. It had struck him when she said her name that fewer and fewer women these days prefaced themselves with the epithet 'Mrs'. It was a title that made him think of his mother. Headscarf and shopping bag and a washerwoman's hands.

Crystal Holroyd did not look like his mother. Not at all. Not one bit.

Tall, blonde, and apparently enhanced in many different ways, Crystal Holroyd was accessorized not with a dog but a child, a girl called Candy, masquerading, if Jackson wasn't mistaken, as Snow White. Or rather, Disney's idea of Snow White – the familiar red and blue bodice and yellow skirt, the iconic red headband with the little bow. Jackson had once been the father of a small girl. He knew these things.

He felt a little spasm of pain at the memory of the last time he had seen Marlee, no longer little, no longer a girl but a grown-up woman now. They'd had a furious row that seemed to erupt out of nothing. ('You're such a *Luddite*, Dad. Why don't you just go and find a picket line to stand on somewhere or join a demonstration and shout "Maggie Thatcher – milk snatcher!"' Yes, it had been a complex and rather long-winded insult. He had been too surprised by his daughter's historico-political analysis – her term – of his character to put up much in the way of a defence.) He should phone her, he thought. Make peace with her before he saw her at the weekend. They were about to undertake (or perhaps endure) one of life's great rites of passage together. They had exchanged only a few chilly texts since this argument a month ago. It was up to him, Jackson knew, to make things better. You could hardly walk your daughter up the aisle if you were at loggerheads with her.

Mrs Holroyd's daughter, in contrast to his own, seemed a placid, well-behaved sort of child. She was eating apple slices with one hand, and with the other was holding a soft toy that at first Jackson had taken for a white horse but on closer inspection turned out to be a unicorn, its horn a spiralling rainbow cornet. He thought of the girl on the Esplanade. Inevitably. He had a duty of care that he was failing to fulfil.

'Are you all right, Mr Brodie?'

'Yes, yes, Mrs Holroyd, thanks.'

'Call me Crystal.'

He ordered another pot of coffee and she ordered a mint tea. Jackson always felt slightly mistrustful of people who drank herbal tea. (Yes, he did know this was utterly irrational.) He was about to fold up the *Yorkshire Post*, ready to get down to business, when she put her hand on his arm and said, 'Hang on.' She took the newspaper off him and read intently. Her lips moved when she read, he noticed. They were very nice lips, not apparently subjected to surgery like some other parts of her – not that he was necessarily an expert in these things. She wore pink lipstick. The lipstick matched her (very) high heels, a classic kind of court shoe that implied a woman, rather than a girl. You could tell a lot about a person by their shoes. The short, but not immodestly short, dress she was wearing showed off her great legs. ('Observational conclusions,' he said in his defence to Judge Julia in his head. She presided over the court of women.)

'Wendy Ives. Murdered,' Crystal Holroyd murmured, shaking her head. 'What the duck? I can't believe it.'

'Did you know her?' Jackson asked. He supposed it was a small town.

'Yeah, a bit. Just socially. She's married to Vince, he's a friend of my husband. Nice bloke.'

Vince hadn't mentioned any friends last night, in fact he had seemed remarkably friendless to Jackson.

'They were getting divorced,' she went on. 'Wendy had started calling herself by her maiden name.' She frowned at the newspaper. 'She wasn't particularly nice, not that that's a reason to kill someone.'

'Sometimes it's enough,' Jackson said.

'Well, she certainly gave Vince the runaround.'

'I met him by chance last night,' Jackson confessed.

'Really? How? Where?'

'On the cliffs. He was thinking of jumping.'

'Fuck me,' she said and then clamped her hands over Snow White's ears as if trying to beat the speed of sound and said to her, 'You didn't hear that, sweetheart.' Snow White carried on contentedly eating her apple – one slice for her, one slice for the unicorn. No poisoning ensued, no glass coffin required.

It seemed Crystal Holroyd suspected that she was being followed and she wanted him to find out by who.

'Do you think it could be your husband? Does he think you might be cheating on him?' Jackson sighed inwardly at finding himself on familiar turf. Yet another suspicious spouse. But – to his surprise – this didn't seem to be the case.

'Could be Tommy, I suppose,' she said. 'It seems unlikely, though.'

'Are you?' Jackson asked. 'Cheating on your husband? Just so we're clear.'

'No,' she said. 'I am not.'

'Who else would have a reason to follow you, do you suppose?'

She shrugged. 'That's what I'm asking you to find out, isn't it?'

He got the distinct impression that there was something she wasn't saying. Truth, in Jackson's experience, was often to be found skulking behind the lines. Sometimes, of course, that could be preferable to it charging you from the front with a bayonet.

Jackson couldn't imagine being married to a woman who looked like Crystal Holroyd. *The Only Way Is Essex*, a programme he had come across by accident (truly) when channel-surfing, was full of Crystal types. She wasn't from Essex – she was, if he judged her accent right, from somewhere in the East Riding. It showed how old he was, Jackson supposed, that he still thought in terms of the Yorkshire ridings, done away with years ago when the administrative boundaries were redrawn.

Crystal Holroyd wasn't his type, although Jackson wasn't sure he had a type any more. ('As long as she's breathing, I expect,' Julia said recently. Unnecessarily hostile, he thought.) His ideal woman used to be Françoise Hardy – he had, after all, always been a bit of a Francophile. He had in fact married someone in that mould, albeit English – the treacherous she-wolf Tessa – but he suspected she had been a tailor-made artefact perfectly designed to ensnare him. ('*I* can be your type,' Tatiana said. 'I can be French if you want.' She said it to provoke, not seduce. She seemed to derive a lot of amusement from his bachelor state. It was bad enough that Julia had long ago taken up occupation in his brain, but to have Tatiana now buzzing around in there as well was an unwelcome development. It gave a whole new meaning to the term 'inner voice'. At least between them they had managed to eject his first wife, Josie.)

'And what do you want me to do if I find out who it is that's following you?' he'd asked Crystal Holroyd, fearing another search-and-destroy request like that of Chloe's mother, Ricky Kemp.

'Nothing,' she said. 'I just want to know who it is. Wouldn't you?'

Yes, he would.

'And you *are* experienced at this kind of thing, aren't you?' she asked, a doubtful little frown momentarily creasing her smooth features. Botox? Jackson wondered. Not that he knew the first thing about it except that you paid someone who wasn't medically qualified to stick needles in your face. It seemed like the macabre stuff of horror movies. Jackson liked his women au naturel. ('Warts and all,' he said to Julia, who didn't seem to take the remark in the spirit of a compliment.)

'Don't worry, Mrs Holroyd – Crystal – it's not my first rodeo.'

'But you're not a cowboy, I hope,' she said, giving him a level look. She had startlingly green eyes, the green of glacier waters in the Rockies. (He'd been there, with the daiquiri-drinking woman from Lancashire. She'd been a travel writer – still was, he supposed – which was why their surprisingly antagonistic relationship had been conducted almost entirely on foreign shores.)

'No,' Jackson laughed. 'I'm not a cowboy. I'm the sheriff.'

She didn't seem impressed.

He took down her details. Crystal didn't work, she was 'just' a housewife and a mother, although that was a full-time job, she added defensively.

'Absolutely,' Jackson said. He wasn't going to be the one to stand up and question the choices women made. He had done that once or twice in his life and it had always ended badly. (*Luddite* still echoed in his brain.)

Crystal lived with her husband, the aforesaid Tommy, in a big house called High Haven a few miles from here. Tommy owned a haulage firm and, as well as the mini Snow White, there was a stepson,

Harry, from the first marriage. He was a good boy, Crystal said. Sixteen but 'a bit young for his age. Also old for his age,' she added.

'Was your husband divorced?' Jackson asked, thinking so far, so cliché, the first wife traded in for a newer model, but Crystal said no, she had died in an accident.

'What kind of an accident?'

'She fell off a cliff.'

'A cliff?' Jackson's little grey cells held hands with each other and started to skip with excitement. People didn't fall off cliffs – he himself had recently acquired expertise in this matter – they jumped or they were pushed or they wrenched you over with them.

'Yeah, a cliff. It was an accident. Well, I hope it was.'

The choice of café was his, the choice of car park was hers – 'The one behind the Co-op. Park near the wall by the railway. I'll try and park there as well,' she had told him on the phone. He had complied with this instruction although he hadn't understood it, certainly hadn't interpreted it as meaning that ten minutes after finishing his second coffee and paying the bill he would be slowly tailing her Range Rover as it exited the car park.

It was a big car park and if he had been parked further away from her, he realized, it would have been well-nigh impossible to keep track of her when she left. He liked a woman who planned ahead.

'You leave the café first,' she said. 'I'll follow five minutes later.'

'Okay,' Jackson said. He had no trouble being compliant with a good-looking woman. A willingness that had been the cause of his downfall on more than one occasion.

Crystal had already given him the number plate of her car – a big white Evoque that was easy to spot – and he sauntered past it now, pretending nonchalance, although he was scrutinizing it, inside and out. You could tell a lot about a person by their car. The windows were blacked out but through the windscreen he could see that the interior was pristine, especially considering it was Snow White's carriage. Julia's car was an object lesson in chaos – dog biscuits and crumbs, discarded clothing, sunglasses, stray trainers belonging to Nathan, newspapers, *Collier* scripts covered in coffee stains, half-read books. She called it her 'sluttery', which was an old word, apparently. ('Old words are the best,' she said. Like 'wife', Jackson thought.)

It wasn't the interior of Crystal Holroyd's car that interested Jackson though so much as the outside, where something had been tucked behind one of the windscreen wipers. Not a parking ticket but a white envelope with a name written on it. *Tina.*

Jackson gently prised it free. ('You know what killed the cat, don't you?' Julia said. Yeah, Jackson thought, but it had eight more lives left, didn't it? Did he? He'd fallen off a cliff, been attacked by a mad dog, almost died in a train crash, nearly drowned, been crushed in a garbage truck, blown up – his house had been, anyway – and that wasn't counting a couple of near misses when serving in the police and the Army. His life had been a litany of disasters. What if he was already on his ninth life? The last go round. Perhaps he should be more cautious.)

The envelope wasn't sealed and he was able to slip the contents out. Not a note or a letter, but a photograph of Snow White – in a different princess costume, a blue dress. It was a candid snap of her on a swing somewhere. A long lens, by the look of it. Who took photos of kids in parks with long lenses? Perverts, stalkers, private detectives, that was who. He turned the photo over. On the back someone had written, *Keep your mouth shut, Christina.* Interesting. Until he looked at the back of the photo he had thought that perhaps it was innocent – someone Crystal knew who wanted her to have a photo they'd taken of her daughter. But there was nothing innocent about *Keep your mouth shut,* was there? Whoever had written the message hadn't bothered to add *or else* at the end. They didn't need to.

And Tina and Christina – were they both Crystal? Three women in one. A holy trinity. Or an unholy one?

There were always more questions than answers. Always. Perhaps when you died all the questions were answered and you were finally given the gift of that clichéd thing 'closure'. Perhaps he would finally find out who murdered his sister, but then it would be too late to get justice for her and that would be almost as frustrating as not knowing who killed her. ('Let it go, Jackson,' Julia said. But how could he?)

He replaced the photograph, returned the envelope to the

windscreen and hustled back to his car before Crystal could catch sight of him. He glanced around. If someone was following her – and, given the photo, it seemed more likely now – then they would have seen him looking at it. Had he just made a rookie mistake or would it give whoever was after Crystal Holroyd pause for thought? Whether he liked it or not, she was under his protection now. Whether she liked it or not, as well.

He watched Crystal as she approached her car, holding Candy by the hand, the two of them chatting away to each other. She stopped short at the sight of the envelope and then plucked it warily from behind the windscreen wiper, opened it even more warily. She looked at the photo and then turned it over and read the message on the back. It was difficult from this distance to discern the exact expression on her face, but her body language was talking loudly. She went rigid, a statuesque statue, staring at the message as if trying to decipher a foreign language. Then she hoisted Candy up in her arms as if she might not be safe on the ground. A Madonna and child, although Jackson supposed Our Lady had never sported pink heels like Crystal Holroyd. Jackson's mother had dragged him to Mass every Sunday in a vain attempt to instil religion into him. A Madonna who looked like Crystal Holroyd might have made it more likely.

Crystal snapped back into life. She put Candy in the child seat in the back of the Evoque and within seconds was driving off at speed like a woman on a mission.

Jackson followed her out of the car park. Strictly speaking, of course, it wasn't Crystal Holroyd that Jackson was following out of the car park, it was the silver BMW that was slinking slowly out behind her.

Initially, he had suspected Crystal Holroyd of paranoia as the claim she had made over her mint tea had seemed a tad dramatic ('I'm being followed'), but, lo and behold, it turned out that she was right.

Their little three-car convoy snaked its way out of town and along the A174, Jackson bringing up the rear. He was good at discreet surveillance – he should be, he'd done enough of it in his time.

He had taken a photograph of the BMW's number plate, another application to the DVLA.

Ahead, Jackson could see the Evoque indicating right. He had put High Haven into his GPS so he was pretty sure this was Crystal heading for home. The silver BMW had obviously escorted her as far as it wanted to, or needed to, and now sailed on past the turning with Jackson following it.

Was it a private detective, like himself, behind those blacked-out windows? A private detective who had just witnessed his quarry having a clandestine meeting with a strange man in a café who was now following him? Had they been photographed together? It wouldn't look good if, despite her doubt, it turned out that it was the suspicious husband who was having her followed. That photo could well have been a message from him – a threat that he would go after custody of his child, for example. Or perhaps he was the kind who decided to punish an errant wife by killing the kids. Jackson had dealt with one of those once – a guy had driven his two-door hatchback into a river with his two little girls strapped in the back. Even thinking about it now years later made him feel sick.

And no matter that it was entirely innocent, had he inadvertently made himself look like the man Crystal Holroyd was having an affair with? Or – and this was a complicated thought for the little grey cells to take on board – had Crystal Holroyd herself made Jackson look like the man she was having an affair with? Why would she do that? In order to dangle a big fat red herring in front of someone? He was over-thinking it, wasn't he?

A couple of miles further along and they hit roadworks being policed by temporary traffic lights. The BMW roared through on amber, Jackson got stuck on (an unnecessarily long) red. Conceding that the pursuit was over, he did a U-turn when the lights changed and headed back. He checked his watch – still a couple of hours to go before his rendezvous with Ewan. Plenty of time.

As he neared the turn-off for High Haven again, he caught sight of the Evoque, this time pulling out on to the main road. It was being driven fast, very fast, as if there were a getaway driver at the wheel rather than a woman who defined herself as a housewife and a mother. The Evoque was not a car Jackson would have chosen himself. It was designed to be a woman's car, albeit a well-off woman. Still, he admitted reluctantly, it had pretty good technical and performance specs. Some of the models – this one, apparently – could do 0 to 60 in just under seven seconds. You had to give it credit for that, and besides, a man driving a mid-range Toyota wasn't really in a position to judge.

Where was Crystal Holroyd going in such a hurry? Had she pretended to go back along the road to High Haven in order to shake off the silver BMW? Or to shake off a mid-range Toyota? But that would make no sense at all. The woman was a puzzle all right, he thought. She was already almost out of sight when he put his foot on the accelerator and set off in pursuit of her. The little grey cells were taken by surprise and had to run in an attempt to keep up.

Transylvanian Families

Crystal settled Candy in front of *Peppa Pig* when they got back home. There was a TV in the kitchen, so she could keep an eye on her from the conservatory where she was smoking an urgent cigarette. Not that Candy was about to go anywhere, Peppa was like heroin to her. Candy was still in disguise as Snow White, but Crystal had kicked off her heels and pulled on a pair of jeans and an old T-shirt. She felt the need to do some cleaning. Cleaning would help her think about the photograph and its message. *Keep your mouth shut, Christina.* Who called her Christina any more? No one, that was who. Tina was long dead and buried as well, resurrected as Crystal, as shiny and polished as glass. And what was she supposed to keep her mouth shut about? No one had asked her anything. It had to be something to do with the silver BMW, didn't it? Was it keeping an eye on her to make sure she didn't open her mouth (but not saying about what)?

As she had predicted to a sceptical Jackson Brodie, she was followed from the car park. In the rear-view mirror she could just make out Jackson Brodie's Toyota. It made her feel marginally safer – but only marginally – to think that someone was watching the person watching her. Perhaps someone was watching him too, an endless trail of people with her in their sights. Nothing to do with Tommy, she felt sure of that now. It felt bigger and nastier than that. It felt like the past. Well, it was true, wasn't it? If she opened her mouth about the past then all the demons in hell would fly out.

Was Jackson Brodie any good? she wondered. *Not my first rodeo*, he had said. Typical man, full of his own sugar. She'd been at the whim of swaggering men all her life, men who treated her like a doll – and

185

not in a good way. ('Braggadocio,' Harry said. 'From the Italian.' Sounded like a racehorse.) Crystal preferred quiet men with low opinions of themselves – Vince Ives, for example. He seemed like one of the good ones. Had Wendy really been murdered? Why? Had *she* failed to keep her mouth shut about something? Did she have a past, too? It seemed unlikely. She shopped from the Boden catalogue and was proud of having grown a horrible stunted little tree.

The front door crashed open. Tommy. He'd never learned how to enter a house quietly. He'd come in late last night and left before six this morning, slipping out of bed without waking her. It wasn't like Tommy to go without his breakfast, nor did he usually let her sleep on undisturbed. She was used to being prodded awake by him with a request for a cup of tea. It was part of her job description, apparently. On Mother's Day, Harry and Candy had brought her breakfast in bed – a tray with a flower picked from the garden in a little vase, a pot of coffee, croissants, jam, a perfect peach. (That was Candy – a perfect peach. Not yet bruised by life.) And a card that Harry had helped Candy to make. A crayon drawing of a stick family – mum, dad, two kids. 'To the best Mummy in the world,' it said. Harry patted her awkwardly on the shoulder and said, 'Sorry, didn't mean to make you cry.' 'Tears of happiness, Harry,' she said. How often did you get those? Not often, that's how often. It was good to know her eyes hadn't completely dried up.

'Crystal?' Tommy yelled. 'Where the fuck are you hiding yourself?'

Crystal sighed. You only have to look, she thought. She stubbed out her cigarette and tossed a mint in her mouth. 'In here!'

Slapping on her best happy smile when Tommy came into the kitchen, she said, 'Well, look at you, babe – home in the middle of the day. Here's a turn-up for the books.'

'Have you been out?'

'Out?'

'Yeah, out. I came back earlier and you weren't here.'

'I popped down to Whitby to run a few errands.'

'Dressed like that?'

'I changed. Did you hear about Wendy?'

'Wendy?' Tommy looked blank.

'Wendy Ives – Vince's wife. She's dead. Someone killed her.'

'Fucking hell. How?'

'Dunno.'

'Vince, do you think? I wouldn't blame him, she was a tight-arsed cow. How about something to eat? A sandwich?'

Was that it? Was Wendy's murder less important than Tommy's lunch? It was alarming how easily he could dispel the thought of a dead wife. Perhaps a living one, too. 'No problem,' Crystal said. 'Pork and pickle or roast chicken?'

'Whatever. Chicken. I'll have it in the office.'

He seemed out of sorts, not the usual happy-go-lucky Tommy.

'Problems at work?' she commiserated. Sympathy was also part of her job description.

'You could say that. I've got to get on,' he said, muttering something about paperwork. But then he had the grace to grunt an apology. 'Bad morning,' he said and gave her a peck on the cheek. 'Sorry.'

'S'okay, babe.' He wasn't himself at all. Who was he, then?

He shut the study door.

She took a pack of cooked chicken slices from the fridge. She peeled back the plastic and wrinkled her nose at the smell of the meat. Dead animal. Was that how Wendy would smell now? *The way of all flesh.* That was from something, wasn't it? The Bible or Shakespeare, probably. Harry would know. Harry knew everything. Sometimes Crystal worried that he knew too much. *Keep your mouth shut.* The words kept ricocheting around her brain.

She put the sandwich on a plate and garnished it with a sprig of parsley, not that Tommy would appreciate this touch. The nearest she had ever come to a garnish when she was younger was a sachet of tomato ketchup on her chips. It was depressing to think that she had reached an age when she could say 'when I was young'. Although not as depressing as remembering what it had been like to be young. She hoped that when Candy was older she would look back on her childhood and remember nothing but happiness. *Keep your mouth shut.*

In the office she found Tommy staring at his blank computer screen. Crystal did sometimes wonder if he knew how to turn it on – he did everything on his iPhone. Or iPhones in the plural, because he had two – the one she was supposed to know about and the one she wasn't supposed to know about, or at least the one she'd never been told about. She had found the second one when she had taken his jacket into the cleaner's a few weeks ago and her heart had dropped at the sight of it. Her first thought, obviously, had been that he was having an affair, which to be honest, as she'd said to Jackson Brodie, would have surprised her because, despite his macho bluster, he wasn't really the type. Tommy liked being married, it made his life easy, infidelity made life complicated. 'Dad's uxorious,' Harry said. (Guess where he got that word.) 'Uxor,' Harry said. 'It's the Latin for wife.' Sounded like something to do with cattle or pigs to Crystal's ears.

To her relief, the phone seemed to be entirely work-related and consisted mostly of text messages – *Fresh stock due to dock at 4.00 am.* Or *Consignment on its way to Huddersfield.* There were no names in the address book and messages went to and from people with initials only – A, V, J, T, and several others so that almost the entire alphabet was covered. Drivers mainly, she supposed. *Unloaded cargo in Sheffield, boss. No problems.* None of his workers ever turned up at the house. 'Work and pleasure,' Tommy said. 'Never mix the two.' She supposed the same rule applied to his phones.

Tommy's 'office' was a small room near the front of the house that must have served as some kind of reception room for visitors in the old days. (The house was Edwardian, according to Harry. 'About 1905,' he added, because he knew she had no idea about dates.) The office was quite different from Tommy's expansive den in the basement. The den was full of men's toys – a snooker table, massive TV, fully stocked bar. The office, on the other hand, was all dark wood and green leather and brass desk lamps. A heavy metal filing cabinet, a serious computer and a box of expensive cigars on display. It felt like the idea of an office rather than the real thing. The idea of an office dreamt up by someone who had started life in the boxing ring. And it was hard to say just what Tommy did in there, because they both knew that the real office was the Portakabin he kept in the Holroyd Haulage yard. No dark wood and green leather there, instead there was a beer fridge, a Pirelli calendar and a litter of tachograph printouts and bills and invoices covered in cup stains that Tommy's accountant came by for every month and transformed into something respectable. Or as near as respectable as he could get.

She had dropped in there once – early on in their relationship when she thought she would surprise him on Valentine's Day. She had arrived with a cake – heart-shaped – from Marks and Sparks food hall (in the old days of dirty eating), but he had hustled her out of the Portakabin as quickly as he could. 'No place for a lady,' he said. 'The guys'll enjoy that, though,' he said, taking the cake from her, and she hadn't the heart (ha!) to point out that it was a romantic gesture aimed at him and not the couple of overweight blokes smoking and playing cards whom she had glimpsed inside the Portakabin.

'Thanks,' he said, taking the sandwich off the plate and biting into it without even looking at it. Crystal spared another thought for the chickens. God only knows what they had gone through in order to keep Tommy Holroyd fed. Best not to think about it. *Keep your mouth shut.*

'Anything else, babe?' she asked.

'Nah. Close the door again on the way out, will you?'

The entryphone buzzed while she was still in the hallway and Tommy shouted through the door, 'Get that, will you?'

When Crystal peered at the monitor next to the front door she could see a girl standing in front of the camera. She was so short that only the top half of her head showed. Crystal pressed the button on the microphone and said, 'Hello?' The girl held up something, a wallet or a card, Crystal couldn't make it out. 'I'm DC Reggie Chase,' she said. 'I'm here with my colleague DC Ronnie Dibicki.' She indicated someone else, out of sight of the camera. 'We'd like to have a chat with Mr Holroyd. Mr Thomas Holroyd.'

Detectives? 'It's a routine enquiry,' the detective said. 'Nothing to be alarmed by.' *Keep your mouth shut, Christina.* But they weren't here for her, they were here for Tommy. Crystal hesitated, more from a natural aversion to the police than any anxiety about Tommy's wrongdoing.

'Mrs Holroyd?'

Crystal let them in, she didn't have a choice really, did she? She knocked on the door of the office and said, 'Tommy? There are two detectives here. They'd like a word with you.'

'A chat,' one of the detectives amended sweetly. 'Just a chat.'

Crystal led them into the living room. It was a room that had several huge windows with fantastic views of the sea – the wow factor, Tommy called it. Neither of the detectives seemed to notice the wow.

Tommy appeared, looking more bulky than usual beside the two girls. He could have picked one up in each hand.

'Make us a coffee, will you, love?' he said to Crystal. 'And for the ladies here too?'

The ladies smiled and said no, thank you.

Crystal went out of the room, but left the door ajar and lingered on the other side of it. Was Tommy in trouble? She was expecting it to be something about the trucks, or the drivers. An accident of some kind, a traffic misdemeanour. It wasn't the first time the police had turned up at the house with questions about the trucks, but any problems usually quietly disappeared. As far as Crystal was aware, Tommy was pretty law-abiding. So he maintained, anyway. 'Not in my interests as a businessman to be on the wrong side of the law,' he said. 'Plenty of money to be made keeping to the right side of it.'

Or perhaps it was something about Wendy. They would be interviewing everyone who knew her, wouldn't they? Wendy had been to High Haven a few times – the pool party for her birthday, Christmas drinks, that kind of thing. She was always snooty, as if she was better than them. Better than Crystal, anyway. ('Oh, I wish *I* was brave enough to wear such a *tiny* bikini!' 'Just as well she's not,' Tommy said. 'It would frighten the horses.')

She could hear some kind of preamble on Tommy's part – dropping the names of a couple of senior policemen he 'knocked out a round of golf with' at the Belvedere. The detectives sounded unimpressed.

'Has this got something to do with Wendy Ives?' he asked.

Has this got something to do with Wendy Ives? Reggie exchanged a look with Ronnie. Ronnie silently mouthed the word 'golf' and raised not one but two eyebrows. Vince had said that Tommy Holroyd was a 'golfing friend'. Could he also have been a 'special friend' of Wendy Easton's? A lot hinged on the ownership of that golf club. Had it been tested for prints yet? Was there some weird, as yet unfathomable link between Wendy Easton's murder and their own Operation Villette? So many questions. Someone had once told Reggie that there were always more questions than answers. The same someone she had seen running up the cliff last night. The same someone whose life she had once saved. What was Jackson Brodie doing here? He was a man who brought confusion in his wake. And he owed her money.

'Wendy Ives?' Ronnie said. 'No, that's a major crime investigation. This is nothing to worry about, sir. Just an old case that we're looking into. Your name came up in connection with one of several individuals we're investigating and so we would like to ask you some routine questions, if that's all right? We're trying to build a picture of these individuals, fill in some background details.'

'Of course, anything to help,' Tommy said amiably. 'Who are these "individuals", if you don't mind me asking?'

'I'm sorry, Mr Holroyd, I'm not able to tell you that. Mr Holroyd — have you ever heard of something called the magic circle?'

All three of them heard the sound of a car making its fast and furious escape.

'Did you hear that?' Ronnie puzzled to Reggie.

'What?' Reggie said, mirroring her frown. 'The unmistakeable sound of a car being driven away at speed?'

'Was that Mrs Holroyd leaving?' Ronnie asked Tommy Holroyd, smiling pleasantly. 'It looks like you won't be getting that coffee.'

He frowned at her as if he was trying to translate what she was saying.

Reggie stood up and walked over to one of High Haven's big picture windows. It was at the back of the house. No driveway, no cars, only sea and sky as far as the eye could see.

'Wow,' she said.

Christina and Felicity. Running. Running away.

Christina, Tina to her friends, although she only had the one,

Felicity – Fee. Tina and Fee running down the street, helter-skelter, screaming with laughter, like hostages who had freed themselves, although it wasn't as if the doors of their care home were locked, or even as if anyone was bothered whether they were inside it or not. The Elms, it was called, and there was precious little care on offer.

The Elms was a place for 'difficult girls' and Tina had never understood why she had ended up there because she didn't consider herself to be in the least bit difficult. She'd been taken into care after her mother abandoned her and her father was deemed unfit to look after her, after he had tried to pimp her out to his drinking pals in the pub. The Elms seemed like a punishment for something her parents had done, not her.

Fee had been in foster care since she was five and she *was* difficult. She was a rebel, bold and mouthy – 'a wicked girl', Giddy said. Mrs Gidding – Giddy she was called, of course. She was short and fat – round almost, like an egg. Tina liked to imagine her rolling down the big staircase at the Elms and breaking into bits at the bottom. Giddy had fluffy hair and was always shouting at the girls in her high squeaky voice, but none of them took any notice of her. There was an assistant manager who was a different kettle of fish. Davy – a big burly bloke who always looked as if he wanted to belt the living daylights out of the girls, although he bought cigarettes for them and even cans of lager sometimes. Fee was always wheedling stuff out of him. The Flea, he called her. Tina was Teeny – you wouldn't think it but she'd been a small kid. Sometimes Tina had seen Fee stumbling out of Davy's airless nicotine-stained office looking pale and sick, but when Tina asked her if she was okay she just shrugged and said, 'Top of the Pops,' which was one of her sayings (along with 'Ah, Bisto' and 'Can I have a P, Bob?').

They'd 'escaped' before, lots of times, of course. They'd caught the bus into the town centre a few times and nicked stuff from Woolworths – a New Kids on the Block CD (there was a machine in the rec room), a bottle of nail varnish, a strawberry-flavoured lip gloss and loads of sweets. They'd gone to the cinema as well, sneaking in the fire exit to see *Candyman* and then having nightmares for weeks. They'd hitched to Grimsby (horrid, rightly named) and to

Beverley (bor*ing*), but now they were on a bigger adventure. And not only were they getting away, they were getting away for good. No going back. Not ever. Running.

It was Fee who suggested they go to Bridlington because that was where the two pervy blokes lived. 'Do-gooders,' Giddy sneered, as if people who did good were actually bad (which, of course, they were in this instance). Davy was a pal of the do-gooding blokes – Tony and Mick – and it was Davy who had first invited them to visit the Elms. Tony was the Bassani's ice-cream guy and when he came to visit he brought big unlabelled tubs of ice-cream with him. They were usually half melted by the time he arrived but that was still okay. He'd dish it out himself, getting the girls to line up for it and then saying something to each one of them in turn – 'There you go, sweetheart, get that down your throat,' or 'Have a lick of that, love,' and everyone giggled, even Giddy.

Tony and Mick were local businessmen, according to Davy. Local celebrities too, always in the papers for one thing or another. Not that either Fee or Tina read the papers, but Davy showed them. Tony had a big car, a Bentley, that he took the girls for rides in. Tina had never been in the car but Fee said she'd got all kinds of stuff for going for rides – sweets, cigarettes, even cash. She didn't say what she'd had to do to earn these rewards, but you could guess. Mick owned amusement arcades and seaside attractions and Fee said that if they got to Brid, Tony and Mick would give them jobs, and then they could get somewhere to live and they would be free to do whatever they wanted, whenever they wanted.

The Flea and Teeny. Running away. They were twelve years old.

They got their first lift on a garage forecourt on the outskirts of town from a quiet truck-driver who bought them crisps and cans of Pepsi. They told him they were sixteen and he laughed because he didn't believe them and when he dropped them off at a roundabout he said, 'Have a good time at the seaside, girls,' and gave them a couple of quid to spend. 'Buy yourselves a stick of rock candy,' he said, 'and don't let the boys kiss you.'

The next lift was from a bloke who was driving a big beige station wagon and who said after a few miles, 'I'm not a taxi service, girls, I don't give rides for free,' and Fee said, 'Neither do taxis,' and he said, 'You're a cheeky little bitch, aren't you?' He stopped at a lay-by and Fee told Tina to get out of the car for five minutes, and when she got back in the driver didn't say anything more about being a taxi service and he took them all the way to Bridlington and dropped them off right on South Marine Drive. 'Dirty bugger,' Fee said after they'd clambered out and he'd driven off. When they arrived in Brid they bought chips and fags with the money the first truck-driver had given them.

'This is the life,' Fee said as they leant against the railings on the Prom and smoked their cigarettes while they watched the waves coming in.

Not much of a life, it turned out. Mick gave them a trailer to stay in, it was on the edge of a site he owned and it was one step away from the knacker's yard. And he did give them jobs, of a sort. Sometimes they worked on the funfair or on reception at the trailer site, but mostly they were needed to go to Tony and Mick's 'parties'. Before she went to the first one Tina had imagined balloons and ice-cream and games, the kind of party she'd never had, but she couldn't have been more wrong. There wasn't even any ice-cream, which you might have thought there would be, given who Bassani was. There were games, though. Definitely not the kind of games you got at kids' parties, although there were a couple of other girls there about their age. There were always loads of kids, they came and went all the time. Not just girls, boys too. 'Just think about something else,' one of the girls advised her. 'Something nice. Unicorns or rainbows,' she added cynically.

It wasn't just the parties either, Mick and Tony's friends came to the trailer sometimes as well. The passion wagon, Mick laughingly called it. (Awful to recall. The kind of memory you spend thirty years trying to block out.) 'Don't complain,' he said. 'You've got nowhere else to go. And anyway, you know you like it. You're a right pair of little slags.'

Crystal could feel her brain curdling at the memory. They had been children. Little girls, not so very much older than Candy. No one had come looking for them. Not Giddy, not Davy. Not the police or social workers. They were scrap, not worth bothering about.

She remembered Fee was always telling her that they were lucky because Mick and Tony took care of them, but there was that word 'care' again. Care shouldn't mean a grotty trailer and sweets and fags for doing 'favours' to old men. They'd seemed old, anyway. Looking back, they probably weren't that old at all. Not then, at least. The judge had once said to her that he knew he was getting old when bishops started looking young to him. Bishops, knights, pawns. They were all pieces on the universe's big chess board, weren't they?

She'd been taught to play by one of the judge's friends. Sir Something, a double-barrelled name. Cough-Plunkett. Something like that, anyway. A 'knight of the realm', Tony Bassani said. He was proud of his connections. Cough-Plunkett, or whatever, had brought a chess set with him to the trailer. He said she was 'a clever girl'. He was the first person who'd ever said that to her. It was an odd thing to want to do, when she thought about it now, but then the men had many worse kinks than wanting to play chess. Of course, in the end he'd wanted more than just chess. It was a long time since she'd made herself think about the judge and his friends. The magic circle.

That was what they called themselves. The magic circle. 'Up to tricks,' one of them laughed.

This morning, in the welcome absence of patrons in Transylvania World, Harry was sticking his head in *Cranford*. He liked Cranford, it was a safe place where small events were accorded great dramatic significance. Harry thought that this was better than big things being treated as if they weren't important.

A better attraction than the World, in Harry's opinion, would be Cranford World. A place where for the price of the entrance fee you could call on Miss Matty and drink tea, or have an evening of cards, or sing around the piano with your neighbours. ('A place of safety,' Miss Dangerfield had called Cranford.) He would enjoy listening to the Captain reading aloud from *The Pickwick Papers*. He could—

'Harry?'

'Crystal?' He dropped abruptly out of his Cranford reverie. 'What are you doing here?' She was carrying Candace in her arms and dropped her on to the ticket counter with a sigh of relief.

Harry frowned. 'You're not wanting to take Candace in there, are you?' he puzzled, indicating the dark mouth of the tunnel that led to Transylvania.

'Fudging carrot, no.'

Crystal made this big effort not to swear. It was such an effort that Harry thought she must have sworn a *lot* before she married his dad. It was funny really, because sometimes she made all the silly innocuous words she'd chosen as proxies sound just as bad.

'I need you to look after her for a bit, Harry.'

'Here?'

'Yes, here.'

'I've got to leave for a matinée soon.'

'I won't be long.'

'What the fuck is that?' Barclay Jack asked when he encountered Harry backstage, lugging a bedraggled Snow White in his arms.

'*She's* my sister,' Harry said. 'Not a that.'

'Sister?' Barclay Jack frowned as though having a relative was an outlandish idea. Perhaps Barclay didn't have any. Harry had never heard him mention a wife or a child and it was almost impossible to imagine him as a father, he barely qualified as a human being.

Despite her promise, Crystal had failed to return when it was time for Harry to hand over his shift to Amy, and Amy, almost as blunt as Emily, refused point-blank to babysit, and so Harry had had to bring Candace all the way on the bus, a switchback ride over the moors. She had never been on a bus before and the novelty of it kept her quiet for quite some time, as did Harry's packet of Monster Munch – strictly forbidden by Crystal, obviously, but she needn't have worried if she'd known because Candace threw it all back up again minutes later and then promptly fell asleep on Harry's knee. He did his best to clean up the orange-coloured mess but it was difficult without the bottomless bag of accessories with which Crystal normally travelled – an entourage of wet wipes, sippy cups, changes of clothes, drinks, snacks, face cloths. At the very least, Crystal could have remembered Candace's stroller. ('Yeah, that would have been super-helpful,' Amy said as she watched him hauling his sister out of the World and running for the bus.) And something to amuse Candy with – a toy or a book or, better still, her little DVD player and a selection from the Peppa Pig 'oeuvre', as Miss Dangerfield would have called it, although he doubted that Miss Dangerfield had ever come across Peppa. Where had Crystal been going in such a hurry? In retrospect she hadn't seemed like her normal self. She wasn't wearing heels, for one thing. It was a sign of something.

By the time they alighted from the Coastliner, both Harry and Candace were more than a little the worse for wear.

'Well, keep her out of my way,' Barclay said truculently.

Barclay was 'back from the dead', as Bunny put it. Bunny had (reluctantly) accompanied Barclay in the ambulance to A&E last night, from where he had been discharged after a couple of hours. 'Panic attack,' Bunny reported to Harry. 'Shame, I was hoping it was curtains for him. It was something on his phone that set him off, wasn't it?'

'Don't know.' Harry shrugged innocently. Barclay had dropped his phone when he collapsed and it was only later, after the ambulance had departed, that Harry noticed it had skittered beneath the heavy red stage curtains. As he had bent to retrieve the phone it had lit up with a message. *Just so we're clear, DO NOT ignore my last message.* Intrigued, Harry had opened Barclay's messages. Barclay had no password on his phone – Harry knew because he had helped him remove it after he'd forgotten it for the umpteenth time last week. It could be termed an invasion of privacy, Harry supposed, but then for all he knew Barclay was currently knocking on death's door and his messages might be relevant in some way. 'Or you're just being nosy,' Bunny said. True, Harry agreed. The message that was not to be ignored had been sent at 10.05 last night, pretty much when Barclay's blood had sunk into his boots and he had fallen to the floor. It was from a number, not a name, and was direct enough in its content. *Don't open your big mouth, Barclay, or something VERY bad will happen to you.*

Harry had slipped the phone into his pocket, where it was currently burning a guilty hole. He hadn't returned it to Barclay yet, partly because the sight of it might precipitate another panic attack or even a genuine heart attack, and partly because – well, Harry wasn't sure why. Because there was something compelling about it. Thrilling, even. Like a detective novel. What did Barclay know that had made someone threaten him like that? 'Well, Barclay's always been a man of bad habits,' Bunny said, squinting at the text through a pair of reading spectacles that looked so unfashionable they were probably fashionable. 'Bad habits bring bad men in their train.' Which sounded quite Shakespearean the way Bunny said it.

'Well, anyway, the kid's too young to be back here,' Barclay said, scowling at Candace. 'And by the way, have you seen my phone anywhere?'

'Um.' He was going to confess, he really was, but then Barclay said, 'Make sure you keep that fucking kid out of the way, will you?' and Harry decided to punish him by keeping the phone a bit longer.

'Yes, Mr Jack,' he said. 'I'll do my best.'

Mustn't Grumble

'Are you arresting me?'

'You keep asking that and, as I keep answering, no, we're not, Mr Ives,' Inspector Marriot said. 'You have attended this interview voluntarily and are free to leave at any time, as I'm sure your solicitor will verify.' She nodded curtly at Steve Mellors, who patted Vince on the arm and said, 'Don't worry. It's just procedure.' (*Do you feel you need a solicitor at a routine interview, Mr Ives?* Yes he did!)

'You're not being interviewed under caution, Mr Ives. No one is accusing you of anything.'

Not yet, Vince thought.

'I'm here as a friend, really,' Steve said to DI Marriot, 'not as a lawyer. Although,' he said, turning to Vince, 'it might be a good idea to answer "No comment" to all their questions in case they do arrest you at a future time.'

The police had phoned him first thing this morning, asking him to come in again. Vince had phoned Steve in a panic, spilling out the whole sorry tale of Wendy's murder and the fact that the police were expecting him to come in for a second interview and how he had thought about running away or going over a cliff but then he remembered Ashley and he couldn't deprive her of both parents at once even though it seemed like it was only her mum she cared about, not that he was resentful, he loved her, and he *hadn't* killed Wendy – swear to God – although he'd nearly killed this other bloke up on the cliffs last night—

'Vince, Vince, Vince,' Steve said, 'calm down. I'm on my way over. Everything's going to be fine.' Although as soon as he arrived at Vince's flat he said, 'I'm not a criminal lawyer, Vince,' and Vince said, 'Well, that's good, because I'm not a criminal, Steve.' What was a corporate lawyer exactly? he wondered. It seemed to be mostly defined by what it wasn't.

'Naturally they're going to want to talk to you,' Steve said. ('Christ, is this really where you're living, Vince?') 'You've got to look at it from the viewpoint of the police—'

'I don't want to see it from their viewpoint! I want them to see it from mine!'

'Take it easy, Vince. You don't want them to see you so agitated. It's all about appearances. You were married for – what? Twenty years?'

'Twenty-one.'

'Twenty-one. And you're in the middle of a divorce. The police are going to suspect acrimony, even anger on your part. You're bound to be top of the list of people they want to talk to.'

'And you definitely didn't see Ms Easton – Mrs Ives – your wife' (as if he didn't know who Wendy was) 'when you visited the house the other night?'

'I never went inside the house. I told you that. I've told you everything a million times.' No, he wasn't about to say 'No comment' to everything, he had lots of comment!

When he'd woken this morning, at stupid o'clock – he supposed he would never sleep soundly again – he'd gone for a walk up to the house. No longer the 'marital home' but a crime scene, it was festooned with yellow and black tape. *Crime Scene Do Not Cross.* They still hadn't been able to get hold of Ashley and he imagined her coming home unexpectedly and finding her childhood home wrapped up like a macabre gift. A police officer appeared out of nowhere and said, 'Sir? Can I help you?'

'I doubt it,' Vince said. He doubted anyone could. Nonetheless, it had seemed like a good idea to phone Steve Mellors. Vince had saved his life a long time ago, it was time to call in the favour and get Steve to save his.

He'd phoned him at home and his wife, Sophie, had answered. 'Oh, Vince,' she said, 'how are you? It's a long time since we've seen you. How's Wendy?'

'Wendy?' Vince hesitated. It was only eight o'clock in the morning and in the background he could hear the boy, Jamie, asking where his clean rugby kit was and the girl moaning about something. It didn't seem polite to pollute this unsullied family atmosphere with the grisly facts of his life. 'Good. She's good, thanks. Fighting off a bit of a cold,' he added. He didn't want to make her sound *too* well.

'Well, give her my best. I'll fetch Steve, you just caught him. You and Wendy must come to dinner again soon. I think it's our turn.'

Vince thought Sophie probably wouldn't want Wendy sitting at her dinner table in the state she was in at the moment.

'Smashing,' he said.

There was a young detective sergeant tag-teaming with Inspector Marriot. He kept showing photos of the murder scene to Vince, pushing them across the table towards him for Vince to push them back. And they kept asking him the same questions, again and again, as if he would break down and confess from the sheer relentless tedium of it all.

'I didn't kill Wendy,' he said. 'How many more times?' Steve laid a placatory hand on his arm again but he shook it off.

'We're not saying you did, Mr Ives. We're just trying to find out what happened.'

'I know what happened!' Vince said. 'Someone killed Wendy! Someone that wasn't me! I was in the Belvedere.'

'Except for when you were at your house.'

'I was there for *five* minutes. Literally.'

'Five minutes is long enough for a lot of things to happen, Mr Ives.' Inspector Marriot sighed heavily as if she was disappointed with him. He was alarmed to find that his natural inclination was to make her less disappointed by giving her something she wanted. And what she wanted was for him to say he'd killed Wendy. But he hadn't! He was beginning to understand how people confessed to crimes they hadn't committed. It was easier than continually protesting your innocence.

'I was in the Belvedere all evening. Tommy and Andy will confirm that. Tommy Holroyd and Andy Bragg — I gave you their names yesterday — have you got in touch with them? They can tell you what time I left.'

'I'm afraid that so far we haven't been able to reach either Mr Holroyd or Mr Bragg, but obviously we'll keep trying.' She paused and looked serious, as if she was about to ask something of great import. 'You were in the Army, weren't you, Mr Ives?'

'Yes, Signals, long time ago.'

'So you know how to conduct yourself.'

'Conduct myself?'

'Yes. Conduct yourself. You know, for example, how to handle weapons.'

'Weapons? I thought you said that Wendy was killed with a golf club.'

'Well, it was *used* as a weapon. Anything can be used as a weapon. Just read Agatha Christie.' (But that was fiction, Vince protested silently.) 'We haven't ruled anything out yet. We're at the early stages of the investigation,' Inspector Marriot continued. 'We're still waiting on the pathologist's report for an accurate time of death. That will give us a better idea as to whether that tallies with your movements and with your story.'

'It's not a *story*,' Vince insisted. 'And if I'm free to leave, then that's what I'm doing.' He stood up abruptly, pushing his chair back noisily. He hadn't meant to be so dramatic and now he felt like a bit of a flouncing idiot.

The inspector opened her hands wide in a gesture of helplessness. 'It's entirely up to you, Mr Ives. We'll be in touch again soon. I'd appreciate it if you didn't leave town.'

'You probably didn't do yourself any favours in there by losing your temper,' Steve said, pointing his keys at his car parked on the police station forecourt. The Discovery tweeted meek acquiescence.

'I know, I know, but the whole thing's a nightmare. Like

something out of Kafka.' Vince had never actually read Kafka, but he had a pretty good idea of what people meant when they invoked his name. 'Have they really tried to talk to Tommy and Andy? Why can't they get hold of them?'

'Yes, Tommy and Andy,' Steve said thoughtfully. 'I'm sure they'll say the right thing.'

'The *true* thing, Steve.'

'You've got to admit, it looks pretty bad though, Vince,' Steve said.

'You're supposed to be on my side.'

'I am, Vince, I am. Trust me.'

Vince was about to set off back to his flat, but Steve said, 'Come on, we'll go to the Belvedere, have lunch there. We need to talk strategy.'

'Strategy?' Vince puzzled.

'You're in a war zone, Vince. We have to neutralize the enemy. We need to get your story straight.'

That word 'story' again, Vince thought. His life was turning into fiction. Kafka would be proud of him.

They had barely set off when Steve's phone rang. He answered it hands-free and it was a mostly one-sided conversation of *uh-huh*s and *okay*s. He looked grim when he finished.

'Trouble at t'mill, Steve?'

'Just a bit, lad.'

Comedy Yorkshiremen, Vince thought. Neither of them had ever had a particularly strong accent. Vince's parents had been from further south and had met during the war and then drifted north after it. They had characterless Leicestershire accents that had mitigated the broad cadences of West Yorkshire that surrounded Vince in his childhood. Steve, on the other hand, had had the local accent wrestled out of him by elocution lessons – something he hid from the other boys at school for fear of seeming like a Jessie. Vince knew. He had once been the keeper of Steve's secrets. Steve's mother had been hell-bent on her son 'bettering himself'. And he had, hadn't he? In spades.

('Have you been back to the old home town?' Steve had asked

when he and Wendy had gone over for dinner. 'Not for a long time,' Vince said. His father had died not long after his wedding to Wendy and he had never had a reason to return. 'I have work there sometimes,' Steve said. 'It's not the same. Full of Pakis. Imams and mosques.' Sophie had flinched at the word 'Pakis'. Not Wendy, though. Sophie laid a remonstrative hand on her husband's arm. 'Steve,' she half laughed.' 'that's terrible.' 'We're amongst friends, aren't we?' Steve said, shrugging his prejudices away. 'I'm only saying what everyone thinks. Another glass of wine, Wendy?' 'Always,' Wendy said.)

'I need to make a bit of a detour, if that's okay, Vince,' Steve said. It wasn't really a question, Vince noticed. 'A bit of business I have to see to. It won't take long.' Vince hoped not. The idea of lunch had perked him up. His insides felt hollow, as if they'd been scooped out with a sharp spoon, although that could be fear, he supposed. Despite being under suspicion of murder, he was surprised at how ravenously hungry he felt. Of course, he'd had nothing to eat since the toast in that bloke's house last night. Vince was under such stress that he would have forgotten his name if the bloke hadn't given him his card. *Jackson Brodie – Brodie Investigations.* 'Call me,' he'd said, 'if you need to talk.'

They drove for quite a long time, through an increasingly decaying hinterland of run-down cafés, tattoo parlours, and lock-ups and garages that had, bizarrely, been transformed into funeral homes as if that were a natural evolution for them. He had a sudden, unexpected memory of his mother laid out in a dimly lit funeral parlour that had smelt of beeswax and something less pleasant – formaldehyde, perhaps, although he might have been recalling the preserved specimens in Biology class at school.

His mother had died of some unnamed cancer, something that had seemed shameful from the way it was discussed in low voices by her female friends and relatives. Vince was only fifteen and his mother had seemed old, but he realized that when she died she was considerably younger than he was now. She'd been a good cook, he could still conjure up the taste of her hot-pot and her steamed sponge puddings. After she died, Vince and his father lived off steak pies from the butcher's and boil-in-the-bag cod, a diet that intensified their sense of loss. 'I miss your mother's cooking,' his father said, but Vince supposed what he meant was that he missed the woman rather than her shepherd's pie, although the two were inextricably mixed somehow, in the same way that Wendy was an inextricable mix of bonsai and prosecco. What was Crystal Holroyd made of? he wondered. Sugar and spice and all things nice, probably. He imagined biting into her – a leg or an arm – and hearing the crisp snap of sugar. Jesus, Vince, get a grip, he thought. Was he going insane?

Eventually they reached the outskirts of town, and they were almost into open countryside when Steve took a left and drove down a long, curving driveway, bordered with overgrown bushes and trees. Wendy would have been itching to take a strimmer to it, Vince thought. But then he remembered that she was beyond wanting anything, beyond all feelings in this life. Was she in the next one, he wondered, pruning and lopping away at the shrubbery? He hoped she wasn't in hell, although it was hard to imagine her in heaven. Not that Vince believed in either, but it was impossible to think of Wendy being nowhere at all. He hoped that, for her sake, if she was in heaven, it was staffed by a lower order of angels who would wait on her hand and foot after a hard day in the bonsai fields. (*I'm knackered, Vince, fetch me a glass of prosecco, will you?*) At least his mother had beached comfortably in a Baptist-run funeral parlour, whereas Wendy was still on a cold slab somewhere like a haddock slowly going off.

'Vince – you all right?'

'Yeah, sorry – miles away. Thinking about Wendy.'

'She was a good woman.'

'You think?'

Steve shrugged. 'Seemed like it. I only met her couple of times, of course. It can take a lifetime to get to know a person. Sophie still surprises me.' Vince thought of his cat. His Sophie, as opposed to Steve's Sophie, used to bring Vince the gift of mice in her younger days as a hunter. They were tiny little velvety things that Sophie played with endlessly before biting their heads off. Was Vince a helpless mouse, being toyed with by Inspector Marriot? How long before she bit his head off?

A large neglected building loomed into view as they rounded a corner of the driveway. A weathered sign announced *Silver Birches – A Home Away From Home.* It seemed to have once been an institution of some kind, a mental hospital or a nursing home, long since unfit for any purpose – it had obviously been closed for years. Vince couldn't imagine what kind of business Steve could have here.

'Stay in the car, Vince,' Steve said, leaping out athletically from the Discovery. 'I'll just be five minutes.'

It was turning into a long five minutes, Vince thought, as he waited for Steve to return. He suddenly found himself beset by another memory. It seemed as if the past was being peeled open before his eyes today. When he was a boy, a friend of his father's had an allotment and in the summer he used to give them vegetables he couldn't use from his over-abundant harvest – beetroot, runner beans, lettuces. Bob, that was his name. Uncle Bob. Vince's father often drove over to Bob's allotment in the evening in summer. They didn't have a car, they had a van – *Robert Ives – Plumber* painted by a signwriter on the side. They were straightforward times, people didn't feel it necessary to have clever names or slogans and taglines. (*Strain the Drain* he had seen on the side of a white van recently.)

One evening when Vince was perhaps six or seven years old, his father had taken him along in the van to Bob's allotment.

'See if he's got any potatoes!' his mother shouted after them as they pulled away from the kerb.

'You wait in the van,' his father said to Vince, parking at the entrance to the allotment. 'I'll just be five minutes.' And Vince was left alone while his father went off, whistling, to find Bob in his shed on the far side of the allotments.

Late-summer twilight turned into dark. The allotments appeared to be deserted and Vince began to grow frightened. At that age he was easily scared by thoughts of ghosts and murderers and he was terrified of the dark. He sat there for what seemed like for ever, imagining all the dreadful things that might have happened to his father – and, worse, all the dreadful things that might be about to happen to him. By the time his father reappeared, still whistling, Vince was a quivering tearful wreck.

'What you crying for, you daftie?' his father said, his arms full with a huge lettuce and a bunch of Sweet Williams as well as the requested potatoes. 'Nothing to be frightened about. You could have come and found me.' Vince didn't know that. Didn't know he had free will or independence. He was like a dog – if he was told to stay, he stayed.

Bob was an older man, no family, and in return for the vegetables he was often invited for Sunday lunch. There were caveats from his father. 'Don't sit on Uncle Bob's knee if he asks you to.' It was true that Bob was always trying to cajole him into sitting on his knee ('C'mon, lad, give your old Uncle Bob a cuddle'), but obedient Vince never did. His mother liked Uncle Bob – he was a laugh, she said. 'Him and his shed, it makes you wonder what he gets up to in there.'

Vince hadn't thought about Uncle Bob in years. He'd forgotten about the van altogether. *Robert Ives – Plumber.* He missed his father. Still, you shouldn't leave a little child alone like that.

The clock on the Discovery's dashboard informed him that Steve had been gone nearly half an hour. This was ridiculous, Vince could have walked to the Belvedere by now instead of sitting here like a lemon, twiddling his thumbs.

He had independence these days. He had free will. He didn't always stay when he was told to stay. He got out of the Discovery. He left it unlocked and walked up the steps to Silver Birches. He went in.

Two-Way Traffic

Gdansk. Landed.

About time too, Andy thought. The plane had taken off two hours behind schedule and had made up hardly any of that time. He had seen its status drift from *scheduled* to *delayed* to *estimated* to *expected* as if it was stuck in some endless time-warp, a kind of cosmic holding-pattern. By eight o'clock in the evening Andy himself was in a black hole, having drunk four espressos and read the *Mail* from cover to cover in minutiae. He had even been reduced to attempting the Sudoku – at which he had failed miserably. It felt like days, not hours, since he had delivered the Thai girls to Silver Birches. One of them had struggled and Vasily had plucked her up and held her round her waist while she kicked and bucked in protest. She might as well have been a rag doll. Andy could still see her contorted features as she screamed at him while she was carried away, 'Mr Andy! Mr Andy, help me!' Jesus wept. But, hey, not Andy. Heart of stone. What if it cracked? Had it begun already? Little fault lines every-where. *Mr Andy! Mr Andy, help me!*

It felt as if he had done nothing but drive up and down the A1 all day on a tide of caffeine. His car must have dredged a channel in the road by now. Travelling salesmen spent less time in their cars than Andy did. He supposed that was what he was in many ways. A rep, peddling his wares around the country. No shortage of buyers, that was for sure.

He thought again of those washing-machines, the ones that had fallen from the Holroyd truck. Casualties of the highway. There were only so many washing-machines you could sell, but there was no limit on the trade in girls.

Andy wondered whether Steve's wife – holier-than-thou Sophie – knew about the trailer, her husband's 'other office'. 'Stephen works all the hours God gives,' she said to Andy at a New Year's drinks party. 'Yeah, he's a real workaholic,' Andy agreed. Wendy and Vince had been there too. Wendy had had too much to drink and Andy caught Sophie rolling her eyes at Steve. If only she knew where all their money came from she wouldn't be quite so up herself. 'He does it for me and the children, of course,' she said. 'He's selfless that way.' Yeah, right, Andy thought.

It wasn't about sex, none of them ever touched the goods – well, maybe Tommy occasionally – it was about money. All profit, no loss. For Andy it had always been just a job – enough money to live on and a comfortable retirement at the end of it all in Florida or Portugal, somewhere with a really good golf course. A house with a swimming pool for Rhoda to lounge around, wearing one of her big supportive swimming-costumes, drinking a pina colada. A little paper umbrella. There was something about a little paper umbrella that signalled the good life. He didn't suppose Lottie would share that view.

He had enough put away for this good life, so why carry on? Where was the boundary? Where did it stop? He had crossed so many dodgy frontiers by now that he supposed there could be no going back. He'd gone over the top and he was stuck in no-man's-land. ('Christ, Andy,' Steve said. 'When did you begin to *think*? It doesn't suit you.') It had become like one of Carmody's carousels, one that you couldn't get off. 'Well, you know what the song says,' Tommy said. 'You can check out but you can't leave.'

Steve had tried to bring in a fourth musketeer. Vince Ives. More Dogtanian than d'Artagnan. Vince and Steve went all the way back to school and Steve thought Vince might be 'useful', he'd been in the Army apparently and knew a lot about IT, but neither of those things was of any use to them, both Steve and Andy were pretty skilled at all the internet stuff.

Steve seemed to think that he owed Vince because decades ago he had pulled him out of a canal. (If he'd just left Steve to drown, like an unwanted cat, they wouldn't be in this trade. So really if anyone was to be held responsible for what they were doing, it was Vince.) It was immediately obvious that Vince wasn't the kind of bloke who would have the stomach for the kind of business they were in. The fourth musketeer turned out to be a fifth wheel and they decided to keep him in the dark, although he still tagged along with them on the golf course and at parties. In the end Vince had proved to be more of a liability than an asset, especially now with Wendy's murder attracting police like flies on horseshit. And he couldn't even put in a decent round of golf.

Andy sighed and drained his coffee. Left a generous tip, even though he'd had no service to speak of. He made his way to Arrivals. Their names were on the iPad already, he fired it up and adjusted his face. Mr Congeniality. The doors to Arrivals opened and he lifted up the iPad so they wouldn't miss it.

They were a pair of pretty blondes, Polish, genuine sisters ensnared by Steve. Nadja and Katja. They spotted him straightaway. Massive suitcases – no big surprise. They marched confidently towards him. They looked almost alarmingly strong and healthy and for a second he thought they were going to attack him, but then the taller one said, 'Hello, Mr Price?'

'Nah, I'm Mr Price's representative.' Like the Pope was God's representative on earth, he thought. 'Call me Andy, love. Welcome to the UK.'

A Panda Walks into a Bar

'And I said to her, I'm only looking for your inner woman, love!'
Barclay Jack was in full flow on the stage.

'Christ, he's disgusting,' Ronnie said. Reggie and Ronnie were
standing at the back of the stalls, waiting for the matinée to finish.

'Yeah,' Reggie agreed. 'The guy's a Neanderthal. Sadly, they all
seem to love him. The women particularly. That's the depressing
part.' Reggie sometimes wondered if a day would ever go by when
she wasn't disappointed in people. She supposed that would be uto-
pia, and utopias, like revolutions, never worked. ('Not yet,' Dr Hunter
said.) Perhaps there was somewhere far away from here where it was
different. New Zealand, perhaps. (*Why don't you come, Reggie? Come
for a visit. You might even think about getting a job here.* It would be nice
to live near Dr Hunter, to watch her son Gabriel growing up.)
Upholding justice was a righteous act, but you may as well be Canute
trying to stop the tide coming in. (Was that a historical fact? It
seemed unlikely.)

'What do a road and a woman have in common?' Barclay hol-
lered. 'You in the front row,' he said, gesturing at a woman in a red
top. 'Yes, I'm talking to you, love. You'd better close your legs or
you'll get a through draught.'

'I can see *children* in the audience,' Reggie said. She sighed. 'How
much longer has this got to go?'

'Not long, I think,' Ronnie said. 'Ten minutes or so.'

Although he had been flagged during the original inquiry, Barclay
Jack had been discounted at the time. Bassani's and Carmody's positions in the community had meant that they had rubbed shoulders

with a lot of entertainers over the years – Ken Dodd, Max Bygraves, the Chuckle Brothers – none of whom had come under any kind of suspicion. Carmody used to throw a big summer-season party and invite all the stars who were in town. It was a lavish affair, there was some cine film of one of the parties that Ronnie and Reggie had watched. Bassani's home movies, apparently – the pair of them judging a Bonny Baby competition and some kind of beauty pageant with the women in one-piece bathing-suits. Everyone laughing. Barclay Jack was in one shot at the summer party, drink in one hand, cigarette in the other, leering at the camera. He was just one more person ('Man,' Ronnie amended, 'one more man') who had been mentioned in the endlessly bifurcating fractal that was Operation Villette. Another piece in the jigsaw, another brick in the wall.

'Gender fluid, that's what I call it!' Barclay Jack shouted another punchline to the gods. Reggie had tuned out some time ago.

'You've got to laugh,' Ronnie deadpanned.

Of course, there had been rumours about him down the years, even, once, a raid on his home – despite his noisy embrace of all things northern, Barclay Jack actually lived on the South Coast. He had ceased to be successful a long time ago and yet here he was, larger than life, rouged and primped and prancing around on the stage telling jokes that should have made any self-respecting woman – or indeed a person of either gender or any in between – squeamish with the incorrectness of it all. That was his attraction, of course, he got to say things people usually only thought, although now that there was the internet, a web of hatred and vitriol, you might have thought that comedians like Barclay Jack would have lost their appeal.

'We could probably arrest him on several accounts right now,' Reggie mused.

'Not worth the calories,' Ronnie said.

'Because they both have manholes!' Barclay Jack bawled. 'Anyone in the audience from Scunthorpe?' he continued relentlessly. A man somewhere in the circle responded in a belligerent manner and Barclay Jack said, 'So you're the one that put the cunt in Scunthorpe, are you?' There was a moment's delay while the audience processed the joke and then the whole place screamed with delight.

'Why, this is hell, nor am I out of it,' Reggie murmured.

'Eh?' Ronnie said.

'It's nothing to be alarmed by, Mr Jack,' Reggie said. The three of them were crammed into Barclay Jack's small dressing room. The place was a tip. There was the scent of something foetid in the air. Reggie suspected that it might be the chewed-up remains of a burger that was nestling amongst the spillage on his dressing-table, or perhaps it was Barclay Jack himself, decaying from the inside out. He certainly didn't look the picture of health.

Reggie caught sight of herself in the vanity mirror that was framed by Hollywood-style light bulbs. She looked small and wan, although no more so than usual. 'Peely-wally,' her mother would have said in her native dialect. No wonder her handsome ex-boyfriend's family had looked aghast at her when he brought her home to meet them.

She gave herself a mental shake and continued, 'We're conducting an investigation into a historic case, Mr Jack, and this is just a routine interview. We're looking into several individuals and would like to ask you a few questions, if that's all right? We're trying to build a picture, fill in some background details. A bit like doing a jigsaw. I'd like to start by asking you if you know someone called – are you all right, Mr Jack? Do you want to sit down? Would you like a glass of water? Mr Jack?'

'How do you handle a dangerous cheese?'

'Jesus, kid,' the magician said, 'are all your jokes about cheese?'

'No,' Harry said. 'I went into a shop to buy a cake and I said, "I'll have that one, please"—'

'Is this a joke,' the magician asked, 'or an incredibly boring incident in your life?'

'A joke.'

'Just checking.

'– and the woman behind the counter said, "That'll be two pounds." "And how about that one over there?" I said, pointing at another cake on the shelf. "That one's four pounds," the woman said. "But," I said, "it looks like the same cake as the first one. How can it be twice the price?" And she said, "Oh, that's madeira cake."'

'Weeell,' Bunny said, stretching the word out, 'it's *sort* of funny, if you were maybe ten years old. A lot of it's in the delivery though, Harry. You sound like you're making an insurance claim.'

Harry didn't mind being critiqued (© Bella Dangerfield) by Bunny. Well, he did, sort of, but he knew if Bunny said something negative it wasn't spiteful and was meant to be helpful. He supposed if he wanted any kind of career in the theatre, whether it was behind or in front of the curtain, he was going to have to learn to face criticism, even hostility.

'Wey, aye,' Bunny said. 'It's nothing but pure hate out there. It's a shit life really, but what are you going to do?'

They were in Bunny's dressing room, which he shared with the magician. Out of the two of them Harry didn't know who complained more about this arrangement. ('You should be grateful it's not the ventriloquist – then there'd be three of you in here,' Harry said. 'That's a joke,' he added. 'Is it?' the magician said.)

Bunny was in his stockinged feet and his wig was off, revealing the flimsy monk's tonsure that rescued him from complete baldness. Otherwise he was in full costume and make-up because he didn't bother leaving the theatre in between matinées and evening performances. Bunny and the magician were playing a complicated card game, the same game that they had been playing since the start of the season. It seemed never to reach a conclusion although money frequently changed hands. Apparently the magician had learned it in 'the big house'.

'He means prison,' Bunny said to Harry. The magician cocked his head to acknowledge this fact.

They paused the game so that the magician could pour a measure of whisky into the two smeared glasses. Crystal would have had a fit at the state of them.

'Want a tipple, Harry?' the magician asked.

'No. Thanks, though.' It was the cheaper, blended sort of whisky. Harry only knew that because his father bought an expensive malt. Encouraged by his father, Harry had tried it, but even the smell made him feel sick. 'Yeah, you have to stick at whisky until you get the taste for it,' his father said. Harry thought it might be something it would be better *not* to get a taste for.

'What have you done with the bairn?' Bunny asked.

'Candace? The chorus girls are spoiling her in their dressing room.' The last time Harry had checked he'd found that the girls had made Candace up – eyeshadow and lipstick and sequins stuck on her face. Her fingernails had been painted green by the dancing girls and a feather boa was wrapped round her neck and most of her body. He could only imagine what Emily would have to say about this get-up.

'Sorry,' he'd said to the room in general, as several girls were in a state of undress.

'It's all right, Harry,' one of them sang out. 'Nothing you haven't seen before.' Well, he thought, that wasn't exactly true.

'Those girls'll eat that kid up,' the magician said gloomily.

Bunny produced a cigarette packet, offered one to the magician and said, 'Light us up, Harry, will you?'

Harry obligingly produced his lighter. 'Can you show me a trick?' he asked the magician.

The magician picked up the cards, shuffled them in a grandstanding kind of way and then fanned them out and said, 'Pick a card, any card.'

As Harry approached Barclay's dressing room a girl flew out. She surprised him by saying, 'You're not Harry by any chance, are you?'

'I am.'

'Oh, good.' She was Scottish – she said 'gud'. 'Mr Jack was asking for you. He needs his pills, he can't find them. I can get them if you tell me where they are.'

'Is he all right?' Harry asked. 'He's not had another funny turn, has he?'

'He seems a bit distressed,' she said.

Harry didn't know why Barclay didn't have his pills on him and he had no idea where they might be. He popped his head back in the dancing girls' dressing room and Candace squealed with delight when she caught sight of him. A tiara had been added to her ensemble, one of the girls' cheap rhinestone ones that they wore for a high-kicking routine they did to 'Diamonds Are a Girl's Best Friend'. ('And they are, Harry,' one of them said to him. 'Never forget that.' 'I'll try not to,' he promised.)

The tiara was far too big for Candace and she had to hold it to stop it slipping off. Harry rescued her before she could be eaten. He was going to have to use some of Bunny's make-up remover on her before Crystal saw her. (Where *was* his stepmother?)

No, the girls hadn't seen Barclay's pills, neither had the ventriloquist. Nor had Clucky (according to the ventriloquist). Harry returned, defeated, to Barclay's dressing room. There was another young woman in there now and they had been joined by Bunny, so it was a terrific squash.

'Turns out Jessica Rarebit there had them,' Barclay said, holding a bottle of pills aloft for Harry to see.

'Hospital gave me them last night,' Bunny said, 'for safekeeping.'

'Twat,' Barclay said succinctly.

'Are you all right, Mr Jack?' Harry asked.

'I'm freezing to death. Shut that door, will you?' It was stiflingly hot in the dressing room. Harry wondered if Barclay really was ill, he certainly didn't look well, but then he never did. As requested, Harry shut the door and was startled by the expression of absolute horror that washed over Barclay's face. He looked as though he'd just seen some kind of ghastly apparition. Barclay's mouth had fallen open, revealing his ratty, nicotine-stained teeth. He held up one trembling hand and pointed at Harry.

'What?' Harry said, alarmed, thinking of the decomposing son who had appeared at the door in 'The Monkey's Paw', a story that had kept him awake at night recently.

'It's behind you,' Bunny said, in his best pantomime inflexion.

Harry whipped round, expecting at the very least a vampire, but then he saw what had given Barclay a fright. Scrawled on the back of his dressing-room door in messy red paint was one word, in capitals: PEEDO.

Oh, for goodness' sake, Reggie thought. Whoever had written it could at least learn how to spell.

There was a tentative knock on the door, but no one said anything so it seemed to be up to Reggie to say, 'Come in.'

They all had to shuffle round so there was room to let another person in. A ventriloquist's dummy, some kind of repellently unattractive fowl, put its disembodied head round the door.

'Fuck off, Clucky!' the drag queen yelled at it. There was what sounded like a scuffle outside in the corridor, as if Clucky was having an altercation with someone, and then Thomas Holroyd's wife squeezed herself into the dressing room and joined the cast of misfits. This was what the Black Hole of Calcutta must have been like, Reggie thought. Only worse.

'Mummy!' a child, sequinned and feathered and invisible up until now, yelled at Crystal, holding her arms out to be picked up. She sounded relieved, and who could blame her?

'Mrs Holroyd,' Reggie said. 'Fancy seeing you here. It's a small world, isn't it?'

Funny Business

Your name came up in connection with one of several individuals we're investigating and so we would like to ask you some routine questions, if that's all right? Why? Why *Tommy*, of all people? Crystal puzzled. How could he have known about those days? He was only a handful of years older than her and Fee. Had he been one of the kids at their parties? Her heart was popping in her chest and Fee said, 'You all right, Teen? Have a fag. I could make some tea?' She didn't look capable of wrangling a kettle but Crystal said, 'Yeah, go on then. Thanks.' She didn't say anything about herbal or no dairy, she knew how stupid that would have sounded to Fee.

She hadn't even recognized Crystal when she'd opened the door to her. 'It's me. Tina,' Crystal said. 'Christina.'

'Fucking hell,' Fee said. 'Look at you. Miss Universe.'

'Let me in,' Crystal said. 'We have to talk. The police are asking about the magic circle.'

'I know.'

It seemed that the judge had a daughter. Crystal hadn't known that. She was called Bronty, apparently, and the same thing had happened to her as had happened to them. Fee said she remembered her, but Fee had gone to more parties than Crystal. Now, all this time later, Bronty Finch had gone to the police and that was why everything was suddenly unravelling, the past and the present crashing into each other at a hundred miles an hour. 'And Mick, too,' Fee said. 'Seems it's prompted him into naming names. Have they found you yet? They were here, I told them what they could do with themselves. We could tell them lots, couldn't we? Lots of names.'

'I'm not going to talk, not to anyone. I found this on the car.' Crystal showed her the photo of Candy and the writing on the back. 'It's a message. They're threatening my kid.' Fee held the photo for a long time, just staring at it, until Crystal took it back. 'Nice,' Fee said. 'Nice kid. I had something too.' She searched in her bag and came up with a piece of paper. The message on it was less succinct but still pretty straightforward. *Don't talk about anything to the police. You'll be sorry if you do.*

The judge was dead now, of course, a lot of the magic circle were. The knight of the realm – Cough-Plunkett – was still on the go, he'd made a decrepit appearance on TV not long ago. And the MP, now a peer, who liked – no, don't even think about what he liked – he was right at the top of the heap now, blustering on about Brexit. 'Call me Nick,' he said. 'Old Nick. Ha ha.' It gave Crystal the willies every time she saw him on the television. ('Let's not watch the news, Harry, it's depressing.') He still had all sorts of connections, to all sorts of people. People you didn't even know existed until they started threatening you.

Crystal had got away when she was fifteen. Carmody had given her a handful of cash – dirty notes 'from the ponies' – he was the silent partner in an on-course bookmaker's, Crystal's relationship with laundered money went back a long way. Dirty into clean, the story of her life. 'Get lost,' Mick said as she stuffed the money into her bag. She was too old now, he said. So she went to the station, got on a train and left. Simple as that, she realized. You just turned your back on everything and left. Christina, running away.

She'd begged Fee to come with her but she'd chosen to stay, already listlessly hooked on drugs. Crystal should have dragged her kicking and screaming out of that trailer, out of that life. Too late now.

She had got a room in a flat and it wasn't as if her life changed overnight like in fairy tales or *Pretty Woman*, and she had to do some lousy stuff to survive, but survive she did. And here she was now. New name, new life. She wasn't giving it up for anyone.

★

They drank the (weak) tea and smoked without pause.

'You married, then?' Fee asked, dragging hard on her cigarette. She was more animated and Crystal wondered if she'd taken something while she was making the tea. 'An old married lady,' she laughed, amused by the idea.

'Yeah, married now. "Mrs Holroyd",' Crystal said, making rabbit ears and laughing because it suddenly seemed absurd that she should be this person, Crystal Holroyd, when the life she had really been destined for was sitting in front of her twitching to get out on the streets and earn her next fix.

'Yeah?' Fee said. 'Any relation to Tommy?'

'Tommy?' Crystal echoed, little warning flags going up all over the place in her brain.

'Tommy Holroyd. Worked for Tony and Mick in the old days. Oh, wait, I think that was after you left. You were before Tommy's time with them. He did really well for himself after – he's the Holroyd in Holroyd Haulage.'

'Haulage?' Crystal echoed again.

'Yeah,' Fee snorted derisively. 'That's the nice word for it. Don't tell me you married *him*? You did, didn't you? You did. Fucking hell, Teen.'

Crystal had been hit in the stomach once by a bloke, a big bloke looking for a punching-bag and finding Crystal, or Tina as she still was then. The blow had been painful beyond belief. Took her breath away, literally, so she ended up curled up like a bean on the ground, wondering if her lungs were ever going to start up again or if that was the end for her. But that didn't compare to now. Everywhere she looked she saw her world collapsing.

Turned out that Fee had known Tommy a lot longer than Crystal had. Knew a lot more about Tommy than Crystal did as well. Tommy and his associates. 'Do you really have no idea what he's up to? You used to be the smart one, Tina.'

'Not any more, apparently,' Crystal said. 'I'll put the kettle back on, shall I? And then you can tell me everything I don't know.'

The thing about the past was that, no matter how far you ran or how fast you ran, it was always right behind you, snapping at your heels.

'Fuck, fuck, fuck,' Crystal said as the whistle on the kettle screamed.

She gave Fee fifty quid – all that she had in her purse – and Fee said, 'What about your watch?' so Crystal gave her the Cartier too, the one that was inscribed *From Tommy with love*.

Crystal had never stepped inside the Palace Theatre before. It was a cheap version of something more opulent. It had a grand staircase and mirrors, but the paintwork was old and the tartan carpet was worn. The smell of stale coffee had drifted into the foyer from the café. There were already posters up advertising the Christmas panto. *Cinderella*. Rags to riches. No one ever wanted it to be the other way round, did they? Tony Bassani had taken her and Fee to the pantomime, as though they were kids. Which they were. *Peter Pan*. Someone off the telly was playing Captain Hook. Alan something. No one remembered him now. Tony bought them a box of Black Magic to share and they'd sung along to all the songs when they put the words up on a board. It had been a great evening, they'd really enjoyed themselves, and then Tony took them backstage afterwards and introduced them to Captain Hook in his dressing room. 'Christmas present for you, Al,' Tony said when he left them there. 'A token of thanks – it's been a great panto season.'

The place was quiet, the matinée must have finished, and she had to ask someone in the box office where to find Harry. They didn't know who Harry was so she asked for Barclay Jack instead, said she was his niece when they looked doubtful and said, 'Are you sure? He doesn't like visitors.'

'Neither do I,' Crystal said. They directed her backstage to his dressing room and she knocked on the door.

You couldn't have got more people in the room. It was like a game of sardines. The magic circle had liked to play a version of that. Fun and games, Bassani called it. The detectives from earlier were in there, but Crystal shelved this fact, she already had enough to think about. Ditto the fact that Barclay Jack looked as though he was about to expire and that there was also a drag queen, without a wig (this must be Harry's new friend Bunny, she supposed). No sign of Candy, and Crystal felt a spasm of panic until Harry pushed his way out of the scrum with her in his arms. She looked as if she'd been shot by sequins. Crystal shelved that thought as well.

Crystal was a fast driver and a nippy overtaker so it had been a challenge for Jackson to keep on her heels until she reached Whitby. She was good at parking too, magically manoeuvring the Evoque into a spot on the West Cliff that was intended for a much smaller vehicle. Jackson negotiated the less tractable Toyota into a parking bay as far away from Crystal as he dared, before setting off on foot after her. She didn't just drive fast, she walked fast too. She'd ditched the heels and the short dress from earlier and was in trainers and jeans now, toting Snow White in her arms as she passed through the Whalebone Arch and down the stone steps to the harbour and the pier. She set a pace that Jackson found hard to keep up with, let alone Dido, although she was making a game effort.

Crystal strode along, slaloming around the holidaymakers who were jamming the pavements, moving slowly like a tide of mud. Jackson held back, mingling with the crowd, trying to disguise himself as a day-tripper in case Crystal turned around and spotted him.

Music — although it barely merited that term — blared out from an amusement arcade as he passed. Despite the good weather it was teeming with people inside. Nathan loved those places, Jackson had endured several brain-freezing hours hanging around with him while he fed coins into the bottomless maw of a coin pusher or a claw machine. Thus were addictions formed. The museum's mummified Hand of Glory was no match for the Claw. None of the current habitués within the strident walls of the arcade looked like healthy citizens. Half of them were sloth with obesity, the other half looked like they'd recently been released from jail.

Jackson was taken by surprise when Crystal suddenly ducked into something called Transylvania World. A vampire thing, presumably – the town was awash with blood-suckers. It didn't seem a suitable entertainment for a three-year-old – but then what did he know? (*Luddite!*)

Jackson loitered in the gap between a shack selling seafood and the booth of a fortune-teller, on which a sign announced, *Madame Astarti, clairvoyant and spiritualist to the stars. Tarot cards, crystal ball, palm reading. Your future is in your hands.* A glass-bead curtain hid Madame Astarti from the prying eyes of the world, but he could hear the low murmur of voices inside and then the voice of Madame Astarti, presumably, saying, 'Pick a card, love, any card.' It was the stuff of nonsense. Julia would have been in there like a shot.

Jackson tried not to inhale too deeply the scents of the pier – fried food and sugar ('Weapons of mass destruction,' according to Julia) – which despite their unpleasantness were making him salivate. It was lunchtime but he seemed to be running on nothing more than caffeine today. All he had on him was a bag of dog treats and he was still enough meals away from anarchy not to consider them. He gave one to doughty Dido as a reward for her stoicism.

Across the road he could see a menu board outside a pub announcing that they were serving 'Yapas' and it took Jackson some time to fathom that this meant Yorkshire tapas. There was a movement, he had been reading, for 'Yexit' – devolution for the county, in other words. Yorkshire, the argument ran, had a population almost the size of Denmark, a larger economy than eleven EU nations, and had won more gold medals at the Rio Olympics than Canada. It was funny, Jackson mused, how he had considered Brexit to be the end of civilization as he knew it, and yet Yexit played a siren tune on his heartstrings. ('Thus are civil wars and tribal genocide fomented,' Julia said. Julia was the only person Jackson knew who started sentences with 'thus' and her prediction seemed a bit of a savage outcome for something that began with a Yapas of 'shrimp ceviche' and 'sweet and sour whelk meat'. Whelk meat was a (so-called) food he would only be prepared to eat if it were to save the life of one of his children. And even then . . .)

He was distracted by the departure of Madame Astarti's client, a thin young woman who didn't look at all happy with any of the tenses of her life, past, present or future.

And then, at last, Crystal was out of Transylvania World, having ditched Snow White, apparently, and before Jackson had time to catch his breath they were off again, back in their respective cars and on the road.

'Sorry about this,' Jackson apologized to Dido as he gave her a leg-up into the back seat. She fell fast asleep immediately.

Crystal seemed to be going to Scarborough, which was good because that was where Jackson was also bound. If Crystal noticed him, he reasoned, he could claim a perfectly innocent alibi, even though he was following her like a hunter stalking prey, behaving, in fact, exactly like the silver BMW that he was supposed to be investigating. He checked the time again – still an hour before Ewan and Jackson's pubescent alter ego, Chloe, were due to meet.

When they reached their destination, more nifty parking ensued. More walking along streets – Crystal was going at a trot, she'd be cantering soon. Why was she in such a hurry? So she could get back and rescue Snow White from the vampires' clutches?

They had reached the mean streets by now. Crystal stopped short outside a tattoo parlour and checked the name on the bell on the door next to it. A flat was above, Jackson presumed. After a couple of minutes the door was opened and a woman peered out cautiously. It was hard to judge her age as she had the scrawny morbidity of a meth addict. Not really the type you'd expect a self-styled 'wife and mother' to keep company with. She was hugging a man's cardigan around her body as though she was freezing. On her feet were a pair of old-fashioned furry slippers, the kind that Jackson imagined his grandmother would have worn if he had ever had a grandmother – there wasn't much in the way of longevity in his ancestral line. The two women exchanged a few intense words on the doorstep before the cardigan-wrapped woman stepped aside and let Crystal inside.

More loitering ensued on his part, this time in a coffee shop on the other side of the street. Not a coffee shop, more of an apology for a greasy spoon, a run-down place in which Jackson was the only customer, so it was easy to secure a seat near the window from where he could keep a lookout for his client's reappearance. He ordered a coffee (rank) and pretended to look busy with his iPhone until Crystal suddenly flew out of the door. She was halfway up the street before he'd thrown down a five-pound note (a ludicrous overpayment) and cajoled Dido into getting to her feet.

Jackson changed his mind about keeping up the chase. He thought it might quite possibly kill the dog and that was the last thing he wanted on his slate of shortcomings with either Julia or Nathan. Instead he crossed the street to find out the name of Crystal's haggard friend. A piece of paper had been stuck with Sellotape above the doorbell and, handwritten in felt-tip, it said, *F. Yardley.* He wondered what the F stood for. Fiona? Fifi? Flora? She didn't look like a Flora. Jackson's own mother was a Fidelma, a name she had to spell for every English person she ever met. She was from Mayo, which didn't help. The accent was dense. 'Potato speak,' Jackson's brother, Francis – another F – had called it, dismissive of his Celtic heritage. Francis was older than Jackson and had embraced the freedom of the Sixties with relish. He was a welder with the Coal Board and owned a sharp suit and a motorbike and had a Beatles pudding-bowl haircut. He also seemed to have a different girl every week. He was a role model to aspire to. And then he killed himself.

It was guilt that drove him to suicide. Francis had felt responsible for their sister's death. If Jackson could speak to Francis now he would give him the usual police spiel about how the only person responsible for Niamh's death was the man who killed her, but the truth was that if his brother had met Niamh at the bus-stop like he was supposed to, then a stranger wouldn't have raped and murdered her and thrown her in the canal, and for that Jackson had never forgiven his brother. He was okay with grudges. They served a purpose. They kept you sane.

Jackson rang F. Yardley's doorbell and after a considerable wait, and a lot of shuffling and rattling of door keys and chains, the door was finally opened.

'What?' the cardigan woman asked. No preamble there, then, Jackson thought. Close up he could see the look of sunken desperation on her skeletal features. She could have been any age between thirty and seventy. She had changed from the grandmother slippers into a pair of cheap knee-high black patent boots and beneath the oversized cardigan she was wearing a short skirt and a scanty sequined top. Much as he disliked jumping to easy conclusions, Jackson couldn't help but think 'working girl', a bargain-basement one at that. He had always got on well with the oldest profession when he had been a policeman, and he took out his licence and embarked on his usual doorstep patter – 'Miss Yardley, is it? My name's Jackson Brodie. I'm a private detective working on behalf of a client, a Mrs Crystal Holroyd' (The truth, after all.) 'She's asked me to make some enquiries about—' Before he could make anything up she said, 'Fuck off,' and slammed the door in his face.

'If you change your mind, give me a ring!' he shouted through the letterbox before posting his card through.

'Come on,' he said to Dido, hustling her back into the car again. 'We need to get our skates on or we're going to be late for our date.'

It was only when he was nearing the Palace Theatre that he noticed the silver BMW, cruising quietly as a shark behind him.

The car turned right and Jackson hesitated for a moment before doing a dodgy U-turn and following it down a side street. To no avail, he could find no sign of it anywhere, so he drove back to the Palace, parked and took up a position at the bandstand. No band today, no music. The colliery where his father and brother had worked had had a brass band – what colliery didn't, in those days? – and his brother had played the flugelhorn. The young Jackson had thought it was a silly name for an instrument, but Francis was good. He wished that he could just once hear his brother play a solo again. Or help his sister pin up the hem on a dress she'd made. Or have a goodnight peck on the cheek from his mother – the most intimacy she could manage. They were not a family who touched. Too late now. Jackson sighed. He was growing weary of himself. He sensed the time was approaching to let it go. After all, his future was in his own hands.

He waited at the bandstand for half an hour but Ewan proved a no-show. A youth had pitched up at one point, slouchy in a hoody, and

Jackson wondered if his quarry was young after all, but within a few minutes he was joined by his similarly attired confrères, all in hoodies, trackies and trainers, which gave them a criminal air – pretty much like Nathan and his friends, in fact. Jackson caught a glimpse of the face of one of them – the drowned boy from the other day. He looked blankly through Jackson as if he wasn't there and then they all moved off like a single-minded shoal. As he watched them leaving, Jackson realized that he was looking at Crystal Holroyd's Evoque, parked opposite.

'A bit of a coincidence, that, isn't it?' he said to Dido.

'Well, you know what they say,' Dido said. 'A coincidence is just an explanation waiting to happen.' No, she didn't say that. Of course she didn't. She didn't believe in coincidences, only fate.

Perhaps, it struck Jackson, he wasn't following Crystal, perhaps she was following him. He liked a mysterious woman as much as the next man, but there was a limit to the attractions of an enigma and he was reaching it. Before this train of thought could advance any further it was derailed by the reappearance of Crystal herself, followed by a teenage boy – Jackson thought this must be Harry (*a good boy*) – who was carrying Snow White in his arms. She was not the pristine child he had seen earlier. The last time Jackson had seen Snow White she had been in Whitby. How had she got here? Teleportation?

Jackson was debating whether or not to make himself known to Crystal when all hell suddenly broke loose.

Harry carried Candy outside and Crystal unlocked the Evoque. Harry got in the back so he could strap his sister into her car seat. Crystal wanted him to come with them but he said, 'I can't miss the evening performance.'

'It's not a matter of life and death, you know, Harry,' she said. She wished he would come with her. The most important thing now was to keep Candy safe, but Harry needed to be kept safe as well, didn't he? He was still just a kid. Crystal had no idea what she was going to do, but she knew what she wasn't going to do – she wasn't going to stand up in court and talk about the past. What kind of a stain on her kids' lives would that be? *Keep your mouth shut, Christina.*

On the other hand, she was no one's pawn any more. Of course, that was something else the judge's chess-playing friend, Sir Cough-Plunkett, had taught her. In the endgame a pawn can change into a queen. Crystal had a feeling there was an endgame in play, she just wasn't sure who her opponent was.

Crystal had just opened the driver's door when it happened. Two men – big brawny blokes – ran up and took her completely by surprise, and one punched her in the face.

The Wing Chun kicked in and she bounced back up to her feet and landed a punch or two, but the bloke was like Rambo. It was over in a second and she found herself on the ground. The bloke who had hit her was already in the driving seat and the other one was slamming Harry's door shut, with Harry still inside, not to mention Candy, and then throwing himself into the front passenger seat. They drove off with a showy squealing of tyres and, just like that, the entire content of Crystal's life disappeared up the road.

She struggled to her feet and ran after the car, but there wasn't much point. Even at her fastest she wasn't going to beat the Evoque. She could see Harry staring out of the rear windscreen, open-mouthed in shock. *His little face,* she thought, a tug of something cataclysmic in her heart.

Jackson Brodie appeared out of somewhere. He'd been following her all day. Did he really think she hadn't noticed?

'Are you okay?' he asked.

'My car's just been hijacked with my kids in it, so no, I would say, not all right. Some fucking sheriff you are. Where's your car?'

'My car?'

'Yes, your fucking car. We have to follow them.'

En Famille

'Mrs Mellors? I'm DC Ronnie Dibicki and this is DC Reggie Chase. I wonder if we could come in and have a word with Mr Mellors. Is he at home?'

'No, he's not, I'm afraid. Do call me Sophie,' she offered, holding out a hand to shake. 'Is there a problem? Is it something to do with a case he's working on?' she asked, all spousal support.

'Sort of . . .' Reggie said.

Sophie Mellors was a very well-put-together polite fortysomething. She was tall, wearing a neat dress and a modest pair of heels, and everything about her was fifty shades of mellow, from the brown of her eyes to the honey of her dress to the caramel of her shoes. Expensive shoes. Reggie always looked at the shoes first. You could tell a lot about a person by their shoes. Jackson Brodie taught her that. She would like to see him again, despite her initial antagonism at the sight of him on the cliff the other day. In fact she wanted to catch up with him quite badly. For a brief period of time she had masqueraded as his daughter and it had felt nice.

'Come in, why don't you?' Sophie said. 'Gracious' was the adjective for her, Reggie thought. She was wearing what Reggie believed was called a 'tea dress'. She was garden-party ready. Reggie thought of Bronte Finch, dishevelled in her workout gear, encouraging them to eat strawberry tarts. *Small animals only.*

Sophie Mellors led them into a huge kitchen that must have once been the beating heart of a farm. Reggie imagined farmhands in here, sitting round a big table for a harvest supper or a hot breakfast before lambing. A big table groaning with hams and cheeses.

Yellow-yolked eggs, freshly laid by hens pecking in the yard. Reggie knew absolutely nothing about farming except that farmers had one of the highest suicide rates of any profession, so she supposed it wasn't all hams and lambs, just a lot of muck and mud and worry. Anyway, whatever farming had happened here was long gone, the kitchen in Malton was now a hymn to expensive appliances and craftsman-built cupboards. A lasagne was sitting cling-filmed on a counter, waiting to go into the Aga. Of course there was an Aga, you would expect nothing less of a woman like this.

'It's nothing urgent, nothing for him to concern himself with,' Ronnie said. 'We're conducting an investigation into a historic case, former clients of Mr Mellors. We thought that perhaps he might be able to give us some information. Do you know where your husband is?'

'Just now? No, actually I have no idea, but he said he'd be home in time for supper.' She glanced at the lasagne as if it might have an opinion on her husband's punctuality. 'Ida's been hacking all afternoon with Buttons and he promised he'd eat with us when she got back. En famille, as it were.'

Ida's been hacking all afternoon with Buttons. Reggie couldn't even begin to translate that sentence. She presumed that Buttons had nothing to do with Cinderella and, equally, that hacking had nothing to do with computers. Sai had hacked into the global soft drinks corporation whose name was the second most recognized word in the world. So it goes.

'Do you want to wait?' Sophie Mellors asked. 'Would you like a coffee or a tea?' They declined in unison. 'Or a glass of wine?' she said, indicating a bottle of red waiting patiently on the counter. 'Not on duty, thank you,' Ronnie said primly. The wine was already open. Breathing, Reggie thought. Everything in the world was breathing, one way or another. Even the inanimate rocks, we just didn't have the ears to hear them.

Ronnie gave her a little nudge and murmured, 'Planet Earth calling.'

'Yeah,' Reggie sighed. 'I hear it.'

A boy, a teenager, burst into the kitchen, with adolescent energy and burgeoning testosterone. He was dressed in a mud-splattered school rugby kit and was battered and bruised from a game.

'My son, Jamie,' Sophie introduced with a little laugh, 'fresh from the fight.'

Reggie was pretty sure that was a line from 'Holding Out For A Hero'. She had not been averse to karaoke when she was a student and drunk. Those days seemed painfully long ago.

'Good game?' Sophie said.

'Yeah, good,' he said.

'These are detectives who need a word with Dad.'

The boy wiped his hands on his shorts and shook hands with both of them and Sophie said, 'You don't know where he is, do you? He said he'd be back in time for supper.'

The boy shrugged. 'No idea, but . . .' He took out his phone and said, 'He's on Find My Friends. You can see if he's on his way back.'

'Oh, yes, clever boy,' Sophie said. 'I wouldn't have thought of that. We're all on it, but I only use it sometimes to check where Ida is. Looking for your husband seems . . .' – she stared at the lasagne again as if it would come up with the right word for her – 'intrusive,' she decided eventually. (Ronnie sighed audibly. Sophie Mellors was a wordy sort of woman.) She hadn't finished either. 'It's like looking at someone's texts or emails. As if you don't trust them to be honest with you. Everyone has a right to some privacy, even husbands and wives.'

'Yeah, I know what you mean,' Reggie said. Reggie who, after Sai had ended their relationship, had stalked him obsessively on the GPS tracking site they shared, not to mention Facebook and Instagram and anywhere else where he might appear in his Reggie-less future. 'Trust's everything,' she nodded.

'Look, there's Ida,' Sophie said fondly, pointing at a green dot on Jamie's phone moving towards the house. 'She's almost home. Her friend's mother is dropping her off. We take it in turns.'

'And there's Dad,' Jamie said, pointing at a red dot. They all four of them peered at it.

'Looks like Mr Mellors is in the middle of nowhere,' Ronnie said. 'He's not moving.'

'It's just a field,' Jamie said cheerfully. 'He's often there.'

'Really?' Sophie said, the lightest of frowns passing over her face like a summer cloud.

'Yeah,' Jamie said.

'And you've never wondered what he does there?' Ronnie asked, deploying her eyebrow.

The boy shrugged again and with an admirable lack of teenage curiosity said, 'No.'

'Meditating, perhaps,' Sophie suggested brightly.

'Meditating?' Ronnie said, the eyebrow launching into space.

'Yes, he does that. You know – mindfulness.'

There was the sound of a car drawing up and driving off again and seconds later Sophie said, 'Oh, here's Ida,' and beamed as a small, rather put-upon-looking girl slouched sulkily into the kitchen. She was outfitted in jodhpurs and was carrying a riding helmet. She scowled at everyone, lasagne included. Reggie judged that she had missed out on the bland-mannered genes of the other Mellors.

'Good hack?' her mother asked.

'No,' Ida said grumpily. 'It was an awful day.'

I hear you, sister, Reggie thought, I hear you.

'You know what that field is, don't you?' Reggie said to Ronnie when they were back in the car.

'One of Carmody's old trailer parks?'

'Bingo.'

'Let's go and see if he's there, then,' Ronnie said. 'What *is* hacking?'

'I've no idea. I actually don't know *everything*.'

'Yeah, you do.'

Angel of the North

They drove south, tracing the beacon of hope that was Harry's location on Crystal's phone. The Star of Bethlehem had not been followed with such devotion.

'It was Harry that put the app on my phone,' she said. 'One of those family things – I can see him, he can see me. I don't bother with it much, but Harry worries about things like that – after what happened to his mum, I suppose. They didn't find her for a couple of days. He likes to know where everyone is. He's a bit of a sheepdog.'

'Me too,' Jackson said.

The signal had been stuttering in and out of range for the whole journey and Crystal stared at the phone clutched in her hand, as if sheer willpower could keep it from disappearing altogether.

Jackson could see a nasty bruise already formed on her cheek. A black eye was blooming, she was going to have an admirable shiner in an hour or two, he reckoned. She had taken a couple of brutal blows but she didn't go down without a fight – fuelled by adrenaline, Jackson supposed. She had given almost as good as she got, a couple of Ninja moves, one-two straight punches and some good elbow work that she must have learned somewhere. She was an Amazonian but unfortunately her opponent was a fighting machine. Ex-military, by the look of him, Jackson was thinking as he had sprinted towards the fray. Too late, unfortunately. It was over in seconds and by the time Jackson was on the scent the guy had knocked Crystal to the ground, wrenched the Evoque's key fob off her and was driving off up the road. *Some fucking sheriff you are.*

★

Crystal pulled down the sun visor and peered at herself in the vanity mirror. She peeled off her false eyelashes, one after the other, flinching when the one attached to her blackening eye got stuck. It seemed to Jackson that she had perfectly good eyelashes without adding to them, but what did a Luddite know?

'What a fucking mess,' she muttered to the mirror before retrieving a pair of spectacles from her bag. 'Can't see shit without them,' she said. Whither the woman who had seemed to be making such an effort earlier not to swear? 'And the bastard broke my prescription sunglasses when he hit me.' Kidnapped kids trumped vanity, apparently. It was a different woman sitting next to him from the one he had first met a few hours ago. It was as if she was slowly deconstructing, she even seemed to have less hair, although he wasn't sure how that could be. Jackson wouldn't have been surprised if she removed a false leg next.

'There's a first-aid kit in the boot, if you want,' he offered. 'I can stop.'

'No. Keep going. I'll be fine. Can't this thing go any faster?' She was almost feral with worry. 'Do you want me to drive?'

Jackson treated the question with the silent contempt it deserved and instead admitted, 'I looked in the envelope on your windscreen. I saw the photo of your daughter and the message on the back. *Keep your mouth shut.* And not say what, exactly?'

'People are asking questions,' she said vaguely.

'Who? What people?'

She shrugged, fixated on her phone. 'The police,' she said grudgingly after a while. 'The police are asking questions.'

'Questions about what?'

'Stuff.'

Jackson had experienced enough unforthcoming conversations with Nathan to know that dogged perseverance was the only way forward. 'And have they questioned you?'

'No,' Crystal said. 'They haven't.'

'And would you answer their questions? If they asked them?' Enigmatic didn't cover the half of her. He gave Crystal a sideways glance and she said, 'Keep your eyes on the road.'

'Do you know what they're asking questions about?'

She shrugged again. He supposed this was what was meant by keeping your mouth shut. 'They've just passed the turning for Reighton Gap,' she said, looking at the phone.

'So, the man in the silver BMW,' Jackson persisted, 'and the men who drove off with your kids – do you know if they're related?' How could they not be? he thought. It was surely too much of a coincidence that one person would be following you and another quite different person would snatch your kids, wasn't it? A sudden image of Ricky Kemp flashed into his head. *I know some really bad people.*

And for all Jackson knew, there was a third person who was leaving the threatening messages. Some of the little grey cells had fainted with the effort of understanding and were being fanned by other little grey cells.

'Well . . .' she said.

'Well what?'

'They're sort of related and they're sort of not related.'

'Oh, good, that makes everything really clear. Crystal-clear, that is. Are they working in tandem? These people, whoever they are? Are they even aware of each other? What did you *do* to bring about all this, for God's sake?'

'Questions, questions,' Crystal said.

'Well, how about answers, answers?' Jackson said. 'Or we can go to the police, which is what any sensible, law-abiding person would have done by now if their children had been abducted.'

'I'm not going to the police. I'm not putting my kids at risk.'

'I would say they're already at risk.'

'Further risk. And anyway, for all I know the police *are* involved.'

Jackson sighed. He was about to object – he didn't have much time for conspiracy theories – but then the phone in Crystal's hand pinged to announce the arrival of a text. 'Christ,' she said. 'It's from Harry. No, not Harry,' she amended and gave a low moan of despair. She held the phone aloft so Jackson could see the photo of a furious-looking Harry holding Candy in his arms. 'Same message,' she said dully.

'Keep your mouth shut?'

'And more.'

'What more?'

'Keep your mouth shut or you'll never see your kids alive again.'

It seemed to Jackson to be an overly melodramatic message. Kidnappers who held people hostage were rare, unless they were terrorists or pirates, neither of which seemed likely in this case. And kidnappers who killed their hostages were even rarer. And garden variety kidnappings were about money or custody, not ensuring someone's silence (and who on earth would want a three-year-old on their hands?), but there'd been no ransom demand, no request for anything. Just intimidation. It was all a bit Cosa Nostra. Was it possible, he wondered, that Crystal was in some kind of witness protection?

'What about your friend?'

'Friend?'

'The woman you went to see today. The one who lives above the betting shop. Is she part of this whole mysterious Q-but-no-A thing you've got going on? And answer gave she none,' Jackson murmured as Crystal continued to gaze silently at her phone. And then he said what all good TV cops say at this point – Collier himself was particularly fond of the phrase: 'If you want me to help you, you're going to have to tell me everything.'

'It's not a pretty story.'

'It never is.'

And it wasn't. It was a long and winding tale and it took them all the way to Flamborough Head.

They were both quiet as they drove up towards the headland. Jackson was thinking about the cliffs there – very high cliffs – and he suspected that Crystal was thinking about them as well. No place to bring kidnapped kids. Flamborough Head was a known suicide spot and he supposed that a place where people jumped off cliffs was also a good place to push people off. He had a sudden picture of Vince Ives going over the edge.

There was the lighthouse and there was a café and nothing else much, but this was where Harry's beacon had stopped moving nearly fifteen minutes ago. There were a few cars in the car park. Walkers came here to brave the wind and take in the view. 'Looks like they're in the café,' Crystal said, peering at the phone.

No sign of them in the café, of course. The likelihood of simply coming across the kidnappers eating toasted teacakes and rendering up the children was remote in the extreme, but Crystal was already running towards a bloke who was sitting at a table with his back to them, nursing a mug of something.

To the guy's surprise, to put it mildly, before he could do anything about it Crystal had her arm round his neck and was holding him in a chokehold. The contents of his mug – tomato soup, unfortunately – went everywhere, but mostly in his lap.

When Jackson had managed to prise Crystal off the guy – she had a grip like a boa constrictor – she indicated a mobile sitting on the table. It had one of those personalized covers on which Jackson could see a photo of Crystal and Candy, their faces smooshed against each other and both grinning for the photographer, who was Harry presumably.

'Harry's phone,' Crystal pointed out unnecessarily to Jackson.

The guy who was covered in tomato soup turned out to be just your average idiot, the owner of the pimped-out boy-racer car that Jackson had noticed on the way in. A man had come up to him in a service station, he said – once he was able to speak – and offered him a hundred pounds to drive the phone to Flamborough and throw it off the headland. 'A prank – a stag-do thing.' Crystal slammed his head into the table. Jackson glanced around to see how the rest of the café's denizens were reacting to this, but they all seemed to have quietly disappeared. Jackson didn't blame them. Wives and mothers, he thought, you never wanted to get on the wrong side of them. Madonnas on steroids.

'So let me just check this,' Jackson said to the boy racer. 'A complete stranger comes up to you, gives you a hundred quid to throw a phone into the sea, and this stranger then disappears and you're unlikely to ever see him again, but you do what he asked anyway.'

'I haven't. I wasn't going to,' he said, rubbing his forehead. 'I was going to keep the phone, change the SIM.'

His head renewed its acquaintance with the table. 'This is assault,' he muttered when Crystal yanked him back up by the hair. He was lucky his head was still attached to his body. Boadicea eat your heart out, Jackson thought.

'I could sue you,' the boy racer said to Crystal.

'Just fucking try,' she growled.

'Thanks for the help back there,' she said sarcastically when they got back in the car.

'I thought you were doing just fine on your own,' Jackson said.

Babes in the Wood

'I thought we were staying the night in Newcastle? We've left New-castle, haven't we?'

'Change of plan, love. I'm taking you to a B&B for the night – that's a bed and breakfast to you and me.'

'Yes, I know what a B&B is, but why?'

Andy was surprised by how good her English was. Better than his own, really. She was the taller of the two. Nadja and Katja. They were smart – smart and pretty. Not smart enough, though. They thought they were going to work in a hotel in London. What was going to happen to them shouldn't happen to a dog, really. He had a sudden image of Lottie's poker-face. Did dogs have a moral code? Honour amongst dogs and so on.

'There was a bit of an incident, apparently,' Andy said to her. 'A problem with the Airbnb you were supposed to stay in. A gas leak,' he elaborated. 'In the whole building, in fact. Everyone had to be evacuated. No one allowed back in. This B&B we're going to now means that you'll get a bit further on the journey, further south. To London. And then, first thing in the morning, I'll drive you to the station and you can hop on a train at Durham or York. Even Don-caster,' he added, working his way mentally down the East Coast main line. Newark? Or was that on a different line? Why was he even thinking about it? They'd be going nowhere near a station or a train. 'You'll be in London by tomorrow lunchtime. Tea at the Ritz, eh, girls?'

He knew without turning round that they were staring at the back of his head as if he were an idiot. He was supposed to be the smooth operator, but this pair were derailing him for some reason. It was taking a tremendous effort for him to keep the whole show on the road. No one understood what a burden it was.

Yes, there had indeed been an 'incident', but nothing to do with gas leaks or an Airbnb, although Andy still didn't know what the actual nature of it was. Tommy had finally resurfaced on the phone just after Andy had picked the girls up at the airport. He hadn't sounded like his usual easy-going self and he must have been out of range of a signal because whatever he was saying was lost to a hissing garble of white noise.

Another call had followed swiftly on the heels of Tommy's. Steve Mellors this time, saying there'd been an incident at Silver Birches.

'What kind?' Andy asked, trying to keep his tone nonchalant in front of the Polish girls. He could tell that Nadja was paying close attention.

'Not on the phone,' Steve said. (Why not? Was someone *listening* to their phones? Andy had a sick feeling of panic.) 'Get your arse to Silver Birches pronto,' Steve said. 'It's all hands to the pump down here.'

'Well, I've got my hands full, as it were, here, with these lovely Polish ladies that I'm chauffeuring,' Andy said blandly, smiling at the girls in the rear-view mirror. He caught sight of himself. His smile was less of a smile and more of a death rictus.

'Just bring them with you, for Christ's sake,' Steve said. 'It's where they're going to end up anyway.'

Andy stretched his death-rictus grin even further in case the girls were suspicious. Should have been on the stage, he thought. Mr Congeniality. He could have done a turn at the Palace. He'd been to see the summer-season show, the Eighties revival thing – Barclay Jack *et al.* It had plumbed new depths of mediocrity. Andy had been unwillingly dragged there by Rhoda because, apparently, she used to date the magician. 'A lifetime ago,' she said. 'Nothing for you to worry about, Andrew.' He hadn't been worried. Not until she said that anyway. Rhoda and the magician had greeted each other with air kisses and theatrical 'Hello, darlings – which was not the Rhoda that Andy knew. He had felt jealous for a moment, although he suspected it was the jealousy of ownership rather than passion.

'Nice handbag,' the magician said to Rhoda, spotting her Chanel bag.

'It's a fake,' Rhoda said to the magician. 'Can't you tell?'

'Dunno,' the magician said. 'Everything looks fake to me.'

'Angel of the North,' Andy said automatically as they passed the great rusted wings, looming over them in the dark. There was silence in the back of the car and when he glanced behind he saw that both girls had fallen asleep. The smaller one had her head on the shoulder of the taller one. It was a touching picture. They were the right age to be his daughters, if he'd had daughters. Anyone looking at them might think he was their dad, driving them home. From a concert. Or a holiday. He felt momentarily blindsided by the loss of something he'd never known.

The girls didn't stir until they were turning into the driveway of Silver Birches.

'We're here?' Nadja asked sleepily.

'Yeah,' he said. 'We're here.' The place was in darkness apart from the porch light that was casting a dim glow over the front door. Andy drew the car to a halt. No sign of life unless you counted the pale moths throwing themselves suicidally against the light. No trace of an incident, unless it was something that had killed everyone in Silver Birches without any mess. A sound wave or a silent alien force.

'*This* is a B&B?' Nadja asked, giving her sister a shake to wake her.

'Yes, love,' Andy said. 'It doesn't look like much from the outside, I know. But it's nice and cosy inside.'

She gave her sister another shake and said, 'Wake up, Katja, we're here.' The girl's tone was sharper this time, with a note of urgency to it that made Andy uneasy. She tried to open her door but there were child locks fitted at the back. 'Can you let us out, please?' she said crossly.

'Hang on, love,' Andy said, hitting Tommy's number on the phone. 'I'll just find out where the reception committee is.'

Tommy didn't answer the phone, but the front door flew open suddenly and Vasily and Jason appeared. With a practised move they sprinted to the car, opened the back doors and pulled out a girl each.

The Poles were fighters, Andy could have predicted that. They kicked and struggled and screamed. The younger one in particular — Katja — was like a wild animal, a spitfire, he thought. Watching from the car, Andy was surprised to find that there was a part of him that was willing the girls to win. No chance of that — the battle was over when Jason put Katja's lights out by punching her in the head. He slung her over his shoulder like a sack of coal and carried her inside, followed by Vasily dragging a yowling Nadja along by her hair.

Andy had been so absorbed by the scene in front of him that he nearly jumped out of his skin when there was a loud knock on the car window.

'We've got a problem, Foxy,' Tommy said.

Hansel and Gretel

The last thing that Harry had seen was Crystal standing in the road screaming as the Evoque accelerated away from her. Then the man in the passenger seat leant over and told Harry to give him his phone and get down on the floor and keep his eyes shut, so Harry supposed that they didn't want him to see where they were going, or maybe they were afraid that he would try to signal out of the car window for help. At least they didn't put a hood over his head or blindfold him – and if they had intended to abduct him they would probably have come prepared with something like that, wouldn't they? So surely that meant this was just a carjacking gone wrong? After all, the Evoque was a high-end car, it wouldn't be a total surprise if someone wanted to steal it. And, Harry reasoned further (he was doing a lot of reasoning, it was keeping him just this side of sane), after they'd gone a few miles they would let him and Candace out and everyone would go on their way. A happy ending for all concerned.

Candace herself was silent, and when, against orders, Harry squinted through his eyelids he could see that she had fallen asleep, thank goodness. She looked overheated, her hair clinging damply to her forehead. A few stray sequins still glinted on her cheeks. Reassured, he tried very hard to obey and keep his eyes tightly shut, which was surprisingly difficult, as all his instincts were to do the opposite. He crept his hand up blindly and felt for his sister's own warm and sticky one.

He might not be looking, but he couldn't help hearing as the men conversed in gruff, dissatisfied voices. It appeared that he was wrong. Not a carjacking but a genuine kidnapping, with Candace as the target. His father had money and he liked people to know it, so perhaps it made more sense to hold his daughter to ransom rather than simply stealing his car. ('*My* car,' he could hear Crystal's voice in his head correcting him.) Harry, on the other hand, also Tommy's child, didn't seem to count. ('The lad,' the men called him – they didn't even seem to know his name.) He was just 'collateral damage'. Did that mean he was disposable? Would they stop soon and order him out of the car and then make him stand on the edge of a ditch and shoot him? (He had recently seen a documentary about the SS. 'Leave history behind where it belongs,' Crystal had said when she saw what he was watching.)

They came to a stop after about half an hour and one of the men said, 'You can open your eyes now. Get the kid out for us.' Harry's legs wobbled a bit when he climbed out of the car, but no one made a move to shoot him. He unstrapped Candace, who protested in her sleep but still didn't wake up. He couldn't imagine what she would make of this new situation, although she had a fairly phlegmatic personality. ('That sounds like a disease, Harry,' Crystal said.)

It was the first time Harry had had a chance to get a proper look at the men. He had expected a rough-looking pair of dopey criminals, and he realized he had probably watched *101 Dalmatians* with Candace too many times as these men looked tough and professional, almost in a Special Forces way, like the ex-soldiers in *Who Dares Wins* – although Harry couldn't begin to imagine why the SAS would want to kidnap Candace.

They were in a field. Surrounded by fields. He couldn't see the sea, but there was the kind of empty horizon that indicated it might be somewhere close by. The field had been used as a trailer park at some point – there were a couple of dilapidated trailers with rusty weeds and thistles growing up around their wheels, and one that was off its wheels altogether. A newer, smarter one, a mobile home, was parked over in a corner near the gate.

'Don't even think about running,' one of the men snapped at him, and the other one, the one who had Harry's phone, fished it out from his pocket and took a photo of him and Candace, although – again – he was only really interested in Candace. 'Hold her a bit higher. Maybe you could pinch her awake.' Harry held her higher and pretended to pinch her. 'It's no good. She's out like a light,' he said. 'An earthquake wouldn't wake her once she's gone like this.'

Once they had the photo they texted it to someone, conferring on the wording to accompany the photo. Crystal would be able to track his location, he thought, he had put a GPS app on her phone. He felt buoyed up by this thought, but then he heard one of them mutter, 'Need to get rid of this fucking phone before they track it.'

Harry decided to give the two men nicknames so that he could remember them. He imagined himself later, sitting in the back of a police car with a kindly policewoman beside him asking about his ordeal and him saying, 'Well, the one I called Pinky had a scar on his chin, and Perky had a tattoo on his forearm – I think it was of a lion,' and the kindly policewoman saying, 'Well done, Harry. I'm sure this information will help us catch these dastardly villains very quickly.' Of course, Harry knew the kindly policewoman wouldn't use the phrase 'dastardly villains' – neither would he, for that matter – but he liked the sound of it and she was imaginary, after all. ('The thing about the imagination, Harry,' Miss Dangerfield had told him, 'is that it knows no bounds.')

Pinky and Perky were puppets from long ago. Harry had seen them on YouTube – they were unbelievably awful. He wouldn't have been surprised to have found them on the bill at the Palace. He had only heard about them because Barclay had referred to a couple of the stage hands (in a derogatory way, he had no other) as 'Pinky and Perky'.

Harry thought that robbing the kidnappers of their anonymity might somehow make them less threatening, but in fact it made them seem even more terrifying. He tried to focus on the idea of the kindly policewoman, but he kept seeing her standing over the ditch that his lifeless body had been rolled into.

He wondered what Pinky had texted and who he had sent it to. (Or was it 'whom'? Miss Dangerfield was very strict about grammar.) His dad, he supposed, a threatening ransom demand. *Pay up or we kill the kid.* Harry shuddered. There were now two bodies in his imaginary ditch.

Pinky seemed to be having trouble sending the text – he was walking around the field holding the phone above his head as if he was trying to catch a butterfly.

'There's no fucking signal,' he concluded finally.

'Send it later,' Pinky said.

Pinkie was also the name of the character ('protagonist' he heard Miss Dangerfield say in his head) in *Brighton Rock*. Harry was supposed to be reading it for next term. Perhaps he never would now. Whole fleets of world literature would sail unread over his head as he lay bleeding out in that ditch, staring at the sky.

'You!' Perky commanded.

'Yes?' (He almost said 'sir'.)

'Bring the kid over here.'

'My name's Harry,' Harry said. He had read somewhere that you were supposed to humanize yourself to kidnappers.

'I know what your fucking name is. Bring the kid over here. And don't try any funny business or you'll be sorry.'

It was evening, a soft glow of twilight was coming through the trailer's windows. They were imprisoned in one of the wrecks. Candace had woken up not long after they were locked in and had since gone through more than half of her Seven Dwarfs repertoire – grumpy, happy, dopey and sleepy. Hungry, too, but thankfully the kidnappers had left him with a plastic Co-op bag containing a packet of white bread sandwiches and a bottle of Irn-Bru. Harry supposed that Crystal would have made allowances given the circumstances.

Harry passed the time (and it passed very, very slowly) by playing several silly games with Candace, telling her endless jokes that she didn't understand but made an effort to laugh at. ('What's a pirate's favourite cheese? Chedd-*aargh*.') Not to mention reciting every tale in the fairy canon and singing 'Let It Go' on a loop. Now, thankfully, she was back to sleepy again. He used the opportunity to pick some of the dancers' sequins off her face. Once she'd dozed off, Harry was left with nothing to do but ponder the situation he found himself in.

There were things to be thankful for, he told himself. They weren't tied up, they weren't gagged, and if they were going to be killed they wouldn't have been left with food, surely? Nonetheless, they were definitely imprisoned. Harry had tried very hard to break out of the trailer. He had tried smashing the thick windows with an old metal stool that was lying around. He had tried prising the windows out of their frames with a blunt knife he had found in a drawer. He had tried kicking down the door. He had tried throwing his shoulder against it. Nothing had worked. It might look like an antique but the trailer was made of sturdy stuff.

'It's a game,' he'd tried to reassure Candace, who didn't look in the least reassured. In fact, she looked terrified at this new violent aspect of his behaviour.

Harry made a silent vow that if they got out of here – *when* they got out of here – he would stop being so puny and ineffective. He would lift weights and get his dad to give him boxing lessons and he wouldn't be made to feel frightened and helpless ever again.

There was a moment of sheer joy when he remembered that Barclay Jack's phone was still in his pocket, but the butterfly signal remained elusive. He tried texting too, but it couldn't be sent. The disappointment left him wanting to weep with frustration.

Harry was still hungry, but he was saving the last sandwich in the bag for when Candace woke, so he thought that perhaps the best thing he could do would just be to try to sleep. He curled himself around his sister on the one thin nasty mattress that was in the trailer. She was giving off so much heat that it was like lying next to a radiator. He tried to take his mind off the situation they were in with a reverie of comforting thoughts – buying a packet of tea in Miss Matty's Cranford World front parlour (*Dear Harry, do come in*) or opening his A-level results (*All A stars, Harry! Congratulations*). He was in the middle of fantasizing about what it would be like to be the set designer for a National Theatre production of *The Three Sisters* (one of his favourite plays so far) when he heard the unmistakeable sound of a car engine. He leapt up and looked out of the grimy back window. A car drew up near the gate and a figure climbed out. He recognized the Scottish detective from earlier at the Palace. A kindly policewoman! She was joined by the second detective and the two of them walked over to the mobile home near the gate and knocked on its door.

Harry banged on the window. He jumped up and down and shouted and yelled and banged some more. The field was big and the trailer they were in was a long way away from the policewomen, but nonetheless, surely they could hear him? Candace woke up and started crying, which was good, Harry thought – more noise to attract the detectives' attention. But it was as if the trailer had been soundproofed.

The detectives knocked again on the door of the mobile home and peered through the windows as if they were looking for someone or something. He saw one of them shrug. No, please, no, he thought, don't walk away! He was screaming frantically at them, pummelling the window with his fists, but they were blind and deaf to him. For a glorious moment he thought they had heard him because the Scottish one looked around and seemed to be listening, but then they both seemed to notice something that was out of his line of sight and they disappeared.

They returned a minute later with a girl. They were supporting her, one on either side of her, as if she couldn't walk on her own. They helped her into their car and one of them, the Scottish one, got in the back with her and the other one got in the driving seat and they drove away. Harry dropped to the floor of the trailer and burst into tears. He hadn't known it was possible to feel so wretched. To have hope and then to have it snatched away, surely that was the cruellest thing?

Candace put her arms round his neck and said, 'S'all right, Harry. Don't cry,' even though her eyes were big and wet with her own tears. They sat like that for a while, just hugging each other, and then Harry sniffed and stood up and wiped his nose on his sleeve and said, 'Eat that sandwich, Candace, you're going to need all your strength. We're getting out of here,' and when she'd obediently munched her way through it he said, 'Cover your ears,' and he picked up the little stool and hurled it at the window, again and again. All that banging on it earlier in an effort to get the detectives' attention must have loosened it, because the thick Perspex window fell out in one complete piece and Candace shouted, 'Yay, Harry!' and they both did a little jig of triumph.

'We've got to hurry,' Harry said and lowered Candace out of the window, holding her by her hands until she was almost on the ground before he dropped her. She landed softly on a bed of nettles and hadn't even started crying by the time Harry scrambled out and picked her up.

He ran. A difficult thing to do with a three-year-old child in your arms, especially a nettle-stung one, but sometimes it really was a matter of life and death.

It had grown almost dark by now. They were sitting by the side of a small road that seemed to have no traffic on it, but Harry didn't think he could go any further. He had a signal now and he kept trying Crystal's phone, but she didn't answer. It had taken him for ever to remember her number and he thought that, after all, he must have got it wrong. From now on, he thought, he would memorize all the important numbers in his contacts rather than relying on his phone to do it for him. He couldn't remember his dad's number at all. There was only one other number that Harry knew by heart, so he phoned the next best thing to a parent – Bunny.

As soon as he'd dialled, a car appeared, so Harry cut off the call and jumped around at the side of the road, waving his arms around. He was quite prepared to throw himself in the path of a moving vehicle if that was what it took to get home, but he didn't need to as the car glided slowly to a halt a few feet ahead of them. The rear passenger door was opened by an invisible hand and Harry picked Candace up and ran towards it.

'Thank you for stopping,' Harry said when they had climbed into the car. 'Thank you so much.'

'No problem,' the driver said and the silver BMW drove off into the dark of the countryside.

The Final Curtain

Fee was taking a shortcut. It was a dark alley and the one streetlight was out, but it was familiar territory, she sometimes brought a punter down here for a quickie up against the wall. It stank — there were a couple of big rubbish bins because a fish-and-chip restaurant backed on to the alley. She wasn't working, she was on the way to her dealer, ready to barter with Tina's gold watch, which was hanging loosely on her bony wrist, the safest place for it right now. She would get a fraction of what it was worth, but it would still be more than she could make in a week on the street.

She heard someone entering the alley behind her and picked up the pace. She had a bad feeling, hairs on the back of her neck and so on. She had learned the hard way to trust her gut instinct. There was a light at the end of the alley and she concentrated on that, it was only twenty or thirty steps away. Her breath was tight in her chest. The spiky heels of her boots slipped on the greasy cobbles. She didn't look behind her but she could hear whoever it was getting closer and she tried to run, but her heel caught on the cobbles and she went flying. She was going to die in this dirty place, she thought, just another piece of garbage for someone to pick up in the morning.

'Hello, Felicity,' a voice said. 'We've been looking for you everywhere.'

She wet herself in terror.

❧

The gates of HMP Wakefield opened slowly and an ambulance crawled out. When it hit the main road it started to accelerate and the sirens and lights were switched on, although the occupant, despite the vigorous CPR that was still being applied, was already dead.

The paramedic paused, ready to give up, but the prison nurse who had accompanied the patient in the back took over, pumping hard on prisoner JS 5896's scrawny chest. The warden was keen that everything was done by the book, didn't want anyone accusing them of letting the guy go prematurely. A lot of people would be pleased to see him dead.

The nurse, the burly sort, had found the prisoner when he did his night-time rounds. Michael Carmody was slumped on the floor by the side of his bed, his drip pulled out and oxygen mask yanked off. He looked as if he was trying to get away from something. Death, probably, the nurse concluded. He'd popped into the break room for an illicit fag, but he was pretty sure no one had come into the ward while he wasn't there. He took his vitals, but it was obvious that Carmody was in the process of checking out of the Monster Mansion. There'd have to be an autopsy, of course, but Michael Carmody's death was hardly a surprise.

The nurse paused and the paramedic said, 'He's gone. I'm calling it, okay? Time of death eleven twenty-three. Agreed?'

'Agreed. He was a bastard,' the nurse said. 'Good riddance to bad rubbish.'

'Yeah, a lot of people would agree with that.'

Barclay Jack fumbled on his dressing-table for the tumbler of gin that he was sure had been there a moment ago, but he couldn't find it. It seemed very dark in his dressing room. He shouted for Harry but there was no reply. Where was the idiot boy?

He stumbled out of the dressing room – he really didn't feel well.

Another funny turn. Backstage it was even darker, just a dim light coming from above somewhere. Where was everyone? Had they all gone home and left him here alone?

He found himself unexpectedly standing in the wings. How had he got here? Had he had a bit of a blackout? 'You've probably had a TIA,' he was told last year when he was admitted to the Royal Bournemouth after he collapsed at the checkout in Asda. TIA sounded like an airline, but apparently it meant he'd had a small stroke. Stroke of bad luck. They did a lot of tests, but he didn't tell anyone. Who was there to tell anyway? His daughter hadn't spoken to him in years, he wasn't even sure where she lived now.

They must have accidentally locked him in the theatre. That bloody ASM again, he was supposed to check the place was empty. He searched in his pocket for his phone and remembered he'd lost it.

Then suddenly he was on the stage – another little jump in time, apparently. The curtains were closed. He could sense he was not alone, after all – he could hear the hiss and murmur of expectation out in the auditorium. The audience was waiting. The curtains jerked slowly open and after a second of blackness someone turned his spotlight on. He peered into the dark auditorium, shading his eyes like a man in a crow's nest looking for land. Where was everyone?

Perhaps if he started his set they'd come to life a bit. 'A man goes to the dentist,' he tried, but his voice sounded scratchy. Was it the dentist? Or was it a doctor? Press on. He was a trouper. This was a test. 'And he says I think I've got a problem.' Silence. 'And he says—' He was interrupted by a tremendous roar of laughter, it washed over him like balm. The laughter was followed by wild applause. Fuck me, Barclay thought, I haven't even got to the punchline yet. The invisible audience continued clapping, some of them were on their feet, chanting his name, 'Barclay! Barclay! Barclay!'

Another wave of darkness passed over him, as if the curtain had closed. This time it didn't open again. Barclay Jack couldn't hear the applause any more.

Bunny was in the relatives' room waiting for someone to come and have a word with him about what to do with Barclay Jack's corpse. A comedian corpsing (as it were) indicated a bad joke – the kind that Harry might make – but Bunny was in no mood for levity. He had spent the entire evening chaperoning Barclay on his last journey. The ambulance, A&E, the relatives' room, Bunny had endured them all. He appeared, by default, to have become Barclay Jack's next of kin. It was not a role he would have chosen.

Was he somehow duty-bound to arrange the funeral as well? Would anyone attend? Perhaps some third-rate entertainers from ancient history and the summer acts at the Palace, which was the same thing. The chorus girls would turn out in force, they were good for that kind of thing. They always brought in cake when it was someone's birthday. No more birthdays for Barclay Jack.

Bunny sighed with boredom. There was no one else in the relatives' room, just Bunny, stuck with an electric kettle, a jar of instant coffee and some well-thumbed magazines on a worn veneer coffee table – a couple of copies of *Hello!* from over a year ago and an old Sunday magazine colour supplement. So far he'd drunk several cups of cheap coffee and gleaned a lot of unnecessary information about the Swedish royal family (he hadn't even known that they had one), not to mention how to throw an 'elegant summer barbecue'. Could a barbecue be elegant? Bunny couldn't remember when anyone had last invited him to one, elegant or not.

The ambulance and all the drama of A&E had seemed pointless to Bunny because he was pretty sure that Barclay had already left the planet when the St John Ambulance bloke was applying the defibrillator pads to his grey-haired chest in the crowded corridor outside his dressing room. He'd been helped, but not much, by the ventriloquist, who unexpectedly identified himself as the Palace's official first-aider. 'Barclay!' he kept saying loudly to him. 'Barclay! Barclay!' as if he was calling a dog to come back.

Bunny scrolled idly through the photos on his phone. His only son had recently become a father. The new baby, Theo, had his own Instagram account, to which his daughter-in-law had reluctantly given Bunny access. There had been a christening, just before the start of the summer season. Everything was being done by the trad-itional book for this child – C of E service, full set of godparents, women in silly hats, the top tier of the wedding cake served up at the christening tea. His daughter-in-law was on high alert the whole time. Bunny suspected that she was afraid he would turn up in drag, the evil fairy at the cradle side, cursing her child with his question-able career choices. Of course he hadn't, he'd worn his best Hugo Boss suit and a pair of brogues as polished as his almost bald skull, with not even a trace of Illamasqua foundation on his face.

'It's not that he's a drag queen,' Bunny had overheard his daughter-in-law whisper to someone over the 'quiche fingers'. 'It's that he's such a crap drag queen.'

'Mr Shepherd?'

'Yes?' Bunny jumped up as a nurse entered the room.

'Would you like to sit with Mr Jack for a while?'

Bunny sighed heavily. This must be some kind of etiquette for the dead. More pointlessness. 'Yes, sure,' he said.

He was quietly contemplating Barclay's yellowing sunken features, wondering how long he had to stay before he could make a polite escape, when his phone rang. Bunny looked at the caller ID. It said 'Barclay Jack'. Bunny frowned. He contemplated Barclay again. He was quite silent, the sheet tucked up around his chin. For a moment Bunny wondered if it was some kind of prank, but then Barclay wasn't a prankster. And the entire hospital wouldn't collude in some kind of elaborate *Candid Camera* gag involving a corpse. Would it?

Bunny stared intently at Barclay. No, he concluded, he was def-initely dead. He put his phone cautiously to his ear and said, 'Hello?' but no one answered. 'The rest is silence,' Bunny said to Barclay's corpse, for he was not a stranger to Shakespeare. You had to laugh, he supposed.

Catch of the Day

The *Amethyst* had been out since first light. She was a fishing boat with four Geordies on board. The men always chartered the *Amethyst* and the skipper treated them like old friends. They came two or three times a year and took their fishing seriously, although not so seriously that they hadn't spent the previous evening in the Golden Ball getting plastered, giddily free of domestic duties. Their wives never came on these trips, they remained tethered to their homes further north, grateful to be avoiding the paralysingly tedious subjects of fish, real ale and the competing merits of the A1 and the Tyne Tunnel.

It was set to be a beautiful morning. The sky was full of marshmallow clouds that promised to melt away soon. 'Going to be a lovely day,' someone said, and there were murmurs of happy agreement. A flask of coffee was produced and the contentment settled in for the day.

Their lines were baited with squid. They were looking for big fish – cod, ling, pollock, haddock, maybe even halibut if they were lucky.

The cool morning air had almost succeeded in blowing away the effects of last night's Sam Smith's when the first of them felt a tug on his line. Something big and heavy, yet, oddly, it didn't seem to be struggling to escape capture. When the fisherman peered into the water he could make out the flash of silvery scales. If it was a fish it was enormous, although it was lolling around in the water as if it were already dead. No, not scales, he realized. Sequins. Not a halibut or a haddock – a woman. Or a girl. He yelled for his friends and between them the four managed to hook the dead mermaid and haul her on deck.

Hand of Glory

Out at sea, in the wide mouth of the South Bay, Jackson could see a fishing boat making its way back into harbour. The sea was glassy and reflected the early-morning sun. It looked like a nice day to be out in a boat, he thought. He was taking Dido for her daily constitutional before driving back up the coast to his cottage. He had not gone home last night, instead he had slept in one of the several spare bedrooms at High Haven, having downed a couple of whiskies with Crystal once Harry and Candy had gone to bed. It had been more like medicine than alcohol for both of them, and even if he hadn't had anything to drink he was still riding a tide of exhaustion that would have made climbing back in his car seem impossible. He had fallen asleep with Dido curled on the rug at the foot of the bed and woke to find her stretched out beside him, snoring peacefully in the vast white acreage of the emperor-size bed, her head on the pillow next to him. (*When you last sleep with woman? With real woman?*)

While he drank his coffee, Crystal was drinking a dubious beverage the name of which sounded like something you would shout in a karate class. (*Kombucha!*) Martial arts was something she had taken up, she told him. ('Wing Chun. I know, sounds like something you'd order in a Chinese restaurant.') So were the headbanging moves in the café at Flamborough Head on the Wing Chun curriculum? 'Nah, I just wanted to kill the stupid bugger.'

She cooked sausages for Dido, but all Jackson was offered was buckwheat porridge and almond milk, with the admonition that he should be watching himself at his age. 'Thanks,' Jackson said.

Crystal looked as though she was ready to breakfast on a leg ripped from a cow, but no, a 'raw cacao ball' was the ultimate indulgence for her, apparently. It looked like shit to Jackson, but he kept that opinion to himself in case he found his face mashed into the breakfast table, and instead he ate up his buckwheat porridge like a good boy.

The elusive Tommy Holroyd had not appeared. Jackson was beginning to think Crystal's husband was a figment of her imagination. He wondered what Tommy would have made of a strange man availing himself of his bed and his buckwheat porridge, like an unwanted Goldilocks.

In tribute to the early-morning warmth, Crystal was wearing shorts and a vest top and flip-flops. Jackson could see her bra strap beneath the top and her fantastic legs were on full display. As was her fantastic black eye. 'Here,' she said, dumping the mug of coffee in front of him. Jackson thought that he had never met a woman who was less interested in him.

The Amazon queen sat down opposite him and said, 'I'm not paying you, you know. You've done fuck all.'

'Fair enough,' Jackson said.

When he left High Haven after his workhouse breakfast, both Candy and Harry were still asleep upstairs, worn out by the previous day's events. Harry had sketchily related their exploits before exhaustion got the better of him last night. They had been driven to a field, he said, and been locked in a trailer from which they had subsequently escaped, but Harry had no idea where the trailer was except that it seemed to be near the sea. After they had escaped, a man had given them a lift back to High Haven. He didn't give his name but he was driving a silver car – at least, Harry thought it was silver, it was difficult to tell in the dark, and no, he didn't know what make it was because he had been distressed to the point of collapsing at the time, he said, so could he please be left alone now to go to bed and sleep? And what did it matter anyway as the man had helped them, possibly even saved them. 'He knew my name,' Harry added.

'What do you mean?' Crystal said, frowning.

'He said, "Hop in, Harry." I *know* that was weird and I'm sure you want to discuss it endlessly, but I really do have to go to bed now. Sorry.'

'Don't be sorry, Harry,' Crystal said, kissing him on the forehead. 'You're a hero. Night night.'

'Night. Who *are* you, by the way?' he said to Jackson.

'Just a concerned bystander,' Jackson said. 'I helped your stepmother look for you.'

'You didn't find him though, did you?' Crystal said. 'He found himself. Claims he's a detective,' she said to Harry, 'but he's shit at detecting.'

'What do you make of that?' Jackson had asked Crystal once Harry had dragged himself up the stairs. 'That the guy knew who he was?' (Was it a good thing or a bad thing? Tide in or tide out?)

'I don't make anything of it,' Crystal said. 'I don't *intend* to make anything of anything, and no, you can't look at the footage from our CCTV, because your work here is done. They've made their point. My mouth is shut.' She made an exaggerated zipping motion on those perfect lips and said, 'I'll handle this on my own, thanks, so bugger off, Jackson Brodie.'

After their failure to find Harry and Candy at Flamborough Head, Jackson had driven a defeated Crystal back to High Haven. 'They might call on the house phone,' she said hopefully. 'Or they might bring them back. If they're trying to teach me a lesson they've succeeded, because, believe me, I don't want anything happening to my kids.'

It had been growing dark by the time they arrived at High Haven. Bats were flitting overhead like an aerial escort as they turned into the driveway. A fanfare of lights along the drive came on automatically as the Toyota approached the house. It was an impressive place. Holroyd Haulage must be pretty successful, Jackson reckoned.

He was just reiterating to Crystal that the only course open to her now was to go to the police, and she was just reiterating that he should fuck off, when a security light above the front door snapped on.

Crystal gasped and Jackson said, 'Oh, shit,' because they both saw that something had been deposited on the front doorstep. It looked like a bundle of clothing, but as they drew nearer it took on a human shape. Jackson's heart dropped several floors and he thought, Oh, please, God, not a body. But then the figure stirred and resolved itself into two figures, one larger than the other. The larger figure stood up, blinking in the bright lights. Harry.

Crystal was out of the car before Jackson had hit the brakes, running towards Harry and flinging her arms round him before scooping up Candy from the step.

Jackson climbed stiffly out of the car. It had been a long day.

He took the funicular up to the Esplanade to save Dido's legs, although his knees were grateful as well. When they came out of the cabin at the top Jackson found the *Collier* film unit swarming everywhere. No sign of Julia though, so he made his way to the unit base. He was keen to know when he was going to get his son back. Jackson had texted Nathan several times since he last saw him, asking him how he was. (*How's it going?*) The incident with Harry had made him think about Nathan, and how he would feel if a malevolent stranger drove away with him. He had received just the one curt response to his query. *Good.* How come his son could spend hours chatting about nothing with his friends, but had no conversation whatsoever for his father? Where was Nathan, exactly? Still with his friend, presumably, although, infuriatingly, he had turned off the location services on his phone so that Jackson couldn't track him. He was going to have to give him a lecture about how important it was.

No sign of Julia at the unit base either. He finally tracked down a second AD, a woman Jackson had never come across before, who told him Julia wasn't on set today. Really? Jackson thought. She had said she had no time off at all. 'I expect she's with Nathan,' he said and the AD said, 'Who? No, I think she went off for the day. Rievaulx Abbey, I think she said. With Callum.'

Callum?

Jackson ate a welcome bacon roll in the dining bus. No sign of buckwheat porridge here. Breakfast was always the most popular meal on set, Julia told him. Dido received another sausage from the cook. 'You should be watching yourself at your age,' he said to her.

He was joined by the actor who played Collier – Matt/Sam/Max. Munching his way through an egg roll, the actor said, 'In your expert opinion, what do you think is the best way to kill a dog? I'm supposed to shoot one in a scene soon, but I thought a bit of hand-to-hand combat would be more visceral. Or hand-to-paw, I suppose.'

Jackson had had to kill a dog once, not a memory to dwell on, but he refrained from saying this – not in front of Dido anyway. 'Stick with the gun,' he said. 'God knows, a gun's visceral enough for anyone. Who's this Callum bloke, by the way?' he added casually.

'Julia's boyfriend? He's the new DOP. I think she likes him because he lights her really well.'

Jackson digested this news along with the bacon roll.

More irritating than the appearance of this unexpected person Callum in Julia's life was the fact that she had gone with him to Rievaulx. The Terraces at Rievaulx were one of Jackson's favourite places on earth, it was where he was going to live in the afterlife if there was one. (Unlikely, but he wasn't against hedging his bets. 'Ah, Pascal's Wager,' Julia said mysteriously. Tide in/tide out, Jackson guessed.) In fact, he had introduced Julia to Rievaulx. And now she was introducing someone else to it. Jackson didn't know about Pascal, but he would be willing to bet that she wouldn't tell Callum they were canoodling in her former paramour's favourite place.

He was homeward bound, on Peasholm Road, just passing the entrance to the park, when the ice-cream van appeared, approaching from the opposite direction. A Bassani's van, pink like the last one he had seen and still creakily pumping out the same music. *If you go down to the woods today, you're sure of a big surprise.*

It gave Jackson the chills and started him thinking about all the lost girls over the years. The ones lost in woods, on railway lines, in back alleys, in cellars, in parks, in ditches by the side of the road, in their own homes. So many places you could lose a girl. All the ones he hadn't saved. There was a Patty Griffin song that he played sometimes, 'Be Careful' it was called. *All the girls who've gone astray.* It had the power to make him irreducibly melancholic.

He hadn't thought about his latest lost girl for at least twenty-four hours. The girl with the unicorn backpack. Where was she now? Home safe? Being berated by loving parents for having come back late and for losing her backpack? He hoped so, but his gut told him differently. In his (long) experience, your brain might mislead you, but your gut always told you the truth.

He might have been remiss where the girl was concerned, but there were still people out there who needed him to protect and serve them, whether they liked it or not. The men who had snatched Harry and Candy hadn't voluntarily released them, so what was to stop them going after one or both of them again? Crystal might have said that those perfect lips were zipped, but the kidnappers had no way of knowing that. Should he let sleeping dogs lie? Were they sleeping or were they prowling around waiting to pounce again? His own sleeping dog was in a post-sausage slumber on the back seat and had no opinion on the matter.

He sighed and took the turning for High Haven. He was the shepherd, he was the sheriff. The Lone Ranger. Or Tonto, perhaps. ('You know *tonto* is Spanish for "stupid", don't you?' Julia said.) He might be shit at being the shepherd, but sometimes he was all there was. 'Heigh-ho, Silver,' he murmured to the Toyota.

Women's Work

Ronnie and Reggie stayed the night at the hospital, in the small side ward where the girl they had found had been berthed. Someone ought to keep guard over her and no else seemed to be available. In fact, they were having a hard time garnering any kind of police concern about her, even though she had been beaten up and had heroin in her system, according to the doctor.

The duty sergeant had almost laughed when they phoned in last night. They were too 'resource poor', he said, to come out and interview the girl, and they would just have to wait until the morning like everyone else.

'Another transfusion of coffee?' Ronnie asked and Reggie sighed an assent. The hospital coffee machine was up for an award for the world's worst coffee (quite a competitive field), but they had completely replaced their blood with it by now so one more paper cup wasn't going to have much more effect.

The girl had been half-naked when they spotted her cowering in a corner of the field last night. She was covered in bruises and had a badly swollen lip, but mostly she had just been terrified. Muddy and scratched by thorns and brambles, her appearance, not to mention her demeanour, gave the impression that she'd been hunted, running through fields and ditches and hedges to escape. Like prey. It was the kind of ghoulish plotline you got on something like *Criminal Minds* or *Collier*, not in real life. And yet here she was anyway, the one that got away.

All thoughts of looking for Stephen Mellors went out of their heads when she appeared, not that there was any sign of him in that field anyway. There had been a couple of old trailers — total rust buckets — as well as a newer mobile home, but no one answered when they knocked on its door. All the blinds were drawn and it was impossible to tell what went on inside it. Stephen Mellors practising mindfulness seemed unlikely.

They had concluded that it was probably some kind of glitch in the GPS on Jamie Mellors' phone and that Stephen Mellors was already en famille, chowing down on lasagne and chugging back his breath-taking red. Reggie had once located Sai in the middle of the English Channel, although he had turned out to be in a pub in Brighton when she phoned him to check. 'Are you stalking me?' he laughed, but that was when they were together and he found the idea of stalking cute, not sinister, which was what it became later, apparently.

They had got as far as a name with the girl — Maria — and had managed to ascertain that she was from the Philippines. It took much longer for it to dawn on them that the 'Maria' she kept repeating so agitatedly wasn't herself. Ronnie, reduced to pidgin English, pointed at herself and said, 'Ronnie, I'm Ronnie,' and then pointed at Reggie and said, 'Reggie,' and finally pointed at the girl and raised the questioning eyebrow.

'Jasmine.'

'Jasmine?' Ronnie repeated and the girl nodded vigorously.

There was another name that she also kept repeating. They couldn't decipher it properly but it could have been 'Mr Price'.

'Did Mr Price do this to you?' Reggie asked, pointing at the girl's face.

'Man,' she said, and raised her hand above her head.

'Big man?' Ronnie said. More vigorous nodding, but then she started crying and talking about Maria again She made an odd dumb show of tugging on something invisible around her neck. If they had been playing charades, Reggie might have guessed 'The Hanging Gardens of Babylon', but she was pretty sure that wasn't what Jasmine was miming. She and Sai had played charades a lot, just the two of them. There had been a lot of wholesome, innocent fun in their relationship, childish sometimes even. Reggie missed that more than she missed all the other stuff. Or sex, as it was also known.

They had put in a request for a translator but weren't holding out much hope, certainly not until office hours kicked in. Ronnie went off to scour the hospital and came back with a Filipino woman, a cleaner – with a name badge that said 'Angel' – and asked her to talk to Jasmine for them. As soon as they began to talk a torrent of words flowed from Jasmine, accompanied by a lot more crying. You didn't need to speak Tagalog to know that it was a wretched tale she was telling.

Unfortunately, before they were able to glean any real information, a dark presence chose that moment to darken the doorway of the side ward.

'Hey up, it's Cagney and Lacey.'

'DI Marriot,' Reggie said brightly.

'Have you heard the news about your boyfriend?'

'Boyfriend?' Reggie echoed. Marriot couldn't possibly mean Sai, could she?

'Michael Carmody?' Ronnie hazarded.

'And the prize goes to the girl in blue.'

'What about him?' Reggie asked.

'Dead,' Marriot said succinctly. 'Last night.'

'Murdered?' Reggie and Ronnie asked in unison, but the DI shrugged and said, 'Heart attack, as far as anyone can make out. He won't be missed. Is this your girl?' she asked, nodding at Jasmine. She sounded sympathetic, Reggie gave her Brownie points for that. Not that she'd ever been a Brownie, something she regretted now, she would have made a good one. ('You *are* a Brownie, Reggie,' Ronnie said. 'Right down to your fingertips.')

'Where's she from?' Marriot asked.

'The Philippines,' Reggie said. 'She speaks hardly any English.'

'Fresh off the boat and straight into a massage parlour?'

'I don't know. This lady, Angel, is translating for us.'

'Well, it so happens we've got another dead Asian lass on our hands,' Marriot said, ignoring Angel. 'Found last night. Dumped at sea, I'm afraid. No ID. Looks like she was strangled, still waiting on the autopsy. It's like buses, you wait ages for one dead foreign sex worker and then . . .'

Reggie took back the Brownie points, 'Ours isn't dead,' she said, 'and you don't know she's a sex worker.'

'She's a woman,' Ronnie added. 'And she needs help.'

'Yeah, hashtag MeToo,' Marriot said. 'Anyway, dead or alive, she's not yours any more, we're taking her. You can get back to your sleuthing.'

They said goodbye to Jasmine. She clung on to Reggie's hand and said something that Reggie thought must be goodbye in Tagalog, but Angel said, 'No, she said thank you.'

'Oh, by the way,' Ronnie said to Marriot as they were leaving the ward, 'you might find your "dead Asian lass" is called Maria.'

'Wow. Gender and racial stereotyping all in one go,' Ronnie murmured as they left the ward.

'Yeah, bonanza,' Reggie said.

Just before Marriot had appeared and ejected them, Jasmine had paused for a drink of water. She had to sip it through a straw because of her split lip and they used the brief hiatus to ask Angel if Jasmine had said anything useful yet about what had happened to her.

'She say same things again and again.'

'I know,' Reggie said. 'Maria and Mr Price.'

'Yes, and something else. I don't know what. Sound like "siller-burtches"?'

'Angel,' Ronnie said.

'It's a popular name in the Philippines,' Reggie said. 'It would be funny, wouldn't it, if it wasn't her name – if it was her job. Perhaps after you've earned your first angel badge you work your way up, rise through the nine ranks of angels and retire at the top of your profession as one of the seraphim. I like the idea of having a badge that says "Angel". Or a warrant card. "DC Ronnie Dibicki and Angel Reggie Chase. We'd just like to ask you a few questions. Nothing to worry about." Of course, you can be an angel as well. Angel Ronnie Dibicki.'

'You've had too much coffee, sunshine. You need to lie down in a dark room. Hang on.' Ronnie put a hand on Reggie's arm and held her back. 'Look. Isn't that the drag act from the Palace?'

A man was standing at the reception desk filling out some paperwork. Dressed in jeans and a grey sweatshirt and a pair of moccasin shoes that had seen better days, he was virtually unrecognizable from the grotesque parody of a woman from yesterday. He looked as if he ought to be mowing his lawn and discussing the best route to Leeds over the garden fence.

'Wonder what he's doing here?'

'Sillerburtches? Silver birches, do you think?' Reggie puzzled as they made their way back to the car.

'As in trees?'

Ronnie trawled through the more abstruse outer circles of the internet on her iPhone. 'All I can find is something in the *Scarborough News* from years ago. Silver Birches was a nursing home, closed after some kind of scandal – followed by a court case, I think. Mistreatment of residents, inadequate facilities, blah, blah, blah. It had a long local history, apparently, started life as a mental hospital, a showcase of Victorian reform. There's a suggestion that it was the model for the mental asylum where the character Renfield was incarcerated. Renfield?'

'He's a character in Bram Stoker's *Dracula*,' Reggie said.

'Oh, yeah, it says that next. "Bram Stoker's visit to Whitby was the inspiration for . . ." blah-blah-blahdy-blah. It's not far from here – shall we swing by? Even though it's absolutely nothing to do with us and Marriot would give us a right bollocking if she thought we'd gone rogue.'

'No harm in a quick shufti though,' Reggie said.

'No, no harm at all. It'll just take five minutes.'

Be the Wolf

Vince was dry-eyed with sleeplessness by the time the first light seeped through his thin curtains. The dawn chorus had cranked up before it was even dawn. Someone should have a word with the birds about their timing. It was a surprise to Vince to think that there even were birds where he was living. He wondered if they had to sing louder to hear each other above the racket of the amusement arcade. He wondered, too, if he would ever sleep properly again. Whenever he closed his eyes he could see her. The girl.

Five minutes inside was all it had taken yesterday. There was an entrance foyer in which there was still evidence of Silver Birches' former life as some kind of nursing facility – fire doors and exit signs and a couple of old Health and Safety notices about keeping doors locked and getting visitors to sign in. On the walls there lingered a limp piece of paper with a typewritten request for more volunteers to help with an outing to Peasholm Park, alongside a small, time-weathered poster announcing a *summer fête*, decorated with (badly) hand-drawn pictures of balloons, a tombola, a cake. The thought of confused, senile old people being jollied along like children with balloons and cake made Vince feel even more depressed than he already was. If that were possible. Better to go over a cliff than to live out the scrag-end of your life in a place like this.

He pushed his way through one of the wired-glass fire doors on the ground floor and found himself in a corridor. The corridor was lined with doors, all of which were closed except for one that stood wide open like an invitation. Inside the small room were two old hospital bed frames on which lay bare filthy mattresses.

There was only one occupant of the room – a girl. A girl who lay crumpled and lifeless on the floor beneath one of the barred windows. There was a thin scarf round her neck, knotted tightly. The ends of the scarf had been cut just above the knot and the remainder of the scarf was still tied to one of the window bars. Her face was swollen and purple. It was a pretty self-explanatory scene.

She was a speck of a thing, Thai or Chinese or something. She was wearing a cheap silver sequinned dress revealing legs covered with bruises and was quite obviously dead, but Vince crouched down and checked her pulse anyway. When he stood up he felt so dizzy he thought he might faint and he had to hold on to the door jamb for a few seconds to steady himself.

He left the room, backing out and closing the door quietly. It was the nearest he could get to a gesture of respect for the dead. In a daze, he tried the other doors in the corridor but they were all locked. He wasn't sure – because his brain seemed suddenly untrustworthy – but he thought he could hear noises from behind the doors: a soft moan, a little sob, small scuffling, snuffling sounds as if mice were in the rooms. It was the kind of place that Vince thought of as existing in other countries, not this one. The kind of place you read about in the newspaper, not the kind of place that someone you had known most of your life had 'business' in.

He could hear a man's voice coming from somewhere at the back of the building and he followed the thread of sound like a sleep-walker. It led him to the large back door. It was a double door, accessorized with all kinds of bolts and locks, but its wings were standing wide open to reveal the concreted back yard beyond. Tommy was framed in the diptych of light. Vince's heart sank. Tommy. He was talking to his dog, the big Rottweiler, Brutus, that put the wind up Vince. He was being loaded by Tommy into his Nissan Navara. Sitting in the passenger seat was the Russian bloke who worked in Tommy's yard. Vadim? Vasily? More of a brute than Brutus. The dog looked eager, as if it were about to set out on a hunt.

Vince stepped into the yard. The bright sun dazzled after the chill of the darkness inside. He had forgotten what summer was. He had forgotten what daylight was. He had forgotten everything except for the girl's discoloured, swollen face. Tommy caught sight of him and said, 'Vince?' He was staring at him as if he'd just met him and was trying to assess him as friend or enemy.

Vince's mouth was so dry that he didn't think he could speak, but he managed to bleat, 'There's a girl back there.' His voice sounded odd to his ears, as if it was coming from a place far away, not from inside him. 'She's dead. I think she hung herself. Or hanged,' he corrected himself absently, although why he was worrying about grammar at a time like this was beyond him. He waited to hear Tommy give a reasonable explanation for the circumstances they found themselves in, but Tommy explained nothing, he just kept staring at Vince. He'd been a boxer once. Vince supposed he knew how to psych his opponent out before the fight began.

Finally Tommy growled, 'What the fuck are you doing here, Vince?'

'I came with Steve,' he managed. That much was true. The sun was dazzling, like a spotlight aimed at him. He'd walked on-stage and found himself in the wrong play, one he didn't know the words to.

'Steve!' Tommy yelled without looking round.

Steve appeared from around the corner of an old outhouse or garage. The yard was surrounded by an assortment of semi-derelict buildings. Steve was in a hurry and didn't spot Vince at first. 'What is it?' he said. 'Because you need to get a move on, Tommy, she's going to be miles away by now. Have you phoned Andy?' In reply, Tommy silently tilted his head in Vince's direction.

'Vince!' Steve said, as if he'd forgotten about him. 'Vince, Vince, Vince,' he repeated softly, smiling regretfully. He might have been talking to a child who had disappointed him. 'I told you to stay in the car, didn't I? You shouldn't be here.' Where should I be if not here? Vince wondered.

'What's going on?' Tommy snapped at Steve.

'I don't know,' Steve said. 'Why don't we ask Vince?' He drew nearer to Vince and put his arm around his shoulder. Vince had to suppress the instinct to flinch. 'Vince?' Steve prompted him.

Time felt as if it was standing still. The bright sun fixed in the sky was never going to move again. Steve, Tommy and Andy. The Three Musketeers. Everything fell into place. It wasn't entertaining enough for the universe that he had lost his job and his house, or that he was under suspicion for murdering his wife, for God's sake. No, now he had to discover that his friends (*golfing* friends, it was true) were involved in something that was – what *were* they involved in, exactly? Keeping sex slaves? Trafficking women? Were the three of them psychopathic serial killers who by chance had found they had the same taste for murdering women? At that moment all bets, however outlandish, were off to Vince.

He hadn't realized that he'd voiced any of these thoughts aloud until Steve said, 'Traffic's just another word for the buying and selling of commodities, Vince. It says so in the *Oxford English Dictionary*.' Vince was pretty sure the dictionary had other definitions of it too. 'Profit with no loss,' Steve added. 'Plenty of money in the bank and always more to come. Do you know what that feels like, Vince?'

The sun was dazzling his brain. He closed his eyes and breathed in the heat. He was in a new world now.

It was suddenly very clear to Vince. There was no meaning to anything. No morality. No truth. It was pointless for him to object if there was no longer any consensus about what was right or wrong. It was something you had to decide for yourself. Whichever side you chose, there would be no repercussions from divine authority. You were on your own.

'Vince?' Steve prompted.

'No, Steve,' Vince answered eventually. 'I don't know what that feels like. I imagine it feels pretty good, actually.'

He laughed suddenly, startling Steve into removing his arm from Vince's shoulder. 'I *knew* you three were up to something!' Vince said triumphantly. 'It all makes sense to me now. You secretive buggers, you might have let me in on it.' Vince grinned, first at Tommy and then at Steve. 'Room for a fourth musketeer?'

Steve clapped him on the back and said, 'Good man. Great to have you on board, Vince. I knew you'd get here eventually.'

⁓

The digital bedside clock said 5.00 a.m. He may as well get up. He had a lot to do today. It felt good to have a purpose for a change.

Blood Poisoning

'Kippers.'

'What?'

'Can you pop into Fortune's this morning and pick up kippers?'

'Kippers?'

'Jesus, Andrew. Yes, kippers. I'm not speaking a foreign language.' (She may as well have been.) 'For tomorrow's breakfasts. The couple in Biscay asked especially for them.'

Andy had got home just after five in the morning after being out all night with Tommy looking for Jasmine, their runaway. And failing to find her. Where was she? Picked up by the police and spilling the beans on them all? He was hoping to make a silent re-entry, but the larkish Rhoda was already up.

'Where've you been?' she asked.

'Went for an early-morning walk,' he bluffed.

'Walk?' she said disbelievingly.

'Yes, walk. I've decided to get fit.'

'You?'

'Yes, me,' he said patiently. 'Wendy's death's made me realize how precious life is.' He could tell that she didn't buy any of it. He didn't blame her. And anyway, what was precious about life? It was a throw-away thing, a bit of paper and rags. He thought of Maria, lifeless like a toy, broken beyond repair. Tiny as a bird that had fallen from the nest before its time. His first thought was that she must have over-dosed. Or been slapped around too much. 'Hung herself, the stupid bitch,' Tommy said.

'You're sure you haven't been out on the boat?' Rhoda said. 'You smell . . . odd.'

I smell of death, Andy thought. And despair. He was feeling sorry for himself.

They hadn't just been trying to find one girl, they had been trying to lose another. 'The other one got away,' Tommy had told him when he'd arrived last night at Silver Birches with the Polish girls and found that Maria had killed herself.

'Jasmine?'

'Whatever. We've been out looking for her for hours with no joy. You're going to have to help. And we have to get rid of the dead one.'

'Maria.'

Andy kept a little boat down in the marina, nothing much, a skip with an outboard motor (the *Lottie*) that he took out fishing occasionally. Tommy came out sometimes, always wearing a lifejacket because he couldn't swim. Unmanned him a bit, in Andy's opinion.

Under cover of darkness they had put Maria in Tommy's Navara and then transferred her to the *Lottie* and chugged out into the North Sea. When there was a decent distance between the boat and the shore they picked Maria up – Tommy by the shoulders, Andy by the feet – a sparrow-weight, and swung her overboard. A shimmer of silver in the moonlight, slick as a fish, and she was gone.

Shouldn't they have weighted her down with something? 'She'll just float back up, won't she?' Andy said.

'Probably,' Tommy said, 'but who's going to give a shit? She'll just be one more Thai druggie whore. Who's going to care?'

'She was from the Philippines, not Thailand.' And her name was Maria. A Catholic, too. Andy had taken the crucifix from around her small neck after he'd unwound what was left of the scarf that she'd hanged herself with. He put it in his pocket. The scarf was a flimsy thing, but it had done the job. Tommy had sawed through it with his Stanley knife, but he'd got to her too late. Andy recognized the scarf as the one she'd bought in Primark in Newcastle yesterday. Seemed like a lifetime ago – certainly was for Maria. He untied the remnant that remained knotted around the window bars, treating it with the tenderness befitting a relic, and reunited it with the other piece in his pocket.

After they'd tipped her into the sea, Andy threw the crucifix in after her and said a silent prayer. For a brief moment he considered pushing Tommy out of the boat too, but the lifejacket would save him. With his luck he would bob around until the lifeboat found him or a foundlands were built for, paddling their strong legs through the waves to drag things – people, boats – back to shore. Lottie wasn't here though, only Brutus, Tommy's dog, asleep in the Navara.

'Foxy?'

'Yeah.'

'Can you turn this thing around now instead of daydreaming?'

Tommy was mystified as to how the girls had got out of the plastic ties that attached their wrists to the bed. And why did one stay and one go? Andy wondered. Did Jasmine wake up and find that Maria had killed herself and then run, or did Maria kill herself because Jasmine had deserted her? He supposed he would never know.

Jasmine was tougher than she looked, Andy reckoned. Where would she go? What would she do? He remembered the happy expression on the girls' faces when they were watching *Pointless*, their squeals of delight in the supermarket. He felt suddenly, violently sick and had to hang on to the edge of the boat while he heaved his guts out into the North Sea.

'Didn't know you got seasick, Andy,' Tommy said.

'Must be something I ate.'

And Vince! 'What the fuck, Tommy?' Andy had said when Tommy recounted what had happened at Silver Birches in his absence. One girl dead, one girl absconded, and Vince Ives suddenly being brought into the fold by Steve. The police suspected him of murdering his wife, for God's sake. He was going to bring all kinds of unwanted attention their way.

'Oh, come on, Foxy, Vince didn't kill Wendy. He hasn't got it in him.'

'But he's got *this* in him?' Andy asked as they'd heaved Maria over the side of the boat.

'Well, I'm not particularly chuffed about three becoming four either, but if it keeps him quiet . . . And Steve vouches for him.'

'Oh, that's all right, then,' Andy said sarcastically, 'if *Steve* vouches for him.'

As soon as they were off the boat, Steve was on the phone.

'Steve. How's it going?'

'Andy, how are you?' (He never waited for an answer.) 'I think it's best, given the circumstances, that we move all the girls out first thing, transport them to the place in Middlesbrough. Close down the op at Silver Birches.' You would think he'd been in the military, the way he spoke. And he was the captain and they were the lowly foot soldiers.

Andy imagined freeing the girls, opening the door, throwing off their chains of slavery and watching them run across a wildflower meadow like wild horses.

'Andy, are you listening to me?'

'Yeah, sorry, Steve. We'll start getting them loaded up first thing.'

Cranford World

'Are you all right?' Bunny said. 'You missed last night's performance.'

'Was Barclay cross with me?' Harry asked.

'No, not cross, pet. He can't be cross, he can't be anything, he's dead.'

'Dead?'

'As a dodo.'

'Right,' Harry said, trying to absorb this unexpected news.

'Sorry to be blunt. It was a massive heart attack. He was dead before he got to the hospital.'

Harry was shocked by the news of Barclay's death, but he wasn't entirely surprised by it. After all, Barclay hadn't exactly been the picture of health, but still . . . 'Shall I tidy up his dressing room a bit?' he said, at a loss as to how to proceed. That's what people did after a death, didn't they? Tidied up a bit. After his mother died he remembered her sister, who was someone they hardly ever saw, arriving to go through her things. Harry had tried to help his aunt, but it had been too overwhelming to see his mother's clothes being piled up on the bed and her jewellery box being sorted through in a rather callous manner. ('Look at these bracelets. She never had great taste, did she?')

It was presumed that Harry would want none of his mother's things. Perhaps that was why he had so few memories of her. It was objects, wasn't it, that bound you to someone's history? A hair-clip or a shoe. Kind of like a talisman. (A post-Dangerfield word he had learned recently.) When he thought about it now, he realized that was the last time he had seen his mother's sister. 'They weren't close,' his

276

father said. Perhaps they would say that about him and Candace when they grew up. He hoped not. There were so few people in Harry's world that he intended to keep them all as close as possible. Harry's World, he thought. What kind of an attraction would that be? No vampires, for sure, or pirates for that matter, just lots of books, pizza, TV. What else? Crystal and Candace. And what about his mother? He felt duty-bound to bring her back to life in his World. What if that meant she was a zombie though? And would she get on with Crystal? He realized he had forgotten to include his father. How would he manage with two wives? And then there was Tipsy, of course, he would probably have to choose between her and Brutus. *Et tu, Brute*, he thought. Harry had played Portia, Brutus's wife, in Miss Dangerfield's 'gender-blind' production of *Julius Caesar*. Emily had relished being Caesar. She had the soul of a dictator. She would push her way into his fantasy World too, if he wasn't careful. Harry was not unaware that his mind was quietly unravelling.

'Knock yourself out,' Bunny said, interrupting Harry's thoughts.

Knock himself out doing what? Harry wondered.

'His dressing room's a complete tip.'

Harry realized, rather shamefacedly, that he'd already forgotten that Barclay was dead.

'Yeah, it is,' he agreed. 'It won't be very nice for whoever's going to take over from Mr Jack to find it like that. Have they got someone yet?'

'There was talk of trying to get Jim Davidson. But not in time for the matinée. Yours truly's going to step in. Top of the bill, eh, pet?'

Hadn't Bunny ever been top of the bill before?

'Oh, yeah, but you know, shit cabaret, shit gay clubs, shit hen nights. And now – ta-daa! – the shit Palace.'

'Better than being dead, I suppose,' Harry said.

'Not necessarily, pet. Not necessarily.'

The dressing room smelt of cigarettes, even though smoking was strictly forbidden in the theatre, and Harry did indeed find an over-flowing ashtray stashed in one of the drawers of the dressing-table, which seemed like the worst kind of fire hazard. A half-empty bottle of Lidl's own-brand gin didn't even bother to try and hide it-self. Harry took a swig from the bottle in the hope that it might perk him up a bit or settle him down – one or the other, he didn't really know how he was feeling. He'd never taken drugs, just the odd drag on someone else's joint at a party (it made him feel sick), but he was beginning to see why so many of the kids in his school took stuff – not the Hermiones, they were as puritanical in their attitude to 'substance abuse' as they were towards everything else. Now he found himself craving something to blur the memories of the last twenty-four hours.

His adventures with Pinky and Perky yesterday had left Harry feeling disoriented. And now Barclay's sudden death, coming hard on the heels of his own kidnapping, made everything seem uncertain and slippery, as if the world had tilted slightly. Every so often he got a flashback to the horror of yesterday. *I know what your fucking name is.* He was sure he could still taste the Irn-Bru, sickly in his mouth. The next time he heard 'Let It Go' there was a chance his head would explode. He probably had PTSD or something. And nobody had even tried to give a satisfactory explanation of what had happened, of why two extremely unpleasant men had plucked him and his sister out of their lives and held them captive in an old trailer. For what reason? Money? Had they asked Crystal or his dad for a ransom? And if so, how much were they worth? he wondered. Or, to be more specific, how much was Candace worth? ('Priceless, both of you,' Crystal said.) Why had no one called the police? And who *was* the man who was hanging around with Crystal?

Just a concerned bystander, he'd said. *I helped your stepmother look for you.*

You found yourself, Crystal had said. Technically speaking, the man in the silver BMW had found him (*Hop in, Harry*), but Harry knew what she meant. Would they try to snatch them again? And what would Candace do if they took her on her own, with no one to make it seem as if it was just a harmless game? No one to tell her the story of Cinderella and Red Riding Hood and all the other fairy tales that Harry had entertained his sister with yesterday. No one to provide a happy ending for her.

He sat on the stool at Barclay's dressing-table and stared in the mirror. It was weird to think that Barclay had been here yesterday, sitting at this very dressing-table, looking in this very mirror, daubing himself with foundation, and now the mirror was empty, which sounded like the title of an Agatha Christie novel. Harry had read them all last summer while at his post in Transylvania World.

Harry didn't think he looked like himself at all. At least, he consoled himself, he *had* a reflection. He hadn't joined the undead like Barclay.

Jackson Brodie had a dog, an old Labrador with soft ears. Harry didn't know why that dog suddenly came into his mind – thinking about Brutus and Tipsy, he supposed – and even more mystifying was the fact that the thought of the old Labrador caused him, without any warning, to burst into tears.

The magician chose that moment to put his head round the door. 'Christ, Harry,' he said, 'I didn't know you liked that bastard Barclay so much. Are you all right?' he added gruffly. 'Shall I get one of the chorus girls?'

'No. Thanks,' Harry snivelled. 'I'm fine. I just had a bad day yesterday.'

'Welcome to *my* world.'

The magician must have gone off and fetched Bunny to come and console him, because he appeared a couple of moments later looking concerned and bearing a mug of tea and a Blue Riband biscuit. 'You can hang around with me if you want, pet. I could do with a hand with my costumes. I've got a lot of sequins need replacing. They're always falling off. Some days it looks as if I sweat glitter. That's showbusiness for you.'

Tonto

There was no sign of Snow White and her Ninja mother at High Haven. The place was lifeless, or certainly appeared lifeless. No sign of the Evoque, of course. Given her avoidance of the police, Jackson wondered if Crystal had reported it stolen. It was probably lying burnt-out in a field somewhere. The Holroyds would have more than one car to their name, he presumed. There were two big garages on the property – converted from stables, by the look of them – and both were closed and impenetrable.

There was a dilapidated building that had resisted conversion, some kind of outhouse, or a wash house perhaps as there was still an old copper boiler in the corner, unused for decades. The place was full of cobwebs and on a wall inside someone had chalked *The Batcave* and drawn a cartoon of a vampire bat dressed in a Dracula cloak holding a protest sign that read, *Leave the fucking bats in peace.* It was signed 'HH' so Jackson presumed it was Harry who had drawn it. It was quite good, the boy had talent.

He was a funny kid, Jackson reflected, older than Nathan and yet in some ways he seemed more of a child. (*A bit young for his age*, Crystal had said. *Also old for his age.*) Nathan regarded himself as cool, Harry definitely didn't come into that category.

It took a while for Jackson to register that the drawing might be referring to actual bats. Gazing up at the rafters he realized that he was looking at a roosting cluster of tiny grey bodies hanging like dusty washing on a line. They didn't seem as if they were planning to suck his blood so he left them in peace.

Was Harry with Crystal? he wondered. The sight of the bats

jogged his memory – the Dracula place on the front. He had wondered at the time why she had abandoned Candy there, entering with her, exiting without her, but then later she had told him that Harry worked there.

Transylvania World, that was what it was called. ARE YOU PREPARED TO BE SCAREDB As taglines went, it was rubbish. It was where he had followed Crystal to yesterday.

Was Harry safe? (Was anyone?) Was there someone keeping an eye on him? Leaving him in peace?

There was a girl manning the attraction – if that wasn't a contradiction in terms. She was a rather superior sort of girl who looked as though she might object to that assignation of gender to a verb. She had her nose in a copy of *Ulysses*. (*The Girl with Her Nose in a Book* – another Scandinavian crime novel Jackson never wanted to read.) Jackson had opened a copy of *Ulysses* once and looked inside, which is a different thing to reading. Harry always had his head in a book, Crystal had told him yesterday when he'd asked, 'What's Harry like, then?' in an attempt to assess the boy's survival instincts. No chance of Nathan being swallowed by books like Harry and his friends. He wouldn't even go near one without shuddering. His translated, simplified copy of the *Odyssey* that he was supposed to be reading had barely been opened. Odysseus and Ulysses were the same person, weren't they? Just a man trying to get home.

Did the girl reading *Ulysses* know where Harry Holroyd was?

'Harry?' she said, removing her nose (also rather superior) from the book and giving him a suspicious once-over.

'Yes, Harry,' Jackson said, standing his ground.

'Who's asking?'

So much for manners, Jackson thought. 'A friend of his stepmother's. Crystal.'

The girl made a funny little moue that seemed to indicate she wasn't impressed by this information, but, reluctantly, she gave up Harry's whereabouts. 'He's got a matinée at the Palace.'

Harry had a stage act? Jackson puzzled to himself. But of course, it was the Palace Theatre that he had been coming out of yesterday with his sister and his mother before the all-hell-let-loose scenario kicked in.

'Thanks.'

'Sure I can't sell you a ticket to Transylvania?' the girl said. *'Are you prepared to be scared?'* she deadpanned.

'This world's scary enough, thanks,' Jackson said.

'Yeah, I know, it's like the Wild West out there,' the girl muttered, her nose already back in the book.

The Tree of Knowledge

It had been so late by the time they had unravelled the events of the day that Crystal had suggested to Jackson Brodie that he should stay the night at High Haven. Tommy's expensive malt whisky had been a factor too, of course. Neither of them was a serious drinker and the whisky swiftly did its job of temporarily numbing the trauma of the kidnapping, and the pair of them – plus Brodie's dog – had shuffled up the stairs afterwards like zombies to their respective beds.

Tommy had come home in the early hours. The unmistakeable sound of the Navara pulling into the driveway had woken Crystal and she had listened to the garage door opening and closing, followed by Tommy banging about downstairs, doing God knows what. All went quiet for a while and then he appeared suddenly at the side of the bed – she could tell he was making a futile effort to be quiet – and gave her a kiss on the forehead. He smelt the way he did when he'd been out in Andy Bragg's boat – diesel oil and something brackish like seaweed. She had murmured a greeting, feigning sleepiness, and he'd whispered, 'I've got a few things on today. I'll see you later, love.'

She wondered how he would have felt if he had known there was a strange man and a dog tucked away out of sight in one of the spare bedrooms. Despite her conclusions about Jackson Brodie's general incompetence, Crystal felt safer with his presence in the house, although she would never have admitted that to him.

Once upon a time, Tommy had been the solution for Crystal.

Now he was the problem. *You were before Tommy's time with them*, Fee had said. Tommy had no idea about his youthful shared history with Crystal. It would be funny, wouldn't it – funny peculiar, not funny ha ha, as Harry would say – if for a moment in time in those bad old days their paths had crossed, slipping past each other like sliding doors. One of them into that life, one of them out of it. Tommy might even have arrived in Bridlington on the same train that she had left on. Perhaps they'd walked past each other on the station platform, him all cocky with his new job with Bassani and her with her cheap Miss Selfridge handbag stuffed with Carmody's dirty money. Crystal running away from her past with Bassani and Carmody, Tommy running towards his future with them. But then she remembered that he said he'd got his first motorbike when he was seventeen. 'My first set of wheels.' And just look at him now. He was all wheels. Wheels spinning everywhere.

She thought about that second phone. *Fresh stock due to dock at 4.00 am . . . Consignment on its way to Huddersfield . . . Unloaded cargo in Sheffield, boss. No problems.*

Haulage, Fee had said. *That's the nice word for it.*

Nothing to do with the trucks at all, or the cargo they carried. Tommy was dealing in a different kind of trade.

Which was worse – Bassani and Carmody's old regime of abuse and manipulation or the cold-blooded lies of Anderson Price Associates? Apples and oranges. Two sides of the coin. Pleasure and business. Tommy, Andy, Stephen Mellors, they had all worked for Bassani and Carmody after she got on that train that took her away from them. Tommy had been young, almost a kid himself, when he hooked up with Bassani and Carmody. Did that make him less to blame in some ways? He had been a bit of muscle for them, someone who could lean on people and keep them in line, keep things running smoothly for the big men at the top. Now *he* was one of the big men at the top and blamelessness didn't come into it.

Crystal heard Tommy leave, in the S-Class this time, by the sound of it. A man getting a fresh horse to ride out on. The house settled back down into sleep, but within its walls Crystal remained wide awake. High Haven. A haven was a safe harbour. Not any more.

What a wally. Didn't he realize that she could see him on the CCTV? Jackson Brodie was nosing around outside. He even disappeared into the old wash house for several minutes. God knows what he was doing in there, he'd better not be disturbing the bats, Harry would be very upset. Harry had woken up late and insisted on going to work at the theatre this afternoon, even though the idea of him being out and about made her nervous. 'Once you're inside, don't leave,' she said. 'Get that big trans bloke to keep an eye on you.'

'I don't think he's trans,' Harry said.

'Whatever. I'll come in and pick you up later.'

She gave him a lift to the bus stop and saw him on to the bus and then tracked him all the way on her phone. He had been surprised to be reunited with his own phone, even more surprised that it had journeyed to Flamborough Head without him. 'Who *were* those men?' he said with a frown as they waited for the bus to come into view.

'I don't know, Harry,' she said. 'I think it was maybe a case of mistaken identity.'

'But why wouldn't you call the police?'

'Didn't need to, did I? Look, here comes your bus.'

As the bus sailed away with Harry safely on the top deck, she held Candy up so she could wave goodbye to him. He wasn't stupid, he was never going to stop asking questions. Perhaps she should tell him the truth about everything. Truth was such a novel idea to Crystal that she found herself still staring after the bus had disappeared up the road.

And here was Jackson Brodie back, trying the doorbell again. Crystal watched him in close-up on the little screen on the entry-phone system. He had a shifty look about him. He thought he was being helpful, but really his presence just made things more complicated. Mostly because, like Harry, he never stopped asking questions.

Crystal had kicked him out this morning as swiftly as she could, but you could tell he was like a dog with a bone now, not willing to let things go, and lo and behold, she was right, because here he was sniffing around as if he might find her hiding somewhere on the property.

He gave up eventually and she listened to him drive off, leaving her free to make plans. It was going to be a busy day.

Showtime!

The yellow and black crime-scene tape that had wrapped Thisldo was still there, although it had come loose in several places and was flapping about with a life of its own. There was an air of desolation about the house, as if it had been standing empty for years rather than days.

Vince was supposed to be going in for another police interview this morning. Perhaps they planned to arrest him today. Inspector Marriot was going to be disappointed not to see him, but he had better things to do with his time.

There was no sign of the police at the house, so Vince used his key to open the front door. He felt like a burglar even though it was still his house, or at least half his house, and as the owner of the other half had been killed while still technically married to him, he supposed it was all his now. He had been going to give Wendy his share in the divorce settlement. 'Mm,' Steve said yesterday as they made their way to the police station (how long ago did *that* seem!), 'you have to admit it looks suspicious, Wendy dying just before you lose the house, before you lose half your pension, your savings.'

In the divorce settlement *you* brokered, Vince thought. You had to wonder how Steve had managed to do so well for himself when he seemed like a pretty crap lawyer. Only of course, no, he didn't have to wonder any more, did he? Because now Vince knew how Steve's good fortune had been earned. (*Plenty of money in the bank and always more to come. Do you know what that feels like, Vince?*)

The keys to Wendy's Honda were still hanging in the hallway next to the ugly barometer that had been a wedding gift from one of Wendy's relatives, its forecast stuck relentlessly on 'Poor'. If there was one gift worse than a barometer, it was a barometer that didn't work. 'Perhaps it does work,' Wendy had said a few weeks ago. 'Perhaps it's the barometer of our marriage.' She had gone through a particularly spiteful period when the divorce papers were being drawn up, a barrage of communications about the division of their marital possessions, 'division' as in Wendy got everything and Vince got nothing. Not a peep of complaint out of her since she was bludgeoned with his golf club.

'You must admit, Vince,' Steve said, 'that you were provoked by her. It's understandable that you would kill her.' What was Steve – the witness for the prosecution? Wendy had haggled for custody of the dog but she didn't want the barometer. 'You can have it,' she said, as if she were being generous. *Tell you what, Vince, I'll keep the dog and you take the barometer.* No, she hadn't actually said that, but she might as well have done. He must try to get Sparky back. He would have no idea what was going on. Neither did Ashley, of course. Still no word from her. Where was she? Was she all right? Was she still with the orang-utans?

Ashley would return to this house, her childhood home, and find it had been transformed into a murder scene. He ought to leave her a note in case he wasn't here. He tore a piece of paper off the pad they kept by the telephone and scrawled a message for his daughter on it. He propped it up in front of Wendy's bonsai. The little tree already looked bigger, as if it was free of the straitjacket of its jailer.

Wendy's car was in the garage. The route to the garage took you past the lawn and Vince couldn't help staring at it. This was where she died. She must have been running, trying to flee from her attacker. For perhaps the first time since it had happened, Wendy's death felt real to him. It had been only a handful of days (he had lost track of time) since her murder, but the grass had already grown higher than she would have found tolerable.

In the garage he found the small stepladder that lived on a hook on the wall and positioned it beneath one of the joists. To anyone watching, he might have looked like a man about to hang himself. The image of the girl's face in Silver Birches flashed up before him and he wobbled precariously for a moment, but then he regained his balance and ran his hand along the top of the dirty joist. A splinter jabbed into his palm but he carried on searching until he found what he was looking for.

He got in the car, started the engine and backed out of the driveway. I'm in the driving seat now, he thought. He laughed. He knew he sounded like a maniac, but there was no one to hear. He surprised himself by remembering the route to Silver Birches.

When he arrived, he marched inside without any trepidation. He was a man on a mission. The first person he encountered was Andy. Andy stared at him in horror. 'Vince?' he said. 'What the fuck do you think you're doing, Vince? Vince?'

Sometimes You're the Windshield

Andy had picked up the requested kippers on the way to Silver Birches. He was starving, he couldn't remember when he'd last eaten, although not starving enough yet to eat a cold kipper. Could you even eat them cold — like some kind of weird sushi?

He was meeting Tommy here — he could see his Mercedes slewed casually in the drive. Tommy was an arrogant parker. Silver Birches appeared to be in the calm after the storm. There was still the problem of the missing Jasmine, but apart from that, the hatches seemed to have been securely battened down, ready for decommissioning. If they were going to move the girls and shut down the place they would need Vasily and Jason, but there was no sign of their vehicles.

It was as quiet inside the building as it was outside. It was suffocatingly warm, as though the good weather of the past few days had entered and been trapped in here and had transformed into something torpid, an almost tangible thickness in the air. The place was deathly quiet too — the whole atmosphere was beginning to make Andy feel uneasy. There was no one in the rooms downstairs. Where was Tommy? Where were Vasily and Jason? Where were the girls, for that matter?

And here was — not Tommy, but Vince. Vince, who was striding purposefully along the corridor towards Andy, aiming a gun at him. A gun! Vince!

'Vince?' Andy said as Vince continued to advance. 'What the fuck do you think you're doing, Vince? Vince?'

Without any warning, Vince pulled the trigger. The force of the shot propelled Andy backward, sending him flying in a kind of comedy cartwheel, arms and legs flailing, until he dropped to the floor. He'd been shot. He'd been fucking shot! He screamed like a rabbit in its death throes. 'You fucking shot me!' he yelled at Vince.

Vince paused for a moment, regarding him dispassionately, and then he was on the move again, still coming towards Andy, still with that mad look on his face. Andy scrambled to his feet and stumbled on, despite the burning pain in his – in his what? Lung? Stomach? His *heart*? He realized he knew nothing about the anatomy of his own body. Bit late to start learning now. Fired by nothing but fear, he lurched along the corridor, bounced off a couple of walls, into another corridor and then dragged himself up the stairs, all the time expecting a hail of bullets to follow and finish him off. None came, thank God, and now he was taking shelter in one of the rooms. A room that, to his surprise (although for surprise nothing could top being shot), was also housing all of the girls. Tommy must have herded them in here, like cattle, to make moving them easier.

The girls were still handcuffed with their plastic ties and were in various states of lethargy, which was a relief to Andy because he was the prey now, wasn't he? Foxy had gone to ground. If they had been in better shape the girls might have turned on him like hounds and ripped him to pieces.

The two Polish girls from last night were huddled together by the window. They felt like old acquaintances, but he didn't suppose they would give him help if he asked for it. One of them, Nadja, half opened her heavy-lidded eyes and gazed sightlessly at him. Her pupils were great black funnels. He was frightened they might drag him in and swallow him whole. 'My sister?' she murmured to him. 'Katja?' and he said, 'Yeah, yeah love, she's right there next to you.' Nadja muttered something in Polish and then fell asleep again.

He took out his phone, very slowly, while trying to disassociate himself from the excruciating pain – and dialled Tommy. The signal was always terrible inside Silver Birches. He wondered if it was something to do with the walls being so thick. It was the kind of thing that Vince would know. No answer from Tommy. He dialled Steve and got his voicemail. (Did *no one* ever answer their phone any more?) 'Steve, Steve,' Andy whispered urgently. 'Where are you? You've got to get to Silver Birches. Right now. Vince has gone postal. He's got a *gun*. He fucking *shot* me. Get here, will you? And find Vasily and Jason.' He muted the phone, he'd seen enough horror films to know that your phone always rang loudly and signalled your whereabouts just as the deranged killer was about to give up hunting you. Vince on the rampage. Jesus, who would have believed it? Wendy, perhaps. Rhoda was right, he must have killed her as well. All this time they'd been playing golf with a psycho murderer. One with a crap handicap.

He heard the sound of a car engine starting up and managed to get himself over to the window in time to see Tommy's Mercedes crunching gravel and gears and disappearing round the drive. The bastard must have heard the gunshot, surely? And now he was leaving him here alone to die. So much for friendship.

He could actually see the blood pumping out of his side like an uncapped oil well. He had nothing to stanch it with, but then he remembered the pieces of Maria's scarf, still in his pocket. He managed to extricate them, every little movement an agony, and pushed them up against his wound. He regretted not keeping her crucifix as well. He had forgotten about God during the course of his life. He wondered if God had forgotten about him. He knew every sparrow, didn't He? But did He know the rats?

His phone vibrated angrily and Lottie's poker-face flashed up on the screen. He wished it *was* Lottie on the other end of the phone, she'd probably be more helpful than Rhoda, she'd certainly be more sympathetic to his current predicament if he tried to explain it to her. ('You've been shot? By Vince Ives? Because you're a sex trafficker? Because a girl is dead? Well, good luck with that, Andrew.')

The conversation now raised Katja from her apathy. She started muttering in Polish and Andy whispered, 'Go back to sleep, love,' and was surprised when she obediently closed her eyes.

'Who are you speaking to?' Rhoda asked sharply. He adjusted the arm that was holding the phone and pain shot through his body like a lightning bolt. When he was a child his mother had never comforted him if he hurt himself, instead she always held him responsible. ('Well, you wouldn't have broken your arm if you hadn't jumped off the wall, Andrew.') If she'd kissed and cuddled him, his life might have turned out differently. He whimpered quietly. 'Is that you making that noise, Andrew?' Rhoda said. 'What are you *doing*? Did you remember to get the kippers? Are you there? Andrew?'

'Yeah, I'm here,' Andy sighed. 'Don't worry, I got the kippers. I'll be home soon.' In a body bag most likely, he thought. 'Bye, love.'

Those were probably his last words to her. He should have told her where all the cash was stashed. She'd never be able to sit by the pool with her piña colada now. She'd be surprised when she found out where his life had ended. Or perhaps she wouldn't. It was hard to tell with Rhoda, she was like Lottie in that respect.

He was either going to die here or he was going to have to try and get help and risk Vince shooting him – in which case he would die anyway. Staying and waiting to be killed didn't feel like much of an option, so, inch by painful inch, he began to caterpillar along the floor towards the door. He thought about Maria and Jasmine. One had stayed, one had run. He wished they'd both chosen to run. He wished he could wind time back, to the Angel of the North, to the Quayside flat, to the airport, the plane, the moment they had googled 'recruitment agencies UK' or however it was that they had found Anderson Price Associates. He wished they were still sweating over sewing-machines in Manila making Gap jeans, dreaming about a better life in the UK.

His agonizingly slow progress towards the door was impeded by the Polish girls. He had to climb over them, mumbling an apology all the while. 'Sorry, love,' he said as Nadja woke again. She struggled to a sitting position and he could see that her eyes were no longer black holes. Her pupils had narrowed to pinpricks, designed to bore into his soul. She frowned at him and said, 'You're shot?'

'Yeah,' he agreed. 'Seems like it.'

'With a gun?'

'Yeah.'

'Where is it? The gun?'

Thisldo

A Browning 9mm, the standard Army-issue sidearm until a few years ago when it was replaced by the Glock. *Royal Signals. In another lifetime.* That's what Vince Ives had said as they fell off the cliff together. He must have smuggled his pistol home, on an Army transport probably, after his last deployment. Jackson knew guys who'd done that – more as a souvenir than a weapon. Something that reminded you that you were once a soldier. There was always the feeling – usually confirmed later, unfortunately – that when you left the Service you were leaving behind the best days of your life.

Vince had said something about Kosovo. Or was it Bosnia? Jackson couldn't remember. He wished he could, because it might have helped the current conversation. It was one thing to talk a guy out of jumping off a cliff, but it was quite another thing to persuade him to put down the gun that he was pointing at you, especially when he had a wild look in his eye, like a horse that had been spooked.

'Vince,' Jackson said, raising his arms in surrender, 'it's me, Jackson. You phoned me, remember?' (*Call me if you need to talk.*) Perhaps he ought to stop distributing his card so liberally if this was what it led to.

He'd received a panicked phone call some half an hour ago, Vince giving garbled instructions about how to get to this place, saying that he was in trouble – or that there *was* trouble, Jackson wasn't sure which. Perhaps both, he thought. Was Vince having a breakdown – standing on the edge of a cliff again, about to jump? Or perhaps he'd been arrested for his wife's murder. The last thing Jackson had been expecting was that the guy would have a gun or that he'd be holding it straight and level directly in line with the invisible target that was Jackson's heart. *A gun's visceral enough*, he'd said yesterday to the Sam/Max/Matt guy who played Collier. Certainly was.

Jackson had an uncomfortable vision of himself on the mortuary slab with Julia weighing his heart in her hand. *Healthy male. No sign of heart problems.* According to that seafront clairvoyant, his future was in his hands. But it wasn't, it was in Vince Ives's hands.

'Sorry,' Vince said, lowering the arm that held the gun, having the grace to look shamefaced. 'Didn't mean to scare you.'

'That's okay, Vince,' Jackson said. Keep the guy calm, keep him focussed. Get the gun off him.

'It's a mess,' Vince said.

'I know, but it'll be all right,' Jackson mollified. 'You can come back from this' (a *Collier* cliché) 'you just need to put the gun down.' He was searching his memory for a suitable country lyric or even another helpful phrase from *Collier*, but Vince said impatiently, 'No, not *me*, I'm not the mess, I mean *this* place. What's happening here.'

'What *is* happening here?'

'See for yourself.'

Vince conducted a tour of the downstairs for Jackson's benefit – the cell-like rooms, the stained mattresses, the foetid atmosphere of despair. Vince seemed detached, like an impartial real estate agent. Jackson suspected he was in shock.

The normally placid Dido, who had accompanied Jackson inside Silver Birches – dogs die in hot Toyotas, and so on – was twitching like an agitated sniffer dog. He decided to tie her up in the reception area. She'd seen enough, and whatever was happening here wasn't her business.

When he returned to Vince, he found him standing in one of the rooms, lost in thought. There had been a dead girl here yesterday, he said. No girl now, dead or alive. No girls at all. Jackson began to wonder if this whole thing had been produced by Vince's over-wrought imagination.

'Maybe they've moved them,' Vince said. 'One of the girls

escaped, they'll be worried that she's able to identify this place. They don't keep the girls here for long anyway, apparently.'

They? Anderson Price Associates, Vince explained. There was no Anderson and no Price, it was run by people he knew. 'Friends,' he added grimly. 'Tommy and Andy and Steve.'

Sounded like children's TV presenters, Jackson thought, but then the antennae on his little grey cells twitched. 'That wouldn't be Tommy Holroyd, would it? Crystal's husband?'

'Yeah,' Vince said. 'Crystal deserves better. Do you know her? Have you met her?'

'Sort of.'

'Tommy Holroyd, Andy Bragg, Steve Mellors,' Vince said. 'The Three Musketeers,' he added sarcastically.

'Steve Mellors? Stephen Mellors? A solicitor in Leeds?'

'You know him as well?' Vince said suspiciously. 'You're not in cahoots with them, are you?' Jackson noticed him tightening his grip on the gun. Was it just for show? The man had been in the Signals, for heaven's sake, had he ever fired a gun in combat? More to the point, did he really have the nerve to shoot someone in cold blood?

'Christ, no, Vince,' he said. 'Relax, will you? It's just a coincidence. I do some work for him occasionally. Fact-checking.' He wasn't entirely surprised. There was a narrow line between the wrong and right side of the law and Stephen Mellors was the type who managed to straddle it successfully.

'Pretty big coincidence,' Vince muttered.

It was, wasn't it? Jackson thought. Even in a lifetime of coincidences this one was outlandish. He wondered if he had somehow been unwittingly pulled into this hellish conspiracy. But then he never needed to look for trouble, as Julia frequently reminded him, trouble would always find him.

'And where are they now? he asked Vince. 'Tommy and Andy and Steve?'

'I don't know where Steve is. I just saw Tommy leaving. Andy's somewhere in the building. He can't have got far. I shot him.'

'You *shot* him?'

'I did.'

Not for show, then. 'I'd feel much better if you put the gun down, Vince.'

'I'd feel much better if I didn't, to be honest.'

As they walked along the corridor Jackson noticed occasional smears of blood on the walls, and as they started up the stairs he saw a bloody hand-print on the wall, hardly a good augur. In Marlee's nursery class the children had made a tree that had been hung on the wall. The leaves were the prints from their hands, dipped in different shades of green paint and with their names written on them by their teacher, Miss Carter. 'The Tree of Life' she had titled it. He wondered if Marlee remembered that. She was part of his tree of life. And now she was starting her own tree, putting down roots, growing branches. He sensed himself getting lost in a tangled forest of metaphors.

All thoughts of trees and metaphors disappeared abruptly when Vince opened the door to one of the rooms. And there they were. Women. Jackson counted seven, in various states of disrepair, doped up to the eyeballs and handcuffed with plastic ties. He could detect the ferrous smell of fresh blood. The place felt like an ante-room to an abattoir.

'I'm going to phone the emergency services, is that okay, Vince?' he said. Best to let a man with a gun think he was in charge. Because, let's face it, he was.

'Not the police though,' Vince said.

'The police are what's needed, Vince. I can count at least three major crimes taking place here, and that's without the guy you shot.' Jackson felt as if he'd spent the last twenty-four hours trying – and failing – to persuade people to reach out and grasp the hand at the end of the long arm of the law.

'No police,' Vince said calmly. 'I'll see to it.'

See to it? What did that mean? Jackson wondered as he pushed nine three times on his phone. 'No signal in here,' he said to Vince, holding up his phone as if to demonstrate. 'I'm just stepping out into the corridor, okay?' Jackson wasn't about to let the emergency services walk into an ambush. Vince had already shot one person, who was to say he wasn't prepared to shoot everyone? To go for the classic murder/suicide blaze-of-fury ending and take everyone down with him like a kamikaze pilot.

Cupping the phone in his hands to muffle the conversation, Jackson recited his old warrant number to the dispatcher, hoping it wouldn't be checked. It was a crime to impersonate a policeman, but in the hierarchy of crimes much greater ones were being committed all around him. Unfortunately the dispatcher's voice at the other end started to break up and wander off into the ether, and the game was up when Vince appeared at his side. 'You didn't ask for the police, did you?' he asked, motioning Jackson back into the room with the gun as if he was directing traffic.

'No,' Jackson said truthfully, 'I didn't.'

Jackson went round with his trusty Leatherman, slicing through the plastic ties. The girls were nervous of him, and of the knife, and he kept saying, 'It's okay, I'm a policeman,' which seemed more positive than the past tense, although it hardly made any difference to them as English wasn't their first language. His tone of voice seemed to soothe them eventually. He checked for injuries. Mostly bruises, the kind you got from being beaten. Jackson thought of Crystal Holroyd and the blows she had taken yesterday. It still made him wince to remember it. He couldn't imagine that she knew about this place, that she knew how Tommy made the money that allowed her to live in a style that she had not been accustomed to before she met him. He liked to think that she was one of the righteous.

Vince holstered his weapon casually, tucking it into the back of his belt while he gave the girls water and murmured, 'You're safe now, don't be afraid.' Jackson eyed up the gun. How quick on the draw would Vince be? he wondered. Would he really shoot him? Watching the way he gently tended to the girls, it seemed unlikely, but was he prepared to take that risk?

They worked like battlefield medics – swift but steady. The room did bear a resemblance to a war zone. One more battle in the war against women.

A tale as old as time. Disney, Jackson thought. He had watched *Beauty and the Beast* with Marlee on a Blockbuster video when she was little. (Video! Dear God, like something from the Ark.) And now she had met her Prince Charming, was about to bite into the happy ever after. The poisoned apple. (*Why can't you be pleased for me,*

Dad? What the hell is wrong with you?) Marlee was twenty-three, she could easily be one of the girls held captive in Silver Birches. These girls all had stories – lives, not stories – yet here they'd been reduced to anonymous commodities. The thought made his heart hurt. For them. For all the girls. All the daughters.

Jackson had one ear out for the sound of approaching sirens, but could hear nothing but silence. He kept finding himself kneeling in blood, sticky, fresh stuff that didn't belong to the girls. The man Vince had shot, presumably. Andy. Tommy and Andy and Steve. The gang of three.

'Right,' Vince said, standing up suddenly. 'I'd better go and find that bastard Andy and finish him off.'

As it turned out, Vince didn't need to go and look for Andy as moments later Andy found them, staggering into the room before collapsing against a wall. He was clearly the source of all the blood.

'Help me,' he said. 'I'm fucking dying.' Jackson told him that an ambulance was on the way, but when he made a move towards him to help him Vince pointed the gun at him again and said, 'Don't. Just don't. Let the bastard bleed to death.'

'Andy? Vince? What the hell is going on?'

Stephen Mellors. Last seen by Jackson in a bar in Leeds, eyeing up Tatiana's assets. Tommy, Andy and Steve. Who would be next to enter the room? Tatiana herself, perhaps? Accompanied by her father, the clown? Because this was clearly a circus. Stephen Mellors had, like Vince, come armed to the party, holding a baseball bat in his hands, like any common thug. He suddenly noticed Jackson and frowned at him. '*Brodie?* What are—?'

'This isn't a fucking tea-party, Steve,' Vince interrupted. 'We're not here to introduce ourselves to each other. We're not about to play pass the parcel and eat ice-cream and jelly. Over there,' he said, gesturing with the gun. 'Go and sit on the floor, in the corner, old *chum*,' he sneered.

'Calm down, Vince,' Stephen Mellors said, which, as everyone knows, is just about the worst thing you can say to someone waving a gun around. 'Okay, okay,' he said when Vince steadied his aim on him. He sat down resentfully on the floor.

'And put the stupid bat down,' Vince said. 'Good. Now kick it over to me.'

'Dying here,' Andy muttered, 'in case anyone hasn't noticed.'

'You're just winged,' Vince said. 'Stop making such a fuss.'

'I need extreme unction.'

'No, you don't. Whatever that is.'

Jackson, lapsed Catholic that he was, wondered about explaining the term, and then thought better of it as Vince was now pointing the Browning steadily at Stephen Mellors' head, so it looked as if he might be the one who was about to need extreme unction. 'Don't shoot him,' he said. 'You don't want to do this, Vince.' (Another frequent *Collier* aphorism.)

'Yes, I do.'

'The police are on their way.'

'You're lying. Doesn't matter now anyway. You know,' he said conversationally – they might have been two blokes in the pub – 'when I was in the Army there were some guys who said they'd rather die in combat – go down fighting – than live out their four score and ten. Trudge through it,' he added with a little laugh. 'And I never understood how they could think like that.'

'And now you do?'

'Yeah. I bet that's how you think, too.'

'No,' Jackson said. 'Once upon a time maybe, but not now. Personally I'm happy to trudge to the end. I'd like to meet my grandchildren. Put the gun down, Vince.' Keep him talking, Jackson thought. People who were talking weren't shooting. 'Think about your daughter, Vince – Ashley, isn't it? The police will come with a SWAT team. They might shoot you, and if they shoot they'll shoot to kill.'

'The police aren't coming,' Vince said.

Seemed he was wrong. Seemed they were already here. Two young women entered the room, hardly a SWAT team, but nevertheless it was now a proper three-ringed circus.

'DC Ronnie Dibicki,' one of them said, holding up her warrant card. 'I'm asking you to put that gun down, sir, before anyone gets hurt.'

'*I'm* hurt,' Andy Bragg said.

Jackson was impressed by their joint steadfastness in the face of a loaded weapon. They were brave, he thought. Men fell down. Women stood up.

'This man needs urgent medical attention,' one of the DCs said, kneeling down next to Andy Bragg.

She was about to speak into her radio but Vince said, 'Leave it. Stand up, get away from him.'

'It's okay, an ambulance is on the way,' Jackson said. Several ambulances, he hoped.

'Shut up,' Vince said, 'all of you.' Not surprisingly he was growing increasingly edgy. He was wrangling a lot of people now with that gun, including two police officers, both of whom seemed to know him already. (*Mr Ives, do you remember me? Ronnie Dibicki.*)

'Can someone explain what's happening here? Mr Brodie?' one of them said to Jackson.

'Beyond the obvious? No.' He paused, registering the 'Mr Brodie'. How do you know my name?' he puzzled.

'Mr Brodie, it's *me*. Reggie. Reggie Chase.'

'Reggie?' Worlds were colliding all over the place. Jackson thought he might actually have gone mad. Or that he was hallucinating. Or that this was an alternative version of reality. Or all three. (Reggie! Little Reggie Chase!)

'Arrest him,' Vince said to her, pointing the gun at Steve Mellors. 'He's called Stephen Mellors and he's the mastermind behind all this.' Andy Bragg grunted something that seemed to be disagreement about the word 'mastermind'.

'Because if you don't arrest him, I'll shoot him,' Vince said. He moved closer to Mellors and said 'Arrest him' again, the gun now inches away from Mellors' head. 'I promise I'll shoot him if you don't arrest him. It's one or the other, you choose. I'd rather shoot him, but I'll settle for arrest.'

'For fuck's sake,' Mellors said to no one in particular. Jackson seemed to be the only one who saw Ronnie Dibicki slip out of the room while everyone's attention was on the gun and its proximity to Stephen Mellors' head.

'Stephen Mellors, I am arresting you on suspicion of . . .' Reggie said. She glanced at Jackson and he said, 'Try GBH for starters. I expect you can throw in the Modern Slavery Act later. As well as a few other choice things.'

'Stephen Mellors,' Reggie said, throwing Jackson a black look, 'I am arresting you on suspicion of assault causing grievous bodily harm. You do not have to say anything but it may harm your defence if you do not mention when questioned something which you later rely on in court. Anything you do say may be given in evidence.'

And then one of the girls suddenly stumbled to her feet and pointed at Stephen Mellors like a character accusing someone in a melodrama. 'Mark Price,' she said. 'You're Mark Price.'

Haulage

She was dreaming about plums. Just a few days ago they had sat knee to knee – Nadja and Katja and their mother – on the small balcony of their mother's apartment, eating plums from an old plastic bowl. The plums were the colour of bruises. Big purple bruises.

They had picked the plums on a visit to their grandfather's farm. Not really a farm, more of a smallholding, but he grew everything. Plums, apples, cherries. Cucumbers, tomatoes, cabbages. When they were little they used to help him make his sauerkraut, squeezing the salt into it until the leaves went limp. He kept a big wooden tub of it on his porch. A thick mat of mould on the top kept it from freezing in the winter. It used to disgust Katja. She never had a strong stomach – their mother said she was a fussy eater, but she was mostly just obsessed with her weight.

Katja didn't like to go shooting with their grandfather either. It wasn't so much the killing that she didn't like, it was the skinning and gutting afterwards. Their grandfather could strip a rabbit of its fur in seconds and then slit it open and let its steaming innards slip out. His dogs devoured the entrails before they even hit the ground. Nadja was his willing apprentice, following him through the woods and fields, stalking the rabbits.

Foxes too, although Katja said if he didn't shoot the foxes the foxes would eat the rabbits and then no one would have to go about like cowboys shooting everything in sight.

Nadja was a good shot. Only this weekend she had bagged a fox, a big brown dog with a huge brush. Her grandfather nailed the best skins on to the door of his woodshed. 'Trophies,' he said.

Nadja was his favourite. 'My strong girl,' he called her. Katja didn't care. She never cared about anything much except skating. Nadja gave up ballet so their mother could afford all the expense. Nadja wasn't resentful – perhaps it was a relief in a way because she no longer had to keep proving herself. She loved her sister. They were close – best friends. She went to all Katja's competitions. Hated it when she lost or when she fell, because she could be beautiful on the ice. When she had to give it up it hurt Nadja almost as much as it hurt Katja.

They'd picked all the plums, scavenging even the last of the small, imperfect ones. Their grandfather made his own slivovitz. It could take the top of your head off. They should take a bottle to London with them, he said. Show the English what a real drink was. He had never forgiven Churchill for his betrayal of the Poles after the war. Katja couldn't care less about history. 'Modern times now, Grandpa,' she said.

Nadja had been roused by something and then she'd fallen asleep again. Andy had been there. For a moment she thought he was going to look after her, and then she remembered what had happened to her. To her sister.

She woke again and heard Katja say, 'You're Mark Price.' Her sister shook her and said, 'Nadja. It's Mark Price.'

The plums were purple. Like bruises. She could almost taste them. She was awake now.

House of Mirth

'Jesus Christ,' Ronnie murmured. 'What *is* this place?'

'Watch out, there's blood here,' Reggie said. There was a bloody hand-print on the wall, like a cave-painting, and more stains and drops on the heavy old lino on the staircase. 'Fresh. Don't slip in it,' she added as they followed the trail. Bloodhounds, Reggie thought. They'd had a look around downstairs and even without the blood there were enough signs to tell them that something very nasty was going on in this place.

There was a dog tied up in reception and they had eyed it warily at first, before realizing it was a patient old Labrador who wagged her tail in welcome when she saw them enter the building.

'Hello, old girl,' Reggie whispered to her, rubbing the velvet bone of her head.

Upstairs, the door to the first room they came across was wide open, and inside they caught a glimpse of a hellish tableau of broken, frightened women. There was a man bleeding on the floor who was moaning, probably too articulate to be dying, as he was vociferously claiming.

'DC Ronnie Dibicki,' Ronnie said, holding her warrant aloft like a shield. Reggie followed her into the room and it was only then that they saw the gun. 'Vincent Ives,' Ronnie murmured. Reggie considered a karate move on him, kicking the gun out of his hand (*Hi-yah!*), but it seemed too dangerous given the number of people in the room and the likelihood of one of them getting shot in the process.

Ronnie chose the softly-softly approach. 'Mr Ives,' she said gently, as if she was a kind teacher talking to a schoolboy, 'do you remember me? Ronnie Dibicki. We talked the other day, in your flat. I'm asking you to put the gun down, before anyone gets hurt. Can you do that?'

'No, not really. Sorry. Can you come in the room, please?' Vince indicated with the gun, quite politely, like a cinema usher. Reggie remembered how he had swept the crumbs off his sofa before they sat on it the other day. She glanced at Ronnie. Were they really going to walk willingly into a hostage situation?

Apparently, yes.

Inside, the room was crowded. It reminded Reggie of Barclay Jack's dressing room at the Palace yesterday – a nightmare version of it with, as far as Reggie could tell, a completely new cast of characters. Thankfully there was no ventriloquist's dummy this time. Finding Jackson Brodie at the heart of this melee seemed par for the course, somehow. He was a friend to anarchy.

Vincent Ives was pointing the gun at a man who was cowering in the corner of the room. 'Arrest him,' he said to Reggie. He moved closer to the man and held the gun over his head, execution style. 'He's called Stephen Mellors and he's the mastermind behind all this. Because if you don't arrest him, I'll shoot him . . . It's one or the other, you choose.'

There was no harm in arresting the man, Reggie supposed, she could always de-arrest him later if it turned out he hadn't actually committed a crime, although what were the chances of that, given the circumstances they all found themselves in? It seemed more likely that other crimes would be added, not subtracted. So, after a moment's consideration, she complied. 'Stephen Mellors, I am arresting you on suspicion of . . .' Reggie hesitated, unclear as to what exactly she could charge him with. She was furious with herself because she glanced over at Jackson Brodie, looking for authority. Somehow he was still the senior policeman in the room. The senior person, if it came to that.

She sighed with frustration at herself, at him, but took his advice. 'Stephen Mellors, I am arresting you on suspicion of assault causing grievous bodily harm. You do not have to say anything but it may harm your defence if you do not mention when questioned something which you later rely on in court. Anything you do say may be given in evidence.'

They say that in moments of crisis time slows down, but for Reggie it suddenly sped up. Everything happened so quickly that it was difficult later to piece it back together.

It began when one of the girls gasped loudly and wobbled unsteadily to her feet. She looked like someone waking from a long, long sleep. She was tiny – shorter even than Reggie – and was sporting two black eyes and a bloodied nose. *Small animals only.* Having levered herself to her feet, she stared fixedly at Stephen Mellors before pointing at him and saying, 'Mark Price. You're Mark Price.'

She leant down and shook the girl who was slumped on the floor next to her. They were so alike they had to be sisters. 'Nadja,' she said, trying to rouse her. Reggie could make out the words 'It's Mark Price,' but the rest of the conversation was in what she was pretty sure was Polish. Reggie turned round, looking for Ronnie to translate, but Ronnie, she realized, had disappeared. She must have gone to try and get help.

The other girl – Nadja – rose up from the floor and, in a surprisingly energetic move for someone who had appeared to be half-comatose moments before, she grabbed the gun out of Vince's hand. Stephen Mellors, who seemed to recognize the girl, twisted round, trying to scrabble away from her, but there was nowhere to go. He was already up against the wall in more ways than one and there was no mousehole for the rat to take shelter in. Nadja raised the Browning, her arm steady, her aim true, and shot Stephen Mellors in the back with it. Then she raised her arm again and said, 'For my sister,' and shot him a second time.

The sound was deafening, ricocheting around the room for what seemed forever. It was followed by a moment of profound silence. Time, which had been moving so quickly, was suddenly suspended, and in that space the two girls stood silently with their arms around each other, staring at Stephen Mellors' lifeless body. Then Nadja, the girl who had just shot a man in the back in cold blood, turned and looked straight at Reggie and nodded to her as if they were members of some secret sisterhood. Reggie couldn't help herself, she nodded back.

'Reggie Chase,' Jackson Brodie mused.

'Yes. Detective Constable Chase, actually.'

'You're a *detective*? In *Yorkshire*?'

'Jeeso. You don't own the county. Could you stop being amazed by everything, Mr Brodie?'

They were sitting in a major incident van waiting for someone to take a statement from them. They'd been given tea and biscuits by a PCSO. Clearly the whole situation was going to take hours to unravel. When the dust had settled, Stephen Mellors was dead and Vincent Ives had disappeared. Andrew Bragg had been carted off in an ambulance. ('That was *our* Mr Bragg?' Ronnie said. 'We looked everywhere for him.')

The trafficked women were handed over to the MSHTU and a place of safety. 'Modern Slavery and Human Trafficking Unit,' Reggie said, explaining the acronym to Jackson in case he didn't know. But there was nothing modern about any of it, was there? Reggie thought. From the pyramids to the sugar plantations to the brothels of the world, exploitation was the name of the game. *Plus ça change.*

'You became a detective? In Yorkshire?'

'Again, answered, yes and yes. And don't flatter yourself that you had any influence over either of those things.'

'And who *is* he exactly?' Ronnie asked, staring rather belligerently at Jackson.

'Just someone I used to know,' Reggie said crossly, answering on Jackson's behalf before he had a chance to explain himself. 'Used to be a policeman. Used to be from Yorkshire,' she added. Used to be my friend, she thought. 'I saved his life once.'

'She did,' Jackson affirmed to Ronnie. 'I remain indebted,' he added to Reggie.

Ronnie had managed to escape and alert the authorities and thus missed the details of the denouement.

'It was pandemonium,' Reggie reported to Ronnie, dunking a

digestive in her mug of tea. 'And over in seconds. Vincent Ives dropped the gun and Andrew Bragg managed to grab it off the floor and shoot Stephen Mellors with it.'

'He didn't look capable of grabbing anything,' Ronnie puzzled. 'He seemed ready for the Last Rites. And why would he shoot his friend?'

'Who's to say?' Jackson said. 'Criminals, they're a law unto themselves. They turn on each other all the time. In my experience.'

'He's seen a lot,' Reggie added helpfully. 'He's very old.'

'Thanks. Thanks, Reggie.'

'You're welcome, Mr B.'

Fake News

'A detective?' He was having trouble getting his head round this grown-up version of Reggie. A very antagonistic version, it had to be said. It turned out he owed her money and he did have a vague recollection, hooked up from the seabed of memory, of borrowing money from her shortly after Tessa, his evil fake wife, had drained his bank account. It was only after he had signed an IOU in her notebook that Reggie relented. A little. 'It's good to see you, Mr B.'

'Good to see you too, Reggie.'

Most of the witnesses in the room weren't in a state to have actually witnessed anything and only Jackson and Reggie were able to give anything approaching a coherent version of events, and even then there were some confusing loopholes in both their accounts.

Jackson had good witness credentials – ex-military police, ex-Cambridgeshire Constabulary, currently working as a private investigator. He had been present, he said, when Stephen Mellors arrived at Silver Birches armed with a baseball bat. Vincent Ives had brought the gun to the scene with the apparent intention of protecting the girls who had been trafficked. 'Armed siege' was a slight exaggeration. Vincent Ives's motives, Jackson maintained, had been for the greater good – wasn't that the standard by which everyone should be judged? Unfortunately Ives had dropped the gun and it had been picked up by Andrew Bragg, who proceeded to shoot Stephen Mellors, albeit in self-defence, when he tried to attack him with the baseball bat. This sequence of events didn't entirely satisfy the police (Where was the gun? Where was the baseball bat? Big question marks), but it satisfied Jackson. Bad people were punished, people with good intentions weren't crucified. And girls who took justice into their own hands weren't penalized when they had already suffered more than anyone should. Killing in self-defence was one thing, but shooting someone in the back, not once but twice, was unlikely to be ignored by the Crown Prosecution Service.

Andrew Bragg had already been wounded before they arrived, he testified, but had no memory of the event. He was rushed from the scene by ambulance to the hospital, where he underwent an emergency splenectomy and a transfusion of several pints of blood. 'Not as bad as it looked,' the surgeon said when he came out of the operating theatre. The patient remembered nothing about what had happened, not even who had shot him.

'You should write crime novels,' Reggie said to Jackson. 'You've got a real talent for fiction.'

By the time the Armed Response Unit had arrived, Stephen Mellors had already been dispatched to the great necropolis in the sky and both Vincent Ives and the gun had disappeared.

It was at the bottom of the sea now, thrown off the end of the pier at Whitby during high tide, everyone's fingerprints washed away for good. Jackson's, Vince Ives's and those of the girl who shot Stephen Mellors. After she had killed him, Jackson gently prised the gun out of her hand and quietly pocketed it. Nadja. Nadja Wilk and her sister, Katja. They came from Gdansk, where they had worked in a hotel. Real people with real lives, not just ciphers for the tabloid newspapers. *Foreign sex workers released from House of Horrors in police raid.* And *Girls trafficked into prostitution involved in violent shoot-out.* And so on. The news' afterburn went on for a long time. The triumvirate – Tommy, Andy and Steve – had been the top dogs in a trafficking network, a web, the strands of which reached far and wide. Untangling it took some time. It was too late for most of the girls they had brought over, already long disappeared into places where no torch was bright enough to find them. But the seven in the room in Silver Birches were rescued and all went home eventually. Taking their harrowing statements took a long time. Jasmine flew home on the same plane as the coffin of her friend Maria.

Perhaps they would recover, perhaps they wouldn't, but at least they were given that chance, and the person who had given them that chance was Vince Ives, so Jackson reckoned he ought to be allowed to avoid the gallows of the media and the courts.

'Do the right thing here, Andy,' he had said to Bragg as he knelt by his side, listening to the approaching sirens growing louder. And to make his point he pressed his thumb into Andy Bragg's gunshot wound. Ignoring his shrieking, Jackson said, 'You don't remember anything that happened. Complete amnesia. Okay?'

'Or?' Bragg groaned. He was a bargainer, Jackson reckoned. Did he want to bargain with God? Was that what Pascal's wager was?

'*Or*, I'll finish you off right now and you'll go straight to hell. Do the right thing,' Jackson said again. 'Take some responsibility for all the pain and suffering you've caused. Confess your sins,' he said, appealing to the man's inner Catholic. 'Find redemption. Absolution. And Andy,' he added, putting his lips closer to his ear, 'if you don't keep your mouth shut about who shot Stephen Mellors, I'll hunt you down and tear your heart out and feed it to my dog.'

When he retrieved Dido later she gazed at him enquiringly. She didn't look as if she would be a particularly eager participant in the promised gore fest. He gave her a dog treat instead. She really did seem to prefer the ones shaped like bones.

High Noon

Love was hard to come by, but money was easy. If you knew where to find it. In a safe, of course, where else? When they renovated High Haven, Tommy had installed one, a sturdy, old-fashioned one, a vault. It stood in the corner of the office, drilled into the floor, and came with a big key and an even bigger double-handed lever on the front, just asking to be turned. It could have played the central character in a heist movie. It was a safe that said, 'Look at me, don't bother looking for anything else.' It contained, however, only a thousand pounds or so in cash, which was small change to Tommy.

The safe also contained some odds and ends of jewellery, trinkets really, alongside a few documents that looked as if they might be important but weren't. 'So then,' Tommy had explained to Crystal, 'if someone breaks into the house in the middle of the night and holds a knife to your throat' (why were they holding the knife to her throat and not his? Crystal wondered) 'and tells you to open the safe, it won't matter.' (A knife to her throat wouldn't matter?) 'You can open this one and they'll think they've got away with our loot.' (Loot? It was Tommy who thought he lived in a heist movie, not the safe.) He kept the 'important things' – their passports and birth certificates, his 'investment' Richard Mille watch (criminally expensive), Crystal's diamond bracelet and her diamond pendant necklace and twenty thousand pounds or so in twenty-pound notes – in a different, somewhat smaller safe, one that had been drilled into the wall of the study and that hid itself behind an indifferent print of yachts at sea called *Sails at Dawn*. 'A safer safe' was what Tommy called it, pleased with this ruse.

'Your old man must be really paranoid,' the man who had fitted the safe had laughed. He was from the straightforwardly named Northern Safe Installers ('All our engineers have enhanced DBS checks and vetting to BS 7858 standards') and spent most of the day hammering and drilling in the study. 'It's like Fort Knox in here,' he said.

'I know,' Crystal said, handing him a well-sugared mug of coffee and a four-finger KitKat. She kept a special supply of treats for workmen. They respected her for it and proved eager to please her with all sorts of extra little jobs. ('While you're here, do you think you could just fix . . .?' and so on.) Tommy said it wasn't the four-finger KitKat that made them want to please her, it was her tits and her arse. Crystal wondered sometimes – if she was substituted overnight by a replica, a really good robot (a 'high-functioning android', Harry supplied), would Tommy notice? 'Two safes,' she said. 'I know. You'd think we were hiding the Crown Jewels.'

'Three,' the safe-installer corrected, intent on labelling the various sets of keys.

'Three?' Crystal queried lightly. 'He has gone overboard, hasn't he? He's a one, Tommy. Where's he putting the third one? There's hardly any room, surely?'

The second phone. The third safe. The fourth musketeer. Five gold rings. Just one, actually, and it was brass, not gold – a recessed ring pull, fitted flush into a floorboard.

'Better safe than sorry, I suppose,' Crystal said.

'Funny,' the safe-fitter said.

Later that evening, when she looked in the study, she found that Tommy was in the process of hanging *Sails at Dawn* in front of the second safe. She could see that he had covered the hiding place of the third safe with the heavy metal filing cabinet. It was too bulky to move on a regular basis so she supposed the third safe was intended for long-term storage, not everyday use. She wondered if he had already filled it, and if so, with what?

'Good, eh?' Tommy said, standing back to admire *Sails at Dawn*, or rather what it concealed as he had no interest whatsoever in art. 'You would never know anything was there, would you?' No, she agreed, she wouldn't. He was cheerful, almost gleeful. They had only just moved into the house and she was pregnant with Candy at the time. Crystal Holroyd, the newly crowned Queen of High Haven.

He handed her two sets of keys and said, 'They're the spares, for if you need to get into one of the safes for your jewellery. And just take whatever cash you need when you want it.' When she first married him she had found it hard to believe how generous he was. Really landed on my feet, she thought.

No mention was made of the third safe beneath the filing cabinet. It had a spare key too – the safe-installer, full of the joys of coffee and a KitKat, had given it to her when she'd asked for it. He didn't seem to know that husbands kept secrets from their wives. Or indeed that wives kept secrets from their husbands.

'Did you watch him fitting the safes in here?' Tommy asked casually, finally satisfied with the position of *Sails at Dawn*.

'Nah, he took hours. I've been getting the nursery ready.' She had loved that word 'nursery'. It implied so much – love, care, money. 'I'm going upstairs to finish off, okay, babe?' They already knew Candy was a girl. 'Sugar and spice and all things nice,' Crystal murmured as she arranged the cradle in the nursery. It had cost an arm and a leg, a proper old-fashioned one like you got in fairy tales, draped with lace and silk. She'd made the mistake of watching *Rosemary's Baby* recently on TV, late at night on a horror channel, and now she was having a sudden disturbing flashback to the scene where Mia Farrow peers into the crib – a black version of their baby-to-be's – and realizes she's given birth to Satan's baby. Candy would be an angel, not the devil, Crystal reminded herself. And Tommy wasn't Satan, she thought. (She'd changed her mind about that now.)

She had put the spare key to the third safe beneath the crib mattress. It seemed unlikely that Tommy would be changing the little sheets when they were stained with vomit and shit. Babies weren't really made of sugar and spice, Crystal knew that, they were flesh and blood and should be cherished accordingly. Since then, the third key (it was like a mystery novel, *The Third Key*) had travelled around the house to whatever place Crystal deemed the most Tommy-proof, although it had come to rest for some time now inside a bag of frozen edamame beans in the Meneghini, because the day that Tommy looked inside *that* would be the day hell itself froze.

'All right?' Tommy had said, coming into the nursery just as she'd finished smoothing the sheet on the crib's mattress. He'd fiddled with a mobile of sheep above the crib, sending them spinning round dizzily.

Crystal had been knocked up when she was with the Bassani and Carmody show and they'd given her money for an abortion in Leeds. Fee had gone with her. Not a memory to cherish. She'd been so relieved when it was out of her. 'Devil's spawn,' Fee said, passing her a fag as they waited for the train back. They had enough money left over from what Mick had given them to buy a curry and a half-bottle of vodka. They were fourteen years old. She wondered afterwards why no one in the clinic had asked her age or what had happened to her. Why no one *cared*. She would care so much about her daughter that no harm would ever come to her.

The sheep had finally stopped spinning and she said, 'Yeah, everything's good, Tommy. But we need more pink in here. Lots more pink.'

The filing cabinet was a bugger to move and Crystal had to shuffle and tilt, shuffle and tilt, as if it were a particularly clumsy dance partner, or an upended coffin that she was having to manoeuvre around the floor. She knew what was in it, or at least what was in it the last time she'd looked, because this wasn't the first time she had done this particular dance with her awkward metal partner. Tommy liked his money to look like money, not like plastic. 'Keep it liquid,' he said. The trouble with liquid money was that it could get washed down the drain when someone mopped it up. And there was lots of it in the safe. Lots and lots of mopping to do. Mrs Mopp, Crystal thought.

She was sweating by the time she had heaved the cabinet far enough to uncover the brass ring. She pulled on the ring until a neatly glued-together section of floorboards lifted. 'Open sesame,' she murmured to herself. Of course, Tommy – Tommy, who had barely seen the inside of his home in days – would choose that moment to return to it, so she had to hastily reprise the dance with the filing cabinet, shoving it hard into place, and by the time she heard him enter the house ('Crystal! Where the fuck are you?') it was back, more or less, in place and she was in the conservatory.

He gave her a peck on the cheek and said, 'Have you been smoking again?' but didn't seem particularly interested in the answer. He looked exhausted and she said, 'Why don't you put your feet up and I'll pour you a drink?'

'Nah,' he replied. 'Thanks, love, but I've got stuff to do.'

He went in the study and shut the door. Listening at the door, she heard the unmistakeable sound of the filing-cabinet waltz.

'Shit,' Crystal said, because he was about to discover that his larder was bare. She caught sight of Candy standing in the doorway, clutching her unicorn and dressed as Belle. She looked worried – she *was* worried, had been upset ever since the kidnapping. As you would be.

'Naughty word, Mummy,' she reprimanded.

'Yeah, you're right, it is,' Crystal said. 'Sorry.'

'Mummy? You all right?'

'Top of the pops, sweetheart. Top of the pops.'

That's All, Folks

'Crystal? Are you all right?' Vince had found the front door of High Haven wide open and no sign of any occupants apart from Candy, who was in the kitchen watching *Frozen*. He knew it was *Frozen* because he'd watched it with Ashley last Christmas. She told him it was a feminist film, but it just looked like Disney to Vince.

'Hello, darling,' he said to Candy. She had her headphones on and took them off when he spoke to her. 'Are Mummy and Daddy here?' he asked.

'The pool,' she said and replaced her headphones.

Vince no longer had his gun, of course. He had intended to shoot Tommy with it and now he would have to improvise. He had Steve's baseball bat though and was intending to crack Tommy's skull open like an egg. He thought of Wendy. A golf club had done the same for her.

Steve was dead, Vince was pretty sure of that, so all bets were off now. He was disappointed that he hadn't killed him himself, but he supposed there was a certain justice in the way it happened, killed by one of the girls. And with any luck Andy might bleed to death before the ambulance got to him. That just left Tommy to be dealt with. All hell had broken loose after the girl shot Steve, and Vince had slipped out of Silver Birches and was back in the Honda and driving away before you could say, 'Just like that.' On the other side of the road the first police car, all sirens blaring, was sprinting towards Silver Birches.

★

Crystal was standing on the edge of the pool, dressed in shorts and a strappy top. She was soaking wet so she must have been swimming like that rather than in a costume. Tommy's dog, Brutus, was sitting placidly next to her. She was smoking a cigarette and looking thoughtful. 'Oh, hi, Vince,' she said when she saw him. 'How are you?'

He hesitated, unable to think of an answer that could encompass his day so far, then said, 'Did you know your front door's open?'

'That'd be Tommy, I'm always asking him to make sure he's closed it when he comes in. He never does. He's a careless so-and-so, Vince.'

Distracted by the sight of Crystal's breasts in her wet top, it took Vince a moment to realize that there was someone in the pool. Not just someone, but Tommy – and he wasn't swimming, he was floating, face-down.

'Jesus Christ, Crystal,' he said, dropping the baseball bat and pulling off his shoes, preparing to jump in and save Tommy. So he could kill him later.

Crystal put a hand on his arm and said calmly, 'Don't bother, Vince. He's gone.' She took a final long drag on her cigarette and threw the stub into the pool.

Gone? What had happened here? 'What's going on, Crystal?'

'Just cleaning up a bit, Vince. How about you?'

Don't Just Fly

The water looked so inviting, but she wasn't here to swim, attractive though that idea seemed.

She had knocked on the door of the study when she heard the filing cabinet being moved and said in an urgent voice, 'Tommy, you need to come and see this, babe. Down at the pool. There's something wrong. Can you hurry up?' And then she'd parked Candy in front of the TV with her little pink headphones on and run down to the echoing chamber that contained the pool. The artificial daylight was reflecting off the blue water and the gold mosaic. She inhaled the smell of chlorine. She loved it here.

By the time Tommy got there, Crystal was standing at the edge of the pool. 'Here, over here,' she said, gesturing to him. 'Stand next to me and then you'll be able to see it.'

'See what? Where? I don't see—'

She slipped swiftly behind him and gave him an almighty push that left him thrashing around in panic in the water. He made a grab for the side of the pool, he could easily haul himself out, but that was something Crystal had already considered and so she jumped in beside Tommy, getting behind him and holding him up in the water as if she was performing a lifesaving manoeuvre. He said something to her, but he was choking on water and it was hard to decipher the words. It could have been 'Thanks' or 'Help' or 'What the fuck, Crystal?' for all she knew. Instead of helping him to the side, she towed him further out, into the deep end, and then she swam swiftly away, carving her efficient breaststroke through the water. By the time she was out of the pool he had slipped beneath the water.

'Just cleaning up a bit, Vince,' she said when she saw him. 'How about you?'

'Yeah,' Vince said as they watched Tommy's body drifting towards them like an inflatable raft on a current. 'The same.'

'Give you a lift somewhere, Vince?'

Just the Facts, Ma'am

Words never actually spoken by Joe Friday in *Dragnet*, as any girl who knows everything knows. 'You know too much,' Ronnie said.

'No, I don't know enough,' Reggie said.

The third man, as he was known – although there were actually several 'third men' – was finally unmasked, thanks to Operation Villette.

Nicholas Sawyer's Christmas card to colleagues and friends was a family portrait that featured his wife, Susan, sons Tom and Robert, and grandchildren George, Lily, Nelly Isabella and Alfie. His daughters-in-law were absent from the photograph, as if perhaps only his direct bloodline was of any importance. Or perhaps they were just busy that day. Or camera shy. The photograph was unseasonable, taken in summer, in an unnamed field that Nicholas claimed was in his old rural constituency although it could have been anywhere.

The photograph had the cheerful, casual feel of a family snap but had been taken by a professional photographer as Nicholas Sawyer was a man who liked to control his image. He liked to control everything. He was seventy-five and had been an MP for forty years in the same constituency in Kent, a Cabinet minister, in and out of government for twenty, finishing in Defence, and ten years ago had been elevated to the House of Lords, where he had chosen to sit on the cross benches. He still introduced himself and his wife as 'Nick and Susie', although Susie herself was more inclined to use 'Lady Sawyer'. Nicholas consulted with several of the *Financial Times*'s UK 500, defence contractors being his speciality, and Susie was on the board of many charities, the majority of which favoured the arts rather than social justice.

The couple had an apartment in Chelsea, a *maison de maître* in Languedoc, as well as the constituency home, Roselea, in Kent, which they had kept after Nicholas left the House of Commons and where nowadays they spent most weekends. Roselea was a picture-book thatched cottage in a covetable village and had, over the years, been featured in several lifestyle articles in the broadsheets. It was where they were when the police came and asked Nicholas to accompany them to the nearest police station, where he was interviewed under caution. Three weeks later he was arrested and charged with several offences under the 2003 Sexual Offences Act, the offences dating as far back as the Eighties. A charge of conspiracy was thrown in for good measure. The scandal was a complete fabrication, he told everyone – he was being thrown to the dogs, a sacrifice on the altar of political correctness, it was a conspiracy by the gutter press to discredit him, they hated him because he supported curbing their freedom. And so on.

On the same day that Nicholas Sawyer was arrested, several others were picked up by the police. Sir Quentin Gough-Plunkett was one of them, a veteran and vocal anti-Europe campaigner. Sir Quentin was also a noted chess player – he had qualified in the Western zonal round of the World Chess Championship in 1962 and for many years had been the patron of a charity that encouraged underprivileged children to learn to play chess.

Also questioned, and eventually charged, was a retired senior police officer from Cheshire, a former circuit judge and the aged boss of a family-run construction company. They had all once been members, it was claimed, of a shadowy group known to each other as 'the magic circle'. There is no statute of limitations in the United Kingdom for sexual offences.

The Crown Prosecution Service praised Bronte Finch, the daughter of a High Court judge, for her evidence. Her 'brave' testimony in open court had helped convict a 'brutal predator'.

Another witness, Miss Felicity Yardley, gave evidence in the cases of all of the accused. She refused anonymity and later sold her story to the tabloids for an undisclosed figure. Miss Yardley, a former prostitute and drug addict, claimed that she had been persuaded by MI5 to give evidence. She claimed that 'a man in a silver BMW' had taken her to a safe house, where she had given a statement about the 'foreigners' she had met when in the company of Nicholas Sawyer. She had been told that he had sold defence secrets for years to the Russians and the Chinese and anyone else prepared to pay. MI5 were very keen to find a way to 'neutralize' him' – their words, she said. She was offered witness protection by them, but 'the bastards' had welshed on the offer.

These shadowy figures in the Security Service told her that the magic circle were like 'the Illuminati' (it took her several attempts to pronounce the word) and had tentacles that reached far and wide. They were prepared to kill anyone who might reveal their secrets. She herself, she claimed, had been threatened with serious harm if she talked to anyone who was investigating the magic circle, as had a friend who had also been a victim of the same men and had been similarly threatened and even had her children kidnapped, Miss Yardley said. The prosecution was unable to produce this witness. 'Well, they would say that, wouldn't they?' Fee said, in an unconscious echo of another scapegoat of the great and the good.

The team for the defence said Miss Yardley was an unreliable witness and her evidence was that of a publicity-seeking fantasist who was hawking her story round to anyone who would listen. Nicholas Sawyer was a patriot who would never betray his country, let alone abuse underage children.

After three days' deliberation, the jury brought in a verdict of guilty.

'This is a travesty of justice,' Nicholas's wife, Lady Susan Sawyer, said, adding that an appeal had already been mounted.

Gough-Plunkett died in mysterious circumstances before his case came to trial. The senior officer with the Met killed himself by jumping off the top of a multi-storey car park. The CEO of the construction company suffered a massive heart attack at his desk and was dead before his PA could run to him with the defibrillator that was kept next to the women's washroom.

★

Andy Bragg was arrested while still in hospital, on charges arising from the Modern Slavery Act – human trafficking into the UK for sexual exploitation, arranging travel with a view to sexual exploitation and controlling prostitution for gain – as well as on suspicion of association with criminal organizations and money-laundering offences. If he was convicted he would never see the outside world again.

'Seems fair,' he said to Rhoda.

'Stupid plonker,' was her own guilty verdict. She only came to visit him once in hospital.

While in the hospital, Andy Bragg managed to convey to Rhoda where the money was hidden and she was able to relocate to Anguilla, where she bought citizenship and a villa with a pool. She drank a lot of piña coladas. Lottie got a passport and a new life which she disliked intensely, although you would never have known from her expression.

Andy Bragg's 'little black book', full of incriminating evidence against the magic circle, was sent anonymously to Bronte Finch (although the envelope containing the memory stick was stamped with an Anguilla postmark), to be used in evidence against Nicholas Sawyer's appeal. It did nothing to mitigate Andy Bragg's case as he died of complete organ failure due to sepsis a week after he was admitted to hospital. 'Blood poisoning,' the sister said when she told Rhoda. The cause might well have been the dirt on Maria's filthy scarf he had stanched his wound with. Reggie liked to think so anyway. Justice served.

Thomas Holroyd drowned in the swimming pool at his home. The coroner ruled an open verdict. Mr Holroyd was unable to swim and it was believed that he had slipped into the pool and was unable to get out, but the possibility that he'd died by his own hand was not ruled out.

Darren Bright, forty-one, was caught in a sting by the self-appointed 'paedophile hunter' group Northern Justice. A spokesman for the group, Jason Kemp, said they had formed the group after there had been an online attempt to groom his daughter. The men posed as an underage girl, Chloe, and arranged to meet Bright, whose online profile was that of a teenage boy called Ewan. Using stock photographs from the internet, Ewan was 'a very convincing avatar', the court was told. The encounter was filmed by another member of the group and the video later appeared on YouTube.

After the video was uploaded to the internet, Mr Bright's home was surrounded by a baying mob shouting 'Kill the paedo!' and he had to be rescued by the police.

A police spokesman said, 'We do not approve of vigilante groups as it is easy to compromise evidence or attack wrongly identified victims, but we are happy that Mr Bright has been brought to justice.'

Vincent Ives is no longer being sought by the police for the murder of his wife, although they would still like to question him about his involvement in the siege at the House of Horrors (not their term). He is believed to have moved abroad.

When Ashley returned home to discover both her mother and her father lost to her, she found a note from her father that read, 'Sorry about all this. Can you get Sparky back from the police? He needs walking twice a day and likes to sleep with his blue blanket. Love you lots, Dad xxx.'

Sophie Mellors landed on the National Crime Agency's 'Most Wanted' list, and for good measure was also the subject of a European Arrest Warrant, for her involvement in an organization that went by the name of Anderson Price Associates. Anderson Price Associates was a front for a group of criminals, including Mrs Mellors' husband, Leeds-based solicitor Stephen Mellors, now deceased, that was responsible for trafficking girls into the UK. They brought in innumerable girls under false pretences and the girls were then sold into the sex industry. The three 'associates' – Thomas Holroyd, Andrew Bragg and Stephen Mellors – all also had links to the case known as Operation Villette, but none of them were subject to prosecution in either case as they were all deceased.

Neighbours said that they hadn't seen Sophie Mellors or the couple's children for several weeks.

Sophie Mellors ('*widow of the murdered House of Horrors gang boss*') was long gone, of course, on a Brittany ferry to Bilbao with her two confused offspring in tow. Ida threw up for the whole of the crossing. When she wasn't throwing up she was weeping because she had been forced to leave her pony, Buttons, behind, and the promise of a replacement in whatever country they settled in was no comfort whatsoever. There would never be another horse like Buttons, she wailed. (True, as it turned out.) Jamie had long since retreated into silence. He had read everything on the internet about Bassani and Carmody, as well as everything about the trafficking case his parents had spearheaded. He hated them for what they had done and despised them for getting caught.

Sophie had always been sarcastic about Tommy and Andy's devotion to cash. Stephen's share of the Anderson Price profits was salted away in a variety of untouchable Swiss accounts. She hadn't spent years as an accountant without learning a trick or two. She holed up in Geneva while considering the safest refuge. Most of the countries that did not have extradition treaties with the UK were singularly unattractive – Saudi Arabia, Tajikistan, Mongolia, Afghanistan. She briefly considered Bahrain, but in the end opted for simply buying new identities for them all, the cost of which would have bankrolled a small war. Then she enrolled her children in very expensive boarding schools in Switzerland and bought a farmhouse in Lombardy which she spent her time renovating, more or less happily. Ida never forgave her for the loss of Buttons, or anything else, for that matter.

So who did kill Wendy Easton?

Craig the lifeboatman. Craig Cumming killed Wendy 'in a jealous rage', according to the prosecution at his trial. He had gone round to the victim's home, Thisldo, in the hope of rekindling his relationship with her. In evidence, Detective Inspector Anne Marriot said that Craig Cumming killed Mrs Ives (who also went by the name Easton) with a golf club which was kept in the garage. The golf club might indicate a spur-of-the-moment act of rage, the prosecution argued, but the golfing gloves that Cumming was wearing – it was a warm evening at the height of summer – were evidence of premeditation rather than spontaneity. Cumming's phone records showed that he called the victim fourteen times in the two hours previous to the killing.

Wendy Ives, who was separated from her husband, Vincent, had previously confided in a friend that she was scared of her former boyfriend, after he started following her to work. Reading from a written statement outside the court after the trial, Mrs Ives's daughter, Ashley, nineteen, said, 'I am pleased that justice has been done, but no one can replace my mother, taken so cruelly from us by this man. She was the kindest, most loyal, most generous person in the world.'

Craig Cumming was sentenced to life imprisonment with a recommendation that he serve a minimum term of fifteen years.

Trouble at t'Mill

On the way, they made a detour up to Rosedale Chimney Bank to stretch their legs and look at the sunset that was flooding the vast sky with a glorious palette of reds and yellows, orange and even violet. It demanded poetry, a thought he voiced out loud, and she said, 'No, I don't think so. It's enough in itself.' The getting of wisdom, he thought.

There was another car parked up there, an older couple, admiring the view. 'Magnificent, isn't it?' the man said. The woman smiled at them and congratulated the 'happy couple' on their wedding and Jackson said, 'It's not what it looks like. She's my daughter.'

Marlee chuckled when they got back in the car and said, 'Right now they're probably on the phone to the police, reporting us for incest.' She had startled the woman by giving her the bridal bouquet. The woman had looked unsure, as if it might be bad luck.

'I know I'm egregiously cheerful,' Marlee said to Jackson (he filed the word 'egregiously' away to look up later), 'but I expect it's just hysteria.' She didn't seem hysterical to Jackson. He'd seen a lot of hysteria in his time. 'You know what it's like,' she continued. 'Demob happy, school's out and all that.'

'Yeah, I know,' Jackson said, although he didn't, because he'd never personally jilted anyone at the altar. His life might have been better if he had.

Josie had already been pregnant when they married, so Marlee would still exist (the non-conception of beloved children always a stumbling block to the if-I-could-live-my-life-over-again fantasy). He and Julia had never married, never even come close to it, but

Nathan would have happened anyway. And if he had never married the evil, thieving Tessa, he would probably still be a rich man and would have been able to afford the wedding his daughter had wanted, instead of allowing 'the in-laws' as Marlee had already been calling them, only mildly ironically, to pick up the tab. 'Why not?' she said. They were 'filthy rich' and, having only sons and no daughters themselves, they wanted to make a big deal out of this 'union', as they called it. 'And anyway,' Marlee added, 'they love me like a daughter.'

'No, they don't,' a curmudgeonly Jackson responded. '*I* love you like a daughter. They "love" you like the prospective mother of their grandchildren. You're just a brood mare for their bloodstock, so they can continue to inherit the earth ad infinitum.' Yes, it had been a particularly bad thing to say, but he had met them and didn't like what they stood for, even though they were perfectly pleasant (extremely pleasant, in fact) and Jago – yes, that was the name of the groom – was a harmless type (he had brothers Lollo and Waldo – go figure), although he had a bit too much charm and polish for Jackson to feel he was trustworthy. He was 'something in the City', a phrase that always baffled and irritated Jackson in equal measure.

'We can't possibly let you pay,' the in-laws said when they were introduced to Jackson. 'The kids want an enormous do and it would be our pleasure to foot the bill.' Jackson had demurred, but to no avail. He had only met them the once and was finding it hard to believe his blood was going to flow with theirs – in 'union' – for the rest of eternity, or however long the planet lasted. They came from an ancient and aristocratic lineage, with a huge country pile outside Helmsley and a townhouse in Belgravia. They had the kind of serious and discreet old money you never hear about.

There had been a 'small party' – champagne and strawberries – in the garden of the London house to celebrate the engagement. Jackson had asked Julia to come with him for moral reinforcement, and even though it was her only weekend off from filming she had agreed quite cheerfully. She wanted to 'see how the rich lived', she said. Jago's parents seemed to be under the misapprehension that Jackson and Julia were still a couple. Jago's mother was a fan of *Collier* and

330

was quite excited at the idea of welcoming a 'celebrity' into the family.

Jackson was contemplating a plate of tiny canapés when Jago came up behind him, put his arm around Jackson's shoulder and said, 'I can't keep calling you Mr Brodie. Shall I call you Jackson? Or' — he laughed at this point — 'should I call you Dad?'

'You could try,' Jackson said. 'But I wouldn't advise it.'

'I know my timing's awful,' Marlee said. 'I didn't *intend* to jilt him, Dad. And certainly not at the altar.'

'And yet you did.'

'I know, poor Jago. It's such an awful thing to do to someone. I'm a complete cow. Is this the debrief now? Are you going to castigate me for leaving a trail of destruction in my wake, or congratulate me on regaining my freedom?'

'Well, actually, I was going to commiserate with you for marrying someone called Jago.'

'Posh boy?'

'Yeah, posh boy,' Jackson said. After a couple of miles he glanced at her and said, 'Shouldn't you be more upset?'

'Time enough for that,' Marlee said. She laughed again and said, 'And after Julia went to all the trouble of buying a fornicator.'

'A fornicator?'

'It's what I call a fascinator. They're so stupid, I hate them,' Julia said.

'And yet you're wearing one?'

'Oh, well, you know, it's not every day that your son's half-sister gets married.'

Actually she looked rather fetching. The fascinator wasn't ludicrous, not a royal-wedding one, but a discreet little black cap with an alluring net veil that made her look old-fashioned and French, especially as she was wearing a two-piece suit that 'shows I still have a waist'. Time had been called on her role in *Collier* — the 'popular pathologist' had met a grisly end in her own mortuary after being dragged around a lot of East Coast scenery, which viewers always appreciated seeing. Julia had let slip to Jackson that she was going to the gym on a regular basis. It was such an unlikely thing for Julia to be doing that Jackson could only presume she had answered the call from *Strictly Come Dancing*. He hoped it wasn't because of Callum. 'It's nothing, just sex,' she said airily when questioned. Jackson wondered if he was supposed to take comfort from that.

She definitely looked more stylish than Josie, who had opted for a floral dress and jacket that screamed 'mother of the bride'. ('Jacques Vert,' Julia murmured. 'Very ageing on her.') No fascinator for Josie, instead a large ornate hat. She looked uncomfortable. Perhaps she knew her daughter was about to make the mistake of her life. Not that Jackson had had much more than a glimpse of the wedding party from the church door. The church was near the groom's home, and was Norman and pretty, full of the same pink roses that made up Marlee's bouquet.

Marlee had spent the night in the hotel where the reception was to be held, along with the in-laws and Josie, but Jackson, Julia and Nathan had opted for the Black Swan in the main square in Helmsley. Two rooms. Julia and Nathan in one, Jackson in the other. Nathan had eaten with them, slumped over his phone and barely looking up from whatever game he was playing. It seemed easier to let him than berate him to sit up straight, eat properly, join the conversation and all the other little building blocks of civilization. 'The barbarians aren't at the gate,' Julia said, 'they're rocking the cradle.' It didn't seem to bother her as much as Jackson felt it should.

'Good time with your friend?' Jackson asked when he picked Nathan up after finally managing to free himself of the aftermath at Silver Birches.

He shrugged. 'S'pose.'

Jackson had picked him up from the *Collier* set, where his mother was in her final death throes. He had swapped him for Dido. 'Fair exchange,' Julia said. He missed the dog immediately – perhaps he should get one of his own. He had briefly been in charge of a rather unsatisfactory dog with a stupid name. Perhaps he could get a more manly dog – a collie, perhaps or an Alsatian, called Spike or Rebel.

Nathan threw himself carelessly into the passenger seat of the Toyota and immediately took his phone out. After an interval he looked up and turned to Jackson and said, 'It's good to be back though.'

'Back?'

'With you, Dad. I was thinking . . . maybe I could live with you all the time.'

'Your mother wouldn't let you,' Jackson said. Happiness had risen up inside him like a big bubble and he hung on to it before it – inevitably – burst. 'But I'm very happy that you want to.'

'S'okay,' accompanied by another shrug. Nathan's indifference deflated the bubble a little, but not entirely, and Jackson reached out a hand to cradle the back of his son's head. Nathan batted the hand away and said, 'Daa-aad, keep your eyes on the road.' Jackson laughed. Everything was all right, everywhere. For a little while anyway.

A vintage Bentley, pink ribbons on the bonnet, took Jackson and Marlee the short distance from the hotel to the church. She had wanted everything about this wedding to be stylish and in 'good taste'. Style not substance, Jackson thought. Even the hen party had resisted tackiness, according to Julia, who had been invited. No drunken knees-up in York or Ibiza, instead it had been a pink-champagne afternoon tea in a private dining room in the Savoy. 'Very sedate,' Julia reported back. 'Not an inflated penis-shaped balloon in sight. Bit of a disappointment, really, I was rather looking forward to the blow-up penises. It was ferociously expensive too, I expect.' Jackson supposed the in-laws paid.

'It's just a *wedding*,' Jackson had complained to Julia. 'It's too much emphasis on one day.'

'It does rather raise expectations about the marriage that comes after,' Julia had said.

'She's too young to get married anyway.'

'She is,' Julia agreed, 'but we all have to learn from our mistakes.'

Had she learned from hers?

'Every day's a learning experience,' she laughed. It was the kind of thing that Penny Trotter would say. It was all quiet on the Trotter front. The Penny/Gary/Kirsty eternal triangle was low down on

Jackson's list of priorities at the moment. He had been more preoccu-
pied with the fact that he was going to have to buy a new suit.

'Why?' he moaned to Julia. And, yes, he sounded like Nathan.

'Because,' she said.

The Bentley dropped them off outside the gate to the church. 'Lych
gate,' according to Marlee. The car was booked for a one-way
journey only, and after the ceremony the wedding party would walk
back the couple of hundred yards to the hotel where the reception
was to be held. It involved crossing a field. 'I thought it would be
nice,' she said, 'like an old-fashioned country wedding.'

'What if it rains?' Jackson asked. And, on a more practical level,
what if there were people with mobility issues?

'There aren't and it won't,' Marlee said. He admired the certainty of
her optimism (not gained from his genes, obviously). Nonetheless he
had parked the trusty Toyota behind the church, on the off-chance of
rain or sudden disability or both. 'Or in case you want to run away at
the last minute,' he joked to Marlee. How they had laughed.

They made their way slowly up the path towards the church,
where a cluster of bridesmaids in various sizes but all in the same
(tasteful) shade of pink were waiting for them. Nathan had refused
point-blank to be a page boy. Jackson didn't blame him.

'She's your sister,' Julia had cajoled.

'Half-sister,' he corrected her. 'And I hardly know her.' Which
was true and something that Jackson regretted. 'I suppose there is
quite an age gap between them,' Julia said, but there'd been an age
gap between Jackson and his sister and that hadn't stopped them
being close. She should have been there, he thought, sitting in the
front pew, wearing an unflattering hat and an outfit that aged her,
looking round, trying to get a first view of her niece as she pro-
gressed along the aisle towards her future.

Except apparently there was to be no progression and the future
was about to be changed.

'I don't think I can, Dad,' Marlee murmured as they arrived at the
church.

★

'I know you think I'm too young,' Marlee had said. 'But sometimes you just know when something's right for you, you know?'

And then a bit later you know it's wrong for you, Jackson thought, but buttoned his lips tightly so the thought couldn't escape into the refined air of the 'shoe floor' of the London department store to which he had escorted his only daughter a month before the 'big day'. (*Every day's a big day*, a greeting card in Penny Trotter's shop said.) It was a far cry from the Clarks of Marlee's childhood where Jackson had occasionally been press-ganged into attendance by Josie.

The shoe floor was so big that Jackson thought it probably had its own postcode. You could be lost in here for days and never be found. The sound of one shoe dropping. If a shoe drops in a shop and there's no one to pick it up . . . but there would be someone, because the place was overrun with assistants wanting to serve them. The shoes were tended by a fleet of Prince Charmings of one gender or another (and then another, ad infinitum nowadays, it seemed to Jackson. He remembered when it was just men or women. The cry of *Luddite!* could be heard in the distance, growing nearer).

Shoe-shopping (*wedding*-shoe-shopping, just to add an extra layer of neurosis to the affair) was his punishment for being an inadequate father and not taking enough interest in Marlee's pre-wedding plans. And probably for not paying for the wedding either.

'What can I do to help?' he'd offered when they had met in London. ('Just the two of us – lunch,' she'd said. 'It'll be nice.')

'Well, I'm still fretting about shoes,' she said. 'I've left them until the last minute.' The last minute for Jackson would have been literally the last minute, popping into a shoe shop en route to the church, not a month before his nuptials. 'You could come with me and help me choose,' she said.

'Well, I don't think I'll be much good at the choosing part,' he said, 'but I'm very happy to pay for them.' A brave offer, it turned out. They cost not much shy of a thousand pounds. For shoes! They looked uncomfortable. 'Are you sure you can actually get down the aisle in them?'

'It's like being the Little Mermaid,' she said lightly, 'suffering for the love of my life. I know you don't really like Jago, but I do. And he's a good person, he really is. Give him a chance, Dad,' she said when they had finally retired from the retail fray and were having tea and cake in Ladurée in Covent Garden.

'You're just so young,' he said helplessly.

'And one day I won't be and that'll make you worry as well.'

'I'll be dead by then, I expect,' Jackson said. 'Nathan thinks so anyway.' He watched her cut a delicate *religieuse* in half. It was not a masculine cake.

She was a clever girl – private education, sat the Baccalaureate, Law degree from Cambridge, and now she was planning a career as a barrister. She was only twenty-three, too young to settle down. Too young to buy into the whole traditional path. Degree, marriage, children. ('What in God's name is wrong with that?' Josie had asked. The argument had spread. 'Do you want her hanging about on a beach in Bali or in a drug den in Thailand?' Of course not, but that didn't mean he didn't want his daughter to spread her wings and live a little. Live a lot, in fact. Not constrained by other people's expectations. By Jago's expectations. By the in-laws' expectations. 'Well, it's great that you've become a feminist so late in your life,' Josie had said sarcastically. He'd always been a feminist! He bristled at the injustice of the remark.)

Marlee offered him a forkful of the *religieuse*. Despite it not being manly, it was a cake that Jackson had eaten in Paris, in a café in Belleville with Julia, and the memory made him suddenly nostalgic for the dusty summer streets and the good coffee. And for Julia, too.

'Proust and his madeleine,' Marlee said. 'That's a cake, not a girl-friend,' she added. She always presumed his ignorance before he had a chance to prove it. 'I'm crazy about Jago.'

'Crazy doesn't last,' Jackson said. 'Trust me, I've been there. Also who wants to be crazy? Being crazy is the same as being mad.' And now in the space of a month she had gone from being crazy about her fiancé to dragging her feet to the altar. Which proved his point. Crazy was crazy.

And then somehow it had gone downhill from there, the whole dad/daughter bonding experience ending up as an analysis of his politics, his character, his beliefs, all of which apparently belonged to a less enlightened age. 'You're not enlightened,' Jackson protested (foolishly). 'You just think you are.'

'You're such a *Luddite*, Dad.'

But what if the Luddites had been right all along?

'Just last-minute nerves,' he reassured as their pace slowed down even further as the entrance to the church neared. 'I'm pretty sure every bride gets them.'

He'd forgotten how much he loved Marlee. Not forgotten, you could never forget. She was pregnant, she'd informed him over the *religieuse*. He was horrified. One more gate snapping shut behind her on the path of life. No return.

'You're supposed to say congratulations.'

'You're too young.'

'You really are a shit sometimes, Dad. You know that, don't you?'

I do, he thought. Something, it turned out, that his daughter wasn't about to say to the groom.

She looked so lovely. The cream silk of the dress, the delicate pink of the roses in her neat bouquet. He couldn't see the outrageously expensive shoes beneath the dress, she could have been wearing wellingtons for all he knew. Her lace veil was fixed with a diamond-and-pearl tiara, a family heirloom – Jago's family, obviously.

'Take a breath,' he said. 'Ready?' Ready to run, he thought, the Dixie Chicks song. He could hear the "Wedding March" wheezing up on the organ inside, slightly out of tune as the bellows got their breath.

His daughter faltered and then stood still, didn't put one expensively shod foot any further forward. There was a slight Mona Lisa smile on her lips but it didn't seem to indicate happiness, it was more like the fixed expression of someone who was paralysed. Sleeping Beauty. The woman turned to stone, or a pillar of salt.

Jackson could see Julia, sitting at the end of the front pew, leaning out and craning her neck to get a glimpse of the bride. She frowned questioningly at him and he gave her a little reassuring thumbs-up. A bit of stage fright on Marlee's part, he thought. Julia of all people would understand that. He could see Nathan, who had been persuaded into chinos and a linen shirt, squashed awkwardly between Josie and Julia, and from the angle of his head he got the impression that he was looking at his phone. Jackson's heart was suddenly flooded with love for his son, for his daughter, for his anonymous *grandchild*. One on his arm, one in his sight, one invisible. My family, he thought. For richer, for poorer. For better or worse.

The organ was in full-throated Mendelssohn mode now and he glanced at Marlee to see if she was ready. The smile had gone, he noticed. She turned to him and said, with so little drama that he thought he must have misheard her, 'I'm serious, Dad. I'm not doing this. I can't. It's wrong.'

'Let's go, then,' he said. There was only one side in this scenario and he was on it. He was there to support his daughter, not anyone else. Not a church-load of people in their finery with all their expectations. Not a groom who was a 'good man' and who was about to be devastated, not to mention publicly humiliated. Keep calm and don't carry on. 'What we'll do,' he said, 'is we'll just turn round and walk back down the path as if it were the most natural thing in the world.'

'And then we run?'

'And then we run.'

Know When to Hold Them

'Are you sure?'

'Yes, honestly, thank you.'

Crystal had offered to drive Vince to the airport or to the ferry. He was going to go abroad, he said. Grow a beard, disappear. 'Get contact lenses,' she advised.

'Borneo, maybe,' he said.

'Borneo? What's there, Vince?'

'Orang-utans.'

'Really?'

'No, not really. My daughter, actually, but I think she's probably on her way home now. You know . . . her mother. Wendy. I didn't kill her, you know.'

'Never thought you did, Vince.'

'Thanks. I thought I might try and help, you know, people. Women, girls. Maybe help build a school or something. Teach computer skills. India, Africa, Cambodia, somewhere like that. Somewhere far away from here.'

'Good for you, Vince.'

Vince was in the passenger seat next to her. Candy was in the back, watching a DVD. Brutus the Rottweiler was sitting next to her. He was surprisingly companionable. Anyone looking at them would have thought they were a family.

She was going to the Palace to pick up Harry. Obviously she was going to have to tell him that his father was dead, but not yet. Right words, right time. There was no hurry. Tommy was going to be dead for a long time. She wouldn't tell Harry what an evil bastard he'd been. He'd find out one day, but that day could wait. Candy need never know. A change of name, a change of place. A new truth or a new lie. Same thing, in Crystal's opinion.

Crystal had no idea where they were going to go or what they were going to do when they got there. The road was open, all the way to the horizon. Christina running.

She would have taken Vince further but he was eager to 'get on', and when they reached the station she said, 'Sure?' and he said, 'Yeah, yeah, really, this'll do, Crystal,' so she dropped him on the station forecourt and watched as he ran inside without looking back.

'We have to go,' she said to Harry.

'Go?'

'Yeah, go. Leave. Leave town.'

'You're leaving?' He looked distraught.

'No, *we're* leaving, Harry. The three of us.'

'What about Dad?'

'He's going to join us later, Harry.'

'There's just one thing before we go though,' Harry said.

'What's that, Harry?'

Getting the Hell out of Dodge

They took the long way round, driving on the back roads over the wiley, windy moors. Ronnie had reclaimed her own car, no more blues and twos for a day or two. Operation Villette was over. All that was left was the paperwork. An awful lot of it. 'The third man' had been arrested. Nicholas Sawyer. There was a rumour that the Intelligence Services were involved, that for years he had been selling secrets to anyone who would buy them and, failing other routes, this was their way of getting him. The wall around this rumour was impenetrable. It was 'a meta-jigsaw piece', Reggie said.

'Eh?'

Operation Villette and the House of Horrors case were knotted together and had still not been entirely untangled, but it was not theirs to puzzle over any more.

'Just let it go,' Gilmerton said at his retirement do a few days later. (A nasty booze-up from which they made their excuses and left early.) 'You'll come out of it smelling of roses, not shit. That's the important thing.'

'What next?' Ronnie asked Reggie.

'Thought I might put in for an exchange abroad next year.'

'Abroad?'

'New Zealand.'

'Wow.'

Reggie had seen Jackson take the gun from the hand of the Polish girl, Nadja, after she killed Stephen Mellors. And then he'd knelt down and said something she couldn't hear to Andrew Bragg as the sirens drew nearer and nearer. Ronnie had managed to get out and phone for help. It was brave to run, she couldn't have known that someone wouldn't shoot her in the back. Shooting someone in the back never looks good to the police and the judiciary. It entrammels you in procedure, the law, the media, immigration. It takes away your choices. It taints you. Reggie knew that was why he did it. The girls had been through enough.

And yet if Ronnie had been there and not outside on her police radio, Reggie would never have gone along with his lie. It was something between the two of them now, a barrier.

Just before the Armed Response Unit crashed up the stairs with none of the delicacy you might expect in a hostage situation, Jackson had murmured to Reggie, 'So Bragg shot Mellors.'

And after a pause she said, 'Yes, he did.'

And without the gun no one could say for sure. There would be gunshot residue, of course, but the lack of forensic evidence on Andrew Bragg was compromised by the amount of blood he had lost. And anyway no one questioned the witness statements of a detective constable and an ex-detective inspector. Because what possible reason could there be for them to lie?

'A righteous compromise,' Jackson said. 'Truth is absolute, but the consequences of it aren't.'

'Sounds like a specious argument to me, Mr B.'

'And yet this is where we are, Reggie. You do what you think is right.'

She hated him for doing this to her. And she loved him for it, too. Somewhere, deep down, she still yearned for him to be the father-figure in her life. The dad she'd never known. She hated him for that, too.

And they were old hands at covering up, of course. When Dr Hunter killed the two men who had abducted her and her baby, Jackson had destroyed the evidence and Reggie had lied about what she knew to be the truth. So that it wasn't something that would follow Dr Hunter for the rest of her life, Jackson had said. So Reggie already knew how easy it was to step over the line from law to outlaw.

She had a sudden flashback to seeing Dr Hunter walking down the road, walking away from the house that contained the two men she had killed. Dr H had been covered in blood, her baby in her arms, and Reggie had thought how magnificent she looked, like a heroine, a warrior queen. The two Polish sisters had stood with their arms around each other, looking defiantly at the body of Stephen Mellors. They had the straight, strong backs of dancers. Heroines, not hand-maids. They were beautiful. *For my sister.*

When she'd saved Jackson Brodie's life on the railway tracks all those years ago, Reggie thought that he would be in her thrall until he repaid the favour, until he saved her life in return, but that wasn't so. It was Reggie who had been in thrall to him. And now they were joined in compromise for ever. 'Righteous compromise,' he reminded her.

And as Dr Hunter once said, 'What does justice have to do with the law?'

It was so wrong that it was right. That sounded like the title of one of Jackson Brodie's God-awful country songs. Reggie knew that she had some thinking to do before she could walk a straight line again.

She sifted through Ronnie's music on her iPhone and put on Florence and the Machine. When 'Hunger' came on Ronnie started singing along softly, and by the time they got to the second chorus they were both belting out *We all have a hunger* at the top of their lungs. And then they grabbed each other's hands and made fists and held them up in winners' triumph. They were like Thelma and Louise about to drive off the cliff, except they weren't going to do that, they were driving home.

They were Cagney and Lacey. They were the Brontë sisters. They were the Kray twins. They were police. They were women.

'See you around, then,' Ronnie said when she dropped Reggie off in Leeds.

'You betcha,' Reggie said.

What Would Tatiana Do?

'Mr Brodie?'

Sam Tilling reporting for duty on the phone.

'How's tricks, Sam?'

'Tricky. I don't know how to say this. Well, I do, I'm just . . .'

'Spit it out, Sam.'

'It's our Gary, Mr Brodie. He's dead.'

'Dead? How?'

'His diabetes, apparently. He fell into a coma in a hotel room in Leeds and was dead when housekeeping found him the next morning.'

'And where was Kirsty in all this?' Jackson asked.

'Not with Gary. He was on his own. And Mrs Trotter was at the Great Yorkshire Show with her sister and thirty thousand or so other people.'

'Which hotel was he in?'

'The Malmaison in Leeds. Drinking in the bar beforehand. He did have quite a bit of alcohol in his system, according to the autopsy.'

'And there's been an autopsy already?' Jackson was surprised at the speed with which Gary had been all done and dusted for eternity.

'Yep. Already done, according to Mrs Trotter. Death due to hypo-glycemia. They ruled it as natural causes.'

❦

'And I say, you buy lady drink? If you lady, he say, pleased with himself. Oh, funny man, I see, I say. I like funny men. My father was great circus clown, although, true, not funny. Not in Russia. Vodka for me. *Pozhaluysta.*

'You're not from round these parts, are you? he say. Ha, ha. Yes, you real comedian. I can tell, I say. I ask him if he have wife, he say *nyet.* I ask him if he have mistress, he say *nyet.*

'A couple more drinks and I lead him by tie up to room – executive suite, nice, thank you – like dog on lead. More drinks from minibar. We watch TV, I say I can't miss *Collier.* He lie down on bed and start turn white and say, Love, I'm a diabetic, you see. Shouldn't have drunk so much. Let's just stop a minute.'

'Oh, and interrupt our fun? I say, straddling him on bed like I'm rider and he horse. (No sex, don't worry!) No, please, love, really, he say. His voice fade. He really not well. And then I pull medicine into syringe and jab him—jab! jab!—with needle and he saying no, no, what is that, it's not insulin, is it? That's the last thing I need, love, and then he pass out and I get off bed and wipe everything clean. Then sit with him. Vigil. Until sure he gone.

'*Da,* Mrs Trotter, definitely. Dead. Final curtain. Show over. Bye-bye! Condolences, blah, blah, blah. Pleasure doing business with you, Mrs Trotter. Recommend me to your friends.'

Kill the Buddha

'You'll have to give the tiara back,' Jackson said.

'I suppose. And it's a shame about the honeymoon. The Maldives. Would have been nice,' she said wistfully.

'Maybe Jago can take Waldo?'

'Or Lollo?'

'The future's in your hands,' Jackson said. 'That's what Madame Astarti says.'

'Who?'

They had hidden out for a couple of days at a hotel in Harrogate. 'So I can get my head together,' she said. 'I feel like a criminal.'

'Me too,' Jackson said, although of course he actually technically was a criminal as he had covered up an unlawful killing. Twice. First when Dr Hunter killed her abductors and next when the Polish girl killed Stephen Mellors. He had no regrets. None. He wasn't a vigilante. He really wasn't.

He was saying goodbye to Marlee on the platform of York station. She was going back to London to 'face the music'. He wanted to urge her to tell Jago about the baby, but he was working very hard at not giving his daughter advice. He thought of how Julia had kept Nathan a secret from him. History repeating itself. But then that was all that history ever did, wasn't it?

She was going to keep the baby, she said. He hadn't even known there was a question on the table. She was going to bring up a baby on her own at the same time as pursuing an incredibly demanding career?

'Listen to yourself, Grandad,' she laughed. 'You're such a Luddite.' But at least this time it was said with affection. 'Besides which, I'll have great child-care. The almost-in-laws will fork out huge sums of money to keep their brood mare close.' She gave him a dig in the ribs (quite painful) and said, 'Here's my train coming.' And then she was gone. She was brave, he thought. He must keep her close too from now on.

He checked into a budget hotel for the night. He didn't need anything fancy, just clean sheets and no hairs in the shower. He needed to be fresh for the fight tomorrow.

Jackson set off early next morning. He put on Miranda Lambert. 'Runnin' Just In Case'. *There's trouble where I'm going but I'm gonna go there anyway.* Sounded like the story of his life. He made a phone call from the road. He didn't have a number for her any more. She had moved jobs and he googled her new workplace and asked the switchboard at her station to put him through, which they did, although it took some persuading on his part – she was senior now, she didn't just take phone calls from strangers, because that was what he was now. A stranger to her. There'd been something between them once – a spark, a possibility. They could have been great together, but they were never together. He wondered if she still had the dog. He had given it to her instead of giving himself. ('Fair exchange,' Julia said.) It seemed a long time ago now.

He didn't use his own name. He said he was DC Reggie Chase, because he suspected she might remember Reggie and would take that call.

She answered after a couple of rings. Cool and efficient. 'Superintendent Louise Monroe. Can I help you?' So perhaps she hadn't clocked Reggie's name after all.

He realized he had no idea what he wanted to say to her or whether he really wanted to say anything. He suspected that whatever he said would be definitive somehow. This was a crossroads now and he had to make a choice. Tide in or tide out?

'Hello?' she said. They both listened to the hollow silence, a

moment of odd togetherness, and then she startled him by her powers of divination. 'Jackson?' she said, almost in a whisper. 'Jackson, is
that you?'

In the end, it was easier to make no choice at all. He said nothing
and ended the call.

The words of another song came into his mind. *Freedom's just another word for nothing left to lose.* But so was commitment. He just
wanted something simple. No strings, no complications.

A mile or two further down the road, he made another call.

'Mr Private Detective,' the voice at the other end of the line
purred. 'You not at lovely wedding with beautiful daughter?'

'Do you want to meet for a drink?'

'With you?'

'Yeah, with me.'

'Just drink?'

'Don't know,' Jackson said. (Did he honestly think this was going
to be uncomplicated? Who was he kidding? Himself, obviously. Tide
neither in nor out, more like a tsunami.)

'Okey-dokey. *Da.* Now?'

'Tomorrow. I've got something to do first.'

'Where?'

'Dunno. Not the Malmaison.'

'Okey-dokey. *Poka.*'

A terrace of houses in Mirfield. It was not unlike the one he had
been raised in. Built from gloomy Millstone grit, it had an unwel-
coming aspect. In the Brodie house there had been a small scullery
at the back where his mother spent her time, a 'posh' parlour at the
front of the house with an uncomfortable sofa that was hardly ever
sat on.

And a door in the hallway that led down a steep narrow staircase
to the coal cellar.

The grey Peugeot was parked in the street outside. It belonged to
someone called Graham Vesey. Forty-three years old. The number plate
photographed by Nathan. Enhanced by Sam Tilling. Supplied, eventually, by a helpful woman called Miriam in the DVLA in Swansea.

Jackson rang the doorbell. A man's home was his castle. Always start with the polite method and work your way up to a battering-ram and a giant catapult. Or just one good punch to the gut.

He was big and sweaty and had tattoos on his bull neck and he could crush a girl like a fly if he wanted to.

'Mr Vesey? Mr Graham Vesey? My name's Jackson Brodie. Can I come in?'

Darcy Slee

She heard the doorbell ring and started screaming as loud as she could to get attention. When she paused for a breath she heard a lot of noise upstairs – fighting, by the sound of it. She was about to scream again when the door to the cellar opened. In the wedge of light from the open door she could see someone coming down the stairs. Darcy's heart clenched with terror. She had been here seven days and nights, she knew what terror was.

It was a man, but it wasn't the man with the tattooed neck. That didn't mean he didn't intend her harm. He might be an even worse man, for all she knew.

When he got to the bottom of the stairs, he crouched down to speak to her as though she was a frightened cat and he said, 'It's all right now, it's over. My name's Jackson Brodie. I'm a policeman.'

The Fat Lady Sings

The wings were crowded. Everyone seemed to want to watch Bunny take his position at the top of the bill. On the other hand, there were lacunae (Miss Dangerfield's word, of course) made by the empty seats in the auditorium. A lot of people had only booked to see Barclay Jack, some had even demanded a refund from the Palace because of his no-show. 'No-show?' the man in the box office said. 'The bloke's dead, for God's sake. Give him a break.'

Bunny, however, was very much alive. Resplendent in a bright-blue sequinned frock and a feathered headdress that was even bigger than the ones the chorus girls wore. One of them wolf-whistled him when he came on-stage. He dipped a little curtsey to her.

His set followed the usual pattern. He made a hash of several popular operatic arias – *'L'amour est un oiseau rebelle'* from *Carmen* and *'Un bel dì vedremo'* from *Madame Butterfly*. ('It's an audience of philistines,' Bunny said, 'but it's stuff they might recognize.') They were arias for women, of course, sopranos, and Bunny attacked them with screechy high notes, falling about in his heels, pretending to be drunk, pretending to be lovelorn, pretending to be a terrible singer.

They were musical interludes – his act was basically stand-up, mainly about the travails of being a woman. The thinned-out audience responded as usual – hostility turning to tolerance and then to admiration ('T'fucker's got balls,' Harry heard someone say), until eventually all the animosity towards Bunny had dissipated.

This was the point at which he paused. A long pause and the

audience grew completely silent, unsure, even a little nervous, of what was to come. Bunny was gazing out over them, yet he seemed to be looking inward. Had he died on-stage or was he about to do something memorable, climactic?

'Just wait,' Harry whispered to Crystal. He could already feel the hairs standing up on the back of his neck before the music was even cued. It was a good backing tape – the one thing that the Palace could boast, for no reason known to any of them, was a really great sound system.

Harry could see Bunny taking a deep breath and then he started to sing, quietly at first as the words, about sleep, demanded, but nonetheless the audience recognized the music almost immediately. That plangent note near to the beginning seemed to reassure them. They were on home turf – it was football. And, more than that, they were in a safe pair of hands – the bloke had an amazing voice. He was flying. The audience stirred like birds and settled, they knew they were in for a treat.

It was an aria that had become a cliché, the party piece of *X Factor* and *Britain's Got Talent* contestants, an ubiquitous tune, but it was easily lifted out of its World Cup familiarity. All you needed was a big man with a big voice.

Harry never failed to be moved by Bunny's performance. Tears pricked his eyes. 'Tears of happiness,' he reassured Crystal as the music started to grow.

The recorded female chorus, coming in like an angelic counterpart, slowed everything down for a moment. But only a moment and then it was building again. Building and building. The stars trembled. There was the beautiful control of the first *Vincerò* and then it swelled to the next

Vincerò

and then stepped off into that last great elongated soaring crescendo

Vincerò!

Bunny raised his arms to the gods in triumph. The gods looked down on him and laughed. The stars twinkled like sequins.

Everyone jumped to their feet and cheered him. They couldn't help themselves.

'*Vincerò*,' Harry said happily to Crystal. 'It means "I will win".'

'And so you will, Harry,' Crystal said. 'So you will.'

BRIDLINGTON

Acknowledgements

I'd like to thank the following:

Lt Col M. Keech, BEM, Royal Signals (retd).

Malcolm R. Dickson, QPM, formerly Assistant Inspector of Constabulary for Scotland.

DI Andy Grant, the Metropolitan Police.

Reuben Equi.

Russell Equi, who retains his title of God of All Things Vehicular.

Thanks are also due to Marianne Velmans, Larry Finlay, Alison Barrow, Vicky Palmer, Martin Myers and Kate Samano, all at Transworld. Camilla Ferrier and Jemma McDonagh at the Marsh Agency, Jodi Shields at Casarotto Ramsay, Reagan Arthur at Little Brown (US), Kristin Cochrane at Doubleday Canada and Kim Witherspoon at Witherspoon Associates. And last but by no means least, my agent, Peter Straus.

I have possibly slightly mangled the geography of the East Coast, mainly so that characters, especially Harry, could move about with more speed and ease than is usually the case.

I own all mistakes, intentional or otherwise.

My apologies to the people of Bridlington. I have nothing but happy memories of the place and would like to think that nothing bad ever happened there.

Song References

Reference on p. 20 to 'Don't You Want Me' written by Jo Callis, Philip Oakey and Philip Adrian Wright.

Reference on p. 38 to 'What's Love Got To Do With It' written by Terry Britten and Graham Lyle.

Lyrics on p. 48 from 'The Teddy Bears' Picnic' written by Jimmy Kennedy.

Lyrics on p. 151 from 'The Bug' written by Mark Knopfler.

Lyrics on p. 151 from 'The Gambler' written by Don Schlitz.

Lyrics on p. 151 from 'I'm So Lonesome I Could Cry', 'I'll Never Get Out Of This World Alive' and 'I Don't Care (If Tomorrow Never Comes)' by Hank Williams.

Lyrics on p. 151 from 'The Blade' by Marc Beeson, Jamie Floyd and Allen Shamblin.

Lyrics on p. 169 and p. 341 from 'Wuthering Heights' written by Kate Bush.

Reference on p. 209 to 'Hotel California' written by Don Felder, Don Henley and Glenn Frey.

Lyrics on p. 212 from 'Another Brick In The Wall (Part 2)' written by Roger Waters.

Reference on p. 231 to 'Holding Out For A Hero' written by Jim Steinman and Dean Pitchford.

Lyrics on p. 343 from 'Hunger' written by Florence Welch, Emile Haynie, Thomas Bartlett and Tobias Jesso Jr.

Lyrics on p. 347 from 'Runnin' Just In Case' written by Miranda Lambert and Gwen Sebastian.

Lyrics on p. 348 from 'Me And Bobby McGee' written by Kris Kristofferson and Fred Foster.

Kate Atkinson won the Costa (formerly Whitbread) Book of the Year prize with her first novel, *Behind the Scenes at the Museum*. She has written four previous bestselling literary crime novels featuring former detective Jackson Brodie, *Case Histories, One Good Turn, When Will There Be Good News?* and *Started Early, Took My Dog*, which became a BBC television series starring Jason Isaacs. She has since written three critically lauded and prizewinning novels set around World War Two: *Life After Life* and *A God in Ruins* (both winners of the Costa Novel Award) and, most recently, *Transcription. Big Sky* is her twelfth book.